SWEET DREAMS

A shape appeared in his window. Any shark would have envied this creature's mouth. Maniakes got the idea it could stretch quite a ways—lined with perfectly meshing, sharp-edged teeth from end to end.

Then his eyes met those of the creature. Caught by a will not his own, Maniakes walked toward the window. He understood the creature floating in the darkness had not the power to enter while the mage's charm remained in place. But if he were to sweep that charm aside, nothing would keep the creature from coming in . . . and showing him just how wide its jaws could open.

Each step closer to the window came more slowly as he struggled against the creature's will. When he reached the windowsill, he knew he would brush away the protection the mage had set there.

He knew what would happen afterward . . .

By Harry Turtledove
Published by Ballantine Books:

HAMMER AND ANVIL

Book Two of
The Time of Troubles

Harry Turtledove

A Del Rey® Book
BALLANTINE BOOKS • NEW YORK

A Del Rey® Book
Published by Ballantine Books

Copyright © 1996 by Harry Turtledove

All rights reserved under the International and Pan-American Copyright Conventions. Published in the United States by Ballantine Books, a division of Random House, Inc., New York, and simultaneously in Canada by Random House of Canada Limited, Toronto.

http://www.randomhouse.com

Library of Congress Catalog Number: 95-96185

ISBN: 0-345-38048-7

Map by Christine Levis

Manufactured in the United States of America

First Edition: August 1996

10 9 8 7 6 5 4 3 2 1

HAMMER
AND ANVIL

IN THE TIME OF TROUBLES

PARDRAYA

MYLASA RIVER

DEGIRD RIVER

VEK RUD RIVER

VEK RUD STRONGHOLD

MYLASA SEA

PAPAK'S STRONGHOLD

NALGIS CRAG STRONGHOLD

HARPAR

KOLPHIS R.

OGLOS R.

RIVER

MAKURAN

DILBAT

TIB R.

NASHVAR

SHIPPURAK

ER-KHEDUR

KHURREMBAR

MASHIZ

TUTUB R.

VASPURAKAN

SHAHAPIVAN

ERZERUM MTS

VIDESSIAN SEA

PITYOS

PR

 EREKHATTI

ISKANSHIN

POSKH

RHAMNOS

SERRHES

EMPIRE

LYSSAION

RESRINA

VRYETION

HANZITH

AMORION

ITHOME R.

ARANOS R.

SEA OF SALT

LAND OF THE THOUSAND CITIES

SAILOR

I

When the younger Maniakes looked west from the governor's residence—a polite name for a fortress—in Kastavala, he could see only ocean. Even so, staring out at that ocean did not bother him unduly: he knew that beyond it lay the town of Opsikion, and beyond Opsikion the rest of the Empire of Videssos.

He and his father, from whom he drew his name, had lived on the island of Kalavria half a dozen years now. It was exile, but polite, honorable exile: the elder Maniakes was governor of the island. The Avtokrator Likinios had named him to the post, and Genesios, after murdering Likinios and all his sons and seizing the imperial throne for himself, had seen fit to leave him undisturbed. In his day, the elder Maniakes had been a soldier to reckon with; Genesios was no doubt just as glad to keep him busy far, far away from Videssos the city, the great capital of the Empire.

The younger Maniakes stirred restlessly. He knew just how far Kalavria was removed from the center of the imperial stage. In his six years here, he had ridden over almost every inch of the island. He had camped by a fire on the eastern shore and looked out to where the Sailors' Sea ran on . . . forever, as far as anyone knew. The view east shouldn't have looked different from the view west, but somehow it did. Realizing you had your back to everything you would ever know seemed to change the way your eyes worked.

A voice came from behind him: "Woolgathering again, I see."

"Father! I didn't hear you come up," the younger Maniakes said.

"Proves my point, doesn't it?" The elder Maniakes chuckled raspily. He was a solidly made man in his middle sixties. A great fleshy beak of a nose dominated the rest of his features. He had aged about as well as he could for a man of his years. He still had most of his teeth, and his eyes and ears worked well enough. Along with his big, thick, bushy beard, his hair was white, but he had most of it, too. His wits, if anything, were sharper than they had ever been.

"I wasn't woolgathering," the younger Maniakes insisted, though his voice rose a little in embarrassment. "I was thinking." He had fewer than half his father's years, but most of the same features, including the impressive nose and the heavy beard that grew up almost to his eyes. Both were signs of the Vaspurakaner blood the two Maniakai shared: the elder Maniakes' father had left the land of the princes to take service with Videssos, and his scions had prospered there.

Now the elder Maniakes laughed out loud. "And what were you thinking that was so all-fired important you didn't even notice me?"

The younger Maniakes looked around, and listened, too. No, no servants were in earshot. You couldn't be too careful these days. Lowering his voice, he said, "About Genesios."

That got his father's attention. "Were you?" the elder Maniakes said, also quietly. He strode forward to stand by his son and look west with him. The governor's residence stood on a height above the town of Kastavala proper. From it, the red tile roofs of houses and shops and the golden spheres that topped Phos' temples seemed spread out as if on a chart of parchment.

Beyond the houses, beyond the temples, lay the harbor that was Kastavala's true reason for being. By the sea squatted sun-bleached wooden warehouses and fish-drying sheds. When the wind blew out of the west, as it did more often than not, everyone in Kastavala was reminded of those sheds without any need to see them.

Wooden piers jutted into the sea. Most of the vessels tied up at them were fishing boats. The men who took them out day after day brought back the mackerel and squid that helped feed Kastavala. The merchant ships that came from Opsikion and sometimes even from Videssos the city loomed over them like bulls over calves.

At the base of one of those piers stood a spear, its butt jammed into the sand. Suspended from the point of the spear was a skull. A little skin, a little hair still clung to it. At Genesios' command, that spear and its burden had stood in place there for more than five years. When it came to Kastavala, the skull had been a head: the head of Hosios, eldest son and heir to the overthrown Avtokrator Likinios.

Softly still, the younger Maniakes said, "Genesios Avtokrator hasn't done all the things he might have for Videssos."

Beside him, his father snorted. "Tell the truth, son. As far as I can see, Genesios Avtokrator hasn't done *any* of the things he might have for Videssos." Scorn filled his voice. Even so, he did not raise it. One thing Genesios was good at: scenting treason growing and rooting it out before it came to flower.

The younger Maniakes said, "Between the civil war, the Kubratoi, and the Makuraners, I wonder if there will be anything left of Videssos after a few more years. Here on this island, we're away from trouble, too."

"If it hadn't been for the Kubratoi, Likinios would still be Emperor today, or Hosios after him," the elder Maniakes said with a sigh. "Better he should have lost against the nomads than won a victory that made him think he could win more by ordering his troops to stay north of the Astris River through the winter and live off the land." He shivered at the thought of it. "If I'd been in that army, I might have rebelled, too."

His son shook his head, not believing it for a moment. The elder Maniakes had the grace to look abashed. Duty ran deep in him. He might complain about the onerous parts of a soldier's life, but he would never shirk them.

The younger Maniakes said, "Since Likinios fell, it hasn't been just the Kubratoi running wild up in the northeast." He stopped, bemused by a perspective based on the view from Videssos the city. Kubrat lay north of Kalavria, but also west, not east. But then, from Kalavria just about everything lay to the west. He went on, "The men of Makuran have caused the Empire even more grief, I think."

"And whose fault is that?" The elder Maniakes pointed first at his son, then at himself. "Ours, no one else's."

"No, Likinios', too," the younger Maniakes said. "If he hadn't ordered us to help Sharbaraz—" In Videssian fashion, he pronounced the name of the Makuraner King of Kings as if it were *Sarbaraz*. "—get his throne back from that usurper,

Makuran would be in no position to fight a war against Videssos. They'd have their own troubles to deal with, out there in the far west."

"Likinios Avtokrator may have ordered it, but we accomplished it, you and I," his father answered. "Sharbaraz was properly grateful, too; I'll say so much for him. And now he uses gratitude as an excuse to avenge his benefactor—and swallow up as much of the Videssian westlands as he can."

The younger Maniakes turned and stared out the window again. At this distance, the standing spearshaft and the skull on it were invisible, but he knew where they stood. Half to himself, he said, "I wonder if the Hosios Sharbaraz claims to have with him might actually be Likinios' son."

"No." The elder Maniakes' voice was hard and flat. "Whatever else Genesios Avtokrator may be, he is an effective butcher. If he claims he massacred Likinios' whole clan, you may rely on him to speak the truth there—even if nowhere else. And I recognized that head when it still had flesh on it. Didn't you?"

"Yes," the younger Maniakes admitted unwillingly. "But still—"

"—You wish we had some legitimate choice besides Genesios and his endless murders and betrayals," his father finished for him. "By Phos the lord with the great and good mind, so do I. But with Genesios holding Videssos the city, we don't, so what point even to thinking about it?"

The younger Maniakes left the window. His sandals clicked over the mosaic tiles of a hunting scene as he walked to the doorway. He looked out into the hall. It was empty in both directions. All the same, he closed the door before he went back to his father. When he spoke, it was in a whisper. "We could go into rebellion."

"No, by the good god," the elder Maniakes said, almost as quietly. "Do you know how many rebels' heads adorn the Milestone in the plaza of Palamas these days? A couple of dozen, maybe more. If an Avtokrator who holds the capital is even slightly awake to the world around him, a revolt in the provinces—especially in a Phos-forsaken province like Kalavria—is foredoomed to failure. Videssos the city is too hard a nut to crack."

"Yes, Father." The younger Maniakes sighed. They had this discussion about twice a year, or whenever word of some new disaster of Genesios' came into Kastavala, whichever was more frequent. By now, they both knew all the steps in it as well as a standard opening sequence in the Videssian board game.

But now, like a skilled player trying a variation on one of those sequences, the elder Maniakes said, "Or are you still pining for that fiancée of yours back in Videssos the city?"

Swarthy though he was, the younger Maniakes knew he was flushing. "You know bloody well it's not that," he said. He had been engaged to Niphone, the daughter of Likinios' logothete of the treasury, and assotted of her, as well. But when Likinios named his father governor of Kalavria and packed both Maniakai off to the island, they had had to leave in too much haste for a wedding. The younger Maniakes had wept bitter tears most of the way to Kastavala.

"I didn't think that was it," his father said with a twinkle in his eye, "but I did want to check. I'm sure Rotrude will be glad to hear it."

The younger Maniakes flushed again. Rotrude had been his leman for four years now. She had stayed behind in Kastavala when her husband, a trader in furs and amber from up in cold Halogaland, died of a flux of the bowels. Her exotic good looks had caught the younger Maniakes' eye: almost no Videssians had golden hair and eyes the green-blue color of the sea.

"Hard to believe Atalarikhos will be three soon," he said. He gave the boy's name the Videssian pronunciation and ending. Rotrude had wanted to name her son after her dead husband, and in the Haloga fashion simply called him Athalaric.

"He's a likely enough lad, but one of these days you should get yourself a legitimate heir," the elder Maniakes said.

His son turned that one against him like a board-game player bringing a captured piece back into action on his own side. "By the good god, where am I to find a girl of proper noble birth here on Kalavria?"

"A point." The elder Maniakes conceded that it was a good one by dipping his head and changing the subject. He pointed out to sea and said, "Isn't that a sail coming in from the west?"

"By Phos, I think it is," the younger Maniakes answered. "Nothing wrong with your eyes, Father, that's plain enough."

"Nothing wrong for looking out over the ocean, anyhow. When I try to read, it's another matter. I have to hold everything at arm's length, and then, half the time, the letters are too small to make out."

"That's a good-sized ship," the younger Maniakes said, gauging it against a fishing boat bobbing in the chop not far away. "I think I'll go down to the pier and see what cargo it brings." Watching a merchantman unload was more interesting than most things that happened in Kastavala.

"Pick up the news from the mainland, too," his father said. "It won't be good—it never is any more—but we should have it."

"I'll do as you say, Father."

The younger Maniakes hurried downstairs. At the doorway that opened onto the path leading down into town, he almost ran into his cousin Rhegorios. The two of them looked enough alike to be brothers: not surprising, since Rhegorios' father Symvatios, the elder Maniakes' younger brother, could almost have been his twin.

"Where away in such a hurry?" Rhegorios asked.

"Down to the harbor. I was on the top floor and saw a merchantman coming in," the younger Maniakes said. "Want to come along?"

"Why not?" his cousin answered. "Wait here a moment—let me get my swordbelt." He trotted down the hall toward his chamber.

Maniakes was already wearing his sword, belted on over a robe of brocaded silk. When winter came and snowstorms rolled across the sea and into Kastavala, he changed to tunic and trousers and thick sheepskin jacket, as did everyone else in town. Many men, maybe most, wore tunic and trousers the year around, but nobles were expected to be respectably conservative.

Rhegorios hurried back, still closing the heavy gold buckle on his swordbelt. He liked display better than Maniakes did. But then, he'd seen less fighting than his cousin: a fancy-decked soldier only made a juicier target for his foes.

A servant came up to bar the door behind Maniakes and Rhegorios. The wind was rising, and from out of the west. Maniakes coughed a little—it threw the reek of the fish-drying sheds full in his face. Rhegorios laughed, understanding him. "Think on the bright side, cousin," he said. "It stinks, aye, but it brings that ship in faster."

"True enough," Maniakes said. The slope of the rise lengthened his strides and sped his pace into town. He knew the slog back would be long, but was young enough not to worry about that till he had to do it.

Kastavala had no wall. Danger here came from the sea, not from the island. Soon Maniakes and Rhegorios were in among houses, most presenting to the world only whitewashed fronts with narrow, shuttered windows and stout doors; taverns and inns and brothels that catered to sailors; eateries smelling of fried fish; and shops of all sorts, most with trades connected to the sea—sailweavers, ropemakers, carpenters, coopers, with here and there a silversmith or a jeweler: a good many sailors carried their wealth on them.

Sailors and artisans, merchants and farmers from the hinterland crowded Kastavala's narrow, winding streets. Only the road that led from the harbor up to the governor's residence was cobbled; dust rose from the others in a hovering, eye-stinging cloud. Maniakes and Rhegorios picked their way through the crowd, now and then dodging a wagon heading up from the quays with a rattle of iron-clad wheels and horseshoes on cobbles and the hideous squeak of ungreased axles.

In dodging, Maniakes almost bumped into a priest. "Your pardon, holy sir," he said.

"No harm done. Phos bless you, young man." The priest sketched the good god's sun-circle above his left breast. He wore a gold-embroidered circle there on an otherwise plain robe of sky-blue wool. That garb, his shaven pate, and an untrimmed beard normal for a Vaspurakaner but unusual among all Videssians save clerics were the badges of his office.

Maniakes and Rhegorios returned the gesture and pressed on. A moment later, Maniakes glanced around and saw his cousin was no longer with him. He whirled around. There stood Rhegorios, ogling a pretty girl. By her plain linen tunic and disordered hair, she was probably a laundress or cook rather than a tart seeking to draw men's eyes.

"Come on," Maniakes called.

Rhegorios came, still looking back over his shoulder. "I want to see which shop she goes into," he said. The road bent. He sighed. "She's gone—lost forever." He clapped a melodramatic hand over his heart.

Maniakes let out a snort. "You can take a pandoura into a tavern here and sing of your vanished love. Bring a sailor's cap along and you'll cadge enough coppers for a night's worth of wine. Meanwhile, watch where you're going. You almost stepped into a pile of horse turds there, and didn't even know it."

"You're a cruel, hard man, cousin of mine." Rhegorios staggered, as if wounded.

"What are you miming—being pierced by the arrow of common sense?" Maniakes asked. Rhegorios poked him in the ribs with an elbow. They half wrestled their way down to the piers.

Aboard the approaching merchantman, the sailors had put sweeps into the oarlocks fore and aft and were using them to guide the ship toward a good-sized open space on one of the quays. "Pull, lads, pull!" the captain called, his voice easily audible across a narrowing gap of water. "A little to port on the steering oars . . . a little more. Now—back water!" The ship stopped smoothly by the quay. Sailors jumped across to hold it in place with lines.

Rhegorios pointed to a knot of well-dressed men who stood close by the ship's near rail. "Not the usual sort of crowd you find at sea," he remarked. "Wonder what it means that they're here?"

"It means trouble," Maniakes replied. "You see that one in the saffron robe with the red and black brocade?" Without waiting for his cousin to nod, he went on, "That's Kourikos, the logothete of the treasury."

"Your fiancée's father." Rhegorios' eyes widened.

"That's right," Maniakes answered grimly. "Him I'd know anywhere. The others—it's been six years, but I recognize half of them, maybe more. All the ones I do recognize are men who ran things back in Videssos the city before Genesios overthrew Likinios. The ones I don't know have the same look to them, too; I'd bet they're Genesios' appointees to fill the jobs of men he's killed. But your question was the right one: what are they doing *here*?"

Rhegorios drew his sword. He held it with the point down by his right foot, but seemed ready to raise it and strike at any provocation—or none. "You gave it the right answer, cousin: they're bringing trouble."

A little more slowly than Maniakes had spotted him, Kourikos recognized his daughter's betrothed. He waved frantically at Maniakes, then turned and said something to his companions. In an instant, they, too, were waving like men possessed. At the captain's orders, a couple of sailors extended a gangplank from the ship to the pier. The richly dressed men almost fought one another to be first across it; Maniakes was surprised no one fell—or got elbowed—off the plank and into the sea.

Kourikos in the lead, the nobles and government ministers rushed toward Maniakes and Rhegorios. "Eminent, most noble Maniakes!" his fiancée's father cried, bowing low before him. "Take us at once to the dwelling of your wise and heroic father, that we may pour out for him our tale of the woe and horror and despair that have fallen on the city, the queen of cities—" He meant the imperial capital but, like many Videssian nobles, preferred talking around something to coming right out and saying it. "—and have overwhelmed the Empire!"

One of the other men—Maniakes thought his name was Triphylles—said, "Only your father can rescue Videssos from our present calamity!" Everyone else nodded emphatically.

"What's gone and fallen to the Makuraners now?" Rhegorios asked.

"The Makuraners?" Now Kourikos, evidently spokesman by virtue of his relationship to the younger Maniakes, shook his head. "The Makuraners outside the city do dreadful things, too, seizing our land and carrying off prisoners innumerable, but that murderous Genesios does worse than they within."

Triphylles tapped him on the arm and said, "Eminent Kourikos, if you go through the whole tale of woe here, it will delay us in reaching the elder Maniakes, whereupon we shall just have to retail it over again."

"What you say is true, excellent sir," Kourikos answered. He turned back to the younger Maniakes. "Phos grant that you forgive my cutting short intercourse with you here, that we may speak to your magnificent father as soon as is practicable."

"Yes, certainly," Maniakes said after a moment—he was no longer used to the flowery language in vogue among the upper classes at the capital and had to make sure he knew what Kourikos meant. But instead of leading the delegation of grandees straight back toward the governor's residence, he held up a hand. "First you must tell me whether Niphone is safe and well."

"She was well when I left Videssos the city," Kourikos answered, "and as safe as she could make herself: she and her mother have both entered the convent dedicated to the holy Phostina. We all pray that even the monster Genesios will hesitate before dragging out anyone, female or male, who has taken service with the good god."

"May it be so," Maniakes said, and sketched Phos' suncircle over his heart. With any Avtokrator he had ever heard of, the safety of those mured up in monasteries or convents would have been a given. If Kourikos still worried about what Genesios would do, then Genesios probably was a monster. Maniakes took a step toward the base of the pier. "Come with me, excellent sirs, eminent sirs." He pointed toward the mansion on the high ground in back of town. "There dwells my father. He will hear you with great attention, I am sure."

Together, he and Rhegorios led the nobles from Videssos the city back through Kastavala. The Kastavalans stared curiously at the newcomers, who stood out not only because they were strangers but also by virtue of their rich and splendid robes. Seeing such obvious wealth, a couple of tarts called sweetvoiced invitations. The nobles took no notice; they were undoubtedly used to better.

By the way they looked at Kastavala, that attitude applied to more than just the easy women of the town. Next to the capital, Kastavala was small and drab and dirty and smelly. Maniakes knew that perfectly well. But the same applied to any provincial center. He had seen a great many such towns, all through the Empire of Videssos; Kastavala was typical of the breed. After a while, he realized some of the grandees hadn't seen anything outside Videssos the city save perhaps their country estates and hunting lodges. For them, a provincial town had to be something of a shock.

"Coming out!" somebody called from a second-story balcony, and emptied a jar of slops, *splat!* in the middle of the street. Kourikos and the rest jumped back in alarm and disgust, tugging at the hems of their robes to makes sure the stinking stuff didn't splash them.

"That woman should be clapped in irons," the logothete of the treasury declared.

"Why?" Maniakes asked. "She warned us before she let fly."

Kourikos stared at him in horror that only grew when he realized his prospective son-in-law was serious. Most of the houses and blocks of flats in Videssos the city had drains that connected them to underground sewers. That was an unimagined luxury in Kastavala.

Several of the grandees from the capital were puffing and

red in the face by the time they reached the governor's residence. Maniakes didn't need to open the door and usher them inside: someone had seen them coming, and quite a crowd had gathered in front of the residence to greet them and learn what word they brought.

Voice doubtful, Kourikos asked, "Eminent Maniakes, is that your father there?"

Maniakes didn't blame him for being wrong; the resemblances was striking. "No, that's my uncle Symvatios, father to Rhegorios here. He and my father have always been like as two peas in the pod. And that's his daughter there beside him—my cousin Lysia."

Lysia was still too far away to have heard him speak her name, but chose that moment to wave to him. He waved back, smiling as he did so. He had hardly known her before Symvatios and his family sailed with the Maniakai to the island of Kalavria, but the two of them had grown close since: so close that Rotrude had teased him about it once or twice. He hadn't risen to the teasing as he usually did; it left him nervous.

As Maniakes and the nobles drew near, Lysia called, "What interesting people you've brought us, cousin! Phos' blessing on you for that." Symvatios nodded vigorously. So did more than a few of the grooms and cooks and serving women who had come out with their masters. The prospect of fresh faces and fresh news piqued everyone's curiosity.

Maniakes pointed to a servant. "Aplakes, go fetch my father at once. The eminent Kourikos here and these other excellent sirs and eminent sirs have come from Videssos the city to confer with him on an urgent matter."

Aplakes dashed back into the mansion. Everyone else started buzzing. The grandees looked like important people. Hearing just how important they were set tongues wagging. Lysia stared at Maniakes, her eyes shining in a face slightly rounder and less craggy than that of her brother Rhegorios. Better than the servants, she could guess one reason why the nobles might have come from the capital to Kastavala.

Aplakes hadn't bothered closing the entry door after him. He soon emerged, the elder Maniakes a pace behind. As soon as the elder Maniakes appeared, Kourikos and his companions, instead of bowing as the younger Maniakes had expected, dropped first to their knees and then to their bellies, touching their foreheads to the dirt in the full proskynesis normally reserved for honoring the Avtokrator of the Videssians alone.

The younger Maniakes simply gaped. His father's bushy white eyebrows climbed toward his hairline. He spat on the ground, as if in rejection of the dark god Skotos. "Get up, the lot of you," he growled, anger and fear in his voice. "If you think you'll trick me thus into treason against Genesios Avtokrator, you can bloody well think again."

As the grandees rose, they looked at one another with mixed horror and dismay. "Most noble Maniakes, you misunderstand," Kourikos said, a quaver in his voice. "We are the ones guilty of treason, at least in Genesios' eyes. We have fled here from Videssos the city to beg you to take the crown and save the Empire. Without you, it will surely fall, either from the ravages of the Makuraners or simply from the insane excesses of the tyrant whose bloodstained backside now defiles the imperial throne."

The two Maniakai exchanged glances. Not long before the ship that had brought Kourikos and his comrades to Kastavala came into sight, they had talked about rebellion against Genesios. The elder Maniakes had rejected it then. Now—now he looked thoughtfully at the group of nobles and asked, "What has Genesios done to turn you against him after you followed him like dogs these past half-dozen years?"

Several of the grandees hung their heads. Kourikos had more spirit—or perhaps more desperation—than most; he said, "If you speak of following like dogs, Lord Maniakes, I noticed you've not taken poor Hosios' head down off its pike in all these years. D'you bark with the rest of us, then?"

"Mm, put that way, maybe I do." The elder Maniakes stroked his beard. "Very well, eminent sir, say on: why would you sooner see my backside on the throne than Genesios'?"

"Why?" Kourikos clapped a dramatic—and possibly rehearsed—hand to his forehead. "Were Skotos to come up to Videssos from his hell of ice—" He spat as the elder Maniakes had. "—he could hardly serve it worse than Genesios the poxed, the madman, the butcher, the blundering, bungling idiot who is about to cast centuries of imperial splendor onto the dungheap forever."

The elder Maniakes bowed slightly. "You can curse with any man, eminent sir. But what has Genesios actually *done*?"

Kourikos took a deep breath. "Let us leave to one side the disasters against Makuran and the misfortunes against Kubrat.

You surely know of those already. Not long ago, Genesios spoke to the city mob in the Amphitheater, currying favor with them because he knew everyone else hated him. But some of their leaders jeered him because of his many failings. He sent soldiers in among the seats, seized a dozen men, maybe more, ordered them stripped naked, and put them to the sword in front of the crowd.

"When the general Sphrantzes failed against the Makuraners—and how could he do otherwise, with neither men nor money enough to fight?—Genesios whipped him to death with leather lashes. Elpidios the prefect of the city exchanged letters with Tzikaste, Likinios' widow. Genesios cut off his hands and feet and then his head. Then he slew Tzikaste herself and both her daughters at the same spot where he'd murdered Likinios Avtokrator and his sons. At this rate, not a man nor woman will be left alive in Videssos the city by the time winter comes, save only the tyrant and his toadies. Save us, save Videssos, I beg you, most noble Maniakes!"

"Save us!" the rest of the nobles chorused.

"Eminent sirs, excellent sirs, if you expect me to jump into your ship and sail back to Videssos the city with you, I'm afraid I'm going to leave you disappointed," the elder Maniakes said. "But I'll not deny you've given me much to think on." He peered down toward the harbor. "Will your servants be fetching your baggage here to the residence?"

"Most eminent Maniakes, we found the opportunity to flee, and we took it," Kourikos answered. "We brought no servants; the more who knew of our plan, the likelier we were to be betrayed to the monster. As for baggage, what you see is what we have."

The elder Maniakes' eyebrows rose again. For Videssian nobles to travel without baggage was a truer measure of desperation than any woeful tale, no matter how heartrending. The revelation startled the younger Maniakes, too. He did notice the grandees had fat leather pouches at their belts, pouches that might well be filled with goldpieces. They might have come as fugitives, but they probably weren't beggars.

"Well, well," the elder Maniakes said. "In that case, come in and be welcome. I shan't turn you over to Genesios; that much I promise you. If he has a ship on your heels, you can flee into the countryside and escape. For now, though, more gladsome things: Aplakes and the other servants will show you to chambers. We have room and to spare, that we do, by Phos. And at supper in the courtyard this evening, we'll speak further on these matters. Meanwhile . . ." He used his eyes to gather up his son, Rhegorios, and Symvatios.

The servants led the nobles into the governor's residence. As the younger Maniakes went up to his father, Lysia set a hand on his arm. "Isn't it marvelous!" she exclaimed, her black eyes flashing with excitement. "At last, Phos willing, Genesios will get what he's long deserved. And then—"

"And then," Symvatios broke in, his voice almost eerily like that of the elder Maniakes, "we have to figure out what to do next, if we decide to do anything at all. Are you going to plot with us here?"

Lysia made a face at her father. "I would if you'd let me, but I don't suppose you will." Symvatios slowly shook his head. His daughter made another face. She stood on tiptoe to kiss the younger Maniakes on the end of his nose—he was used to that; because his beard was so thick and full, she did it a lot—then went into the residence herself.

The two older brothers and their sons put their heads together. Rhegorios said, "Uncle, they aim to set you on the throne." His eyes snapped with the same high spirits that had filled Lysia's.

"I know that," the elder Maniakes answered matter-of-factly. "What I don't know is whether I want to sit there. Way things look to me now, I have my doubts, and big ones."

His son, brother, and nephew all gaped in amazement. In the middle of their gaping, the door to the mansion opened. The cook came out. He sent the elder Maniakes a dirty look and headed down the slope toward the markets of Kastavala almost at a run. Symvatios laughed. "That's what you get for inviting a whole raft of people to supper on short notice," he said, resting a hand on his paunch for a moment; he was heavier than his brother.

"If a glare is all I get, I'll count myself lucky." The elder Maniakes chuckled. "I just hope it's not nightshade in the soup, or some such." He sobered. "Back to it. Look at me, all of you. I'm an old man. I've done nothing but fight since I was fifteen years old, except these past few years here in Kalavria. I hated Likinios when he sent me here, but do you know what? I've come to like this place and to enjoy the easy life. I don't want to fight any more, and I don't care to sit on a throne and know half the people watching me are trying to

figure out how to throw me off it. What do you think of that?"
He looked defiantly at his kinsmen.

"Let it all be as you say, Father," the younger Maniakes answered. "Can we sit out here on this island and watch the Empire get dragged down to the ice? If Genesios is as bad as this, even Videssos the city may fall to the Makuraners—or to the Kubratoi. One day a fleet may sail for Kalavria with the red lion of the King of Kings of Makuran painted on the sails."

The elder Maniakes chuckled again, but without humor. "And wouldn't that be strange, when the two of us led the Videssian army that helped put Sharbaraz back on his throne? But you're right. If he saw the chance, he wouldn't hesitate, not even for a heartbeat."

"Well, then," the younger Maniakes and Rhegorios said together.

"Well, then—what?" the elder Maniakes answered.

"You have to take the throne," his son explained, as if the necessity were as obvious as a geometric proof.

"Nonsense," the elder Maniakes said. "I don't have to do any such thing. What's more, the more I think about it, the less I want to do any such thing. I'm perfectly content to rusticate, and, as best as I can recall, I've never been perfectly content before. Governor of Kalavria suits me fine. If you think the Empire needs saving, son, *you* save it."

Symvatios and Rhegorios looked from the elder Maniakes to the younger. For a moment, he didn't understand why they were looking at him as they were. Then he did, and ice and fire might have coursed together through his veins. "Father," he said slowly, "if I go, will you help me?"

Now it was the elder Maniakes' turn to hesitate before he replied. "You mean this," he said. It was not quite a question. The younger Maniakes nodded. The elder sucked in a long breath, then folded his son into an embrace that still had a good deal of strength in it. "Of course. The whole clan will." His eyes swung to his brother and nephew.

"Aye," Symvatios said at once.

"Aye," Rhegorios agreed. "If Maniakes here hadn't spoken up, I would have myself." Now the younger Maniakes stared at his cousin. He was far from Avtokrator as yet, but did he already have a rival?

"We shall essay it, then," the elder Maniakes said. That should have been a ringing declaration. Instead, as had his earlier words, it came out almost as a query. A moment later, he showed the reason for his doubt: "If we fail, we die. The whole clan dies, all the kinsfolk we have whom Genesios can reach. We had best not fail. We don't need to move on Videssos the city tomorrow, and we'd be mad if we did. We think it through before we try it."

"Yes," the younger Maniakes said. Beside him, Rhegorios twisted like a restive horse. He didn't want to wait. He wanted to charge right at Genesios. The younger Maniakes remarked, "Sometimes the straightest way is not the shortest one."

"My boy!" his father said, now full of pride. "You've learned something after all." He hugged the younger Maniakes again.

Symvatios said, "Now that we know we are going to do this thing, let's go in and get ready for supper. I want to see Kourikos' face when he finds out he's going to be father-in-law to an Avtokrator right away."

The elder Maniakes chuckled, but the younger said, "Genesios will find that out, too. I hope it doesn't put Niphone in any danger; Kourikos said she was in a convent in Videssos the city."

"One more thing to worry about," the elder Maniakes said. "On campaign, you'll add something to your list a hundred times a day. But for now, Symvatios is right. We've done what we can for the time being. Let's get ready for supper."

One more thing to worry about, the younger Maniakes thought as he walked toward the tables and chairs that had been hastily set up among the flowers of the courtyard. Rotrude was on his arm, with Atalarikhos walking along holding his mother's hand. How Kourikos would react on seeing his soon-to-be-son-in-law with not only a leman but also a bastard boy was liable to be . . . interesting.

By rights, the logothete of the treasury had no cause for complaint. He could hardly have expected Maniakes to have stayed celibate as a monk when he had been far away from his intended bride all these years. He might have expected Maniakes not to show his woman here so openly. Maniakes had thought about that. If he had left Rotrude behind, it would have said he was ashamed of her, which not only wasn't true but would have infuriated her had it so much as crossed her mind.

Most of the nobles fled from the capital were already in the courtyard, talking among themselves, drinking wine, and pretending to admire the plants. The younger Maniakes knew they were politely insincere there; the formal gardens of Videssos the city outshone this one as the sun did a dim star.

Talk of the garden ceased when they saw Rotrude. Few women of the Halogai came into the Empire. Her golden hair drew a Videssian man's eye like a lodestone. Once you stopped staring at that, you noticed the eyes, the strong chin, thrusting cheekbones, and short straight nose, the sheer size of her—she was almost as tall as the younger Maniakes, who was not short—and her shape, womanly despite her inches.

The grandees' stares gave him a certain amount of pride. They irked her. Turning to him, she said, "I am not one of the big beasts from the Hot Lands, the ones with snakes for snouts." Her Videssian was clear but slow, with the half-drawled accent of her homeland.

"They're admiring you," Maniakes said. "If you'd been born in the Empire, you'd be preening for them."

"If I had been born in the Empire, I would have the same seeming as they and you, so they would not need to gape." She reached down and ruffled Atalarikhos' hair. "So your son does."

"Mostly," Maniakes said. The hair through which Rotrude ran her fingers was as black as his own, but straight, not wavy like Maniakes'. But Atalarikhos had some of his mother's coloring: Maniakes was slightly swarthier than the average Videssian, his son slightly fairer. The shape of his face was more like Rotrude's, too, though even at less than three he gave signs of developing a nose of impressive proportions.

Kourikos strode toward Maniakes and his companions. Behind the logothete, the other nobles grew suddenly quiet, watching to see what he would do. Kourikos bowed to Maniakes. "Good to see you again, eminent sir," the grandee said, his voice politely neutral. "Will you be so kind as to perform the introductions here?"

"Of course," Maniakes said, matching his courtesy. "Eminent Kourikos, I present to you my lady Rotrude and her son—our son—Atalarikhos." There. The truth was out. Let Kourikos make of it what he would.

"Your—lady," Kourikos said carefully. "Not, I take it, your lady wife?"

"No, eminent sir," Maniakes answered. "How could that be, when I am affianced to your daughter?" Rotrude knew about his engagement to Niphone. She had a fierce, direct way of looking at the world; keeping things of importance from her was unwise. Up till now, the engagement had never bothered her; a woman far away in Videssos the city remained quite nicely hypothetical. But if Kourikos was real, that made his daughter realer, too.

As if Rotrude were not standing before him, the logothete of the treasury said, "Of course you will put your—lady—aside when your father is anointed and crowned Avtokrator of the Videssians."

Rotrude looked not at Kourikos but through him. He might have abruptly ceased to exist. Dodging part of the question, the younger Maniakes said, "It's not for me to discuss my father's plans. He is more than able to do that for himself—and here he comes now."

Kourikos and the rest of the nobles cried, "Thou conquerest, Maniakes Avtokrator!"—the traditional acclamation of a Videssian Emperor. They began to prostrate themselves, as they had in front of the governor's mansion.

"Stop that!" the elder Maniakes said testily. "I'm not Avtokrator and I don't intend to become Avtokrator, so stop treating me as if I were. If you think you can flatter me into donning the red boots, you can bloody well think again."

Kourikos' expression said the elder Maniakes might have just taken an image of Phos from the iconostasis of a temple and set a torch to it. The rest of the grandees looked similarly downcast. Triphylles said, "But your maj—uh, most eminent sir—"

"All I'm going to say now is that you won't get left in the lurch." The elder Maniakes waved to the servitors behind him. "First we sup. Then we talk."

Sulkily, the nobles from Videssos the city took the places to which Aplakes led them. They kept on murmuring among themselves. The younger Maniakes watched their eyes flick this way and that. Sometimes those glances rested lightly on him, sometimes on his father, sometimes on Symvatios and Rhegorios. Whenever you caught a noble staring, his gaze would flit away like a frightened fly.

From down the table, Lysia caught the younger Maniakes' eye. Her eyes gleamed; her father or brother must have told her what they had decided. Maniakes smiled at her, glad to find someone who could look his way without seeming guilty about it.

The cook might have been dismayed at the prospect of having to serve a flock of unexpected guests of high rank, but he acquitted himself well. His first course was a salad, carrots and parsnips lightly cooked in olive oil and cumin, then served with salted olives and hard-cooked eggs on a bed of endive. Atalarikhos devoured his egg and the olives and started to cry when Rotrude tried to make him eat some carrots.

"Don't force him, not tonight," the younger Maniakes told her. "Let's keep him quiet if we can."

She sucked in her underlip, as she did when she disapproved. "He needs to eat to grow strong," she said. Then she sighed. "I yield. One night's food does not matter—much."

After the salad came an earthenware casserole full of leeks and fava beans stewed in broth and then wrapped in cabbage leaves. At the sight of that, Atalarikhos said something in the Haloga language he had learned from his mother. The younger Maniakes was glad none of the grandees from the imperial city understood enough of that speech to realize he had called the casserole a big chamber pot.

For the main course, the servants brought from the kitchen trays of steamed young mackerel stuffed with a mixture of mint leaves, pepper, chopped almonds, and honey. Atalarikhos enthusiastically ate up his stuffing but wanted no part of the fish in which it was contained. Now it was the younger Maniakes who avoided Rotrude's probing eye.

The sweet was apple slices, apricots, and grapes, candied together in honey. Atalarikhos swept his own bowl clean, then started stealing grapes from his mother. Rotrude sighed. "He is not starving," she said, as if reminding herself.

Servants swept away dishes, knives, and spoons while supper guests licked their fingers clean. More servants lit torches all around the courtyard. The sky above darkened from bright blue toward black. The first stars began to glisten.

Grunting a little and patting his belly, the elder Maniakes got to his feet. The nobles stared expectantly at him. He swigged from his cup of wine, set the silver vessel down with a clang, and cleared his throat. "I'm not much for speechmaking," he said, which was a crashing lie; his son had never seen anyone better at rousing troops to go forward even when some of them were sure to die. But the lie served its purpose here: it let him say what he wanted without having to festoon it with curlicues of rhetoric. He went on, "You are gracious enough to say you wanted me to wear the crown. Very well, lords, I shall give you a Maniakes Avtokrator."

"Thou conquerest, Maniakes!" Kourikos shouted. In an instant, all his companions took up the cry. So did some of the servants, their voices rising in excitement. Maybe they dreamt of escaping Kastavala for the fabled splendor of Videssos the city.

The elder Maniakes held up a hand. He coughed once or twice, a habit of his when he thought he had outsmarted someone. "I told you this afternoon, lords, I wasn't sure I cared to be Avtokrator. I've spent the day thinking on it and, as I said before we sat down to sup, I have to tell you I've decided I don't. But I won't deny this carbuncle on the arse of Videssos named Genesios needs casting down. And so, my friends, I give you—Maniakes Avtokrator." He pointed to his son.

As the elder Maniakes sat down, the younger rose. He had known this moment was coming, but knowing that and living it were not one and the same. The grandees studied him now, their glances sharp as swords. They were older than he, and more experienced. Some of them would want to rule him, or rule through him—probably the ones who least looked like it, for they would be the most accomplished dissemblers.

He would sooner have gone into battle against the fearsome cavalry of Makuran, its men and horses glittering alike in armor of iron, than face these cagey, devious lords. But if he could not master them, how was he to hope to rule Videssos?

He said, "If Phos has not altogether despaired of the Empire, he will give Videssos a ruler who can end the civil strife that has so long consumed us, who can reclaim from the King of Kings the cities and provinces Makuran has stolen from us, and who can hold in check the ferocious horsemen of Kubrat. Doing any one of those things will be hard. Doing all three at once . . . I wish the lord with the great and good mind had not brought Videssos to such a pass. But since he has, I shall do all I can do to rescue the Empire from those who threaten it, whether on the borders or in Videssos the city itself."

It wasn't the sort of speech to send men rushing into battle, throats full of cheers, swords held high. The Empire's problems were too great for the younger Maniakes even to think about making a speech like that. If he could win the throne, he knew what he wanted to do. How he would do it, unfortunately, was another question altogether.

The grandees courteously heard him out. He was not surprised when Kourikos was again first to cry out "Thou conquerest, Maniakes Avtokrator!"—his prospective father-in-

law naturally hoped to use his accession for himself. But all
the nobles acclaimed him, their voices fulsome if not necessarily sincere.

The younger Maniakes raised his goblet high. ."To
Videssos!" he shouted, and drank.

"To Videssos!" shouted his family, the servants, and the
grandees, all together. The younger Maniakes wondered for
how many that toast actually meant, *To me!*

A single lamp burned on the night table next to Rotrude's
bed. Atalarikhos slept in the next room, with an unbarred con-
necting door between them. Once or twice, that had proved
embarrassing for the younger Maniakes. He hadn't been used
to a little boy wandering in at an awkward moment, needing to
piddle or to be comforted after a bad dream.

Rotrude took such interruption in stride. From what she had
said, in Halogaland several families often lived together in one
big room under the same roof. Privacy was a Videssian notion
to which she had had to acclimate herself.

Now she sat at the edge of the bed, brushing out her long,
golden hair. Maniakes watched the lamplight play off it. Shadows filled and magnified little lines at the corners of her mouth
and by her eyes; she hadn't many fewer years than he.

She tossed the bone-handled brush onto the night table. The
flame from the lamp jumped for a moment, then steadied. Her
face still full of the intent concentration it had held while she
was brushing, she turned to Maniakes and said, "If you win
your fight for the city, you will marry the maiden Kourikos
sired?"

He bit his lip. He hadn't thought she would put it so bluntly.
But the men and women of Halogaland, from what he had
seen of them in the capital and here in Kastavala, were a
straighter-spoken folk than most Videssians. Rotrude simply
sat, awaiting his reply. He sighed. "Yes, I suppose I shall," he
said. "Before I came here, as I've told you, I was very much
in love with her."

"And her father stands high among the Emperor's counsel-
ors," Rotrude said, "and would have reason for wrath were she
cast aside."

"That also," Maniakes agreed soberly.

Rotrude bit down on the nub of it. "And so what of me?
And so what of our son, child of our flesh?"

Again, Maniakes had hoped that question would not come

so soon, or would have been phrased to give him more room to talk around it. None of the answers he came up with struck him as good enough. He did the best he could: "Come what may, both of you will always be dear to me. If you want to stay on Kalavria, you will want for nothing—by Phos I swear it." He sketched the sun-circle over his heart.

Rotrude shrugged. She didn't mock Phos, but she didn't worship him, either; her reverence belonged to the gloomy, bloodthirsty gods of her homeland. "And if we fare forth to Halogaland once more, what then?" she asked.

"I wish you would promise not to do that," Maniakes said slowly. The thought of how much mischief a Haloga chieftain could work with an Avtokrator's bastard for a tool made his blood run cold. "So long as you stay, you can have anything here you wish."

"What I wish here mostly is you," she answered. He hung his head. Most Videssian women, just then, would either have dissolved in tears or started throwing things. Rotrude did neither; she measured him with her eyes as a warrior might have over the top of his shield. "What if I were to find another man who suited me?"

"If you wanted to wed him, and if I thought he would treat you and our son well, you would have my blessing," Maniakes said.

Rotrude studied him again. "I wonder if you tell me this because you care for me not at all or because you care for me very much," she said, perhaps half to herself, and then went on, "You have said what will be, and not wrapped lies in honey to make them sound sweet. For so much I give you credit. Not all men of my folk would have done as much, and few of you southrons, from what I have seen. So I shall choose to believe you. You are one who counts the needs of your folk before those of yourself, is it not so?"

"I hope I am, at any rate," Maniakes answered. It gave him an easier escape than he had looked for. If he wasn't that sort of man, he thought, now would be a good time to try to become such.

"You shall not sail on tomorrow's tide," Rotrude said. "To ready a rebellion to topple the tyrant, you will need to think before you do. What shall become of us before you wander west from Kastavala, from Kalavria?"

Maniakes said, "I leave that up to you. If you find you want nothing more to do with me now that you know I'm going to fight Genesios—" That seemed a better way to put it than *now that you know I'm going to leave you.* "—I can hardly blame you. I won't force myself where I'm not wanted." He would have felt more virtuous about that speech had he not known any number of women would throw themselves into an Avtokrator's bed, some simply because power drew them, others in the hope of the advantage they might wring from it.

Rotrude glanced down at her robe. "This sleeve has a seam that wants fixing," she remarked. Instead of reaching for needle and thread—sewing, like reading, was best done by daylight—she got to her feet and pulled the robe off over her head. She stood a moment in her linen drawers, then slid them down over her legs and kicked them aside. Almost defiantly naked, she stared a challenge at Maniakes.

Her body was thicker than those of most Videssian women, but shapely in its own way. Where the sun never saw it, her skin was so pale and fair, it seemed to glow in the lamplight. Even after she had nursed Atalarikhos for close to two years, her nipples were a delicate pink, hardly darker than the full, heavy breasts they topped. The triangle of golden hair at the joining of her legs matched the long locks that fell over her shoulders.

Maniakes' mouth went dry as he looked at her. If he tore a seam getting out of his own robe, he never noticed. Only when he yanked down his drawers did he realize he was still wearing sandals. He pulled out his feet without unfastening the catches, and threw the shoes against the wall. That was foolish; it might have wakened Atalarikhos. This time, luck went with him.

The coupling reminded him as much of battle as of lovemaking. When Rotrude bit the strip of flesh between his shoulder and neck, he wondered if she had drawn blood. His hands roamed rough over her body, squeezing, demanding. Their kisses smashed lips hard against teeth.

At last, both of them afire, she straddled him. When she impaled herself on him, she groaned as if pierced by a veritable lance rather than one that would presently lose its hardness. Something like triumph was on her face as she slowly began to move. "You will never forget me," she whispered, her breath warm and moist against Maniakes' cheek. "Never."

For a moment, even through growing ecstasy, he knew alarm, wondering if she was trying to bewitch him. They had wizards and witches in Halogaland, even if their magic was different from that of Videssos. Then she lowered her head to kiss him again. Her breasts brushed against the thick mat of hair on his chest. His arms tightened around her back, pulling her down to him. Women could work magic even when they used no spells.

Their lips were joined once more when she moaned and quivered above him, and a moment later when he, too, cried out. The bedchamber was not warm—even summer in Kastavala was mild, and summer nights often cool and foggy—but sweat soaked both of them.

He ran a hand along the slick curve of her back. "I will never forget you," he said, "but you're heavy on top of me." He laughed. "You've told me that, often enough."

"That's so," she admitted, and got up on her elbows and knees. Their skins made small, wet, squelching noises as they separated. Her hair spilled down onto his face. Through the strands, he saw her intently looking at him. "You are a warrior," she said at last. From a woman of the Halogai, he could expect no higher praise.

"On the battlefield, one side or the other must lose," he said. "This fight, we both won."

She stretched out beside him. "Also true," she said. "And here, we can quickly struggle again." She let a hand rest on his chest for a moment, then teased his nipple with thumb and forefinger, as he had with her a little before. Her hand wandered down, closed on him. "For as long as you are here by me, I shall be greedy of you, and take all you can give."

"Whether I can give again so soon—" Maniakes shrugged. When his beard was newly sprouted, he had been as randy as a he-goat. He remained proud of what he could do, but thirty wasn't seventeen, no matter how he wished it could be. His lance needed longer now to regain its temper.

But rise again he did. He and Rotrude joined with something close to the desperation they had shown in their first round. They were both worn and gasping when they finished. After such frenzy, Maniakes wondered what sort of appetite he would be able to conjure up for his promised bride if all went well and he cast Genesios down from the imperial throne.

He didn't wonder for long. Sleep swallowed him before he could raise his head to blow out the bedside lamp.

* * *

The two Maniakai, Symvatios, and Rhegorios strode along the beach north of the harbor of Kastavala. The younger Maniakes looked back toward the town and toward the governor's residence on the rise beyond it. He and his kinsmen had come too far for him to see the grandees up on the wall there, but he knew they were staring out toward him as he peered their way.

Symvatios half turned back toward the residence, too, but only for a moment. He made a slashing, contemptuous gesture with his left hand. "They have their gall," he said scornfully. "This is family business now, and they can bloody well keep their beaks out of it."

"Beaks indeed," the elder Maniakes said, chuckling. He set a hand on his own great nose. "They've lived in Videssos the city all their lives is their trouble; they think it gives them the right to give orders anywhere in the Empire. Not a proper soldier among 'em, either, which is too bad. Help worth having we could have used."

"They help us," Maniakes said. "If his own chiefest men can stomach Genesios no more, Videssos the city may drop into our hands like a ripe orange falling off a tree." He sighed. He missed oranges. They would not grow on Kalavria: summers did not get hot enough for them to flourish.

"If the orange doesn't fall from the tree, we'll cut it off." Rhegorios drew his sword and slashed at the air.

"If we think this fight will be easy, we are doomed before we begin," the elder Maniakes said. "How many rebels have thought the city would fall to them?" He opened and closed his hands several times to answer his own question. "And of that great flock, how many have seized the throne so?" He held up one hand, the fingers curled in a fist, none showing. "The usual way for an Avtokrator to lose the throne is by treachery within Videssos the city itself."

"Well, what of Likinios?" Rhegorios said. "Genesios took the city from without."

"Only because his own men wouldn't fight for him," the elder Maniakes answered. "If I'm keeping the accounts, that also goes down as treachery from within."

"By all the stories, Genesios' men hate him, too," the younger Maniakes said. Rhegorios nodded vigorously. He made more cut-and-thrust motions. His impulse was always to go straight at a foe.

"Not all of them," the elder Maniakes answered. "If

enough of them hated him, his head would go up on the Milestone, not those of all the rivals he's slain." He set a hand on his son's shoulder. "I don't want to see your head there, lad. When we move against Genesios, that's not something we can take back if it's not going as we'd like. We have only the one chance."

The younger Maniakes nodded. He had been through enough battles, and had enough years on him, to know things could go wrong. You did what you could to keep that from happening, but not everything you did was going to work.

Symvatios said, "What the fleet on the Key does will be the key to whether we rise or fall."

No one misunderstood him. The island called the Key lay south and east of Videssos the city and was indeed often the key to the city's fate. Its fleet was next in power after that based at the capital itself. With it, the rebels would stand a fair chance of success. Without it . . .

"You have spoken truth," the elder Maniakes said to his brother. "And it is a truth that worries me. I have—we all have—connections wide and deep within Videssos' army. Some we've not used in a while, but they're there. I expect we can take advantage of them. But few men of Vaspurakaner blood have taken to sea. The grand drungarios of the fleet and his captains have no reason to back us."

"Save that Genesios is a beast," Rhegorios said.

"Genesios has been a beast for some time," the elder Maniakes replied. "He has also been an enthroned beast for some time."

Thoughtfully, the younger Maniakes said, "Perhaps some of our, ah, guests back at the residence have relations serving in the fleet. We should look into that."

"A good notion," his father agreed. "We shall look into that. We'll also have to gather ships and fighting men from all around Kalavria to make the core of our force. We'll have enough ships to get the men and horses across to the mainland, I expect: we need a decent-sized fleet hereabouts to put down the pirates who drip into Videssian waters."

"We sail for Opsikion, I suppose," Symvatios said. "There's a fine highway from there to take the soldiers straight west to Videssos the city. If we leave them at Opsikion, they can attack by land while the fleet sails around the cape and then up to invest the sea walls."

"See what the clan can do when we put our heads together?" the elder Maniakes said. "Seems to me that's the only way to take Videssos the city, if it can be done at all: assail it from all sides at once, stretch the defenders too thin to guard everything, and pray all the powerful mages are either dead or fled from Genesios like the grandees. If we have to sit for weeks outside the city's walls, some deviltry will land on us, sure as Genesios is bound for Skotos' ice."

Rhegorios looked at the younger Maniakes. "You'll command the fleet, I suppose. That will be our striking arm and probably reach the city before the overland forces can. Give me leave to lead the infantry and cavalry, then. I'll get them across from Opsikion as fast as I can. Phos willing, I'll bring plenty of troops from the garrisons along the way, too."

Symvatios coughed. "I'd thought to play that role myself, son." Rhegorios looked stricken. Symvatios coughed again. "It may be that you're right, though." He patted his belly. "I may be too old and too round to push ahead as hard as would suit us best. Have it your way."

Rhegorios whooped and sprang in the air. The elder Maniakes slipped an arm round his brother. "I'm not going, either, Symvatios," he said. "Better the young, strong ones come to power now than that we seize it and have them hating us and counting the hours till we die. Having your sons sitting around hoping your eyes will roll up in your head and you'll fall down dead off the throne—that's no way to rule. Worrying whether your sons might give you something to make your eyes roll up in your head—that's worse."

"We'd never do such a thing!" the younger Maniakes cried. Again Rhegorios nodded.

"You say so now," the elder Maniakes answered, "but you're liable to find never is a long time. Suppose *I* seized the throne now—just suppose. And suppose I live another fifteen years or more, till I'm past eighty. It could happen, you know—nothing's killed me yet." He chuckled wheezily. "You'd be pushing on toward fifty by then, son. Would you be getting impatient, waiting for your turn? Suppose I found some pretty little chit in the city, too, and got a son on her. His beard would be starting to sprout. Would you peer at him out of the corner of your eye and wonder if he'd get the prize you'd wanted so long? What do you think? Answer me true now."

Rhegorios and the younger Maniakes looked at each other. Neither of them felt like meeting the elder Maniakes' eye. The younger Maniakes did not care for what he feared he saw in his own heart. His father was right: he hadn't looked far enough ahead when he shouted out his protest.

The elder Maniakes laughed again, this time long and deep. "And that's why Symvatios and I, we'll stay back here on the island and give the two of you good advice while you're doing the hard, dirty work it'll take to throw down Genesios."

"How many men and ships can we realize from the island?" his son asked; like the elder Maniakes, the younger yielded points by changing the subject.

"In terms of numbers, I can't begin to guess until I go through the records and see just what's spread out in the harbor and garrisons," the elder Maniakes answered. "In terms of what we can do with what we have, my guess is that it amounts to this: we'll get enough here to begin the job but not enough to finish it. If all the top soldiers and sailors in the Empire decide they'd rather see Genesios on the throne than you, you're a dead man. We're all dead men."

"From the news that trickles out to Kalavria, Videssos is liable to be a dead empire if they decide that," the younger Maniakes said.

"Which doesn't mean it won't happen," his father told him. "If men weren't fools so often, the world would be a different place—maybe even a better one. But Skotos pulls on us no less than Phos. Sometimes I wonder if the Balancer heretics of Khatrish and Thatagush don't have a point—how can you be *sure* Phos will triumph in the end?" He held out his arms, the palms of his hands out before him, as if fending off his kinsmen. "I'm sorry I brought that up. Don't start arguing dogma with me now like so many theology-mad Videssians, or we'll never get back to the residence."

Rhegorios said, "I don't know whether our generals and ship captains are fools, but I can name two men who aren't: Sharbaraz King of Kings and his brother-in-law Abivard, his chief general."

"That's true," the two Maniakai said in the same breath. The elder went on, "And it was thanks to the infinite wisdom of Likinios that we helped put Sharbaraz back on the throne of Mashiz and gave Abivard the chance to show what he could do: do to us, I should say."

"No, the two of them aren't fools," the younger Maniakes agreed. "That means just one thing: if we're going to keep them from swallowing up all the westlands—maybe even keep them from swallowing up all the Empire of Videssos— we'd better not be fools, either."

II

LYSIA STRODE RAPIDLY THROUGH THE COURTYARD, NOW GO-
ing almost to one of the doors that led to the mansion, now
coming straight back to the younger Maniakes. At last she
stopped in front of him and burst out, "I wish I were going
with you."

He took his first cousin's hands in his. "I wish you were,
too," he said. "I'll miss you. Nothing like living in each other's
belt pouches for the last half-dozen years to make us friends,
is there?"

She shook her head. "I'm sick-jealous of my brother, do you
know that?" All at once, she hugged Maniakes. "And I'm worried more than I can say for you. Do you know *that*?"

His arms went around her back. "It will work out all right,
I think," he said. "We have a good chance of winning, else
we'd not so much as try." As he spoke, he noticed, maybe for
the first time with the top part of his mind, that not all his feelings for Lysia were chaste and cousinly. She was, without any
possibility of doubt, a woman in his arms.

Lysia's eyes widened slightly. Had his arms around her
tightened more than they usually did? He didn't think so. Was
she feeling some of the same things he was? He didn't know,
or know how to ask. If she was, was this the first time for her?
He couldn't begin to guess.

In a small, shaken voice, she said, "Phos grant that it be as
you wish. May your bride be safe in Videssos the city, and
may the two of you pass many glad years together." She pulled
away from him; with a forefinger, she drew the good god's
sun-sign over her heart.

Maniakes imitated the gesture. "May it be so," he said. He made a wry face. "If I don't go down to the ships now, they're liable to sail without me." He laughed to show that was a joke. Down at the harbor, his father would have had liquid fire flung at any ships that proposed to sail without him, not that any would have.

Lysia nodded and turned away. If she was crying, Maniakes told himself, he didn't want to see. He turned, walked out of the courtyard, and headed for the doorway that led out of the governor's mansion.

He had already said his good-byes to Rotrude and Atalarikhos. He was not surprised, though, when he found her waiting by the door with their son. He was fond of the boy; he scooped him up, kissed him, mashed him in a hug, and set him down. Then he embraced Rotrude and kissed her for what would probably be the last time. Atalarikhos grabbed them both by the legs. If there was going to be any hugging going on, he wanted to be included in it.

"Be bold," Rotrude said. "Be bold and you will be safe. If you think too much of safety, it will escape you."

She spoke matter-of-factly; Maniakes wondered if he was entitled to draw omens from her words. Haloga magic was often so low-key that a Videssian, used to showier sorcery, would hardly notice it was there. Omen or not, he thought she had given him good advice, and said so.

"Though you leave me, though you go to another, still I wish you well, and I have no thought of revenge," she answered. From one of Haloga blood, that was as great a concession as a Videssian's yielding a doctrinal point.

He nodded to show he understood. "I'll miss you," he said. He rumpled Atalarikhos' hair, dark like his own but straight like Rotrude's. "I'll miss both of you. Now I have to go."

Rotrude nodded. She kept her face very still; Haloga women reckoned public tears as great a disgrace as did the northern men. If she cried after he was gone, no one would know but her pillow.

Maniakes opened the door, closed it after him. One book of his life had just ended. As he took his first steps down toward the harbor, he began to unroll the papyrus of a brand-new book.

Ships filled the harbor. Almost every warship Kalavria boasted was tied up alongside one of the piers. Only a handful of vessels remained in the north to defend against piratical inroads from Khatrish or Thatagush or Agder or even distant Halogaland. With all the Empire of Videssos at stake, Kalavria would have to fend for itself at the moment.

With warships jamming the docks, the fishing boats that normally moored there had been forced aside. Most of them were out to sea now, trying to feed not only Kastavala's usual populace but also the influx of sailors and soldiers who had come into town with the ships. When evening came and the fishing boats returned to harbor, they had to beach themselves. If a big storm blew in, Kastavala would go hungry—and Genesios would no longer need to fear rebellion from out of the east.

Maniakes walked down from the governor's residence toward the harbor. Only a few weeks before, he and Rhegorios had made that same walk, to see what news the incoming merchantman might bring. Neither dreamed the news would pitch them headlong into a revolt that just moments before the elder Maniakes had dismissed as hopeless.

People stared at the younger Maniakes as he strode through the streets of Kastavala. He had had to endure a certain amount of that for years; the townsfolk were always curious about what the governor's son was doing. But he was no longer merely governor's son. "Thou conquerest, Maniakes Avtokrator!" someone called to him.

He waved acknowledgment. That call came again and again. It was premature, as he knew full well. Only after the ecumenical patriarch had anointed him and crowned him at the High Temple in Videssos the city would he formally become Avtokrator of the Videssians. But he did not fret his well-wishers with formalism. If he did not soon become Avtokrator, he would die. He had no middle ground left, not anymore.

The streets no longer swarmed with sailors, as they had since the Maniakai summoned to Kastavala such might as Kalavria possessed. Now the seamen were down by the ships. If the wind held, they would sail later today. Nothing would be easy. The younger Maniakes had assumed that. Easier to adjust for things going better than planned than for worse.

For the first time in more than five years, the spear that had held up Hosios' head as a warning to those who would oppose Genesios no longer stood at the harbor. Maniakes had ordered it brought aboard his flagship. Not everyone had loved Likinios and his clan, but they gained virtue by comparison with what had replaced them. Maniakes could and would claim to be avenging the house of Likinios.

He kicked at the dirt. From Makuran, Sharbaraz King of Kings trumpeted the same claim. Even Maniakes, who knew better, had wondered whether the Videssian in imperial raiment whom Sharbaraz kept in his retinue might somehow miraculously be Hosios son of Likinios. He might have accepted the pretender as genuine simply to rid Videssos of Genesios. Now, Phos be praised, he did not have to worry about that dreadful choice.

He had renamed the strongest warship in the fleet the *Renewal*, in hope of what he would bring to Videssos the city. In the fleet at the Key, though, the *Renewal* would have been no more than a middling vessel, and in the fleet at Videssos the city less than that. He and all his kinsmen knew their revolt would fail if the Empire's naval forces did not join them.

Maniakes refused to let himself think of failure. He strode toward the *Renewal*, acknowledging salutes as he came. The hierarch of Kastavala, gorgeous in a robe of cloth-of-gold with a blue circle indicating Phos' sun, stood on the dock by the long, lean craft, chanting prayers to the good god to bring it safely through the upcoming fight. Behind him, two lesser clerics in plainer robes swung censers, perfuming the air with sweet cinnamon and sharp, almost bitter myrrh.

"Good day, holy sir," Maniakes said, bowing to the hierarch.

"Good day, your Majesty." The spiritual leader of the town was a skinny, elderly man named Gregoras, whose shaved scalp made him look even more skeletal than he would have otherwise. His words were proper, but his tone left something to be desired. So did the suspicious stare he sent Maniakes.

Maniakes sighed. He had seen that stare from Gregoras before. The hierarch had doubts about his orthodoxy. His father still worshiped Phos after the manner of the Vaspurakaners, believing the good god had shaped Vaspur, the first man, ahead of all others, and that all Vaspurakaners were to be reckoned princes on account of their descent from him.

In Videssian eyes, that was heresy. The younger Maniakes had grown up taking it for granted, but he had also grown up among Videssians who were as passionately sure it was wrong as his father was convinced of its truth. Now he was certain of only one thing: if he wanted to wear the Avtokrator's red boots and rule Videssos, he would have to satisfy not just the ecumenical patriarch but also the people of his orthodoxy. He

could not afford to have Genesios scream from the housetops
that he was a heretic.

He stretched his hands up toward the sun and recited, "We
bless thee, Phos, lord with the great and good mind, by thy
grace our protector, watchful beforehand that the great test of
life be decided in our favor."

Gregoras repeated the creed of Phos' cult. So did the lesser
priests, and everyone who heard Maniakes' prayer. That did
not stop the hierarch from giving him another suspicious
glower. Vaspurakaners recited the creed in the same way as
those who followed what the Videssians called orthodoxy.

But, grudgingly, Gregoras decided not to make an issue of
it. He stretched up his hands once more, saying "May the lord
with the great and good mind bless you and all the men who
sail with you. May you travel in victory, and may you restore
to Videssos the glory of which she has been too long deprived.
So may it be."

"So may it be," Maniakes echoed. "Thank you, holy sir."
Even a prelate as sternly orthodox as Gregoras was willing not
to inquire too closely into the younger Maniakes' beliefs, for
that simple reason that Genesios, while also orthodox, was vile
enough to embarrass those who agreed with him no less than
those who did not.

Maniakes walked over the gangplank from the pier to the
deck of the *Renewal*. The men at the oars and the rest of the
sailors raised a cheer for him. So did Kourikos and Triphylles.
At his father's suggestion, Maniakes had split the grandees
from the capital among several ships. He had told them he
didn't want them all lost in one disaster, which had some truth
in it. More important, though, he did not want them plotting
among themselves.

A sailor with a long, straight bronze trumpet strode up to
Maniakes and waited expectantly. He looked around the harbor. As far as he could see, all the ships were ready. He nodded to the trumpeter. The man took a deep breath and raised
the horn to his lips. His cheeks puffed out like the throat sac
of a chirping frog. The blast he blew meant only one thing: *we
begin.*

Sailors undid lines from the docks, then jumped back into
their vessels. Oarmasters shouted out the stroke. Grunting, the
big-shouldered, hard-handed men at the oars rose from their
benches, stroked, sat again. The seats of their breeches were

lined with leather to keep them from wearing through to the flesh in short order.

The *Renewal* pulled away from the dock. She pitched slightly in the light chop. Maniakes hadn't done much sailing since his journey to Kalavria. Having the deck shift under his feet made him nervous; it put him in mind of the queasy way the ground shook during an earthquake. But an earthquake soon stopped, while this went on and on. He did what he had done when Likinios sent his clan into their genteel exile: he pretended he was not standing, but on horseback. That helped keep his stomach happy.

They had hardly got out of bowshot of the pier when a sailor dashed to the rail and hung onto it for dear life, his head thrust far out over the side. His comrades jeered at him. Maniakes would have thought him too busy puking to notice, but when he came up he said, "There, that's done. Now, Phos willing, I'm good for the rest of the voyage."

To keep their stroke, the rowers began a raucous song. Maniakes grinned in recognition. Foot soldiers sang about the little bird with the yellow bill while they were marching, oarsmen while they were rowing. He wondered if accountants used the same ditty to help them keep their records straight down to the last copper.

The song seemed to have as many verses as it did singers. The rowers' version included a good many Maniakes hadn't heard before. Like those the foot soldiers sang, though, a lot of them had the little bird doing some very salty things indeed.

Glancing over at Kourikos, Maniakes decided accountants didn't sing about the little bird while they pushed pens over parchment. The logothete of the treasury plainly had never imagined, let alone been subjected to, singing like this. Beneath its swarthiness, his face was almost as green as that of the sailor who had vomited when the *Renewal* was leaving its berth at the pier.

He walked up to Kourikos and said, "The men are in high spirits today, don't you think, eminent sir?"

"Er—yes, your Majesty," the logothete answered, as bravely as he could. He was a spindly little man, so much so that the loud, lewd words of the song almost had him literally staggering. "Most, uh, exuberant."

His effort to show enthusiasm left Maniakes ashamed of teasing him. He turned to face the bow of the *Renewal*. The wind blew out of the west, running its fingers through his beard and flipping his hair back from his forehead. He said, "They won't stay exuberant if the wind's against us all the way to Opsikion. That's a long, hard pull across the open sea."

"It can be done, though?" Kourikos sounded anxious.

"Oh, yes," Maniakes said. "Even a—" He shut up. *Even a lubber like me knows that much,* he had started to say. Kourikos exhaled sharply. He might not know much about sailing, but he had had no trouble supplying the words Maniakes had omitted. Scowling at himself far more than at his prospective father-in-law, Maniakes looked back over his shoulder at Kalavria receding in the distance.

The harbor and town of Kastavala passed out of view before the governor's residence on the height in back of them. Idly, Maniakes wondered why that was so. The mages at the Sorcerers' Collegium in Videssos the city had all sorts of arcane knowledge. Maybe, if he took the city, he would ask them. *No, when I take the city,* he corrected himself. *When.*

Above Maniakes' head, the wool sail flapped and billowed in the fitful breeze. The wind had swung round from west to south, letting the fleet from Kalavria sail at a reach. By now, Maniakes took no notice of the sail's noise. All that mattered to him was the dark green line that divided sky from sea in the west: the highlands above Opsikion.

As Kalavria had vanished over the horizon, so the mainland appeared above it. The first Maniakes saw of Opsikion itself was the sun glittering off the gilded globes of its temples. That flash told any incoming seaman he was approaching a town of the Videssian Empire.

Next to Videssos the city, Opsikion was unimpressive. Next to Kastavala, it was a metropolis. Unlike Kastavala, a formidable stone wall ringed it round. The wild Khamorth horsemen had raided farther south than this, back in the days a century and a half before when they spilled off the Pardrayan plain and overran great stretches of the Videssian eastlands. Towns hereabouts needed walls.

These days, the Khamorth had formed themselves into three groups that functioned more or less as nations: Khatrish, nearest Opsikion and aptest at aping Videssian ways; Thatagush, to the north of Khatrish, whose borders did not march with those of Videssos; and Kubrat, south of the Astris and touching the Videssian Sea. The Kubratoi, whatever deficiencies they had from the standpoint of civilization, were monstrously good at war—and alarmingly close to Videssos the city.

Maniakes watched the commotion in the harbor of Opsikion as lookouts spied the approaching fleet. All the ships from Kalavria flew the Videssian banner, a gold sunburst on blue, but he did not blame the soldiers and marines for showing alarm even so. For one thing, pirates could mimic the Videssian emblem and seek to use it to approach with impunity. For another, a fleet's being Videssian, these days, did not have to mean it was friendly. If Opsikion's own fleet held its loyalty to Genesios, then Maniakes' galleys and transports were anything but friendly.

The captain of the *Renewal* was a middle-aged man named Thrax. He was striking to look at: he had gone gray young, and the sun had bleached that gray to glistening silver while baking his skin brown as bread. Coming up to Maniakes, he asked, "Your Majesty, shall we lower the mast and ready for combat? Shall we signal the rest of the fleet to do likewise?" As commander of the flagship, he was in effect drungarios of the fleet.

Maniakes considered, then shook his head. He pointed in toward the harbor. "They don't look to be sallying everything they have against us." In fact, only a couple of small craft, neither one a match for the *Renewal*, were putting to sea. "Signal our vessels to have all in readiness to brail sails and lower masts, but not to do it until I give the order or until the *Renewal* is attacked. As for what we do here, we go forward and parley. Show the white-painted truce shield at the bow."

"Aye, your Majesty." Thrax looked incompletely happy, but turned and loudly relayed Maniakes' commands to the crew.

The *Renewal* glided forward over the gray-green water. The small ships from out of Opsikion approached startlingly fast. Thin across the sea came a questioning hail: "Who comes to Opsikion with such a fleet, and for what purpose?"

Maniakes hurried to the bow. Standing by the truce shield, he cupped both hands in front of his mouth and shouted: "I come, Maniakes son of Maniakes, Avtokrator of the Videssians, for the purpose of casting the murderous, infamous, bloodthirsty wild beast Genesios down from the throne he has drenched with the gore of slaughtered innocents." There. It was done. If the officers on Opsikion had been unaware rebellion was brewing on Kalavria, they were no more. Maniakes added, "With whom do I speak?"

For a couple of minutes, no one answered him from either of the ships. Then a man resplendent in a gleaming chainmail shirt came to the bow of one of them. Wearing armor at sea was a risky business; if you went over the side, you drowned. The fellow said, "I am Domentziolos, tourmarkhos here."

The garrison commander, Maniakes thought. He must have been down by the waterfront, to have boarded ship so quickly. "What say you, Domentziolos?" Maniakes demanded.

"Thou conquerest, Maniakes Avtokrator!" Domentziolos shouted in a great voice. The men aboard his vessel erupted in cheers. So did those aboard the other small ship. And so did those aboard the *Renewal.*

Maniakes felt giddy, almost drunk, with relief. His force was not large. A fight at Opsikion could have ruined him even if he won: it would have given Genesios' retainers the idea that Maniakes could be vulnerable. Ideas like that had a way of becoming self-fulfilling prophecies. If, on the other hand, everyone joined him against Genesios . . .

"Use our harbor, use our city, as your own," Domentziolos said. "We'd heard rumors this day might come, but knew not how much faith to put in them. Praise the lord with the great and good mind they prove true."

Maniakes hadn't wanted anyone hearing rumors. He supposed fishermen sailing out of Kastavala or one of the other Kalavrian towns from which he had pulled men and ships had met their counterparts from Opsikion on the sea. They wouldn't have kept quiet, not when they were carrying that kind of news. But if Opsikion had heard rumors, the odds were good that rumors had gone on to Videssos the city, and to the ear of Genesios.

"Will the hypasteos of the town grant us the same welcome you have, excellent Domentziolos?" Maniakes asked. Civil officials outranked soldiers in the administrative hierarchy, not least to make rebellions by provincial commanders harder. Likinios had sent the elder Maniakes, a general, to govern Kalavria, but Kalavria was both far from the heart of the Empire and subject to attack by pirates: divided authority there would have been dangerous. In any normal circumstances, an Avtokrator had little reason to fear revolt from Kalavria. If Likinios or Hosios still lived, the Maniakai would have lived out their days on the island.

"Old Samosates? He's over there in the other ship, yelling for you fit to burst." Domentziolos pointed. His vessel had drawn close enough to the *Renewal* for Maniakes to see his teeth skin back in a shark's grin. "Besides, if he weren't for you, your Majesty, we'd soon fix that, the lads and I."

In normal times, a local commander did not casually talk about disposing of the town administrator appointed by the Emperor. Civil war, though, changed all the rules. Maniakes wasn't shocked, as he would have been in peacetime. He was delighted.

"Splendid, excellent Domentziolos," he said. He had no idea whether Domentziolos deserved to be called excellent, and didn't care. If the officer wasn't a noble but performed well in the fighting ahead, he would earn the title with which Maniakes was honoring him now. Maniakes went on, "We'll land infantry and cavalry here, to move overland against Genesios while the fleet, along with your own flotilla, sails round the cape and up toward the Key."

He waited to see how Domentziolos would take that. If the captain was dissembling, he would not want Opsikion to yield tamely to Maniakes' men. He might suddenly decide to fight, or he might cast about for excuses to delay the entry of Maniakes' force into the town or to have the soldiers camp outside.

But he said, "By the good god, your Majesty, come at the usurper every way you can. I've sent up enough prayers that someone worthwhile would rise against him. If you want 'em, you'll have hundreds of men from the soldiery here who'd love to march with you."

"Not with me," Maniakes answered. "I lead the fleet; my cousin Rhegorios will command the soldiers."

That made Domentziolos grin all over again. "Who would have thought a man of Vaspurakaner blood anything but a land soldier? Yet you have the right of it, your Majesty; your fight will be won or lost on the sea."

"My thought exactly." Maniakes turned toward the other ship. "Eminent Samosates!"

A man who was as gray as Maniakes' father and bald to boot came to the bow of the vessel. "Aye, your Majesty?" he called. "How may I serve you?" His voice was not only wary but mushy as well; he couldn't have had many teeth left.

"By yielding up your city and all its supplies to me," Maniakes answered. "Since you've named me your sovereign, you cannot object to that."

Samosates was perfectly capable of objecting, and Maniakes

knew it full well. A recalcitrant hypasteos, or even a reluctant one, would make his stay here more difficult. The bureaucrats of Opsikion would take their cue from their leader and could make nuisances of themselves by nothing more than obstructing supplies. Separating malice from simple incompetence was never easy.

But Samosates seemed suddenly to catch fire. "The city and everything within it are yours," he cried. "Dig up Genesios' bones! To the ice with the usurper! May his head, filled only with thoughts of blood, go up on the Milestone." The hypasteos bowed to Maniakes. "I am your man."

He certainly was. After he had publicly reviled Genesios, the only thing he could expect from the Avtokrator now sitting in Videssos the city was the headsman's sword. He had made his choice, and he had made it plain. For a bureaucrat, that was a miracle of decisiveness.

Maniakes turned to Thrax. "Make signal to the fleet that we are to tie up in the harbor of Opsikion."

"Aye, your Majesty," Thrax said, and gave the order to his trumpeter. Notes rang across the water. The trumpeters in the nearest ships picked them up and relayed them to those positioned farther out on the wings. Thrax spoke two other words, and the trumpeter relayed them, too: "Maintain caution."

"Excellent." Maniakes thumped Thrax on the back. "If they have something nasty in mind—" He shook his head. "You don't get old in this business taking people for granted."

But the Opsikianoi all seemed as delighted as Domentziolos and Samosates to welcome Maniakes and his sailors and soldiers. Of course, taverners threw their doors wide and tarts promenaded in their skimpiest and filmiest outfits: they had profits to make. But carpenters and cobblers, farmers and fishermen, vied with one another to greet the newcomers, to buy them a glass of wine or bread smeared with sea-urchin paste and crushed garlic.

To Maniakes, that said one thing: everybody hated Genesios. Had everyone admired the ruler in the capital, he would have had to fight his way into the town. Had feelings been mixed, he might have got into Opsikion without a fight, but houses and shops would have stayed shuttered against his men. As things were, he worried only that his men would be so taken by the place that they wouldn't care to leave.

Samosates put him, Rhegorios, and the grandees from Videssos the city up in his own residence in the center of town, not far from the chief temple to Phos. The red-tiled building housed not only him but several hundred years of the records of Opsikion; servants hastily carried wooden boxes stuffed with old scrolls out of bedchambers to make room for the noble guests. That affected Maniakes himself not at all; he got the chief guest suite, with Rhegorios installed alongside him.

Supper was tuna and squid and mussels, much as it might have been back in Kastavala. The wine was better here. When Samosates noticed Maniakes thought well of it, he made sure his servitors kept the would-be Emperor's cup full. As more servants cleared away the supper dishes, the hypasteos asked, "How long will you stay in Opsikion, your Majesty?"

Maniakes had drunk himself happy, but he hadn't drunk himself foolish. "A few days, to ready the land forces to move west and to join your local ships here to our fleet," he answered. "How many 'a few' may be, I don't quite know." And if he had known, he wouldn't have told Samosates. The fewer people who were privy to his plans, the fewer who could pass those plans to Genesios.

But Samosates said, "I quite understand, your Majesty. I was just thinking that, since rumor of your rebellion, to which Phos grant success, had reached us here, it might well have traveled on to Videssos the city. That being so, you would be well advised to look to your own safety while you are here."

"D'you think Genesios could have sent assassins out so soon?" Maniakes asked; he, too, had worried about rumors spread west from Opsikion.

"Your own valiant strength, your Majesty, should be protection and to spare against mere assassins," Samosates said. Maniakes knew that was polite nonsense; he wondered if the hypasteos did, too. Evidently so, for Samosates went on, "I was not thinking so much of knives in the night as of wizardry from afar. Have you brought with you accomplished mages to ward against such danger?"

"I've brought a couple of men from Kastavala, the best the island of Kalavria can boast," Maniakes answered. He knew he sounded uneasy; against the best of Videssos the city, those wizards might be a couple of coppers matched against goldpieces. "I'd not expected to need much in the way of sorcerous protection until I reached the Key, if then." He turned to the grandees fled from the capital. "How say you, eminent sirs, excellent sirs? Has Genesios still strong sorcerers who will do his bidding?"

Triphylles said, "Your Majesty, I fear he does. Just this past spring, Philetos the mintmaster died of a wasting sickness that shrank him from fat man to skeleton in half a month's time. Bare days before he'd taken ill, he'd called Genesios a bloodthirsty fool outside the mint. Someone must have overheard and taken word back to the tyrant."

"He has mages, or at least one," Maniakes agreed. "Eminent Samosates, what sort of wizards does Opsikion possess?"

"Our best is a man who commonly calls himself Alvinos, for fear his true name would ring harshly in Videssian ears," the hypasteos replied. "He was, however, given at birth the appellation Bagdasares."

"A Vaspurakaner, by the good god!" Maniakes exclaimed happily. "Send for him this instant."

Samosates called to a retainer. The man hurried away. Maniakes sipped more wine and waited for the wizard to arrive. The nobles from Videssos the city kept up a desultory conversation with Samosates. They tried to act as if they thought him their equal, but could not quite manage to seem convincing. Better they hadn't bothered pretending, Maniakes thought.

After about half an hour, the servitor returned with Bagdasares, sometimes called Alvinos. Sure enough, he had the stocky build and heavy features common in those who sprang from Vaspurakan. He was younger than Maniakes had expected, probably younger than Maniakes himself.

"Your Majesty!" he cried, and went down in a full proskynesis. When he returned to his feet, he rattled off several sentences in the throaty Vaspurakaner language.

That left Maniakes embarrassed. "Slowly, please, I beg," he said, his own words halting. "I have little of this tongue, I fear. My father and mother spoke it when they did not want me to understand what they said. After my mother died, my father spoke it seldom. Videssian goes better in my mouth."

Bagdasares shrugged. He returned to the language of the Empire. "My children, they will be the same, your Majesty. We are a small drop of ink, and Videssos a big pail of water. But now, Phos who made the princes first willing, you want to give all the Empire the coloring of that ink?"

The grandees from the capital muttered back and forth behind their hands. Samosates drummed his fingers on the polished oak of the tabletop. Seldom was heresy spoken so openly in a hypasteos' hall. Heads swung toward Maniakes, to hear how he would respond. If he espoused heresy, too, he would cost himself support—not among the grandees, who were too committed to abandon him for Genesios, but from simpler, more pious folk to whom word of what he said would surely spread, perhaps with exaggerations for effect.

To Bagdasares, he replied, "I fear most of the coloring has already bleached out of me. What the Videssians call orthodoxy suits me well enough."

He wondered if the wizard would rail at him for abandoning the doctrines of his forefathers. But Bagdasares shrugged again. "I know many others from among our folk who share your views. Some of them are good men, some bad, as is true of any other group. I do not condemn them out of hand."

"Good," Maniakes said with genuine relief. Only later would he wonder why a wizard's view should matter to an Avtokrator. He wasn't used to being Avtokrator, not yet. "To business," he declared. "Can you protect me against whatever spells Genesios' mages may hurl from Videssos the city?"

"I think I can, your Majesty," Bagdasares answered. "They'll be stronger sorcerers than I, you understand, but I'll be far closer to you, which also matters in struggles thaumaturgic."

"In these matters, you are the expert," Maniakes said. "Soldiers, as you know, have little to do with magic."

"And for good reason, too," the wizard said. "The stress and passion of the battlefield make sorcery too unreliable to be worth using. Unfortunately, however, it remains a very useful tool for assassins." He preened, just a little; few young men are without vanity, and even fewer can resist the temptation to show off. "As a result of which consideration, you have engaged my services."

"Exactly so," Maniakes said. "I am now going to seek my bedchamber for the night. Will you come with me and do what you can to make it safe against whatever sorceries Genesios can send against me?"

"Your Majesty, I will, if you will excuse me for one small moment." Bagdasares ducked out into the hall. He returned with a stout wooden case with brass fittings. Dipping his head to Maniakes, he said, "Now I am ready to rally to your cause, your Majesty. As well expect a swordsmith to beat out blades with no hammer or anvil as a wizard to work magic without his tools."

"Again, I yield to your expertise." Maniakes nodded to

Samosates. "If a servant will be so kind as to show me to my chamber?"

In Videssos the city, the room would have been reckoned spare; it had bed, table, stools, a chamber pot, and a chest of drawers, but no ornamentation save an icon of Phos. For Opsikion, it was surely good enough.

Bagdasares beamed when he saw the icon. "The good god's protection will make mine more effective," he said, "even if the image is undoubtedly the work of a Videssian heretic."

Half grinning, he glanced over at Maniakes for his reaction. Maniakes was convinced the wizard was trying to get a rise out of him, and held his peace. Bagdasares chuckled, then stalked about the bedchamber muttering to himself, sometimes in Videssian, more often in the Vaspurakaners' native tongue.

At last he seemed to remember his client, and that said client claimed the throne of the Empire of Videssos and deserved to know what was going on. He said, "Your Majesty, this will not be a difficult room to seal. You have but one door, one window, two mouseholes that I found, and one small hole in the roof, probably under a broken tile. Seal those sorcerously and nothing can get in to trouble you. Oh, perhaps the mages in Videssos the city may try to shake down this whole building on your head, but at this distance I do not think they would succeed, though I may be wrong."

Maniakes wished the wizard hadn't added that qualifying phrase. Bagdasares walked up and down the bedchamber, whistling tunelessly between his teeth as he contemplated what needed doing. He began at the window. From his box he took what seemed to Maniakes an ordinary ball of twine. He used a knife to cut off two lengths of it, one of which he stretched across the window frame from side to side, the other from top to bottom. When he pointed a finger at them and spoke imperiously in Vaspurakaner, the two pieces of twine stayed where they were without pins or tacks to hold them in place.

Bagdasares muttered a spell in Videssian. The vertical string burst into gold flame, the horizontal into blue, both so bright that for a moment Maniakes, dazzled, turned his head to one side. When he looked back to the window, the strings had vanished.

"Excellent!" Bagdasares said in self-satisfied tones. "That window is well and truly sealed against unwelcome intrusion from without, whether physical or sorcerous. The morning breeze will get in, but nothing more."

"That's what I want," Maniakes said.

Bagdasares proceeded to treat both mouseholes in the same fashion. He grinned at Maniakes, showing white, white teeth in the midst of his tangled black beard. "The chamber should be clear of vermin for some time to come, your Majesty—it would take sorcery to get them inside now. This is a strenuous way to keep a room free from mice and rats, but no less effective on account of that."

He wiped sweat from his forehead with the sleeve of his robe. Any sorcery was strenuous; had it been easier, the arts of the Empire of Videssos would have been altogether different, with magecraft supplanting mechanic skills in areas as diverse as farming and forgery. But sorcerous talent was rare, and its application limited by the mental and physical strength of the operator.

Bagdasares clambered up onto a stool and sealed the hole in the roof. "If it rains, your Majesty, I think this chamber will not leak there, but I should be reluctant to take oath on it," he said. "I will swear, however, that nothing worse than rain can enter by this path."

"Very good," Maniakes said. "I always enjoy watching a fine craftsman at work, whatever his craft may be. Competence is not so common that we can take it for granted."

"You have spoken truth, your Majesty, and I thank you for the compliment." Bagdasares descended from his perch and turned toward the door. He rubbed his chin. "Here the problem is not so simple as it is with windows and incidental openings. You must be free to go in and out of the chamber, and so must not only your proper comrades but also—I assume—the servants of this establishment." He waited for Maniakes to nod, then went on, "At the same time, we must prevent evil influences from gaining entry. A complex problem, would you not agree?"

He did not wait to learn whether Maniakes agreed or disagreed. He walked over to the doorway. This time, he set two lengths of twine across it and three that reached up from floor to lintel. His first incantation seemed to Maniakes identical to that which he had used before. The upper piece of horizontal twine flared blue, the central vertical piece gold.

"Thus, the sealing spell," Bagdasares said. "Now to modify it: a cantrip of my own invention, I am proud to say."

The cantrip was in the guttural Vaspurakaner language. Every so often, Maniakes would hear a word or phrase he knew, but, while he seized it, the rest of the spell would flow on past him. Then Bagdasares shouted an invocation his father often used: "In the name of Vaspur, firstborn among mankind!" He smiled to recognize that, but failed to follow what Bagdasares wanted the eponymous founder of the Vaspurakaner folk to do.

Till that invocation, the extra pieces of twine had remained in their former condition. After it, though, they, too, began to glow, not so brightly as the other two had, but with soft lights of their own. The additional horizontal piece shone a darker, more nearly purple blue than that of the Videssian colors. To either side of the vertical that had flared golden, the others gleamed, one red, the other orange.

"Ah." Bagdasares rubbed his hands. "All is as it should be, your Majesty. You and your comrades and the servitors of this house may enter and leave as you see fit, but no one else—and no evil influence shall enter with anyone, so far as my skill can prevent."

"I thank you very much," Maniakes said; though he could not know for certain, he had formed the opinion that Bagdasares' skill was considerable. "Have you also protection for me when I am not in my chamber?"

"Aye, I can give you some, your Majesty, though my guess is that Genesios' mage, if any there be, would strike in dead of night, when he was most nearly certain of your location. Still, in your boots I'd not trust a wizard's guess, that I wouldn't." Bagdasares chuckled. He rummaged in his box and pulled out an amulet—a rayed golden sun-disk on a cord of braided blue and gold string. He turned the disk over to show Maniakes a red-brown stone set into the back. "Hematite, your Majesty, or bloodstone, as it's sometimes called. Having an affinity to blood, it will draw the magic that would otherwise spill yours. If you feel the disk grow hot against your skin, you are under assault. It will not long withstand the stronger sorceries, so seek a mage's aid as fast as you can."

Maniakes bent his head and let Bagdasares slip the cord around his neck. "Pure gold," he said, judging by the weight of it. The wizard nodded. "I shall repay it weight for weight in coin, over and above your fee," Maniakes told him.

"Have no fear about that," Bagdasares said. "The fee includes the gold in the amulet." He clapped a hand to his mouth, looking comically aggrieved with himself. "I shouldn't have told you that, should I? I just cost myself some money."

"That's what you get for being an honest man." Maniakes laughed. "If you're a true son of Vaspur, a true prince, I suspect you'll show a profit anyhow."

"I suspect you're right, your Majesty," Bagdasares replied, unabashed. "Going up against these grasping, ready-for-aught Videssians, an honest Vaspurakaner needs all the cunning he can come up with." By every indication, the wizard had enough and to spare. He closed his wooden chest, bowed to Maniakes, and left the chamber.

A few minutes later, Samosates' voice floated down the hall. "Are you there, your Majesty?"

"Aye, I'm here," Maniakes called to the hypasteos. "What's toward?"

"I was just wondering if, while you were in Opsikion, you would—" Samosates got up to the door and started to come through it. The way seemed open—and Bagdasares had gone out—but the hypasteos might have run headlong into a fence. A flash of light came from the open air. "What's this?" he cried, and tried again, with no better luck.

Suspicion flared in Maniakes: Bagdasares had vowed his spell would keep evil influences from entering the chamber, and now Samosates could not come in. Then Maniakes remembered who was allowed into the room—in the mage's own words, himself, his comrades, and the servitors in the hypasteos' residence. Samosates did not fall into any of those groups.

Chuckling, Maniakes said, "Send one of your men after Bagdasares, eminent sir. He can't have gone far yet, and his magic turned out to be a bit too literal." He explained what he thought the mage had done. Samosates did not see the humor in it. Samosates, Maniakes guessed, did not see the humor in a lot of things.

When Bagdasares returned, he was laughing. He chanted in front of the door for a few heartbeats, then bent his stocky frame in a bow to the hypasteos. "Try now, eminent sir, I beg of you," he said. Cautiously, Samosates stepped forward and into Maniakes' room. Bagdasares waved and left again.

"What were you wondering before Bagdasares' protective magic so rudely interrupted you, eminent sir?" Maniakes asked in tones as sympathetic as he could manage.

"I haven't the foggiest notion." Samosates still sounded flustered. He snapped his fingers, either in annoyance or to jar the vagrant memory loose. "Ah! I have it: I was about to ask if

you intended to review the garrison here in Opsikion before in-
corporating it into your own forces."

"I don't think that will be necessary, though I thank you for
the notion," Maniakes answered, diligently keeping his face
straight. People who weren't in the habit of using troops to
fight put great stock in reviews and other ceremonial.
Maniakes was of the opinion that putting men into action did
a better job of testing them.

Samosates looked disappointed. Maybe he had wanted to
see troops all gathered together and glittering in armor. If so,
he had no business being in a post as important as that of
Opsikion's hypasteos. Maniakes shrugged. He would worry
about such administrative changes later, after—and if—he ef-
fected a considerably greater one himself.

Doleful still, Samosates left. When Rhegorios knocked on
the door, he had no trouble passing through it; as Bagdasares
had promised, he had given Maniakes' companions full access
to his chamber. "How soon will you be able to go on the
march, cousin?" Maniakes demanded. "And how many men
from Opsikion's garrison will you take west with you?"

"Whew!" Rhegorios leaned forward, as if into a headwind.
"You *are* in a hurry, aren't you?"

"I begrudge every minute here," Maniakes said. "The longer
we stay in any one place, the longer Genesios has to plan deviltry against me, whether by magic or simply by assassin's
knife. A moving target is harder to hit. How fast will be we be
able to get moving again?"

"Our men and horses are all unloaded," Rhegorios said.
"That's taken care of. I think we can add a couple of thousand
warriors from the local forces without leaving Opsikion in any
great danger from a raid out of Khatrish. All that is as it
should be: couldn't be better, in fact."

"But?" Maniakes asked. "There must be a 'but,' or you
would have answered all my question, not just part of it."

Rhegorios sighed. "Phos grant mercy to the first fellow who
tries to sneak anything past you once you take the throne—
you'll give the wretch a thin time of it. We have men and
horses aplenty, but a shortage of supply wagons. We can't very
well sail our merchantmen along the southern slopes of the
Paristrian Mountains. The Opsikianoi have wains enough for
their own purposes, but not to keep our whole host fed as we
fare west toward Videssos the city."

"A pestilence," Maniakes muttered under his breath. No one

who wasn't a soldier, save perhaps a farmer whose fields had just been ravaged, ever thought about all it took to keep an army—essentially a city on the move—supplied with food, equipment, and weapons. But if you didn't take care of those essentials, the army would be in no condition to fight once it got where it was going, or else wouldn't get there at all.

"I haven't surveyed the town as a whole, to see what we can requisition from merchants and such," Rhegorios said. "I wanted to get your approval before I started anything like that, for I know it'll breed ill will."

"Do it anyhow," Maniakes said. "We'll make their losses good as we may. If we lose the war, goodwill won't matter. If we win, those who grumble can be brought round."

"Aye. When you put it like that, it makes perfect sense." Rhegorios scratched his head. "I wonder if I'm ruthless enough to make a proper captain."

Maniakes slapped him on the shoulder. "You'll do fine," he said. "You have the straight-ahead drive the job needs. You know how to do things that need doing. Before long, you'll see what those things are, too." He was only a handful of years older than his cousin but had vastly more experience as a commander. He felt like some old soldier of his father's generation heartening a recruit whose beard hadn't fully sprouted.

"I'll attend to it, then," Rhegorios said, and hurried away. The odd illusion Maniakes had known went with him, rather to his own relief.

He walked down to the harbor to talk with Domentziolos. He found the leader of Opsikion's flotilla closeted with Thrax, his own naval leader. As he walked in on them, Domentziolos was saying "Word of your rising must have reached Videssos the city by now—Genesios may not be good for much, but by Phos he can spy with the best of them. So—" His finger stabbed out at a map. "—We should expect to have to fight the fleet from the Key not long after we round the cape and head north and west toward the capital."

"Aye, likely you're right," Thrax replied, and then looked up and saw Maniakes. He jumped to his feet, as did Domentziolos. "Good day, your Majesty."

"Good day," Maniakes answered. "So the two of you think it'll come to a sea fight early, do you?" The prospect worried him. If the fleets of the Key and Videssos the city stayed loyal to Genesios, he could gather together every other ship in the Empire and still lose the war.

"Wouldn't be surprised," Domentziolos said. Thrax nodded. Domentziolos went on, "Of course, just because the drungarios of a fleet is loyal doesn't mean his captains will be, and a captain who flouts his crew's wishes will feed fishes if he doesn't know when to ease off."

"You do so much to ease my mind," Maniakes said dryly, which wrung a chuckle from Thrax. "I was hoping to reach the Key without having to fight my way there. That way, the lord with the great and good mind willing, we can get some use out of the grandees: let them soften up the officers, so to speak."

"Aye, well, that would be fine," Domentziolos allowed. "No guarantee it'll happen, though, and fair odds it won't."

"All right," Maniakes said. "How do we ready ourselves to defeat the Key's ships in sea battle?"

Domentziolos and Thrax looked at each other. Perhaps because he had been with Maniakes since Kalavria, Thrax answered the question: "Your Majesty, if the fleet is there in full force and loyal to Genesios, we won't defeat it."

Maniakes winced, then gave Thrax a formal military salute, setting his right fist over his heart. "I am grateful for your frankness. I shall remember and reward you for it. Too many Avtokrators have gone down to ruin, I think, because no one had the courage to tell them a simple but painful truth. Likinios would still be Avtokrator today, and we would have no need of rebellion, had someone only warned him he was mad to order troops to winter north of the Astris."

Domentziolos glanced over at Thrax again and then, with dawning wonder, at Maniakes. "Your Majesty," he said, "may I also speak plainly?"

"You had better," Maniakes answered.

"All right, then," Domentziolos said. But, even after Maniakes' urging, he hesitated before going on. "Truth of it is, your Majesty, I was bound and determined to back any man with the stomach to rise against Genesios, for I think it's as plain as his ugly face on our goldpieces these days that he's dragging the Empire straight down to Skotos' ice. But hearing you talk now, I begin to hope you're not just someone who's better than Genesios—there are as many men answering to that as grains of sand by the sea—but someone who may turn out to be good in his own right, if you take my meaning."

"Phos grant it be so," Maniakes said, and sketched the good god's sun-sign over his heart.

"You had better be good in your own right," Thrax said,

"for if you're not, Sharbaraz King of Kings won't leave much of Videssos for you to rule."

"I know," Maniakes answered. "I know that all too well. He was vigorous half a dozen years ago, when my father and I helped restore him to his throne. He's grown since then. I hope I have, too."

Now Domentziolos murmured, "Phos grant it be so."

"What's worst is that I can't yet worry about Sharbaraz," Maniakes said. "Till Genesios is out of the way, the King of Kings and I don't impinge on each other, not directly." He shook his head. "Funny to think of Genesios as Sharbaraz's buffer against me, but that's what he is . . . among other things."

He unlaced the mouth of a leather pouch he wore on his belt and fumbled in it till he found a goldpiece of Genesios'. The current ruler in Videssos the city had a triangular face, wide at the forehead and narrow at the chin, with a long nose and a thin fringe of beard. So the coin proclaimed, at any rate; Maniakes had never met the man it pictured. But he was willing to believe it gave an accurate portrayal of Genesios; it certainly looked nothing like the images on the goldpieces minted during the reign of Likinios.

"He's not that ugly," Maniakes said, sliding the coin back into the pouch. "Not on the outside, anyhow. If only he had some wit inside that head of his." He sighed. "But he doesn't. He rules by spies and murder, nothing else, and it's not enough. People fear him, but they hate him, too, and won't always do his bidding even when a particular order isn't bad in and of itself."

"Someone should have cast him down long ago," Thrax growled.

"No doubt," Maniakes answered. "But the soldiers weren't the only ones who rejoiced to see Likinios' head go up on a pike. He'd taxed the peasants and merchants and artisans to pay for his wars, so Genesios got goodwill he wouldn't have had otherwise. And then, when people began to see what he was, he put down the first few revolts so savagely that everyone had second thoughts about rebelling."

"And they knew that if Videssian fought Videssian, the only one who gained would be Sharbaraz," Domentziolos suggested.

Maniakes pursed his lips. "I'd like to believe that, and I hope it does hold true every now and again. But you know I have Vaspurakaner blood and heritage, and I sometimes see Videssos from outside, as it were. I speak without intending offense, but, to my way of looking at things, a whole great host of Videssians care for themselves first, their faction next, and after that, if they have any caring left over, they think about the Empire."

"The lord with the great and good mind knows I'd like to say you're wrong, your Majesty, but I fear you're right," Thrax said. "The civil war of a century and a half ago proves that: twin boys born to the Empress, with neither one willing to admit he was the younger. And so, because neither would set aside the wearing of the red boots, they tore the Empire apart."

"They almost put it in its grave, too," Maniakes said savagely. "They were so busy fighting each other, they emptied the frontier fortresses, and the Khamorth swarmed into our lands. And even then, I've heard it said, both greedy fools hired the nomads as mercenaries to bolster their own forces."

Domentziolos gave him a sly look. "Are you saying, your Majesty, that Vaspurakaners don't have faction fights? If that be so, why is the princes' land divided between Videssos and Makuran?"

"It's not," Thrax said. "Thanks to Genesios' blundering, Sharbaraz holds the whole of it these days."

"We have faction fights aplenty, clan against clan," Maniakes said. "That's often how warriors from Vaspurakan come to Videssos: they lose to their rivals in the next valley and have to flee their homes. But war inside a single clan, no, we see that but seldom."

Thrax ran a hand through his silvery hair. "To bring things back to where they were: if, when we round the cape, we find the fleet of the Key awaiting us, and if it still cleaves to Genesios, what then? Do we fight till we're slaughtered, or do we try to flee back to Kalavria? I see no other choices for us."

Maniakes gnawed at his underlip but was again grateful to his admiral for framing things so starkly. "We fight," he said at last. "If we flee, they'd follow and lay Kalavria waste. And we'd get cleaner ends dying in battle than we would were Genesios to take us prisoner."

"Aye, well, you're not wrong about that," Domentziolos said. "I hear he's imported a torturer from Mashiz. There if nowhere else, Sharbaraz is willing to lend him aid."

"That news hadn't got to Kalavria," Maniakes said heavily. "I wish it hadn't got here, either."

* * *

Maniakes worked like a mule, readying both the combined fleets of Kalavria and Opsikion and the cavalry Rhegorios would command for their separate pushes on Videssos the city. That the fleet had no certainty of success—and, indeed, was sure to fail if opposed by the full might of Genesios' navy—only made him work harder, as if his efforts could of themselves magically transmute defeat into triumph.

In the few hours he grudged to his bed, he slept like a corpse. Several of Samosates' serving women were young and pretty; more than one intimated she might be persuaded to do more on that bed than change its linen. He ignored all such offers, partly out of respect for Kourikos' feelings but even more because he was simply too tired to take advantage of them.

After a while, the serving women stopped dropping hints. He caught them talking about him behind their hands: evidently their regard for his masculinity had taken a beating. That would have infuriated some men. He found it laughable; the women's mockery would not make his prowess suffer.

Not long before the fleet was to sail south toward the cape, he awoke in darkness. He stared around, certain someone had rapped at the door. "Who's there?" he called, reaching for his sword. Midnight visitors seldom brought good news.

No one answered. Maniakes frowned. Had one of his officers needed to report some catastrophe, the man would have kept knocking. A skulking assassin, on the other hand . . . He shook his head. An assassin would not have knocked. Whom did that leave? A serving woman, perhaps, bent on revenge for being spurned? It came as close to making sense as anything he could think of.

Then the rapping came again. Maniakes' head whipped around, for the sound was not at the door this time but at the window. The shutters were open to let in cool night air. If anyone or anything stood at that window, he should have been able to see it. He saw nothing and no one.

The hair prickled up at the back of his neck. He sketched Phos' sun-circle over his heart, then clutched at the amulet Bagdasares had given him. He could guess what that rapping was likely to be: magic from the capital, probing at the defenses the Vaspurakaner mage had set up around him. And if it found a weak spot—

He wanted to rise from his bed and flee the chamber. Reason, though, told him that was the worst thing he could do.

Here he lay in the center of all of Bagdasares' wards. If he ran from the sorcery prying at those wards, he would but leave himself more vulnerable to it. But holding still while being hunted came no easier for him than it did for a hare crouching in a thicket as hounds howled outside.

Another round of rapping began, this time on the ceiling. Maniakes remembered the hole Bagdasares had found and hoped he hadn't missed any. When nothing dreadful happened, he decided Bagdasares hadn't.

Before he could begin to relax, though, a mouse burst out of its hole and ran squeaking across the floor, its little nails ticking over boards. Maniakes had forgotten about the mouseholes. Bagdasares, he remembered, had not. His respect for the wizard grew. So did his fear: some stronger magic had forced the mouse through the wards and into his room.

The rapping sound came from each mousehole in turn. Like the rest of the openings into Maniakes' chamber, the mouseholes proved well and truly sealed. Maniakes pulled up the blankets and got ready to go back to sleep, certain now that Genesios' mage had been thwarted.

Reflecting later on what was liable to happen to a mage of Genesios' who failed in his task, he realized he had been naive. A shape appeared in the window. How much of that shape sprung from his own imagination and how much from the sending out of Videssos the city, he never knew. Any which way, it was quite frightening enough.

He could see the night sky through it. Most of it, in fact, seemed thin as gossamer: all but the mouth and the eyes. They were plenty to make up for the rest.

Every so often, fishermen brought sharks into Kastavala along with mackerel and tunny and squid and anchovies. Their jaws fascinated Maniakes: two curved saws of perfectly meshing, sharp-edged teeth. Any shark that swam in the sea would have envied this creature floating weightlessly outside his window now. The thing's mouth was not very large, or rather, not open very far. For some reason, he got the idea it could stretch quite a ways—and be lined with teeth from end to end no matter how far it stretched.

He was glad to take his eyes off that mouth, but doing so almost cost him his life. When his eyes met those of the creature, they were held fast. Try as he would, he could not pull them away. In the westlands and in Makuran, they had lions and even tigers. He had hunted lions a time or two and noted

their lordly golden stare. But a lion with such powers of fasci-
nation in its gaze would have drawn in so much prey as to
make it too fat even to waddle about.

Caught by a will not his own, Maniakes rose from his bed
and walked toward the window. He understood the creature
floating out in the darkness had not the power to enter while
Bagdasares' charm remained in place. But if he were to sweep
that charm aside, nothing would keep the creature from coming in . . . and showing him just how wide its jaws could open.

Each step closer to the window came more slowly than the
one before as he struggled against the will that fought to turn
him to its purpose. But each step was made. When he reached
the windowsill, he knew he would brush away the protection
Bagdasares had set there: the lengths of twine, or their sorcerous residuum. He knew what would happen afterward, too, but
could not bring himself to care.

A mouse, undoubtedly the one disturbed by the prior sorcery
of Genesios' mage, ran over his bare foot. That broke the spell
and startled him, just enough for him to tear his eyes away
from the creature. He staggered back from the window, throwing up an arm to shield himself against the deadly gaze outside.

He heard, or thought he heard, a bestial shriek of rage. It
should have brought men running, swords and bows in their
hands. But Samosates' residence remained quiet and still.
Maybe he hadn't truly heard the rapping that tested his sorcerous defenses, either. Maybe all that, like the creature, existed
only in his mind.

If so, he was convinced his mind had just done its level best
to kill him. Ever so cautiously, he glanced toward the window.
The creature was still out there. Its eyes probed at him again.
Now, though, he had its measure. He felt the urge to let it into
the chamber, but the compulsion that had tried to force him to
action was gone.

If naming the mouse a noble would have helped the little
creature in any way, he would have done it on the spot. Had
Genesios' wizard not probed at his sorcerous protections before attacking, the attack surely would have succeeded.
Maniakes savored the irony of that.

But he was not safe yet. When the creature hanging outside
the window realized it could no longer force him to go tamely
to destruction, it cried out again, even louder and more savagely than before. It drew back. For a moment, he thought that

meant it was returning to the mage who had sent it forth. Then it darted toward the window, swift as a falcon, intent on battering its way through Bagdasares' wards if it could go no other way.

When it reached the pane of the window, where the Vaspurakaner wizard had crossed his pieces of twine, blue and gold lightning flared. Maniakes' eyes were briefly blinded; a clap of thunder smote his ears. He thought the light and noise, if not the anguished wail that came from the creature, plenty to rouse not just the folk of Samosates' residence but half the people of Opsikion with them.

But the night remained still and serene. Maniakes' vision cleared without the blinks he would have needed to recover from a veritable lightning bolt. As cautious as he had been before, he looked toward the window, ready to avert his gaze if the creature tried to lure him forward once more.

He saw no sign of it. Now of his own volition he advanced to the window. He peered out over Opsikion. In the sky to the west he thought he sensed a fading trail of light that might have led back toward Videssos the city, although it faded before he was sure he'd seen it. A dog or two began to bark, off in the distance. They might have sensed the magic that had sizzled around Samosates' residence. On the other hand, they might have smelled or seen a cat. Maniakes had no way to know.

All at once, he stopped worrying about the dogs. A new and urgent question filled his mind: was that the end of Genesios' sorcerous attacks, or only the beginning? His breath came quick and short as fear filled him. From many miles, that first assault had nearly breached Bagdasares' defenses. What could another, more heartily prepared stroke do?

He clutched the amulet Alvinos Bagdasares had given him. It did not seem unduly warm, which meant the wards had not been penetrated. If the wards did fail, it was his last line of defense. He did not like operating from his last line of defense in war, and cared for the idea no more in magecraft.

Nothing happened. A gentle night breeze blew into the room, carrying the sweet, heavy scent of jasmine along with the seaside city stinks of ordure and old fish. The ground did not open and swallow Samosates' residence. The sky did not crack and release a horde of winged demons, each one fiercer and uglier than the thing that had almost seized him.

"Thanks to a mouse—that's the only reason I'm here," he

said wonderingly. "A mouse." He wondered how many great events turned on similar small, unrecorded circumstances. More than anyone guessed, he suspected.

He gradually began to believe that there would be only one attack in the night. Of course, that might have been a ploy to lull him into a false sense of ease before the next sorcerous storm struck, but somehow he did not think so—and, in any case, he was too sleepy to stay on his feet much longer. He got back into bed.

"If something comes in and eats me, I hope it doesn't wake me first this time," he muttered, pulling the covers up over his head.

Next thing he knew, the cool light of dawn came sliding through the window. He yawned, stretched, and got to his feet. At first he saw nothing at all out of the ordinary. Then he noticed four small charred patches on the window frame, at just about the spots where Bagdasares had sorcerously attached his vertical and horizontal lengths of twine. He hadn't seen those places there before. If the wards had indeed flared to protect him against magical attack, something of the sort might have resulted.

"Lucky the building didn't catch fire," he said, and decided he hadn't imagined the ghostly, fanged visitor after all.

He splashed water from the pitcher over his hands and face and, spluttering a little, went downstairs to his breakfast. After he had eaten his fill, he cut a large chunk off the round of cheese Samosates had set out and headed upstairs with it.

"You've made friends with your mice?" the hypasteos asked, chuckling at his own wit.

"With one of them, anyhow," Maniakes said from the foot of the steps. Samosates stared after him as he climbed them.

III

THE HILLS ABOVE OPSIKION DROPPED AWAY TO THE NORTH. Rhegorios had led horsemen and rattling, squeaking supply wagons west toward Videssos the city two days earlier. With luck, his forces would reach the capital at about the same time as the fleet. Without luck, Maniakes would never see his cousin again.

Summer laid a heavier hand on the mainland than it ever did on Kalavria. The offshore wind blew the pungent fragrance of citrus orchards out to the ships that sailed south along the coast. No great mariner himself, Maniakes was just as glad when his captains stayed well within sight of land and beached their ships each night. He hadn't cared for the passage across the open sea that had brought him from Kastavala to Opsikion.

Every so often, the fleet would pass fishing boats bobbing in the light chop, each with a fisherman and perhaps a couple of sons or nephews working the nets. Sometimes the *Renewal* approached so close that Maniakes could see tanned, staring faces turned his way. He wondered what went through the fishermen's minds. *Probably the same thing that goes through an anchovy's mind when a shark swims by after bigger prey,* he thought.

The weather grew ever warmer as they sailed farther south. Maniakes came to understand why so many sailors often went about in nothing more than a loincloth. Had he not been mindful of his dignity, he might have done the same. As it was, he sweated in his robes, feeling rather like a loaf of bread trapped inside its oven.

Then one day the lookout in the crow's nest shouted and

pointed southwest. Maniakes' heart sprang into his mouth. Had the fellow spied Genesios' fleet? If he had, the chroniclers would write briefly of yet another failed rebellion during the reign of Genesios.

But the lookout's shout had words in it: "The cape! There's the cape ahead!"

Sure enough, before long Maniakes, too, could see how the land dwindled away to a single point washed by endless creamy waves. To the south, the sea stretched on forever, or at least to the distant, seldom-visited Hot Lands, home of elephants and other strange, half-legendary beasts.

As the fleet sailed past the point of the cape, Thrax and the other captains bawled orders. Sailors capered this way and that. Water muttered against steering oars that guided ships on a new course. Ropes creaked as the men swung the sails to catch the wind at a different angle. The masts themselves made small groaning noises; bent so long one way, they now were pushed another. The fleet swung northwest, sailing directly toward the imperial city.

"The Key," Maniakes muttered.

He didn't know he had spoken aloud till Kourikos, who stood close by, nodded. The logothete of the treasury said, "Indeed, your Majesty, that island and the fleets based thereon shall be the key to whether we stand or fall."

"I prefer to think of it as the key to Videssos the city and to hope it will turn smoothly in my hand," Maniakes said.

"Phos grant it be so, your Majesty," Kourikos answered. He hesitated slightly each time he spoke Maniakes' title. He had had no trouble bringing it out when he addressed the elder Maniakes, but to acknowledge someone years younger than he as a superior had to rankle. In Kourikos' sandals, Maniakes would have been thinking about having experience earn its proper reward. He wouldn't have been a bit surprised to learn that the same thoughts ran through Kourikos' head. *One more thing to worry about.* That had occurred to him a great many times lately.

Thrax visibly relaxed when the fleet rounded the cape without being assailed. "Now we have a chance," he declared. "If they meet us anywhere else on our way to Videssos the city, there'll be doubt in some of their hearts, and we'll be able to put it to good use. But they could have smashed us like a man setting his boot on a cockroach, and they didn't do it. I begin to think I'm not throwing my life away to no purpose."

"If you thought that, why did you sail with me?" Maniakes asked.

"Because there was always the chance I'd be wrong," his captain answered. "And because, if I do live, I'll do well for myself and I'll do well by Videssos, and both those things matter to me."

Maniakes wondered which mattered more. Thrax had put his own ambition ahead of his concern for the Empire. Maniakes judged that probably honest. He shrugged. As well ask men to give up food and wine as ask them to set anything ahead of their interests.

Every time the fleet put into shore, he had Alvinos Bagdasares renew the protective spells around him. Since that first attack in Opsikion, Genesios had not assailed him with magic. He wondered if that meant Genesios thought him dead, or if the mages at the capital concluded his shielding was too strong for them to penetrate. Neither supposition left him permanently secure. If Genesios thought him dead, sooner or later he would learn he was wrong. And Maniakes was closer to Videssos the city now than he had been in Opsikion. Wards that had sufficed then might fail now.

Every morning he woke relieved to have got through another night unmolested. Maybe, he thought, every wizard Genesios controlled had fled away from the detested sovereign, leaving the man who called himself Avtokrator no way to strike across the long leagues of ocean. Maybe that was so—but Maniakes did not count on it.

When he said as much to Bagdasares, the sorcerer nodded. "You are wise, your Majesty. Never rely on what a wizard may or may not do. We are tricksy, the lot of us." He tugged at his beard. "I wonder if I was wise to include myself in that. Ah, well, had I not, doubtless you would have attended to the matter for me."

"Doubtless," Maniakes said dryly. He had the fleet of the Key to worry about, too. It should have occupied all his thoughts. Instead, he had to spend time wondering whether he would wake up himself or as an earwig. He liked being himself. Gaining a couple of extra legs and a pincer on his backside did not strike him as a worthwhile exchange.

The fleet kept sailing north and west. The only sails the lookouts saw belonged to fishing boats like those that had bobbed in the chop outside Kastavala and Opsikion. Maniakes began to wonder where the fleet from the Key was. He certainly had not wanted to make its acquaintance as his own vessels were rounding the cape. Not seeing it then had been nothing but a relief. Not seeing it now made him fret. What in Skotos' cursed name were the captains based at the Key plotting?

Whatever it was, they didn't have long to put their plot into effect. In another couple of days, his fleet would sail between the Key and the mainland and make for Videssos the city. Was Genesios' plan to have the ships on the Key fall in behind his vessels and cut off their escape? That had risks, even if they did their job perfectly—if his fleet and land forces took the capital, they wouldn't need to escape.

The next morning, a fine bright day with the sun quickly burning off the light sea mist, the watchman in the crow's nest of the *Renewal* cried out, "Sail ho to northward!" A moment later, he corrected himself: "*Sails* ho to northward!" After another few minutes, he declared, "Those aren't fishing boats—sails are the wrong shape, and too big to boot. They're coming on fast."

Thrax cupped his hands into a trumpet: "Ready all for battle!" Horns blared the word to ships behind the leaders. Through their brazen cries, Maniakes heard other captains relay orders and other lookouts report sighting the oncoming vessels.

Then he saw them for himself. No, they were not fishing boats. They were warships like his own, spread across a good stretch of sea ahead. He looked from them to Thrax to his own fleet, trying to gauge numbers. He couldn't, not with any confidence. He keenly felt how much he was a landlubber afloat. At last, he turned and asked Thrax how the opposing forces matched up.

The captain ran a hand through his silvery hair. "Unless there's a whole lot of sail still under the horizon, that's not the whole of the fleet from the Key, nor even any great part of it. We can take 'em, your Majesty, likely without hurting ourselves too bad in the doing." He yelled orders to his trumpeter. "Pass word to widen the line! We'll sweep out beyond 'em to right and left."

Maniakes watched the ships obey the order. He could see they were not as smooth as they might have been. That did not much matter now. In some close-fought engagement, though, it might make the difference between victory and defeat.

"Their lead ship is showing shield of truce!" the lookout bawled.

Thrax peered ahead. So did Maniakes. They both wanted to make sure the lookout was right before doing anything else. When they had satisfied themselves of that, Thrax turned to Maniakes, a question in his eyes. Maniakes said, "We'll show shield of truce ourselves but have our ships go on with their maneuver."

"Aye, your Majesty." Thrax's voice throbbed with approval and relief. At his command, a sailor ran forward with a white-painted shield hung on a spearshaft.

Maniakes looked east and west. On both wings now, his fleet overlapped that from the Key. "We won't start a fight," he said, "but if they start one, we'll finish it, by Phos."

"Well said, your Majesty." Again, Thrax appeared imperfectly trusting of any captains who chose to serve under Genesios.

The fleets continued to approach each other. That from the Key did nothing to keep itself from being flanked, which worried Maniakes. In land combat, passions among soldiers ran so high as to make battle magic chancy at best and more often than not futile. He wasn't sure the same obtained in naval warfare: It seemed a more precise, more artisanly way of fighting than the melees into which land battles generally developed. Ships reminded him more of pieces in the Videssian board game.

He smiled when that thought crossed his mind. With luck, he would capture these ships and put them back on the board as part of his own force.

But would he have luck? No way to tell, not yet. As the fleets drew within hailing distance of each other, a leather-lunged sailor aboard the nearest ship from the Key bellowed across the green-blue water: "Why do you continue to move against us while still showing sign of truce?"

"Because we don't trust you," Maniakes answered bluntly, and his own herald shouted back at the oncoming dromon. He went on, "Genesios the usurper has tried to slay me once, so I have no good reason to trust him or his. But so long as you do not strike at us, we shall not strike at you."

The next question amused him. "Which Maniakes are you?"

"The younger, as I hope you'd see," he answered. Genesios hadn't even known at whom he was striking, then: *opponent* was label enough. Maniakes asked a question of his own. "Who seeks to know?"

After a moment, the reply came back. "You speak with Tiverhios, ypodrungarios of the fleet of the Key. Permission to come alongside to parley?"

"Wait," Maniakes told him. He turned to Kourikos and Triphylles. "Does either of you know this man?"

Triphylles was practically hopping up and down on the deck in excitement. "His brother is married to a cousin of mine, your Majesty. I was a groomsman at the wedding."

Kourikos also had a connection with Tiverhios, in a way perhaps even more intimate than that of Triphylles: "Your Majesty, he owes me seven hundred goldpieces, as well as a year's interest on them."

"Mm." Maniakes was not sure what to make of that. "Would he be more interested—forgive me, I did that by accident—in repaying you, in having you forgive his debt, or in slaughtering you so the matter becomes moot?"

"Oh, the indebtedness would not become moot were I to die suddenly," Kourikos assured him. "It is quite well documented, let me tell you, and would pass down to my heirs and assigns, Niphone receiving her fair portion from any eventual collection."

"You really mean that," Maniakes said in tones of wonder. Even after the six bloody, anarchic years of Genesios' reign, Kourikos remained confident the law would in the end exact payment from a recalcitrant debtor. Indeed, *remained confident* was an understatement; to the logothete of the treasury, no other result seemed conceivable. Maniakes wondered if he should enlighten his prospective father-in-law about the persuasive power of sharpened iron. A moment later, he wondered if Kourikos wasn't trying to enlighten him. He tried a different course. "For the sake of bringing him to our side, would you be willing to forgive his debt?"

"I suppose so," Kourikos said, sounding vaguely surprised. "It is one way of conveying advantage, after all."

"Well enough, then." To his own herald, Maniakes said, "Tell him he may come alongside." His calculation was not based solely upon the likelihood of Tiverhios' switching sides: he had taken the measure of the dromon in which the ypodrungarios of the fleet from the Key sailed and concluded the *Renewal* should have no trouble sinking it or winning any sort of boarding battle. That was reckoning as cold-blooded as any Kourikos made over whether to grant a loan, but made with lives rather than goldpieces.

Tiverhios' ship drew near. It had eyes painted on either side of the bow, to help it see over the waves. Some fishing boats followed that custom, as did some of the dromons in Maniakes' fleet. He wondered if it was magic or merely superstition—then he wondered if those two differed in any meaningful way. If he ever found some leisure, which looked unlikely, he would have to put both questions to Bagdasares.

Like every longtime seaman whose acquaintance Maniakes had made, Tiverhios was baked brown as an overdone loaf by the sun. His fancy robe and his arrogant stance made him easy to spy. As if they were not enough, he also shaved his cheeks and chin bare but wore a bushy mustache to prove his masculinity, an eccentric style by Videssian standards.

"Greetings, Maniakes, in the name of the lord with the great and good mind," he said, his voice all at once oddly formal.

Maniakes started to ask him about greetings in Genesios' name, but hesitated with the sardonic question still unspoken. A great many Videssian officers, probably most, were pious and prayerful men, but few put their piety into that kind of salutation. Tiverhios must have meant something special by it, even if Maniakes could not tell precisely what.

His voice cautious, he replied, "Excellent sir, I return your greeting, also in the name of the lord with the great and good mind. May Phos' sun long shine upon you."

Tiverhios' nearly naked face split into a wide grin. "The good god bless you, sir, you're not the misbeliever they said you were."

Sir was not *your Majesty*; it wasn't even as much courtesy as Maniakes had tendered the ypodrungarios. But, coupled with the grin, it struck Maniakes as a good sign. He asked, "Who are 'they,' and what lies have they been spreading about me?"

"Genesios' men, sir," Tiverhios answered. "They came to the Key, excellent sir, and said you were a rebel, eminent sir, which I see is true, begging your pardon, your Highness, but they also said of you that you were a heretic and a misbeliever and a disbeliever, which I see isn't true at all, your Majesty."

Maniakes stared at him. He felt like some pious layman chosen by an Emperor as ecumenical patriarch and rushed through the grades of the ecclesiastical hierarchy so he would be juridically fit to hold the office to which he had been named. In such promotions, though, a man spent a day at each rung of the ladder. Tiverhios had rushed him to his highest possible title in the space of a sentence. It was dizzying.

"Unless I'm altogether mistaken, they will also have said of me that I'm a cursed rug-peddler of a Vaspurakaner, doomed to Skotos' ice on account of my blood if for no other reason," Maniakes said. "They will have said something about Vaspurakaners always being heretics, too, won't they?"

Tiverhios' head bobbed up and down. It hardly seemed a voluntary motion on his part: more as if the waves that slapped against his ship were making him nod. "They did say something like that, I think, but I didn't pay it any mind. Not me."

That would do for a round, thumping lie until a bigger one came along. Had it been truth, Tiverhios wouldn't have readied his loaded greeting and sprung it like a trap. But Maniakes was willing to overlook it to win the ypodrungarios firmly to his side. Sketching the sun-circle over his heart, he said, "True, my ancestors came out of Vaspurakan, but I am of orthodox faith." He hadn't been, not altogether, but the Videssians would pull him down from the throne and burn him alive if he were mad enough to try to impose his ancestral dogmas on them. Somehow that didn't always stop them from trying to impose theirs on Vaspurakan when they had the chance, but they saw nothing unusual in that disparity.

Tiverhios didn't go down on his belly in a full proskynesis, but he did bow himself almost double. "Your Majesty, I had hoped—I had prayed—that would be what you said. When it is seen to be true all through the Empire, the crown and red boots will be yours. So long as he be orthodox, any man alive is better on the throne than Genesios."

Maniakes had to work to keep his face straight at such back-handed praise. He worried only slightly about what the Empire as a whole thought of his religious views. At the moment, what the fleet thought of them was of paramount importance. Later, if he won his way so far, what the ecumenical patriarch and the people of Videssos the city thought would also matter. So would the opinion of the army, though it was leavened with a good many unconverted Vaspurakaners.

"What do you intend to do now, excellent sir?" he asked Tiverhios. "Will all your ships join me? Will all the Key's ships join me?" He turned his head and in a lowered voice asked Thrax, "What part of the Key's fleet has he here?"

"Perhaps a third," Thrax answered. "A cautious strategy,

coming out to meet us with so few." He sniffed. "In a civil war, caution is mostly wasted."

Tiverhios was also speaking: "Since I did not fully know your views, your Majesty, before setting out I promised—indeed, I swore—no harm would come to captains and crews either willing or unwilling to follow you, that depending on what you turned out to be." He looked anxious. "You will not make me violate my oath, I hope?"

Maniakes wondered how he had expected to be able to fight after giving an oath like that. He shrugged. The scent of heresy might have united the captains behind Genesios as nothing else could. He said, "No, those who prefer a bloodstained bungling butcher who aims to feed Videssos to Sharbaraz King of Kings piece by piece are welcome to go to him. Having such fools as his commanders will but weaken him."

Tiverhios thought that over and then, rather more slowly than Maniakes would have hoped for, got the point and laughed. "Well said! Now that you are shown to be orthodox, few from among my captains here will seek to desert your cause."

"From among your captains here?" Maniakes echoed. "What of the men still back at the Key?"

"More of them, I fear, will incline toward your enemy," Tiverhios said. "I took with me mostly ships whose captains, I thought, leaned your way."

Kourikos stepped up beside Maniakes at the starboard rail. Tiverhios' eyes widened when he recognized the logothete of the treasury. "Aye, I favor Maniakes," Kourikos said. "So do many from among the powerful at Videssos the city. That you do, too, in this hour of Videssos' need makes me set aside your debt to me in recognition of the debt the Empire owes to you."

"You're—very kind, eminent sir, and very generous." Tiverhios bowed almost as low to Kourikos as he had to Maniakes.

The logothete asked, "Is Erinakios still drungarios of the fleet at the Key?"

"Aye, eminent sir, he is," Tiverhios answered. "Genesios, he's slaughtered the generals till there's hardly a one that can tell north from sausage, if you know what I mean. But he hasn't much messed with us sailors. He doesn't trust himself to find better to take our place, unless I'm wrong."

"He hasn't found better to take the place of the generals he's murdered, either," Maniakes said. Lowering his voice, he said to Kourikos, "Tell me about this Erinakios. We Vaspurakaners don't know much about this business of fighting on the sea, either."

"He's a sharp-tempered man—all over prickles, you might say," Kourikos replied. "He's not broken with Genesios this past six years, not formally, but he didn't molest our merchantmen when we sailed by the Key, nor pursue us once we were past, though he might easily have done either. Where he'll stand now, I do not know."

Maniakes plucked at his beard. "What connections do our assembled nobles here have with him?"

"He borrowed money from me three years ago, about the same time Tiverhios did," the logothete answered. "He paid me back ahead of schedule." Kourikos sounded as if that were an affront, not something to be proud of. From his point of view, maybe it was: Erinakios had deprived him of some accrued interest. He went on, "I shall have to inquire. Offhand, I know of no close connections between any of my party and the drungarios."

"Well, we'll see what we can do." Maniakes did his best to keep his voice easy. In fact, he felt like pitching Kourikos and all his prominent companions into the sea. Here they had been boasting of all the important people they knew, but, the first time he really needed them, they let him down. He called across the water to Tiverhios: "Does Erinakios know why you chose the captains for the part of the fleet you led out to seek me?"

"Can't be sure," the ypodrungarios answered. "We didn't talk about it—nothing like that. But if he thinks about who's there and who's gone, he's going to figure it out. Erinakios, he may be spiny, but he's sharp the other way, too, that he is."

It was, Maniakes suspected with a hint of sadness, more than could be said for Tiverhios. Maniakes asked Thrax, "With these ships here added to ours, can we beat what's left of the force the Key has?"

Obviously unaware of what he was doing, the captain of the *Renewal* made several strange, thought-filled faces before answering "Your Majesty, I think we can, provided the fleet from Videssos the city doesn't come down to aid Erinakios. But if he fights with all he has, we'll not get away from the Key with enough to challenge the fleet that anchors at the capital."

Thrax had a way of sounding discouraged whether the situation truly warranted it or not. Maniakes was getting used to that, and included it in his calculations. He asked, "How likely is Erinakios to fight with everything he has?"

"If you're asking me, your Majesty, my guess is that he's not likely to do that," Thrax said. "If he'd intended fighting with everything he had, he'd have met us with his whole fleet a long way south of here. But I'm only guessing. If you really want to know, ask Tiverhios there."

"You're right." Maniakes called the question across the gap of ocean.

Tiverhios tugged at one end of his mustache as he considered. "Your Majesty, I just don't know. Some days, he'd be cursing Genesios up one side and down the other, the sort of curses that, were he a wizard, would slay a man in short order and leave him glad he was dead on account of the pain of his dying. But other times, he'd curse rebels every bit as hard. I don't think he knows himself what he'll do till the time comes to do it."

"That time is coming soon," Maniakes said.

The Key had two central mountain peaks. They loomed up from the sea, green on their lower slopes, the gray-brown of bare rock interspersed above. Neither was tall enough to hold snow in summer.

Maniakes cared nothing for the peaks, save that they marked where in the sea the island lay. His interest centered on the ports, particularly the southern one, Gavdos. The fleet still under Erinakios' command had put to sea and awaited him well out from the port. He would not catch the dromons tied up at the docks or beached nearby. Erinakios gave every appearance of being ready to fight.

Tiverhios' galley lay alongside the *Renewal*, so the ypo-drungarios could tell Maniakes what he needed to know about captains and vessels of the opposing fleet. Maniakes called to him, "Which ship does Erinakios command?"

Tiverhios scanned the oncoming dromons. "It'd be easier to pick out under sail," he said a little peevishly, "but he's brailed up his canvas and stowed the mast for battle, same as everybody else. I think—there! Off to port a bit, the one with the red eyes painted by the ram."

"I see the one you mean," Maniakes said. The rowers on Erinakios' ship powered it through the water with swift, steady strokes. Maniakes couldn't remember seeing such polished efficiency before; it was as if a single hand worked all the oars. As the ship came up and over the waves, he got glimpses of its ram, the bronze turned green by the sea but the point cruelly sharp. That crew would make sure it did all the harm it could.

"Steer toward him," Maniakes said. "We'll show the shield of truce, but if he sprints at us, I want to be ready to fight on the instant."

"We'd better be," Thrax said. "Otherwise we'll be dead." He had also noted what Erinakios' rowers could do—and that the ship in which the drungarios sailed was larger and more formidable than the *Renewal*.

Erinakios' dromon drew closer appallingly fast. Maniakes saw no sign of a shield of truce—only the point of the ram, aimed always at a point just to port of his own bow. The enemy's oars rose and fell, rose and fell.

"A touch to port," Thrax called to the steersmen at the stern. "By Phos, he won't take the angle on us!" The *Renewal* made the slight course adjustment, but Erinakios and his rowers countered. Within moments, the green bronze ram aimed for the same point as before. Thrax bit his lip. "They're good. They're very good."

The two dromons were hardly a bowshot apart when a sailor in Erinakios' ship held up a white-painted shield. "Sheer off!" Maniakes shouted.

"What? Are you mad?" Thrax stared wildly. "It's a trick, your Majesty. Give him your flank and we'll be on the bottom in nothing flat."

"Sheer off," Maniakes repeated. *"Now!"* If he was right, Erinakios was seeing what kind of stomach he had for a tight place. If he was wrong . . . if he was wrong, the little fish and the urchins and the whelks that crawled across the bottom of the sea would feed well.

"Hard to starboard!" Thrax cried, raw pain coming from his throat with the words. They were so close to Erinakios' galley now that even sheering off was risky; if both ships dodged in the same direction, they might still collide.

Just for an instant, the flagship from the Key started to follow the *Renewal*'s movement. Fear turned Maniakes' bowels to water. If Erinakios truly was committed to Genesios, he had the chance to do his sovereign a great service. But then the drungarios' dromon spun to starboard itself and slid past the

Renewal on a parallel track, the tips of its oars almost brushing against those of the ship in which Maniakes sailed.

Across the narrow stretch of water, a hoarse voice bawled, "You want to see how close you can cut it, don't you?"

If that was Erinakios by the port rail, he looked as prickly as Kourikos had described him: a hawk-featured man with a red, angry face and a wolf-gray beard. To him, Maniakes called back, "Isn't that what you had in mind to find out, eminent sir?"

Erinakios' laugh sounded like the sharp, coughing bark of a wolf, too. "Aye, that's what I had in mind. What's it to you?"

Maniakes remembered the sudden, liquid terror he had known. A rush of anger all but burned it away. The first thing he thought of was revenge against Erinakios for reminding him of his mortality. Shame followed, extinguishing rage. Erinakios had a right to be concerned about what sort of sovereign he might get if he abandoned Genesios.

"Do I pass your test, eminent sir?" Maniakes asked.

The distance between the two dromons had lengthened. Erinakios had to raise his voice to answer: "You'll do." After a moment, almost as an afterthought, he added, "Your Majesty."

Maniakes nearly missed the offhand recognition of his sovereignty. He was looking out toward the wings of the two fleets. In the center, where captains on both sides saw their commanders parleying, they, too, had held back from fighting. Out on the wings, they had gone for each other. A couple of dromons had been rammed and were sinking; men splashed in the water, grabbing for oars and planks and other floating wreckage. More than one fire blazed upon the water, which could not extinguish the liquid incendiary the Videssian navy used.

"Will your trumpeter blow truce?" Maniakes asked. "In civil war, hurts cost the Empire double, for it bleeds when a man from either side dies."

"For that all on its lonesome I'd blow truce," Erinakios said. "Genesios hasn't figured it out to this day, and won't if he lives to be a thousand." He turned to his trumpeter. The sweet notes of the truce call rang across the water. Maniakes nudged Thrax, who called to his own hornplayer. In a moment, the call to leave off fighting blared from both flagships.

Not all the captains obeyed the call, not at once. Some of the leaders of the fleet from the Key genuinely favored

Genesios, no matter what their drungarios had to say. And some of Maniakes' captains, already engaged in battle when they heard the truce call, did not care to leave off fights they were winning.

Erinakios and Maniakes sorted things out together. Maniakes' dromons disengaged from battle as they could. Where they still fought Genesios' loyalists, they suddenly discovered allies among Erinakios' ships. Most of the dromons whose leaders backed Genesios soon sank or surrendered. On a couple, mutinies from the crew impelled such surrender.

But a few warships broke free and sprinted northwest toward Videssos the city, oars churning water white as they fled. Desperation lent them speed their foes could not match. "Genesios will be muttering into his mustache tomorrow, when word reaches him of rout and defection," Erinakios said. He bared his teeth. "I like the idea."

"And I," Maniakes said. "But that also means we'll have to look more to our safety from tomorrow on. Have you a wizard whose work you trust? The tyrant has already tried once to slay me by sorcery."

Erinakios made an impatient, disparaging gesture; every line of his body shouted contempt. "I'm a fighting man," he said. "I don't clutter my head worrying about magecraft."

"Have it as you will," Maniakes said, though he did not share the drungarios' scorn of sorcery: After the night in Opsikion, he hardly could. Aye, magic was hard to come by, difficult to execute properly, and of little use in time of battle. All that granted, it remained real, and could be deadly dangerous.

"D'you trust him, your Majesty?" Thrax whispered urgently. "Even without Tiverhios' ships, that fleet is a match for ours. If you add them into the bargain, we could be swamped."

"If Erinakios wanted to swamp us, he could have done it without this mime-show," Maniakes answered. "Having his ships waiting just past the cape would have taken care of the job nicely. We *want* people to rally to our banner, Thrax; we've wanted that from the start. If it hadn't happened, we never could have come this far."

"I understand all that." Thrax stuck out his chin and looked stubborn. "But the thing of it is, we've come this far with people we know are loyal—most of 'em, anyhow. But if we take up this fleet and sail with it alongside ours or mixed together with ours against Videssos the city, and Erinakios turns on us then, why, it'd be like a man walking along on two legs and having one of 'em fall off."

"There's a pretty picture," Maniakes said. "But if we go against the city without the fleet from the Key, we're like a one-legged man setting out."

Thrax winced, but then nodded. "Something to that, too, I suppose. But watch yourself, your Majesty."

"I shall," Maniakes promised. He raised his voice and called to Erinakios: "Have you space at your docks for our ships?"

"Aye, we can take 'em all, in Gavdos or Sykeota around on the north coast," the drungarios of the Key answered. "I suppose you'll want more of my ships to go to one harbor and more of yours to the other, so you can surround yourself with armed men you trust."

He couldn't possibly have heard Maniakes and Thrax talking together. A glance at the distance between the *Renewal* and Erinakios' ship told Maniakes as much. He hadn't thought to give Erinakios any tests for wits, but the drungarios seemed to be setting his own—and passing them handily. Maniakes said, "If you think I won't take you up on that, eminent sir, you may think again."

Erinakios let out a couple of barking grunts of laughter. "You'd be a fool to say no till I prove my worth. Will you take Gavdos or Sykeota? The northern harbor's a trifle larger, but the southern's easier to get in and out of. Either which way, I suppose you'll want me for hostage?" He phrased it as a question, but his voice held certainty.

"Now that you mention it—yes," Maniakes answered, which drew another of those wolfish chuckles from Erinakios. Turning to Thrax, Maniakes asked, "Which harbor do you prefer?"

"Gavdos," Thrax answered without hesitation. "The drungarios is right—it's the easier of the two, and not all our captains and crews have been here before."

Kastavala had a good harbor, Opsikion had a good harbor. Videssos the city had three splendid harbors: north, south, and west. Only those last could stand comparison to the anchorage on the southern shore of the Key: it was as if Phos had scooped out three-fourths of a circle from an otherwise smooth coastline, giving a relatively small entrance to a wide, secure anchorage. Even storms would have their force muted before they smote with wind and wave the ships tied up there.

Had Videssos the city not stood at a crossroads of both land and sea routes, and had the imperial capital not kept itself rich by making potential rivals poor, the Empire might have been ruled from the Key. Maniakes wondered how the world might have looked had the islanders spread out and begun to rule the mainland instead of being ruled from it.

As it was, the town of Gavdos was far smaller than Kastavala, let alone Opsikion, let alone Videssos the city. Most of it seemed to be barracks and storehouses and taverns and brothels: but for the fleet, the place had no life.

"Is it the same at Sykeota in the north?" Maniakes asked.

Thrax did not need to have him explain himself. "Just the same, your Majesty. From time out of mind, this island's been given over to the navy and not much else. They don't grow enough grain here to feed all the sailors, and a city can't live on fish alone."

"So that's the way of it," Maniakes said thoughtfully. "If ever a drungarios of the fleet here decided to rebel, his men would get hungry by and by—provided they didn't win first, that is."

Triphylles came up and examined Gavdos with a jaundiced eye. "What a dreadful hole," he said, adding a shudder redolent of distaste. "I shall be ever so glad when this campaign is over and done and I can return to my villa in the city. Life anywhere else has proved altogether dreary, I fear."

"It would have been dreary to stay in Videssos the city after your head went up on the Milestone, I suppose," Maniakes remarked, deadpan.

"Well, yes, but even so—" Triphylles began. Then he realized he was being made sport of. With a sniff, he took himself elsewhere. Thrax suffered a coughing fit of epic proportions, but valiantly managed to hold back from laughing out loud.

Erinakios' flagship tied up just behind the *Renewal*. Maniakes walked up the gangplank to the dock. After so many days spent mostly at sea, dry land felt wobbly. Sailors with swords and shields came up onto the dock with him, in case Erinakios intended treachery even now.

But the drungarios, though he also got up on the dock as fast as he could—and though he swayed to and fro more than Maniakes—prostrated himself on the rough timbers before the man he had named his sovereign. "Get up, get up," Maniakes said impatiently. "We have a lot of planning to do, and not much time in which to do it."

Erinakios rose. Seen close up, he looked even tougher and grimmer than Kourikos had made him out to be and than he had seemed while aboard his dromon. Maniakes had twenty years fewer than he, but would not have cared to encounter him sword to sword or hand to hand.

But his fierce visage suddenly lightened into a smile, as if the sun had come out from behind thick clouds. "I am already seeing I made the right choice," he said. "Genesios knows nothing of planning. Something happens to him, happens to the Empire, and he goes and does the first thing that pops into his vicious head. Is it any wonder we're in our present state?"

"That we're in it is no wonder, but getting out won't be easy," Maniakes answered. "Falling down a hill is easier than slogging back up it once you've fallen, and straightforward viciousness has one thing in its favor: whoever gets in his way once isn't apt to be around to do it twice."

"Which is the only reason Genesios is still on the throne," Erinakios said. "But if he doesn't manage to murder you, I think you'll beat him. You can think—I can see that already. Most of the others who rose against him were just reacting. He could deal with them; his mind works the same way, and he had the advantages of already wearing the red boots and sitting in Videssos the city like a spider in the center of its web. You'll be tougher."

"May I ask you something?" Maniakes waited for Erinakios' gruff nod, then put his question: "Why didn't you go after the crown yourself?"

"I thought about it," Erinakios said, a dangerously honest answer—a man with imperial ambitions might be reckoned untrustworthy for that very reason. "Aye, I thought about it. But with only the fleet from the Key, I was too likely to lose. And I couldn't count on help from anyone else. I've made too many enemies over the years for that. Why do you suppose Genesios kept me on here? He's shortsighted, but he's not blind."

Maniakes pursed his lips. The drungarios' comment made considerable sense. Genesios had left the elder Maniakes alone on Kalavria, knowing that replacing him would cause more trouble. And he had retained an able but unpopular officer here lest his replacement prove able to forge alliances with other soldiers and sailors. No, that wasn't stupid. If only he had used more of his wits for the Empire's good.

"Going to have to put you up in the barracks," Erinakios said, pointing to a weathered wooden building. "Hope you don't mind—it's where I sleep."

"It's all right with me," Maniakes answered cheerfully.

"Next to some of the places I've slept on campaign, it looks like the imperial palace." He glanced back toward the *Renewal*. "How the excellent Triphylles and the eminent Kourikos will take it is another matter, though. And I've another double handful of nobles from Videssos the city scattered through the rest of my ships."

"Well, if they want to get rid of Genesios, they'll have to take a bit of the rough so as they can have the smooth back," Erinakios said. "And if they don't fancy a couple of nights of hard beds and salt fish, to the ice with 'em."

Maniakes wouldn't have put it so bluntly, but the drungarios' assessment marched with his own. Some of the grandees seemed ready to make the best of their unprepossessing quarters, while others grumbled and fussed.

Erinakios spat scornfully when he saw that. "Pack of half-weaned brats, whining on account of Mama won't give 'em the tit."

"Let them be," Maniakes said, which got him a dirty look from the drungarios. He didn't care. The nobles from the capital might have been discontented with their lodgings, but they were finally doing what he had hoped they would. He watched them going around, mugs of rough wine in hand, to one of Erinakios' ship captains after another; whether through kinship or marriage or acquaintance or gold, they seemed to know most of the fleet's leading officers. The more they talked with those men, the stronger the bond they wove that bound the fleet of the Key to Maniakes.

"By tomorrow," Erinakios said in a appraising tone of voice, "Genesios will know you're here, and he'll know I've gone over to you. I don't think he'll be what you'd call happy about that."

"Then we should sail for the city tomorrow," Maniakes answered. "The faster we move, the less chance he'll have to figure out where we are and what we're up to."

Erinakios raised his cup of wine in salute. "Spoken like a soldier, your Majesty!" He drank again, then studied Maniakes. "The more I hear you talking, your Majesty, the more I like what I hear. Videssos won't prosper—by the good god, Videssos won't survive, the way things are these days—with a slugabed in the red boots."

"If I don't keep moving, I'm liable to be the one who doesn't survive," Maniakes said. "Genesios has already tried once to slay me by sorcery, as I've said. That's why I asked if you had a wizard warding you."

"And I told you, I have no truck with wizards. If sorcery hasn't slain me in all these years, I don't think it will bite on me now."

The logic behind that escaped Maniakes, but he held his tongue. If Erinakios wanted to substitute bravado for brains, that was his affair. And Genesios was in any case more likely to attack his rival Emperor than an underling, however high his rank.

"Do you mind if I send a boat around to Sykeota?" Maniakes asked Erinakios. "I want to make sure my men and ships there are getting on well and also to make sure fleets from both ports will sail against Videssos the city on the same day."

"Yes, that would be a good thing, wouldn't it?" Erinakios gave one of his barking chuckles. He waved a hand in Maniakes' direction, perhaps mocking the delicate gestures of the grandees from the city. "Go right ahead, your Majesty. In your boots, I'd do all the checking I could, too."

Maniakes went over to one of his officers and gave the necessary orders. The captain saluted with clenched fist over heart and went off to do his bidding. Maniakes was confident the fellow would find everything all right; the question had been more intended to find out how Erinakios would react. Had the drungarios tried to talk him out of seeing how things were going at the harbor where his ships were in the minority, he would have had something to worry about. Since Erinakios didn't mind, odds were he wasn't intending to try anything hostile over there.

"I hope all's going well with Rhegorios," Maniakes murmured, half to himself.

Erinakios overheard him. "That's your cousin with the horsemen? I hope it's well with him, too, your Majesty. The thinner Genesios has to spread his men—and his fears, and his hatred—the less he can concentrate on any one thing."

"Just what I was thinking," Maniakes said, and so it was, but only in part. The chief idea in his mind was that in Rhegorios he had a comrade he could trust without reservation. With all the new chieftains, with all the nobles from Videssos the city, he was constantly looking over his shoulder to make sure the hand patting him on the back hadn't first palmed a dagger.

Erinakios said, "Do I rightly remember hearing you also have a couple of brothers?"

"Aye—Tatoules and Parsmanios, both younger than I. They're officers in the westlands, of no great rank. I pray to the lord with the great and good mind that they're well; no word of them has come to Kastavala for a long time. With Sharbaraz rampaging through our lands there, anything might have happened to them."

"Too true—and you say nothing of all the revolts spawned in the westlands. But they won't have heard of your own rising?"

"I don't think so, no," Maniakes answered. "Not unless Genesios has sent for them to take vengeance for my move against him. But I don't think he can do that, either, not with the chaos there. From what I've heard, these days the Videssian armies in the westlands are fighting for themselves and for survival, nothing more. They don't much worry about orders from the capital."

"There you've heard true, your Majesty." Erinakios rolled his eyes to show how true it was. "But they don't work with one another, either, and so come off worse over and over against the Makuraners."

"Videssians do love faction-fighting," Maniakes observed. He couldn't have stated anything more obvious, save perhaps that air was needed for breathing, but several ship captains and three or four of the grandees from the capital looked askance at him nonetheless. He needed a moment to figure out why: he had publicly reminded them of his own Vaspurakaner blood. Many of them had been doing their best to forget about it so they could back him in good conscience.

Erinakios said, "You're sure you'll be able to sleep here in safety tonight, your Majesty?" It might have been real concern about Maniakes' safety; then again, it might have been a taunt. With the drungarios, every sentence came out so drenched in vinegar that it was hard to tell.

Maniakes chose to think of it as real concern. "It should be all right. Genesios won't know tonight where I am, and in any case my wizard Alvinos is with me. His spells warded me in Opsikion and should protect me here, as well."

"Alvinos, eh?" Erinakios glanced over to the mage, who certainly looked more as if the Vaspurakaner appellation Bagdasares belonged to him than the bland, acceptable Videssian moniker he sometimes wore. Maniakes usually called him Bagdasares, too. This time he hadn't, precisely so he wouldn't bring up Vaspurakan in the minds of those who heard him.

Sensing that people were watching him, Bagdasares turned away from the captain with whom he had been talking, bowed, raised his wine cup in salute, and went back to the interrupted conversation. Maniakes smiled. The mage had a certain style of his own.

Servants lit torches to keep the gathering going after sunset. Maniakes stayed on his feet chatting until the man he had sent out to Sykeota returned with assurances all was well. Then Maniakes let out a couple of yawns so perfect, a mime at a Midwinter's Day festival would not have been ashamed to claim them for his own.

When you were Avtokrator of the Videssians, or even a claimant to the throne, such theatrics got results. Within minutes, dozens of captains, yawning themselves, set aside wine cups, went outside to use the slit trenches in back of the barracks, and flopped down on cots. Maniakes didn't expect his cot to be comfortable, and it wasn't. He slept like a log even so.

Breakfast was a rock-hard roll, a couple of little fried squid hot enough to scorch the fingers, and a mug of sour wine. To Maniakes' thinking, it was a naval variation on campaign food. To the grandees from Videssos the city, it might have been just this side of poisonous. Even Kourikos, who usually seemed the most reasonable of the bunch, didn't eat much.

"What are we to do?" Triphylles asked mournfully. He had nibbled a tiny piece off the roll, sipped the wine and set it down with a grimace of distaste, and turned up his sizable nose at the squid, although street vendors sold them in every quarter of Videssos the city.

To Maniakes, Erinakios remarked, "You know, your Majesty, I'm a grandfather now, but I remember when my oldest son was a little boy. He was what they call a fussy eater, I guess. When he didn't fancy something that was set before him, I'd say, 'Well, son, it's up to you. You can eat that or you can starve.' Like I say, I'm a grandfather now, so I guess he didn't starve."

Triphylles let out a loud, indignant sniff. A couple of the other nobles attacked their breakfasts with fresh vigor. Maniakes even saw one of them take a second helping of fried squid. So did Erinakios. His shoulders shook with suppressed mirth.

Kourikos came up to Maniakes and said, "Your Majesty, I don't think it proper that we should be made sport of for no better reason than our being unaccustomed to the rough fare of the military diet."

"Give me a chance, eminent sir, and I expect I could come up with some better reasons than that to make sport of you," Erinakios said with a maliciously gleeful grin.

Kourikos spluttered indignantly. He was used to twisting other people's words, not to having his own twisted. Maniakes held up a hand. He said, "Eminent sir, so far as I can tell, no one was making sport of anyone; the eminent drungarios happened to choose that moment to explain to me how he raised his son. That may prove useful when Niphone and I have children."

Now Kourikos sounded exasperated. "Really, your Majesty, you know perfectly well that—"

"What I know perfectly well, eminent sir," Maniakes interrupted, "is that on the Key there seems to be no food suitable for your delicate palate and those of your companions. Either you will have to take what the cooks dish out for you or you'll go hungry. When we win the war and the lot of you go back to your villas and manors, you can stuff yourselves with dainties to your hearts' content. Till then, you ought to remember the circumstances in which you find yourselves—and remember that, had you stayed in the city, you might be trying to eat through slit throats."

Angrily, Kourikos stomped away. Sulkily, he took a fried squid from a tray. Defiantly, he bit into it—the squid weren't hot any more. His eyebrows shot up in surprise. Maniakes wondered why he was surprised. Squid, bread crumbs, olive oil, minced garlic—nothing wrong with any of that.

Neither Maniakes nor Erinakios wanted to waste time. The sooner they were sailing for Videssos the city, the happier each would be. But sailing into battle without a plan was asking for trouble.

Erinakios led Maniakes to a chart of the capital with the harbors prominently displayed. Maniakes hadn't much worried about them when he had lived in Videssos the city. Even when he had taken ship, they had been just places from which to enter or leave. He hadn't thought about them in the military sense.

"You'll know the Neorhesian harbor on the north coast of the city is the one the navy mostly uses," Erinakios said, pointing to the chart. Maniakes nodded; he did know that much. Erinakios went on, "Now, the harbor of Kontoskalion in the south is every bit as good, mind you, if not as large. Law and custom say trading ships go there and the dromons to the Neorhesian harbor, but in a civil war nobody listens to what law and customs say, anyhow. Are you with me so far?"

"Aye. You've been very clear. When does it start getting complicated?"

Erinakios snorted. "Have no fear, your Majesty. We're getting there." He jabbed a thumb at the third harbor, this one at the blunt westernmost extremity of Videssos the city. "This anchorage is in the palace district, of course. Most of the time, there's not much tied up here: customs boats, a yacht if the Avtokrator happens to like sailing, a few fishing boats to help keep the palaces supplied, things like that. But the place will hold almost as much as the harbor of Kontoskalion. When an army goes over the Cattle Crossing to the westlands, for instance, some of it will go from there, because it's closest and most convenient. Still, because it's not used much, there's a chance the defenders will leave it out of their calculations. And if we can force a landing there—"

"We can seize the palaces and flush Genesios like a partridge from the gorse," Maniakes finished for him.

"That's how it'd work if everything goes the way it should," Erinakios agreed. "Of course, we'll never see the day when everything goes as it should, but the least making a move on the palaces will do is to force Genesios to shuffle his men all around, and that's part of the idea."

"If he spreads himself thin enough, we may be able to get men up and over the sea wall and move into the city that way," Maniakes said. "It's lower than the land wall, after all, and single, not double."

"It could happen," Erinakios said judiciously, "but I wouldn't count on it. If we do pull it off, it'll show that nobody in Genesios' force is standing by him, not his sailors or his soldiers, either. If that's so, we have him."

"If I understand the hints you've thrown around, you want us to make for the harbor of Kontoskalion and the one by the palaces, in the hope that they'll be less heavily defended than the Neorhesian," Maniakes said.

"That's what I'm thinking, all right," Erinakios said. "We

may have a big sea fight before we can get up to the city. Then
again, we may not. Depends on how confident Genesios and
his captains are feeling when they find out we're on our way.
If they hang back, they're afraid of us."

"What would you do in Genesios' sandals?" Maniakes
asked.

"If I knew Erinakios was coming after me, you mean?" The
drungarios puffed out his chest. "Your Majesty, I'd be afraid."

Maniakes was getting used to priests' giving him sour looks
as they blessed his cause. They mistrusted his orthodoxy, but
six years of Genesios had been enough to prove to almost
everyone that orthodoxy alone did not guarantee a decent ruler.

"May the lord with the great and good mind watch over and
protect you and your cause and our sacred orthodox faith," the
priest said to Maniakes, making it clear that in his mind, at
least, you could not be a decent ruler without orthodoxy, either.
"May he grant peace, tranquility, and victory to Videssos. So
may it be."

"So may it be," Maniakes echoed. "Thank you, holy sir." As
far as he was concerned, the blue-robe had got the order back-
ward: without victory, Videssos would know neither tranquility
nor peace. This was, however, neither time nor place nor occasion for quarreling with a cleric.

"Thank you, your Majesty," the priest replied. "After your
triumph, I pray you shall worship at the High Temple in
Videssos the city. With its beauty and holiness, truly it seems
the veritable home of Phos on earth." He sighed. "Ah, were it
granted me to serve the good god in such a place—"

Maniakes had all he could do to keep his face straight. The
priest might mislike his doctrine but was still angling to be
translated from the Key to the capital. Videssians looked out
for themselves, first, last, and always. He said, "When I win
my way to Videssos the city, I shall indeed reward those who
helped me get there."

Beaming, the priest blessed the ships so fulsomely that
Maniakes marveled when they didn't close their painted eyes
in embarrassment at the praise.

"Well, about time that's over and done with," Erinakios said
when the cleric finally fell silent. The drungarios, while undoubtedly a believer, had a distinctly pragmatic attitude toward
matters religious. "Now let's get on with the business of putting Genesios' head up on the Milestone and flinging his body

onto a dung heap—not that I have anything personal against dung heaps, you understand."

"Everyone in Videssos has something personal against Genesios, I think," Maniakes said. "In fact, the only man I know of who doesn't is Sharbaraz King of Kings: Genesios has given away so much of the Empire to him that he's been an even greater benefactor than Likinios was—and all Likinios did, through my father and me, was to set Sharbaraz back on his throne."

"Your Majesty, you're wrong," Erinakios said. "Genesios has also made a whole host of executioners all through the Empire very happy men."

"There you have me," Maniakes said. "Now we need to—" He broke off. His right hand went to his chest. The amulet that rested against his skin there was suddenly burning hot. "Magic!"

The priest who had just blessed the fleet turned and fled, blue robe flapping around his ankles, shaved skull gleaming in the sun. Maniakes wished him dead and spending an eternity in Skotos' ice. In spite of the wish, the priest kept running. Maybe he wouldn't go to the ice, at least not for this. But one thing was certain: he would never, ever come to Videssos the city.

Bagdasares, on the other hand, ran toward trouble, not away from it. He shouted something in the Vaspurakaner tongue that Maniakes didn't quite catch; his hands twisted in quick passes. All at once, faster than metal and stone had any business doing, the amulet cooled again.

"Never mind me," Maniakes said. "I'm all right. Look to Erinakios."

"You're all right *now*, your Majesty," Bagdasares answered, panting. "How you would have been in another moment—"

But with that offhand remark, he turned his attention and his sorcerous skill to the drungarios. Erinakios stood swaying, his eyes wide and staring, lips pulled back from his teeth in a fearsome grimace, hands clenched into fists. As Maniakes watched in dismay, the naval officer's back began to arch so that he resembled nothing so much as a drawn bow.

Do something! Maniakes wanted to scream to Bagdasares. But if anyone had screamed at him in the middle of a battle, he might well have let the air out of the meddler with a well-placed sword thrust. And so, not feeling himself in any immediate danger, he simply stood and watched Bagdasares struggle against the onslaught of Genesios' mage.

"Why wouldn't you ward yourself against wizardry?" he demanded of Erinakios. The drungarios did not, could not, answer. Every muscle, every tendon in his face and neck, hands, and forearms—all Maniakes could see of his flesh—stood out, sharply defined. His back bent more and more. If it bent much further, it would snap.

Bagdasares incanted like a man possessed. He chanted charms in both Vaspurakaner and Videssian, sometimes in what sounded like the two languages commingled. His hands moved faster and more cleverly than those of a man playing a clavier. Greasy sweat ran down his face and dripped to the wood of the dock.

Still Erinakios' back bent.

When it came, the *snap!* reminded Maniakes of nothing so much as a good-sized stick being broken across a man's knee. Erinakios fell, as limp as he had been rigid. The latrine smell of death filled the air. With a groan, Bagdasares collapsed beside the drungarios.

Suddenly, instead of being helped by the mage, Maniakes was helping him. He rolled Bagdasares onto his back, made sure he was breathing, felt for a pulse. To his vast relief, he found one, firm and strong. "Phos be praised," he said shakily. "He's just fainted, I think. Someone flip water in his face."

For all the water that surrounded the Key, getting some in a bucket and splashing Bagdasares with it seemed to Maniakes to take an unconscionably long time. When the mage was finally splashed, he choked and spluttered. His eyes flew open. At first, only horror filled them. Reason slowly returned. "Phos be praised!" he said, sitting up. "Your Majesty yet lives."

"So I do, and glad of it," Maniakes said. "Poor Erinakios, though, wasn't so lucky."

Bagdasares' fleshy nostrils twitched, as if to pick up the death stench and confirm Maniakes' words. The wizard turned around and peered at the drungarios' corpse. "I'm sorry, your Majesty," he said, bowing his head. "I fought with all I had in me, but I could not save him."

Maniakes reached out a hand, pulled the mage to his feet. "Partly Erinakios' own fault, for disregarding sorcery of all sorts," he said.

"Partly, too, that Genesios' mage had time to prepare his attack, while I had to improvise the defense," Bagdasares said.

"I understand that, but failure is never pleasant to contemplate. And Genesios' mage is very strong, to reach so far and to kill in my despite."

"How strong will he seem when we get closer?" Maniakes asked worriedly.

"Stronger than this, unless I miss my guess." Bagdasares' face glistened with sweat, as if he'd been running for miles. Magecraft was not easy, especially magecraft of the desperate sort he'd just been using. In a shaken voice, he went on, "The capital, by the nature of things, draws the best from every art. How good that best can be—" He shook his head. "Better than I had imagined, I can tell you so much."

"And we are now without the man who was plainly the best choice to lead our ships against the fleet from the city," Maniakes said.

The captains who had been staring at Erinakios' body returned with that to the world of the living, the world of rank and preferment. Tiverhios the ypodrungarios took half a step forward, as if to say that someone with appropriate qualifications might not be overhard to find. But, even though Tiverhios had declared for him right away, Maniakes was not keen to name the ypodrungarios his supreme commander on the sea. He strongly suspected an admixture of expedience in Tiverhios' choice. Besides, choosing Tiverhios would make the rest of the captains from the Key jealous.

And so Maniakes said, "Thrax, you'll command against Genesios' fleet. Tiverhios, you'll stay on as ypodrungarios, but ypodrungarios now of my whole fleet, not just the ships from the Key. To help show that's so, I'll raise your pay half a goldpiece a day, effective right now."

"Your Majesty is gracious," Tiverhios said enthusiastically, bowing almost double. If he resented being passed over for command of the whole fleet, he hid it very well. On brief acquaintance, Maniakes doubted he was a good enough actor to dissemble so well. And, if he had got in debt to Kourikos, the extra money had to look good to him. *One problem solved,* Maniakes thought; had Tiverhios proved difficult, everything might have unraveled right there.

"We have to go on," Maniakes said. "Only by casting down Genesios can we be sure outrages like this won't happen all across the Empire at a vicious brute's whim. By the good god, excellent sirs, my brave captains, I am a man, and I own to faults aplenty; only Phos and his sun are perfect things. But you will not need to fear—this—" He pointed to Erinakios' body. "—while I am on the throne."

They cheered him, louder than he had expected: perhaps they were venting the fear they had felt when Erinakios fell before their eyes. At Maniakes' wave, captains and sailors filed aboard their ships.

After Maniakes stood once more on the deck of the *Renewal*, he asked Bagdasares, "How do we protect ourselves if Genesios looses this murderous mage upon us once more?"

"I think we have a few days' grace before we need worry about that, your Majesty," Bagdasares said. "I stumble with weariness merely from having tried to withstand his sorcery. Having instigated it, he will be the next thing to dead this moment, and will need some days to recover before he next thinks about casting a spell."

Maniakes pondered that. It explained the long interval between the attack on him in Opsikion and this one now. He said, "Does that not suggest Genesios is down to a single wizard? If he had more, he would have been continually harassing us."

"It may well be so," Bagdasares answered. "If it is, though, the one he has is very powerful."

"I wonder what became of the others," Maniakes mused. "Would their heads have gone up on the Milestone when they failed to satisfy him?"

"With Genesios, I find that very likely," Bagdasares said.

"So do I," Maniakes said. "Tell me, how it is that an Avtokrator who is no magician himself, save perhaps in the sense of magically creating disaster for Videssos, can dominate sorcerers with great power?"

"The main reason, your Majesty, is that most magic requires slow preparation. If a man has a knife to his throat, or if his family is threatened, he is likely to obey a man who commands such immediate power." Bagdasares' chuckle sounded nervous. "Wizards do not widely broadcast this unfortunate fact."

"Yes, and I can see why," Maniakes said. "Well, Genesios' sorcerer, even if he succeeded against Erinakios, has twice failed to slay me now. Phos willing, Genesios will see that and act on it and solve our problem for us."

"May it be so." Bagdasares sketched the sun-circle over his heart.

Thrax came up to Maniakes and said, "Your pardon, your

Majesty, but shall we sail?" Maniakes nodded. Thrax's trumpeter relayed the call to the fleet. Lines were cast off; oars churned the sea. The ships left the harbor of Gavdos and swung north against Videssos the city.

IV

"**THE CITY! THE CITY!**" THE LOOKOUT IN THE CROW'S NEST cried. He was a Kalavrian lad and, so far as Maniakes knew, had never before set eyes on the imperial capital. But when any Videssian spoke of *the* city, no one could doubt what he meant.

Within a few minutes, Maniakes, too, made out the sparkle of the sun off the gilded globes topping the hundreds of temples dedicated to Phos in Videssos the city. Kourikos and Triphylles sighed like lovers returning to their beloved. "Home at last," Triphylles said, as if he had spent the time since he left the capital among the wild Khamorth of the Pardrayan plain rather than merely in the Empire's outlying provinces.

Then the lookout shouted, "Ship ho!" Fast as lightning, the cry ran through Maniakes' fleet. Thrax's trumpeter began blowing like a man possessed, relaying the drungarios' commands to the rest of the captains. Most of the dromons from the Key moved out to the flanks; a few of the larger, stouter vessels stayed in the center with the ships that had come from Kalavria, stiffening that force against the onslaught fast approaching.

Maniakes had picked the captains whose galleys would go into battle close by his. He had done his best to make sure they were loyal to him. But he did not know the men from the Key as he did those who had been in the rebellion from the beginning. If any of those captains turned on him, the sea fight could be lost all at once.

Or, of course, it could be lost in more conventional fashion. The dromons ahead had already stowed their masts. They were ready to fight. Maniakes' captains did not wait for orders from Thrax to prepare their own vessels.

"Erinakios was ready for war, too, or so he seemed, at any rate, but he and his fleet went over to me," Maniakes said hopefully.

Thrax answered, "True, your Majesty, but if those bearing down on us are about to abandon Genesios, they're running a bluff that puts Erinakios' to shame."

"We'll go straight through them and make for the harbor of Kontoskalion," Maniakes said. "Once we get armed men inside the city, Genesios will have to flee or fall into our hands." He peered east, out past the capital's great double land wall, and clapped his hands with delight at the tents and pavilions that sprouted on the grass there like mushrooms. "Rhegorios has come, by the good god! He'll keep Genesios' soldiers at play while we overwhelm the tyrant's fleet."

"If we overwhelm the tyrant's fleet," Thrax said, imperfectly optimistic. His eyes scanned the sea from horizon to horizon. "They have a lot of ships, and I see no sign of—"

Before he could finish his sentence, a dromon bearing down on the *Renewal* let fly with its catapult. The dart, half as long as a man, hissed between Thrax and Maniakes and fell with a splash into the sea. The crew that served the dart-thrower loaded another missile into it and began winching back its flexion arms to shoot again.

"So much for the notion of their giving up without a fight," Maniakes said.

Thrax did not dignify that with a reply. He said, "Your pardon, your Majesty, but I have to fight this ship now," and ran back to the stern. There the men at the steering oars and the oarmaster could most clearly hear him as he shouted the commands that would keep the *Renewal* fighting—or send her to the bottom or see her smashed to kindling.

Maniakes had never given much thought to sea battles. When he had campaigned in the westlands, ships had sometimes brought supplies and reinforcements to Videssian ports, whence they had come to his army far faster than if they had made the whole journey by land. Kalavria kept up its fleet against pirates from out of the north, but that fleet hadn't been severely tested since he came to the island—and, in any case, he hadn't been aboard any of its vessels when they did see action.

The fight was, in its own way, an awe-inspiring spectacle.

At first, it struck him as cleaner than a land battle. Catapults aboard the larger dromons hurled their great darts. Archers shot again and again whenever opposing vessels drew within range. All the same, the endless chorus of screams and groans that went with a battle of cavalry and infantry was missing here. Men shouted, aye, but in excitement and fear, not torment.

After a while, Maniakes realized that a sea battle was not man against man, as it was on land: here ship against ship was what counted most. He cried out in exultation as one of his galleys rammed a vessel whose crew was shouting for Genesios, then backed oars to let foaming water pour into the hole the dromon's bronze-shod beak had torn.

Men screamed then. Some were thrown into the sea, where they bobbed and began to sink—not all of them, nor even most, could swim. Some of the rowers seized oars and leapt off the stricken galley. Others fought sailors and officers for space aboard the ship's boat. That struck Maniakes as a more savage struggle than the larger battle of which it was a part.

One of Genesios' ships flung from its catapult not a dart but a large pot from which smoke trailed as it flew through the air. It crashed down onto the deck of a galley. Burning oil and pitch and sulfur started a fire on the planking that could not be put out. With cries of despair, men leapt into the sea: drowning was better than burning. Thick black smoke rose from the crackling flames that consumed the dromon.

A firepot from another of Genesios' ships flew wide of a vessel loyal to Maniakes. He cheered out loud when he saw the miss. But the firepot broke as it smacked into the sea and spread a coating of flame over the water. It clung to men floundering in the ocean, so they burned and drowned at the same time.

Few of Maniakes' ships from Kalavria could throw fire in that terrifying fashion: provincial fleets were seldom entrusted with the burning mixture, lest it fall into the hands of foreign foes. But the galleys from the Key answered Genesios' ships firepot for firepot, horror for horror.

"Every ship that burns is one more we won't have when we need them against Makuran or even Kubrat," Maniakes groaned.

Beside him, Kourikos said, "If too many of *our* ships burn, we shall not be the ones who worry about Makuran—or even Kubrat." The logothete of the treasury looked as if he would rather have been anywhere else than on the deck of a galley in the middle of a sea fight, but, having no choice in the matter, he was doing his best to keep up a bold front despite qualms. Maniakes admired him for that.

The pitching deck of a dromon was not Maniakes' familiar haunt, either. He peered this way and that, trying to figure out which side was winning. In a land battle, but for blowing dust, it would have been relatively easy, even for a blind man: the changing cries of friend and foe told who advanced, who gave ground.

Here no dust intervened, but the line of battle extended much farther to either side than it would have on land, and the warships became so intermingled that Maniakes could not tell who was crying out in triumph, who shrieking in terror as his vessel was holed.

Instead of up and down the battle line, then, Maniakes looked ahead toward Videssos the city. The temples and hills and mansions seemed closer than they had when he'd looked before. With that in mind, he did glance at the line once more. As best he could tell, his fleet was moving forward with the *Renewal*.

He went back to the stern with Thrax. "We drive them," he said. "Does that mean we're winning?"

"We're not losing, at any rate," Thrax answered abstractedly. His eyes swung every which way. "Two points to port!" he called to the steersmen, and the dromon swung leftward, toward one of Genesios' galleys. The archers aboard it sent a volley that hit a couple of the *Renewal*'s oarsmen. That fouled the rowers' stroke, slowed the *Renewal*, and let the smaller enemy vessel escape ramming.

Not far away, a dromon crewed by men shouting for Genesios rammed one of Maniakes' ships. When it tried to pull free, though, it stuck fast. Sailors and rowers from Maniakes' galley, armed with knives, belaying pins, and every other sort of makeshift weapon, scrambled onto Genesios' ship and began battling the crew for a platform that would stay afloat. Before Maniakes could see how the fight turned out, other warships surged between it and the *Renewal*.

"There!" Thrax yelled, right in Maniakes' ear, loud and unexpectedly enough to make him jump. The captain pointed to port. "Those are our ships, your Majesty, a whole good-sized flotilla of them. They've broken free, and it looks like they're making for the harbor in the palace quarter."

Maniakes' gaze followed Thrax's outthrust finger. Sure enough, a score of dromons had outflanked their foes and were streaking toward the city, their oars churning the ocean to creamy foam as the oarmasters demanded—and got—the best from their rowers. Faint across the wide stretch of water, the crews' cheers floated back to the *Renewal*.

"Attack!" Thrax shouted. "All along the line, everything we have." The trumpeter blared the command to those ships near enough to hear it. Maniakes clapped his hands in excitement as other dromons' hornplayers relayed the order to more of his vessels.

And then, very suddenly, what had been a hard-fought struggle became a rout. Maybe that was because Genesios' captains saw their position turned and realized they could not keep Maniakes' fleet from reaching the harbors. Maybe, too, those captains saw in the determination of Maniakes' attack a warning of what might happen to them if they kept resisting and lost anyhow. And maybe, as some of them loudly proclaimed once the fight was through, they found themselves unable to stomach serving Genesios any longer. That impressed Maniakes until he remembered how long those captains *had* served his rival.

Explanations came later. Out there on the ocean south of Videssos the city, what he knew was that some enemy galleys were raising all their oars high out of the water in token of surrender. Others turned their sterns to his fleet and fled, some back toward the city, others toward more distant coastal towns or out to the open sea. Still others, stubborn or loyal, fought on, but more and more of them were overwhelmed as Maniakes' captains concentrated several dromons against each one.

"Phos be praised," Triphylles exclaimed. "Soon I'll be able to enjoy octopus in hot vinegar as it should be prepared." Maniakes had other reasons to be pleased at the victory, but he was willing to let the noble find his own.

"On to the harbor of Kontoskalion," he cried. "We'll enter the city and rout Genesios from whatever hole he hides in."

Beside him, Alvinos Bagdasares murmured what might have been a prayer or a spell or a little of both. The Vaspurakaner mage who sometimes used a Videssian name sketched the sun-circle over his heart. A prayer, then. Maniakes whispered Phos' creed, too. He knew Bagdasares was also worrying about Genesios' ferocious mage. They weren't in Opsikion any more, or on the Key. They were coming to Videssos the city, where Genesios' wizard would be almost as close to Maniakes as the mage who protected him.

The harbor swiftly drew nearer. People stared out toward the approaching dromons, pointing and exclaiming. Maniakes wished he knew what they were saying. If they were cursing him as a usurper surely bound for Skotos' ice, he was going to have trouble. Fighting his way through the streets of the capital against an angry city mob was the last thing he wanted.

Closer and closer the *Renewal* came. Maniakes hurried to the bow of the galley and craned his neck toward the docks and the people on them. He scowled in frustration; all he could hear at first was a confused babbling with no distinct words. Then someone unmistakably yelled, "Maniakes Avtokrator!"

Maniakes waved to the crowd to show them who he was. Some of the men and women waved back, as they might have for any incoming sailor. But others got the idea. A great cheer with his name in it rose from the people. He felt he had gulped half a jar of wine all at once.

Along with his name, though, people were also shouting that of Genesios. He wondered why that didn't touch off curses and fights and stabbings between the backers of the Avtokrator in the city and those who favored the man just entering it. All at once, though, a clear shouted sentence pierced the unintelligible racket: "Genesios Avtokrator is trying to flee the city!"

"Phos," Maniakes whispered. Now triumph was a brew more heady than any squeezed from the grape. He had known a moment even close to this only once before, when his forces and his father's had helped Sharbaraz beat Smerdis and take back the throne of the King of Kings of Makuran. But even that did not compare, not truly. Then he had been fighting for someone else's benefit. Now the gain, could he but seize that which so nearly lay in his hands, would belong to him alone.

"Don't let him get away," he called to the shore. "Five hundred goldpieces to the man who brings him to me, alive or dead."

That stirred up the crowd round the docks. Some of them cheered what looked like the fall of a hated ruler. Others, more pragmatic or perhaps just greedier, pushed away to start Emperor-hunting. Maniakes nodded in satisfaction. The thinner the press of people at the shore, the more easily he could disembark his men and take control of the city.

"Back oars!" the oarmaster cried. The *Renewal* slowed, slid-

ing to a stop alongside an outthrust dock. Sailors sprang up
and roped the dromon fast. When the gangplank went out from
ship to land, Maniakes rushed toward it, wanting to be first
ashore but for those sailors. Other men, however, held him
back. One of them said, "You wait, your Majesty. Let us make
sure it's safe up there."

Brandishing knives and bludgeons, a dozen sailors swarmed
up the gangplank. "Make way for Maniakes Avtokrator, curse
you!" they shouted. The crowd of gawkers fell back before
them, though some in that crowd were as well armed as they.

Only after the sailors had cleared some open space on the
tar-smeared timbers of the pier did they wave for Maniakes to
follow them. When he stepped off the gangplank, he drew his
sword and said, "I shall not sheath this blade until Genesios
the tyrant is captured!"

As he had hoped, that drew loud cheers from the crowd.
Several men waved weapons of their own. That took a certain
amount of courage, or at least bravado: the penalty for using a
sword in a street brawl in Videssos the city was amputation of
the thumbs.

Kourikos and Triphylles came across the gangplank after
Maniakes. Triphylles got down on his knees, not to prostrate
himself before the Avtokrator but fervently to kiss the timbers
on which he stood, tar and white streaks of sea gull droppings
deterring him not a bit. "Phos be praised, I'm home at last!"
he cried, which in its manifest sincerity drew a cheer almost as
loud as the one Maniakes had got.

Maniakes pointed to a nearby man who looked reasonably
bright and asked, "How long have the soldiers under my
cousin Rhegorios been outside the city?"

"Since day before yesterday, lord, uh, your Majesty," the fellow answered, adding, "The guards at the wall haven't attacked 'em, but they've held 'em off and not let 'em in."

"They will now," Maniakes declared. *They'd better,* he
thought, *or I'm still in trouble here.* "Please stand aside, my
friends, and let me come take my rightful place in the city."

The throne wasn't exactly his rightful place. He had no
blood claim to it. He did have, though, a great many armed
men who were of the opinion he belonged on it. He also had
as his foe Genesios, which in and of itself went a long way
toward cementing his claim.

More ships were tying up behind the *Renewal* and at the

quays nearby. Sailors swarmed ashore. A cry went up: "Where now, lord?"

"To the palaces," Maniakes answered. "Once we take them, to the High Temple, to give thanks to Phos for letting this day come to pass." Getting the ecumenical patriarch's blessing would start him off on the right foot. If he didn't get the patriarch's blessing, he told himself, he would soon get a new ecumenical patriarch.

Some of the sailors now on the docks bore the shields and swords dromons carried so their men could repel boarders. They pushed the civilians back, shouting "Way! Make way for the Avtokrator!"

"I wish I had a horse," Maniakes said as they made their way up into the twisting maze of little streets north of the harbor of Kontoskalion. A cavalry officer, he didn't feel as if he could see enough from ground level.

"We'll get you one, by Phos," his escorts said. The first mounted man they came upon, they unceremoniously dragged from the saddle. Had the fellow said a word of protest, had he raised a hand to defend himself, they would have done worse than that.

Maniakes hadn't wanted to acquire a mount in such fashion, but didn't see how he could check his men, either—he wanted them enthusiastic on his behalf. To the unhorsed rider, he said, "Come to the palaces after I've driven Genesios from the throne for good. You'll have your beast back, and gold for my use of him."

"Phos bless you then, your Majesty!" the man cried, and people in the street took up the call. That eased Maniakes' mind, too; having the fickle city populace on his side while he seized power could only help him.

From his seat atop the newly acquired horse—a sedate and elderly mare with a very comfortable gait, provided you weren't in any hurry to get where you were going—he could see over the heads of his men and the swarms of locals in the streets. That helped him less than it would have on the battlefield, for the streets themselves twisted too much to let him see far.

He worried about that. His sailors could easily overpower any civilians who might try to stand against them, but if the Imperial Guards or any other troops in the city decided Genesios was worth fighting for, his men would be up against more than they could handle. They wore no armor, they carried only a few spears and bows, and they had no idea how to fight save as individuals. Disciplined soldiers would have massacred them.

But no soldiers appeared to try to bar his way. "We'll go north, toward Middle Street," he called to his men. The main east-west highway of Videssos the city would give him a long straight stretch, on which he could take his bearings.

Finding and then keeping to north in that warren wasn't as easy as when sailing by sun and stars. Many buildings were tall enough to hide the sun from sight. Sometimes balconies almost met overhead above the streets. That was supposed to be against the law, but Genesios had ignored laws far more important, so Maniakes had no reason to think he would have paid any attention to this one.

He had just reached Middle Street and was started down it toward the plaza of Palamas and the palace quarter beyond when a rumor coming from farther east overtook him from behind. "The gates are opening," people said. "No—the gates are open."

"We have him," Maniakes said to nobody in particular. If his own soldiers were in the city, nothing Genesios could do would stop it from falling. And Genesios did not seem able to do much in any case. His supporters had abandoned him outside the capital, and now the same looked to be happening within.

The only ways Maniakes could see losing now were a lone assassin . . . and Genesios' wizard. Against an assassin, he could take precautions. Against the wizard—Bagdasares was tramping along beside him. He didn't know if Bagdasares would be good enough, but he was the best available.

He rode past the red granite pile of the government offices. He had always thought the building squat and ugly when he had been in the capital before. Then his opinions on architecture had mattered to no one but himself. Now, if he wanted, he could change the way Videssos the city would look for generations yet to come.

He laughed at himself. He had more urgent things to worry about.

People stood under the covered colonnades that ran along both sides of Middle Street. Some cheered, some stared, some went about their business. A few people gaped from atop the colonnade, too. He thought that merely a curiosity until he realized it also made an ideal hiding place for a killer. Past

clearing everyone off, which would have made him look foolish, he didn't know what he could do about it.

He reached the plaza of Palamas unassassinated and stared
across the broad stretch of cobbles to the lawns and splendid
buildings of the palace quarter beyond. The plaza was
crowded with people chaffering with merchants at stalls or
booths or wagons or hand-held trays, buying everything from
cloth to jewels to octopus tentacles; Maniakes glanced over at
Triphylles. Other folk, even on a day when the crown of the
Empire of Videssos changed hands, were out for a stroll, either to take the air or simply to see and be seen.

The vast bulk of the Amphitheater marked the southern
boundary of the plaza of Palamas. To the west, just at the edge
of the palace quarter, stood the Milestone, the granite obelisk
from which all distances in the Empire were measured. Heads
in great number were affixed to it, not just at the base as was
usual, but for some distance up toward its pointed top. Plac-
ards, too distant to read across the square, set forth the alleged
crimes of each victim. Unless Maniakes missed his guess, most
of those boiled down to nothing more than falling foul of
Genesios.

Beside the Milestone waited a small, bald, gray-bearded
man in a robe of shimmering blue samite. Even with that fancy
robe, Maniakes would have paid him no special attention had
he not been surrounded by several soldiers in chainmail. They
were very nearly the first soldiers not his own he had seen in
the imperial capital.

He turned to Kourikos. "Who is that fellow there?" he
asked, pointing.

The logothete of the treasury squinted. "That is the honor
guard of the eparch of the city, your Majesty, unless I am mistaken, but I do not recognize the man whose honor they find
themselves guarding."

"Whoever he is, he thinks he's important," Maniakes said.
"Let's go over there and find out if he's right."

Getting across the plaza of Palamas wasn't easy, not even
with the sailors from the fleet doing their best to clear the
crowds out of the way. Some Videssians were intent on getting
a close look at the man who was in the process of becoming
their new Avtokrator, others on finishing the business for
which they had come to the plaza in the first place. No one
wanted to get out of the way. At last, the sailors went from
shoving and shouting to hitting people with belaying pins. That

touched off a few fights, but did eventually persuade the crowd to move back and make way.

The little bald man stared anxiously as Maniakes approached. "Are y-you the man I believe you to be?" he asked, stammering a little.

"That depends," Maniakes said. "But if you believe I'm Maniakes son of Maniakes, then you're right. And who, may I ask, are *you*, eminent sir?" The fancy robe and the armed retinue made the title a sure bet.

He had to wait for his answer; the little man promptly prostrated himself on the cobbles of the square. The delay made Maniakes notice the stench from the grisly collection of heads Genesios had on display at the Milestone. Some had been packed in salt like poor Hosios to keep them recognizable longer, but they still smelled like a butcher's shop much too long forgotten by its proprietor.

At last, the little man arose and said, "Your Majesty, I am Doulikhios. I have the honor to be eparch of the city, at least until you make a different appointment to that position, as is of course your privilege."

"Your Majesty, when my comrades and I left the city, the eparch was a certain Goulaion," Kourikos said.

Doulikhios pointed to the Milestone. "There is Goulaion's head. He was accused of conspiring against the Avtokrator, uh, the tyrant Genesios. And there below it is the head of Goulaion's successor Evdokimos. And there, right at the base of the column, is the head of Evdokimos' successor Levkates. Evdokimos was put to the sword for the same reason as Goulaion; I do not know how Levkates ended up displeasing Genesios, but he did."

No wonder the poor sod is nervous, Maniakes thought. The job he was holding did not seem one where the incumbent got much chance to learn from experience. "Well, eminent Doulikhios, in your place I do believe I'd have fled to a monastery," he said.

"I tried that," the eparch of the city answered bleakly. "Genesios dragged me out and forced me into this blue robe rather than the other."

Maniakes did not care to hear that; if Genesios had gone into a monastery after Doulikhios, he might have gone into a convent after Niphone. He forced himself not to think about that. "Am I to assume, eminent Doulikhios, that even though you are Genesios' appointee, you do not favor him as Avtokrator?"

At the question, Doulikhios drew himself up with the first pride he had shown. "Your Majesty, the mistake Goulaion made, and Evdokimos, and maybe Levkates, too, for all I know, was in plotting against Genesios *and getting caught.* Me, I plotted with Abasgios, the second-in-command of the Imperial Guards—and instead of reinforcing the troops on the land wall against your men out there, they moved on the tyrant this morning."

"You may just stay on as eparch of the city after all," Maniakes exclaimed.

"We botched it," Doulikhios said. "Genesios was to have been slain, but he killed one of our men, wounded the other, and fled to the imperial harbor. I fear he got away in some small boat or another."

"We'll catch him, or at least I hope we will," Maniakes said. "We've had ships heading that way since they broke free of the sea battle."

"May it be so," Doulikhios said fervently.

Kourikos held up a hand. "A moment, if I may. Eminent Doulikhios—" He sounded so dubious about the title, it might have been an insult. "—I have spent my entire adult life among the nobility here at the capital, and I must confess I do not recall your being numbered among us. May I ask from what station Genesios elevated you to the eparchate?"

"Well, if you must know, eminent sir, I ran a fish market and pleased his I hope former Majesty with my wares," Doulikhios answered.

"Your Majesty!" Kourikos cried to Maniakes. "Surely you will not allow such a high office to be filled, surely you will not allow the ranks of the nobility to be polluted, by this, this *fishseller.*" Spittle flew from his lips with the last word.

"If he can do the job, I don't see why not," Maniakes said. Kourikos goggled. Maniakes went on, "He's done me one great service already and deserves a reward for that. Anyhow, I have no time to worry about niceties of rank right now." He turned back to Doulikhios, leaving his prospective father-in-law gaping in dismay. "Tell me at once, eminent sir: do you know what's become of Genesios' chief mage? Can we find him at the Sorcerers' Collegium?" He heard the hot eagerness in his own voice. Genesios had put far too many heads up on the Milestone, but the wizard's was one that deserved to be there.

"I know the man you mean, your Majesty, but no, he's never had anything to do with the Sorcerers' Collegium," Doulikhios answered. "He's never had much to do with me, either, for which I give thanks to the lord with the great and good mind." He sketched the sun-circle above his heart, then shuddered. "He frightens me, and I'll not deny it. He's a tall man, and thin as a lath, and by the look of him he was born before your great-grandfather, but they say he's strong as a soldier in first flush of youth."

"Sounds like a hard man to miss, at any rate," Maniakes said. "We'll know him when we catch him, that's certain."

"Eminent sir—" When Kourikos spoke to Doulikhios now, he had scrubbed the scorn from his voice. That surprised Maniakes until the logothete of the treasury went on, "Have you any news of the fate of my wife and daughter, who took refuge in the convent of the holy Phostina? This affects more than me alone, for Niphone is affianced to his Majesty here."

"I don't know what to tell you, eminent sir," Doulikhios said slowly. "I never heard Genesios mention that name, or any like it, but that doesn't necessarily signify. And who knows what crazy orders he might have given since we tried to kill him but didn't do it, or who might have listened to them?"

"Where is this convent?" Maniakes demanded of Kourikos.

"In the northwestern corner of the city, north of the Makuraner district."

"We'll send men there," Maniakes said. He told off a couple of dozen sailors and, to guide them, found a local who knew where the convent was. That done, he went on, "As for the rest of us, we'll secure the palace quarter. Eminent Doulikhios, you come with us. If any of the soldiers there decide they're still on Genesios' side, maybe you can explain he's fled. The fewer we have to fight, the better."

"As you say, your Majesty." Doulikhios did not prostrate himself again, but he bowed almost double.

As Maniakes was about to enter the palace quarter, unrest broke out on the eastern side of the plaza of Palamas, the side that fronted on the rest of Videssos the city. He looked back over his shoulder. Horsemen in bright chainmail were trying to force their way through the crowd that had re-formed after Maniakes made his way to Doulikhios.

At the head of those horsemen rode someone he recognized, even across the broad stretch of the plaza. From atop his own horse, he waved vigorously. "Rhegorios!" he shouted. "Cousin! To me!"

He didn't know whether Rhegorios heard him through the rack or spied him waving, but his cousin waved in return and booted his horse ahead. Cheering, the men he led followed. The folk of the capital did make way for them: It was that or be trampled.

Maniakes rode back into the crowd. Both men were grinning from ear to ear when they finally met. Rhegorios sheathed the sword he carried. "Cousin!" he cried, and then, "Your Majesty!" He thrust out the hand that had held the blade. Maniakes clasped it.

"Genesios' men are giving up and coming over to us wherever we find them," he said. "The only true fight they showed for him was on the sea south of the city. But even there, once we began to turn their position, they folded up. Videssos the city is ours."

"That it is, by the good god," Rhegorios said. "The men on the walls held us out till you came up with your fleet, though they didn't fight much doing it." He looked awed. "You don't have to do much fighting when you hold those walls and towers and gates. They'd stand off the whole world, so long as the soldiers atop them keep breathing. The soldiers needn't do much more than that, let me tell you."

"I'm glad you and your riders are here," Maniakes said. "If we find holdouts anywhere, they'll be in the palace quarter, and you can do a better job of overawing them than a ragtag and bobtail of sailors."

Rhegorios' grin stretched wider yet. "Do you know what, cousin of mine? When your brothers finally find out what we've been doing, they'll want to piss themselves out of sheer jealousy."

"I just hope they're alive and well," Maniakes answered. "That's first. Second is finding them enough important things to do—and rank to give them the power to do those things—to take away the sting. The state the Empire is in these days, that should be easy."

"Too true." By the way Rhegorios sat slightly straighter in the saddle and did his best to look capable and impressive, he was also looking for both rank and duties. That pleased Maniakes rather than alarming him. As he had said, the

Empire had more than enough troubles to share out among all those who were trying to set them right.

"Come on," Maniakes said. "Let's take the palaces. I was about to do that when you rode up here. The company is better now." He turned back to his sailors. "Onward!" The men cheered. Some of them bayed like hungry wolves. Maniakes went on, "I don't mind you coming away with a trinket or three. The good god knows you've earned that. But I will not stand still for murder. You try killing to get your loot and your head goes up on the Milestones beside Genesios'."

He did not add, *I mean what I say.* The men already knew as much—or if they didn't, they would soon find out.

The palace quarter was a world altogether different from the hustle and bustle of the plaza of Palamas. The generality of city folk were not allowed to disturb the calm quiet of those lanes set amid lawns and gardens and magnificent buildings. Only a few bureaucrats and beardless eunuchs strolled on them when Maniakes' forces brought the outside world crashing in. The bureaucrats fled with cries of horror. So did most of the eunuchs.

One of them, though, came up to the party of horsemen who led the advance. In a grave voice somewhere halfway between contralto and tenor, he asked, "Who among you is Maniakes son of Maniakes?" When Maniakes walked his mare up a couple of paces, the eunuch prostrated himself before him. Forehead still pressed to the cobbles, he said, "On behalf of all the palace servitors, your Majesty, I welcome you to this your new home. May your years be many and your line never fail."

He had probably said the same thing, maybe in the same words, to Genesios after Likinios and his sons met the headsman. Maniakes did not hold that against him; the weak were well advised to keep clear of the quarrels of those more powerful than they. He said, "Thank you, esteemed sir." Eunuchs had their own honorifics, from which he chose the highest. "Rise, please, and give me your name."

"I am called Kameas, your Majesty, and have the honor to be vestiarios at the imperial residence." Kameas deserved that high honorific, then; he headed all the Avtokrator's servants. If the Avtokrator was weak, the vestiarios might become the most important man in the Empire. Maniakes did not intend to let that happen.

He said, "When Genesios fled the palaces, did he take with him whatever family he has?"

"No, your Majesty," Kameas answered gravely. "His wife and his young son and daughter remain in the imperial residence, awaiting your pleasure." He licked his lips. If Maniakes had a taste for blood, he would learn of it right now.

"I don't want to see them," Maniakes said. "If the woman and girl go into a convent and the boy to a monastery, that will satisfy me. Take them that message from me. But tell them also that if they ever try to come out or meddle in politics, their heads will answer for it. I do not want them to confuse mercy for weakness—tell them that, too."

"I shall carry your words exactly as you have spoken them." After a moment, Kameas added, "It will be good to have in the palaces once more an Avtokrator who understands the meaning of the word mercy." With a bow, he set off for the imperial residence.

Maniakes went on more slowly. He rode past the Hall of the Nineteen Couches, where fancy banquets were held. The building's great bronze doors stood open, as if inviting him in. He was hardly more eager to dine there than to see Genesios' family: the couches were for reclining while one ate, an antique style of feasting that had passed away everywhere save the palace quarter. He felt sure he would make a hash of it the first time he tried it.

He turned aside from the straight road to the imperial residence so he could examine the Grand Courtroom. It, too, had portals of bronze, these ones worked with reliefs so perfectly realistic they almost seemed to move. Large wings swept out to either side from the courtroom itself. Bureaucrats peered out from windows in those wings. As long as Maniakes' men did not harm them in this moment of transition, the change of rulers would affect them but little: if they were massacred, who would administer the Empire in their stead?

To one of them, Maniakes called, "What's behind that grove of trees there, off to the southwest?"

"That's a chapel to Phos, sir," the man answered, not realizing he was speaking to his sovereign. "It's been there many years, but seldom used of late: most Emperors have preferred to worship at the High Temple instead."

"I can understand that," Maniakes answered. He had trouble seeing how any man, given a choice, would worship anywhere save at the High Temple.

He stayed there a while chatting with the functionary, both to learn more about the buildings of the palace quarter and to give Kameas a chance to get Genesios' family out of the imperial residence without his officially having to notice them. When shouts and cries came from the west, he feared Genesios' wife and children were raising such a fuss that he would have to let them come to his attention.

But these were yells of joy and excitement, all in men's deep voices. Before long, he caught one rising above the rest: "We've got him!"

He dug his knees into the sides of the mare he was riding. The horse snorted indignantly at such treatment: how dare a rider try to rouse her to speed? Maniakes dared, and forced her into a reluctant trot. "You've got whom?" he called as his men streamed after him. "Have you laid hold of Genesios?"

When someone answered, "Aye, by Phos," his heart leapt within him; Genesios would not get away to stir up yet another round of civil war. His men loosed a torrent of cheers that soon formed words of their own: "Thou conquerest, Maniakes Avtokrator!"

Sailors came capering toward him from the direction of the harbor for the palace quarter. The imperial residence also lay in that direction; again he hoped Kameas had got Genesios' wife and children away; he wanted to spare them this. But whether they were off to convent and monastery or not, he gave the order he had to give: "Fetch Genesios here before me at once."

The sailors peeled back toward the anchorage, shouting his words ahead of them. He rode on after the men. Before long, they came in his direction again, shoving along a man whose hands were tied behind his back.

Maniakes recognized Genesios at once. The engraver at the imperial mint had accurately portrayed the man's features: wide forehead, narrow chin, a short thin fringe of beard, long straight nose. Now, though, Genesios did not wear the crown and rich robes that marked an Avtokrator of the Videssians. He was bare-headed—and, Maniakes noted with a touch of malice, going bald—and wore a plain linen tunic that came down to his knees, garb a fisherman might don before going out to work his nets.

Blood soaked the tunic now; Genesios must have fought before he was captured. He had a deep gash in his left arm and a cut across his forehead. More blood dripped from the slate on which he stood. A trail of it led back toward the harbor. Genesios, Maniakes thought, had left a trail of blood through the Empire ever since he murdered his way into the red boots.

He looked up at Maniakes. His face showed pain but not much fear; Maniakes remembered he had been a combat soldier. "All right, you have me," he said. His voice was deep, with the accent of a peasant from the westlands. He didn't ask what Maniakes was going to do with him—he had to have figured that out for himself.

"Aye, I have you," Maniakes said. "How could you have let Videssos come to such a pass?" He hadn't intended to ask that; it came out almost as a cry of pain.

Murky defiance lit in Genesios' eyes. "You're on top now, and you think you're such a great lord," he said, "but will you do any better?"

"By Phos, I hope so," Maniakes exclaimed. He looked around to the men who crowded close to see Genesios. He raised the sword he had carried ever since he set foot in Videssos the city. Now that the moment was come, though, he gulped. He had done plenty of fighting, but he had never been an executioner before. "Kneel," he told Genesios. When Genesios wouldn't, he spoke to the men who had frogmarched the defeated Avtokrator through the palace quarter: "Make him kneel."

They forced Genesios to his knees. He cursed them and Maniakes and Videssos all together, a torrent of vileness that had men making the sun-sign to turn aside words of evil omen. Maniakes clasped his blade two-handed, brought it up, and swung it with all his strength.

It bit into Genesios' neck with a meaty *chunnk!* His curses cut off in midword. Blood spurted, impossibly red in the bright sun. His body convulsed; his bowels and bladder let go. Maniakes swung the sword again, to sever his head completely.

"Take it through the city," he told his cheering followers. "Let everyone see Genesios is dead. Then it will go up on the Milestone." The cheers grew louder, fiercer. He held up a hand. "But that will be the end of it. We won't stop his slaughter to start our own."

"What shall we do with the body, your Majesty?" someone asked. It was still twitching feebly.

"Burn it," Maniakes answered, which prompted fresh cheers. He hadn't intended that; he had only wanted to get rid of a piece of carrion. But, now that it was done, he wouldn't turn aside the acclaim, either.

He rode on toward the imperial residence. Like the chapel,

it was screened by trees: cherries here. They would be beautiful in springtime when they blossomed; the rest of the year, they were just there. The residence itself was as unprepossessing a structure as any in the palace quarter. Unlike most of the other buildings, it looked like a place where a man might actually live rather than be put on display.

Some of the soldiers who guarded the imperial residence were Videssians, others big blond Halogai who made Maniakes think of Rotrude. Kameas must have already come and gone, for as soon as Maniakes finished winding his way down the path through the cherry grove, all the guardsmen shouted, "Thou conquerest, Maniakes Avtokrator!" They went to their knees and then their bellies, honoring him with a full proskynesis.

"Get up, get up," he said, not wanting to make them resent him—after all, they would be protecting him now. "You served Genesios better than he deserved. I hope you'll serve me bravely, too."

"Thou conquerest!" the guards cried again, which he took for assent.

He swung down off his horse. He wanted to see what the imperial residence looked like on the inside. *I'll be living here the rest of my days,* he thought, *whether those be long or short.* From the shade of the doorway, pale smooth eunuch faces stared out at him. Like the guards, the servitors had to be wondering what sort of new master they would have.

Maniakes had just set his foot on the low, broad marble stairs that led up to the entrance when a breathless voice from behind him called, "Your Majesty, come quick! There's fighting in the northwest!"

He spun round to face the panting messengers. "Can't my officers handle it?" he snapped. "If they can't, what do I have them for?" Then a possible answer occurred to him, and urgency replaced anger in his voice: "Is it at the convent dedicated to the holy Phostina?"

"Aye, your Majesty," the messenger said. "A company of soldiers loyal to Genesios was trying to force their way in. The nuns had shut up the convent against them. They were doing their best to smash down the door when your men came up, but you didn't send enough to check them. They may be inside by now, and the good god only knows what outrages they'll work!"

Kourikos groaned. Maybe only Phos knew what outrages

Genesios' men might commit, but he could imagine. "My daughter!" he cried piteously, and then, a moment slower than he should have, "My wife!"

Maniakes sprang back onto the mare. "I'm on my way!" he said. "Rhegorios, you and all your horses with me." That would leave the palace quarter to the doubtful mercy of the sailors, but it couldn't be helped. Horsemen would reach the convent in half the time folk on foot required.

The mare didn't want to trot, let alone gallop. Maniakes was in no mood to heed an animal's whims. Lacking spurs, he whacked it with the flat of the blade he had used to take Genesios' head. Once her attention was gained, the mare proved to have a fair turn of speed after all.

From behind, Kourikos called, "Wait!"

But Maniakes would not wait. "Gangway!" he shouted as he and his men neared the plaza of Palamas. For a moment after that, he glimpsed a sea of startled faces, all staring toward him. Then, with cries of alarm, people scattered every which way, some of them trampling others to keep the onrushing horses from trampling them.

He didn't think his mount ran over anyone. Horses didn't care to step on the soft, wiggling things people became when they fell to the ground. But from the screams that rose in back of him, some of the animals of his riders had been imperfectly careful about where they set their feet.

He had thundered out onto Middle Street before he realized he didn't know exactly where in the northwestern quadrant of the city the convent dedicated to the holy Phostina lay. He shouted the question back over his shoulder. "I can find it, your Majesty," one of his men said. "I grew up not far from there."

"Come forward, then," Maniakes said, and slowed his mare to let the city man take the lead. The mare snorted indignantly, as if asking him to make up his mind: first he'd called for more speed, so how dared he check her now? The animal complained again when he booted it in the ribs to make it keep up with the horse his guide was riding.

Once they swung north off Middle Street, the journey through the city became a nightmare for Maniakes. The streets were narrow and winding; he couldn't gallop full tilt no matter how much he wanted to. And if a mule-drawn wagon or donkey cart blocked the way, not all his curses or threats would clear the road for him until the driver could find a corner and turn.

At last he heard shouts of alarm and fury ahead that seemed to have nothing to do with the panic his own passage was causing. He muttered a quick prayer to Phos that they meant he was coming to the convent. A moment later, he burst out into the open space of a small square and found his prayer had been granted.

Blood splashed the cobbles of the square. A lot of the sailors he had sent were down, some dead, others thrashing with wounds. Others were down with them, men whose chainmail proclaimed them genuine soldiers. A good many more of them were trying to break into the convent dedicated to the holy Phostina.

They weren't having an easy time of it. Beneath the white-wash, the walls of the convent were solid stone, the windows mere slits too narrow to let a man through. The door was the only vulnerable point—and it didn't seem any too vulnerable, either.

Genesios' men here were all Videssians—they had no axe-wielding Halogai to make short work of the stout timbers. They had found a long, thick board to use as a ram, but, just as Maniakes rode into the square, the nuns poured a large tub of hot water down onto their attackers. The soldiers staggered back from the door, howling with pain.

"Yield or die!" Maniakes shouted at them and at the rest of the guardsmen trying to find other ways into the convent. The soldiers who had followed Genesios to—and past—the end stared in horrified dismay as cavalrymen, some with swords, some with light lances, but most with bows, filled the open space in front of the building.

A couple of Genesios' men stepped away from the convent and toward Maniakes and his followers with weapons still in hand. Bowstrings twanged. The guardsmen fell, screaming and twisting on the cobblestones. That was plenty to give their comrades the idea. Swords clattered as men threw them down. Maniakes waved some of his soldiers forward to take charge of the prisoners. Glumly, they let their hands be tied behind their backs and filed off into captivity.

Maniakes rode closer to the convent wall—but not too close. To the nuns at the second-story window, he called, "I am Maniakes son of Maniakes, now Avtokrator of the Videssians. Genesios the tyrant is dead. May I approach and confer with

your abbess without fear of being boiled like a capon in a holiday stew?"

The nuns disappeared from the window without answering.
After a couple of minutes, another, older, woman appeared
there. "I am Nikaia, abbess of the convent dedicated to the
memory of the holy Phostina," she said, and Maniakes believed her at once: her voice held authority any general would
have been glad to own. She looked him over from beneath the
blue head-scarf that concealed her hair, then went on, "How
may I serve you . . . your Majesty?" By the hesitation, she remained imperfectly convinced he was who he claimed to be.

He said, "I am told by the eminent Kourikos, logothete of
the treasury, that you have taking refuge within your walls his
wife and daughter. As you will probably know, I am betrothed
to Niphone. Now that I am returned to Videssos the city, now
that the eminent Kourikos has accompanied me here, I would
have you tell the noble ladies they are free and safe to come
forth into the world once more, should they so desire."

"We have no 'noble ladies' here, only those who serve the
lord with the great and good mind," Nikaia answered sternly.
"Wait there, if you will." As the nuns had before her, the abbess left the window. She returned in a little while with another nun and pointed out at Maniakes. He heard her ask, "Is
that the man?"

Was that Niphone there? Maniakes stared up at the window
as the nun stared down at him. She was young; he could see
that much. But her head scarf robbed her of much of her indi-
viduality, and, he discovered, the picture of his fiancée he had
carried in his mind these past six years of exile had faded over
time. He remembered Niphone as having a long, rather thin
face, with delicate features and large eyes. That could have
been she at the window, but he would not have dared take oath
on it.

Whoever the woman was, she seemed similarly troubled.
She said, "Mistress, I believe that is the younger Maniakes,
but—I have trouble being certain."

Her voice was not far from what Maniakes remembered
Niphone's sounding like, yet again he could not be sure. He
called her name. She waved and nodded. He waited for a great
surge of love and affection to pour from his heart and warm
him from head to toe. He had been waiting to see her again for
six years, after all. The surge didn't quite come, or rather did
come but wasn't nearly so large as he had expected. He carried

on as if it had been, saying to Nikaia, "Holy abbess, I ask you again: will you release this woman and her mother from the vows they took more to protect themselves from Genesios' evil designs than to resign from the world forever? Not that they are not pious, of course," he added hastily.

Niphone retreated; Nikaia came forward. "I have seen their piety these past months, your Majesty," the abbess said, "and it is far from inconsiderable. But, in any case, I have not the power to release them from vows they took of their own free will. Here in Videssos the city, that power rests only in the hands of the most holy ecumenical patriarch Agathios. If he so orders, and if the women be willing, I shall in obedience let them come forth from my convent. Until that time, I reckon them nuns no different from any others."

Maniakes admired her courage and rectitude, however much of a nuisance he found them. If he tried to disregard the abbess' wishes and take Niphone from the convent dedicated to the holy Phostina without patriarchal leave, he had no doubt boiling water would come rain down on him. He told Nikaia, "I'll see the most holy Agathios, then." To Rhegorios, he said, "Leave a third of your men here, to make sure we have no more problems with diehards—oh, and send a rider back to the eminent Kourikos, so he knows his wife and daughter are safe and well. You and the rest of your men will come with me to the High Temple."

Though both the convent and the High Temple lay in the northern part of Videssos the city, the fastest way to go from one to the other was to drop back down to Middle Street, ride west along it to the avenue that led up to the chief shrine of the Videssian faith, and then travel north along that avenue.

From the outside, the High Temple was massive rather than magnificent; the stout walls of golden stone needed to support the great central dome bore no special ornament. As with most Videssian homes, the treasures were on the inside, hidden from external view. Maniakes called to a priest ascending the low, broad stairs that led up to the entrance: "Holy sir, is the most holy patriarch at his devotions within?"

The priest needed no more than a heartbeat to realize who would approach the High Temple with hundreds of armed men at his back. Bowing, he replied, "No, your Majesty, I believe he is at present in the patriarchal residence nearby." He pointed. The High Temple dwarfed the residence, though anywhere else in the city it would have been reckoned a house of respectable size. A number of cypresses, gnarled and hoary with age, grew around it.

With a word of thanks, Maniakes led his troopers to the patriarchal residence. He dismounted and, Rhegorios at his side, walked up to the entrance and rapped on the door. The priest who answered was not an old man, as he knew Agathios to be, nor decked in the magnificent patriarchal vestments and the sky-blue boots that were as much a prerogative of Videssos' chief prelates as red ones were for the Avtokrator.

As a lot of people had done over the past few hours, the priest asked, "You are his Majesty, the Avtokrator Maniakes?"

Maniakes wondered if he should make a sign and hang it around his neck. He contented himself with saying, "Yes. Here with me is my cousin Rhegorios. And you, holy sir?"

"My name is Skombros, your Majesty," the priest replied. "I have the honor to be synkellos to the most holy Agathios." That meant he was Agathios' secretary, assistant, and, at need, keeper and watchdog for the Avtokrator.

"I am pleased to meet you, holy sir. Take me to the ecumenical patriarch at once."

Bowing, Skombros turned and obeyed. Maniakes followed him, with Rhegorios another pace behind. The patriarchal residence struck Maniakes as pleasant without being splendid; prelates were sworn to poverty, though not all of them took their vows seriously. Oaths aside, a greater display of luxury would not have surprised Maniakes.

Skombros rapped on a closed door. A soft voice answered. The synkellos worked the latch. "The most holy Agathios, ecumenical patriarch of the Videssians, awaits you, your Majesty—and you, eminent sir." He tacked on the last four words for Rhegorios' benefit.

Maniakes went into the chamber, only to be met by Agathios' pointing finger, which the patriarch wielded as if it were a spear. "Will you presume to make alterations in Videssos' pure and holy and orthodox faith?" he thundered, his voice soft no more. His eyes flashed. His long white beard seemed to crackle and stand away from his face, as if lightning had struck nearby. His beaky nose had the curve of a Kubrati scimitar. He was, in short, a most alarmingly holy old man.

He had, however, chosen a question Maniakes could answer without qualm of conscience. "No, most holy sir," he said, and watched Agathios deflate like a punctured pig's bladder.

"Oh, that's very good," the ecumenical patriarch said. His

eyes stopped blazing; even his beard seemed to relax. Sounding much more like a grandfather than a righteous, wrathful cleric, he said, "I was concerned because of your Vaspurakaner blood, your Majesty. Heresy on the throne is a dreadful thing."

"You need have no fears on that account," Maniakes answered. He wondered what his father would say upon learning he had opted for unabashed orthodoxy. Something interesting and memorable, he had no doubt. But he was also sure the elder Maniakes would recognize the need.

"That's excellent, excellent." Now Agathios was beaming. His sudden swings put Maniakes in mind of a weathervane—he seemed liable to blow in any direction and to swing from one to another without warning. The patriarch said, "Would you have me crown you now, then, your Majesty?"

"Later today will do nicely. I would ask something else of you first," Maniakes said. Agathios' bushy white eyebrows rose: what could be more important than an imperial coronation? Maniakes explained what the abbess Nikaia had demanded of him.

"This is truly the wish of these women?" the patriarch demanded.

"Most holy sir, would I lie about such a matter, causing a rift with my own prelate before he has even set the crown on my head?"

"If you are wise, you would not," Agathios said, "but who can tell yet whether you are wise? Meaning no disrespect to you, your Majesty—Phos forbid!—we have seen our share and more of stupidity these past half-dozen years."

"And more," Maniakes agreed.

Before he could again ask the ecumenical patriarch to relieve his fiancée and her mother from the vows they had taken at the convent, Agathios called, "Skombros! Fetch me pen, parchment, and sealing wax—at once!"

"Certainly, most holy sir," the synkellos replied from the hall. Hovering near Agathios was part of his job. He soon returned with the articles the patriarch had asked of him.

Agathios inked the pen and wrote rapidly. When he was done, he showed the note to Maniakes. It was the release he had requested, couched in florid ecclesiastical style. Nodding, he returned it to the patriarch. Agathios rolled up the parchment, tied a ribbon around it, and then picked up a lamp. He used the flame from the wick to melt several drops of his special sky-blue sealing wax so they fell onto the parchment and the ribbon. While the wax was still soft, he pressed his signet ring into it. When he lifted the ring, the mark of his monogram remained in the wax. With a flourish, he handed Maniakes the completed document.

"Thank you, most holy sir," Maniakes said. He turned to Rhegorios. "Take this back to the convent dedicated to the holy Phostina, fast as you can ride. Then, if she will, bring Niphone here to me. The most holy Agathios will wed us and then proclaim us Avtokrator and Empress."

"I like that, by the good god," Rhegorios exclaimed, his eyes sparkling. "You'll put on two different crowns the same day."

Maniakes laughed. "True enough." Videssian custom was for a man and woman who joined together to don wreaths called crowns of marriage.

"It must be Phos' will, your Majesty," Agathios said, "to see you revealed as bridegroom and Avtokrator on the same day."

"I pray it proves a good omen," Maniakes said soberly. He slapped Rhegorios on the back. "While you're at it, bring Niphone's mother, the lady Phevronia, as well. And send riders to the palaces, too. Kameas will know where the true imperial crown is; I'd sooner have the most holy patriarch set it on my head than have him use some substitute. The same goes for the Empress' crown. And we'll need to bring the eminent Kourikos here, as well, to watch his daughter wed."

Rhegorios frowned in concentration. "Let me make sure I have all that," he said, and repeated it back. Maniakes listened, then nodded, pleased with his cousin. Independent command seemed to have made Rhegorios more responsible than he had been. He saluted with a clenched fist over his heart, then left the patriarch's chamber at a run. He almost ran over Skombros in the hallway; Maniakes listened to them exchanging apologies. Then Rhegorios' footsteps receded rapidly.

That made Agathios snap his fingers in annoyance at himself. "Here I sit, forgetting my manners! I crave pardon, your Majesty." He raised his voice. "Skombros! Fetch cakes and wine for the Avtokrator." He shook his head. "These should have come before business, not after."

"Most holy sir, ceremony is all very well in its place, but sometimes business has such urgency that it must lead," Maniakes replied. The ecumenical patriarch looked doubtful; Maniakes wondered if here, unwittingly, he had spoken heresy for the first time.

Skombros returned with food and drink on a silver tray. The cakes left Maniakes' fingers so sticky, he had to lick them clean: honey and chopped nuts between layers of thin, flaky pastry. The wine came golden from the jar into the silver cups that stood on the tray. Maniakes was no great connoisseur of such things, but he knew a noble vintage when he tasted one.

When Agathios emptied his cup, Skombros poured it full again—and, a little while later, again, then yet again and once more. The ecumenical patriarch seemed little affected by all he drank, but Maniakes noted how much that was. He wondered if Skombros had wanted him to note it. A synkellos' loyalty was liable to lie as much with the Avtokrator as with the patriarch.

"I shall pray for your success against the troubles besetting us from every side, your Majesty," Agathios said, only slightly slow speech showing the wine he had taken on. "How shall you drive the Makuraners forth from the westlands while the heathen Kubratoi oppress us from the north?"

That was a good question. It was, in fact, the very question Maniakes had been pondering since he'd rebelled against Genesios. "Most holy sir, the one thing I know for certain is that we can't fight them both at once." Given the parlous state to which the Empire had descended, he wasn't altogether sure Videssos could fight either one of its principal foes, but he did not tell that to Agathios. It was not the sort of thought he wanted noised about, and he was not sure how far he could trust either patriarch or synkellos.

"Will you make peace with one so that you may pursue war against the other?" Agathios persisted.

"It could be so." Maniakes held up a hand. "Till now, I've worried more about casting Genesios down from the throne he stole than what I would do once I held the throne myself." That wasn't strictly true, but it gave him an excuse not to go into details about his plans.

Skombros said, "Since you were benefactor to Sharbaraz King of Kings, perhaps he will give over his war against Videssos when he hears you have become Avtokrator. Phos grant it be so, anyhow."

"Perhaps," Maniakes said, though he didn't believe it. "As custom requires, I shall send him an embassy announcing my accession as soon as I can. Then we'll see."

"And against the Kubratoi?" Skombros asked. He was so long used to keeping track of what the patriarch said and did and planned, he automatically assumed he had the same right with the Avtokrator.

"Right now, holy sir, I don't know what I'll do," Maniakes replied, and in that he was completely truthful. "When I have an answer, be sure you will know along with the rest of the Videssos." Skombros bowed his head, recognizing he had just been reminded of his place in the world.

Heard dimly down the hall, the racket outside the patriarchal residence suddenly swelled. Agathios said to Skombros, "Go see if that betokens the arrival of his Majesty's bride or that of her father."

The synkellos returned with Kourikos, and with Kameas as well. The vestiarios was bearing not only the bejeweled dome of the imperial crown but also a pair of red boots and a stout shield on which the soldiers would raise Maniakes, symbolizing their acceptance of him as commander. He could no more rule without their blessing than without the patriarch's.

"We would not want the ceremony celebrated imperfectly," Kameas said with great seriousness. Maniakes nodded. Stories said eunuchs were often fussily precise. Stories said a good many things, though. Here, for once, they did not seem far wrong. Maniakes resolved to find ways in which Kameas' character could best serve him.

Kourikos said, "Thank you, your Majesty, for sending me word my daughter and wife are safe."

"It was something you needed to know." Maniakes cocked his head. The noise outside was rising again. He smiled. "And, unless I'm much mistaken, here they are now." He turned to Agathios. "Most holy sir, we're ready for you."

V

MORNING SUN SNEAKING IN THROUGH THE SHUTTERS stabbed Maniakes in the eye and woke him. He yawned, stretched, sat up in bed. The motion disturbed Niphone, who also opened her eyes. He didn't know whether she was a naturally light sleeper or simply unused to sharing her bed with a man.

She smiled at him and made no effort to pull up the sheets to cover herself, as she had on the morning after they were wed. He'd laughed then, perhaps too loudly; he hadn't wanted to embarrass her. He had wanted a modest bride, and by all indications had got one. Modesty should have limits, though, or so he thought. He wasn't sure she agreed.

"I hope you slept well, your Majesty?" she said: formal as well as modest. He had thought well of that, too, till he found himself faced with the prospect of being yoked to it for as long as they both should live.

Truth was, he missed Rotrude, missed her openness, her easygoing acceptance, and the mind of her own that she most definitely had. The next opinion Niphone expressed about anything more profound than the state of the weather would be her first.

Very softly, Maniakes sighed to himself. He missed Rotrude for other reasons, too. Niphone's approach to the marriage bed was dutiful, little more; he had grown used to a partner who enjoyed what she was doing. He didn't think that was just because Niphone was only now passing from maidenhood, either. It sprang from a basic bit of who she was. He

115

sighed again. Sometimes you had to make do with what you found in life.

Niphone tugged on a bell pull. Down the hall, a chime sounded in a maidservant's room. The serving woman came in to help the Empress dress. When she was done, Maniakes rang for Kameas with a different bell pull. The vestiarios slept in the room next to the imperial bedchamber.

"Good morning, your Majesty," the eunuch said. "Which robe shall it be today? The red, perhaps? Or the light blue with the golden embroidery?"

"The plain dark blue will do fine," Maniakes answered.

"As you wish, of course, although the light blue would go better with the gown your lovely Empress has chosen," Kameas said, gently inflexible. He nodded politely to Niphone. She returned the gesture. She was modest around Kameas, and Maniakes approved of that. He had watched the way the eunuch eyed women: all longing, with no possibility of satisfying it. Having Kameas in the bedchamber while Niphone robed herself would just have reminded the vestiarios the more strongly of his condition.

"And how will you break your fast, your Majesty?" Kameas asked once Maniakes' robe—the dark blue one; he had got his own way—was draped in a fashion of which he approved. "The cook has some fine young squab, if I may offer a suggestion."

"Yes, they'd do nicely, I think," Maniakes said. "Tell him to broil me a couple, and to bring them to me with bread and honey and a cup of wine." He glanced over at Niphone. "What about you, my dear?"

"Just bread and honey, I think," she answered. "These past few days, I've not had much of an appetite."

By Maniakes' standards, she had never had much of an appetite. "Maybe you got used to short commons in the convent of the holy Phostina," he said.

"It could be so," Niphone said indifferently. "The food here is far better, though."

Kameas bowed to her. "I shall tell the cook as much, and tell him of your requirements—and yours, your Majesty," he added for Maniakes' benefit before he went out the door.

After breakfast, Maniakes and Rhegorios put their heads together. His cousin was serving as his Sevastos—his chief minister—for the time being. He had sent a letter summoning the elder Maniakes and Symvatios to the capital, but it was still on the way to Kalavria. He had also sent letters to the westlands after his brothers, but only the lord with the great and good mind knew when—or if—those letters would get to them. For now, Maniakes used the man upon whom he could most rely.

He flapped a parchment in front of Rhegorios' face. "Look at this!" he exclaimed—rhetorically, for Rhegorios had already seen the despatch. "Imbros sacked by the Kubratoi, half the wall pulled down, half the town burned, more than half the people run off to Kubrat so they can grow crops for the nomads. How am I supposed to fight off the Makuraners if the Kubratoi send everything to the ice up in the north?"

Rhegorios sighed. "Your Majesty, you can't."

Maniakes nodded. "I'd pretty much decided the same thing for myself, but I wanted to hear someone else say it, too." He also sighed. "That means I'll have to buy off the khagan of the Kubratoi. I hate it, but I don't see any other choice. I just pray old Etzilios won't want too much."

"How much is in the treasury?" Rhegorios asked. He managed a wry grin. "If you don't know, I'll ask your father-in-law. He'd tell me, right down to the last copper."

"The last copper is about what's there." Maniakes laughed bitterly. "No, I take that back: there are rats' nests and spiderwebs, too. Not much in the way of gold, though, nor even silver. I hope Skotos makes Genesios eat gold and silver down there in the ice." He paused to spit on the floor in rejection of the dark god, then went on, "For all I know, Genesios was eating them up here, too, for he certainly pissed them away. Maybe Phos knows what he spent his gold on, but I don't. Whatever it was, he got no good from it."

"And, of course, with the Makuraners raging through the westlands and the Kubratoi raiding down almost to the walls of the city here, a lot of taxes have gone uncollected," Rhegorios said. "That doesn't help the treasury, either."

"Too right it doesn't," Maniakes said. "I'm worried Etzilios will decide he can steal more than I'm able to give him."

"Or he might decide to take what you've given him and then go on stealing," Rhegorios put in.

"You're a cheerful soul, aren't you?" Maniakes said. "So he might. I'll offer him forty thousand goldpieces the first year of a truce, fifty thousand the second year, and sixty the third.

That'll give him good reason to keep an agreement all the way through to the end."

"So it will," Rhegorios said. "It will also give you more time to scrape together the bigger sums."

"You're reading my mind," Maniakes said. "I even went over to the Sorcerers' Collegium to see if they could conjure up gold for me. If I hadn't been Avtokrator, they'd have laughed in my face. Now that I think on it, that makes sense: if they could conjure up gold whenever they wanted it, they'd be rich. No, they'd be richer than rich."

"So they would," Rhegorios said. "But tell me you didn't go there for another reason, too: to see if they'd had any luck tracking down Genesios' pet wizard for you."

"Can't do it," Maniakes admitted. "I wish I'd had some luck, but they've seen no sign of him, and their sorcery can't find him, either. They don't want to say it out loud, but I get the feeling they're scared of him. 'That terrible old man,' one of their wizards called him, and no one knows what his name was."

"If he's so old, maybe he dropped dead while you were taking the city, or maybe Genesios took his head for not finishing you but never got the chance to hang it up on the Milestone," Rhegorios said.

"Maybe," Maniakes said, though he remained unconvinced—such endings for villains were more the stuff of romance than real life. "I just hope Videssos never sees him again." In earnest of that hope, he sketched the sun-circle above his heart.

Triphylles rose from the proskynesis he had gone into after Kameas led him to the chamber in the imperial residence Maniakes used for private audiences. "How may I serve you, your Majesty?" he murmured as he took a chair.

Normally that was but a polite formality. Now Maniakes intended to ask important service of Triphylles. "I have a mission in mind for you, excellent sir," he answered. "Complete it satisfactorily and I shall enroll you among those reckoned eminent in the Empire."

"Command me, your Majesty!" Triphylles cried. Striking a dramatic pose while seated wasn't easy, but he managed. "To serve the Empire is my only purpose in existing." Being promoted to the highest level of Videssian nobility might never have entered his mind.

"All Videssos is indebted to your intrepid spirit," Maniakes said, which made Triphylles preen even more. The Avtokrator went on, "I knew I could not have chosen a better, bolder man to take my words to Etzilios, the khagan of Kubrat. With you as my envoy, I am confident my embassy to him will succeed."

Triphylles opened his mouth, but whatever he had started to say seemed stuck in his throat. His florid, fleshy face turned even redder than usual, then pale. At last, he managed to reply "You do me too much honor, your Majesty. I am unworthy to bring your word to the fearsome barbarian."

Maniakes got the idea that Triphylles was more worried by Etzilios' fearsomeness than his own unworthiness. He said, "I am sure you will do splendidly, excellent sir. After all, you so bravely endured the privations at Kastavala and on our return journey to the capital that I am sure you'll have no trouble withstanding a few more as you journey up into Kubrat." No sooner had he said that than he realized Triphylles might not have to travel to Kubrat; for all he knew, Etzilios might still be on Videssian soil after sacking Imbros.

Triphylles said, "I endured these hardships in the expectation of returning here to the capital. If I beard the vicious nomad in his den, what hope have I of faring home again?"

"It's not so bad as that, excellent sir," Maniakes said soothingly. "The Kubratoi haven't murdered an envoy of ours in close to thirty years." For some reason, that left Triphylles inadequately heartened. Maniakes went on, "Besides, you'll be going up there to offer Etzilios gold. He's not likely to kill you, because then he wouldn't get paid."

"Ah, your Majesty, you don't know how that relieves my mind," Triphylles said. Maniakes stared at the noble; he had not suspected Triphylles had such sarcasm in him. When the grandee didn't say anything more, Maniakes kept looking at him. At last Triphylles wilted under that steadfast gaze. "Very well, your Majesty, I shall do as you request," he muttered sullenly.

"Thank you, and may the lord with the great and good mind watch over you and decide the test in your favor," Maniakes said. When Triphylles still looked glum, he went on, "I'm not asking you to do anything I won't do myself. When the agreement is made, Etzilios and I will have to meet face to face to ratify it."

"Aye, your Majesty, *if* the agreement is made," Triphylles

said. "If he chooses to slice me in strips and roast me over a horse-dung fire, though, you won't be coming after me to share my fate."

"I will come after you if that happens," Maniakes said. "I'll come after you with the whole weight of the army of Videssos behind me, to avenge the outrage." *Or as much of the Videssian army as I can afford to commit, what with the Makuraners rampaging through the westlands,* he thought. He did not share the qualification with Triphylles.

Having yielded, Triphylles got up to go. As he headed for the door, he muttered again, this time to himself. Maniakes did not catch all of it, but what he did hear angered him. Triphylles was complaining about having to go off to discomfort again after enduring so much of it in putting Maniakes on the throne.

"Halt," Maniakes snapped, as if to an insubordinate cavalry trooper. Triphylles peered back over his shoulder in alarm. Maniakes said, "If you worked to set me on the throne for no better reason than to let yourself come back to the fleshpots of the capital, you made a mistake. I thought you wanted me to rule to set Videssos' problems to rights. That is what I propose doing, and to do it I will seize any tool that comes to hand— including you."

Triphylles bit his lip, nodded, and took his leave before Maniakes could find any other reason to give him assignments he did not want. Maniakes plucked at his beard, wondering if he should have pretended to turn a deaf ear toward the grandee's grumbles. On reflection, he decided he probably should have, but it was too late to change his mind now. He could only go forward from what he had already done.

When you got down to it, that was all Videssos could do, too. But he was trying to take the Empire forward from what Genesios had done, and, so far as he could tell, Genesios had done everything wrong.

Meeting a returning envoy in the Grand Courtroom meant donning red boots, heavy ceremonial robe, and the even heavier imperial crown. In the hot, muggy weather of Videssos the city in summer, that was a torment Maniakes would just as soon have evaded. But Kameas politely insisted an emissary returning from the court of the King of Kings could not with propriety be met in the imperial residence. Maniakes was discovering that, while he ruled the Empire, his vestiarios was in charge of the palaces.

Fuming and sweating, Maniakes perched himself on the imperial throne and waited for his ambassador to make the long, slow advance between rows of marble columns. Sphrantzes was a man of an old noble family, one of the bureaucrats who did their best to keep the Empire on course even with a Genesios on the throne. Maniakes had sent him to Sharbaraz because he was both persuasive and honest, no more common a combination in Videssos the city than anywhere else.

He prostrated himself before Maniakes, turning what was for most people an awkward gesture of respect into one as flowing and graceful as part of a dance, then rose with the same fluid ease. He was about fifty, with a gray beard and a long, handsome, thoughtful face, one capable of expressing every shade of emotion he felt.

"How did you fare, eminent sir?" Maniakes asked. The logothetes and courtiers and functionaries who lined the way from the entrance to the throne leaned forward to hear better.

Sphrantzes' face grew longer yet. "Your Majesty, I regret I must tell you I failed in every particular," he said. His voice was deep and vibrant, a fit vehicle for the energy that filled him.

"Say on," Maniakes answered. Confessing failure before the Avtokrator and his court took courage. Most men would have claimed at least partial success before admitting such failures as they could not possibly deny.

The ambassador ticked off points on his fingers as he spoke. "Item: Sharbaraz does not recognize you as Avtokrator of the Videssians. He continues the mime-show of believing and claiming that the Videssian in fancy robes he keeps by himself is Hosios son of Likinios. I knew Hosios, your Majesty, and this lout is no Hosios."

"I knew him myself, and recognized his head when it came to Kastavala," Maniakes said, "so I know you are right about that. Go on."

"Item: he will not give over the war he is waging against Videssos, he says, until he sets the false Hosios on the throne you now occupy, your Majesty. This he terms obtaining vengeance for Likinios his benefactor."

"He conveniently forgets the Maniakai his benefactors," Maniakes said. "My father and I led the men who fought and bled to set him back on his own throne, and by the good god I wish we'd never done it."

"Item: he claims all Videssian territory his armies have overrun to be annexed to Makuran; his claim is that he shall hold it in trust for Hosios until the pretender's accession to the imperial throne." Sphrantzes raised an eyebrow in an elegant display of well-bred skepticism.

Maniakes translated without effort. "He'll keep it forever, he means. He wasn't arrogant when he knew he needed our help. Amazing what half a dozen years with nobody to tell him *no* have done." Every word Maniakes said was true. He also felt those words as a warning to himself. Who here in Videssos the city would tell him when he was being cruel or arrogant or foolish? Rhegorios might. The elder Maniakes would, when he got to the city. Past them, though, everyone knew currying favor with the Avtokrator was the way to rise. Nobody had told Genesios *no,* that was certain.

Like a sad bell, Sphrantzes tolled on. "Item: he proclaims all Vaspurakan annexed to Makuran in perpetuity."

Under other circumstances, that would have infuriated Maniakes. As it was, it seemed only to add insult to injury. Laughing, he said, "Let him proclaim, or simply claim, whatever he likes. Videssos and the princes of Vaspurakan will have more to say about that than he does."

"As you say, your Majesty," Sphrantzes replied. Maniakes thought he heard approval in the diplomat's voice. No less than Sharbaraz, Maniakes' own officials were taking his measure in the early days of his reign.

He said, "Did the King of Kings show any interest in my offer of tribute?" Videssos could not really afford to pay tribute to Makuran and Kubrat at the same time, but could afford war with either, let alone both, even less. If he could get a breathing spell no other way, Maniakes was willing to buy one.

But Sphrantzes mournfully shook his head. "Your Majesty, he says that since you are not the legitimate ruler of the Empire of Videssos—I hasten to add that these are his words, not mine—you have no right even to propose tribute to him. He adds that, once his Hosios is installed on your throne, he will regulate such matters to suit his own convenience. And he adds further that you need not pay him tribute, since he takes whatever he wants from Videssos as things stand now."

That made the assembled courtiers mutter angrily among themselves. It angered Maniakes, too. Sighing, he said, "The wretch is revealed to be a man without gratitude. My father and I set him on his throne; now he begrudges me my place on this one. By the good god, eminent sir, if he wants war so badly, war he shall have."

The courtiers cried, "Thou conquerest, Maniakes!" Their acclamations came echoing back from the domed ceiling of the Grand Courtroom. Maniakes, though, knew he had only echoes of the Videssian army that had preserved the balance against Makuran for so long. As far as he could tell, only two reliable regiments remained in the westlands. When he finally did go forth to confront Sharbaraz, he would have to build up his forces from scratch.

To Sphrantzes he added, "Eminent sir, I am grateful for your courage and tact. You have served the Empire well."

"Not so well as I should have liked, your Majesty," Sphrantzes answered.

"Well spoken—a model we can all look up to," Maniakes said. "In these times, though, the Empire is in such a state that no one can do as much as he would like. If everyone does his best, that will have to be enough—and, if everyone does his best, I do not see how we shall fail of victory."

The courtiers cheered again, with apparently sincere enthusiasm. Maniakes had already learned to be wary of that. But trying truly to fire them was part of doing his best. He hoped he could be good enough.

"Delicious!" Maniakes said. The chef had done something interesting with mullet, sauteeing it in white wine and serving it up with a sauce of liquamen and garlic cloves baked in goose fat till they were soft and brown and tender. The garlic and fermented tunny were a perfect complement to the mullet's firm, tender flesh.

Or so Maniakes thought, at any rate. But while he was devouring his portion and soaking a heel of bread in the sauce left on his plate, Niphone picked at her supper and pushed it aside after two or three bites.

"Are you feeling well?" he asked. It was hard to be sure in ruddy lamplight, but he thought she looked pale. She hadn't eaten much at supper for several days, now that he thought back on it, or at breakfast, either.

"I think so," she said listlessly, fanning the air with her hand. "It's close in here, isn't it?"

Maniakes stared at her. The window to the small dining

room was open, and admitted a cool breeze from off the Cattle Crossing. "*Are* you feeling well?" he repeated, his voice sharper this time. Like army camps, cities were breeding grounds for illnesses of all sorts. Videssos the city had the finest sorcerous healers in the world—and needed them.

Instead of answering him in words, Niphone yawned, covering her mouth with her hand. "I don't know what's come over me," she said. "Lately I want to go to bed as soon as the sun goes down and then sleep till noon. There's more to life than a mattress—or so I would have thought till now."

She certainly hadn't had much interest in matters of the mattress other than sleeping; Maniakes had to clamp his jaw shut to keep from saying something sardonic. The last time he had made love to her, she had complained his caresses made her breasts sore, though he didn't think he was doing anything different from the way he had stroked her since the day they became both man and wife and Emperor and Empress.

With that sarcastic retort still sizzling inside him, he wondered if he could find a discreet way to bring Rotrude to the imperial capital. She had never grumbled about his technique, except for a couple of months when . . .

"By the good god!" Maniakes said softly. He pointed a forefinger at Niphone, as if she were the key bit of evidence in a case he had to decide. And so, in a way, she was. Still quietly, he asked, "Could it be you're carrying a child?"

The way she gaped at him said the idea hadn't crossed her mind till now. "I don't know," she said, which annoyed him a little; a precise man himself, he preferred precise people around him. But, even if she didn't keep mental track of things as well as she might, she was not a fool. She started counting on her fingers. By the time she was done, an internal glow lit her face more brightly than the lamps could. "Why, I think I am!" she exclaimed. "My courses should have come ten days ago."

Maniakes hadn't noticed their failure, either, for which he reproached himself. He got up from the table and wrapped his arms around Niphone. "I won't pester you about eating any more," he said, "not for a while. I know you'll be doing the best you can."

A shadow crossed his wife's face, so fast he could hardly be sure he saw it. But he was. Niphone knew how he knew; she knew about Rotrude, and about Atalarikhos. He hadn't spoken of them himself, on the assumption that what he had done before he married her was his business. But she had mentioned them a couple of times, casually, in passing. He didn't know whether Kourikos had told her himself or mentioned them to his wife, who passed the news to Niphone. However it had happened, he was less than overjoyed about it.

By what seemed a distinct effort of will, Niphone made her features smooth and serene. She said, "I shall pray to the lord with the great and good mind that I give you a son and heir."

"May it be so," Maniakes said, and then, musingly, "In Makuran, I think; the wizards have ways to tell whether a child yet unborn will be a boy or a girl. If our Videssian mages can't do as well, I'll be surprised and disappointed." He chuckled. "The wizards won't want to disappoint the Avtokrator."

"Not after living through Genesios' reign, they won't," Niphone said, more spiritedly than she usually spoke. "Anyone who got on his wrong side went up on the Milestone without ever getting the chance to make amends." She shuddered; everyone in Videssos the city had memories of horror from the half-dozen years just past.

"I am not the sort of man, nor that sort of Avtokrator," Maniakes replied with a touch of injured pride. Then he laughed again. "Of course, if they don't fully realize that, and strive especially hard to please me, I won't be altogether unhappy."

Niphone smiled. After a moment, the smile reached her eyes as well as her lips. That gladdened Maniakes. He didn't want her thinking about Rotrude . . . even if he had been doing the same thing himself.

He raised his wine cup in salute. "To our child!" he said loudly, and drank.

After that toast, Niphone's smile showed more than polite happiness. She lifted her own cup, murmured Phos' creed, and spat on the floor in rejection of Skotos. "To our child," she echoed, and drank with Maniakes.

He didn't recall her having been so pious before he had to sail for Kalavria. He wondered if he had failed to notice before—something an assotted young man might well do—or if her stay in the convent dedicated to the holy Phostina had brought out that side of her character. As far as he was concerned, the way you lived made a better proof of piety than ostentatious displays, but he knew not everyone in the Empire agreed. Videssians, he sometimes thought, got drunk on theology as easily as on wine.

So what? he thought. Trying to change the nature of the Empire was the fastest way he could imagine to make a whole host of rebels spring up against him. And if Niphone had found happiness in a close embrace of Phos, that was her concern. She had certainly embraced him, too—even if he had found more joy in the arms of another—or she would not be pregnant now.

"To our child!" he said again. If it proved a son, he would be overjoyed; if a daughter, he would give her all the affection he could . . . and try again as soon as the midwife gave him leave.

"Octopus in hot vinegar!" Triphylles exclaimed when a eunuch servitor brought in the supper Maniakes had ordered to celebrate his ambassador's return from Kubrat. "How kind of you to remember, your Majesty."

"After your weeks in the hinterlands and then in the plainsmen's country, eminent sir, I thought you would like something to remind you that you'd returned to civilization," Maniakes answered. He nodded to himself, pleased he had remembered to address Triphylles by the higher honorific he had promised him for going to Kubrat. Amazing what men would do for a change of title.

"Your Majesty, you know not what truth you speak." Triphylles ate octopus with every appearance of rapture. "Remind me to kidnap your cook—although, after some little while of elderly mutton without garlic, I doubt my palate is at its most discriminating right now."

Since his own mouth was full, Maniakes did not have to reply. He ate his octopus, too, though without feeling the ecstasies it inspired in Triphylles. He found the delicacy overrated: not only was the octopus a queer-looking beast, a man could die of old age trying to chew up each resilient, not particularly flavorful bite.

When supper was done and he and Triphylles were sipping on white wine from the north coast of the westlands, Maniakes said, "I gather from the despatch the couriers brought to me day before yesterday that your dicker with Etzilios went well."

"Fairly well, I'd say," Triphylles answered judiciously. "He is eager to receive tribute—"

"A great deal more eager than I am to pay it, I have no doubt," Maniakes said.

"As to that, I should not be surprised in the least,"

Triphylles said, nodding. "But the mighty khagan—and if you wonder about that, just ask Etzilios' opinion of himself—is, mm, imperfectly trustful of promises from an Avtokrator of the Videssians who overthrew his great friend Genesios."

"Of course he reckons Genesios his friend—Genesios was his lifesaver," Maniakes said. "Likinios was on the point of putting paid to the Kubratoi once and for all when Genesios overthrew him. And Genesios wasn't any good at fighting people who knew how to fight back, so he left Kubrat alone. Etzilios must feel he's lost the best friend he ever had."

"That was the impression he left with me, your Majesty," Triphylles agreed. "Accordingly, he set conditions on his agreement with you."

"What sort of conditions?" Maniakes asked. If Triphylles had taken revenge for being sent off to a barbarous land by acquiescing to onerous terms, Maniakes would think about feeding him to the octopi instead of the other way round, perhaps after first dunking him in hot vinegar.

But his envoy replied, "To assure himself of your goodwill toward him, your Majesty, he insists that you personally bring the first year's tribute to him, at a spot to be agreed upon by future negotiation. I gather he has in mind somewhere not far from the border between Videssos and Kubrat."

"On our side of it, I assume," Maniakes said sourly. He felt no goodwill toward Etzilios; he wished Likinios had succeeded in crushing Kubrat and pushing the Videssian frontier back up to the Astris River, where, to his mind, it belonged. But he had thought the khagan might demand something like that; Etzilios was a smaller menace than Sharbaraz, and so had to be accommodated until the threat from Makuran was gone. He sighed. "Very well. Let that be as pleases the khagan. What else?"

"That was the chiefest point," Triphylles said. "He also requires that your retinue include no more than five hundred soldiers, and swore by his sword to bring no more than that number with him. Among the Kubratoi, no stronger oath holds."

"Which means we either believe him or take precautions," Maniakes said. "I aim to take precautions. I shall swear to bring no more than five hundred men with me to the meeting with Etzilios, but I'll have others standing by not far away in case his strongest oath proves not strong enough."

For a moment, he thought about treachery of his own. If he managed to slay Etzilios, the benefits now might well repay any damage to his soul later: he would have plenty of time to do good works and found monasteries in expiation of the sin. But if he tried to kill the khagan and failed, the Kubratoi would have plenty of reason to ravage his land and sack his towns. From all he had seen, Etzilios was wily enough to have a good chance of escaping any plot. With pragmatism and moral scruples pulling him in the same direction, Maniakes decided against breaking a pledge once made.

Triphylles said, "May it please your Majesty, here you shall have a fine opportunity to overawe the barbarian with the splendor of Videssian court life. When he sees such a magnificent display, he will desire nothing more than to continue gaining the bounty you condescend to grant him."

"That would be good," Maniakes agreed. He found court life more nearly stupefying than awe-inspiring, but then he was stuck in the middle of it—like a fly stuck in honey, he sometimes thought. But indeed, to a sheep-raising nomad, the gold-encrusted robes, censer-swinging priests, and slow, stately eunuchs might be impressive. Unquestionably, Etzilios would never have seen anything like them.

"The last item the khagan demands, your Majesty, is twenty pounds of peppercorns a year in addition to the tribute of gold." Triphylles made a face. "The lord with the great and good mind alone knows what he purposes doing with the pepper, for he seemed utterly ignorant of its use in cookery."

"We shall survive that," Maniakes said. "We can give him his spice."

"Excellent, your Majesty." Triphylles beamed for a moment, then suddenly looked anxious. "Uh, your Majesty—I trust you won't need me to hammer out the details of your forthcoming visit to the borders of Kubrat?"

"I think the services you have already rendered the Empire will suffice for the time being, eminent sir," Maniakes said, and Triphylles' fleshy face filled with relief. "High time now for you to enjoy the comforts of Videssos the city, as you have indeed labored so long and hard to keep them safe."

"Phos bless you, your Majesty," Triphylles said. His mobile features bore a different message: *it's about time*.

Not every day did an ordinary, rather battered galley pull up to the quays of the little harbor in the palace quarter. But then, not every day did the father and uncle of the Avtokrator return to Videssos the city after years of exile. When word the ship was approaching came to the palaces, Maniakes set aside the tax register he had been studying and hurried down to the water's edge. Had anyone asked him, he would have admitted he was glad for an excuse to set aside the cadaster. No one presumed to ask. That was one of the nice things about being Avtokrator.

Waves sloshed through one another and slapped against the sea wall. The sound of the ocean pervaded Videssos the city, surrounded by water on three sides as it was. These days, Maniakes often had to make a conscious effort to hear it. Time in the capital, and before that in seaside Kastavala, had dulled his awareness.

Rhegorios came hurrying down to the docks. "Are they here yet?" he said. "Oh, no, I see them. Another few minutes. Look, there's Father in the bow—and your father, too." He waved. After a moment, so did Maniakes. As often happened, his more spontaneous cousin got him moving.

The elder Maniakes waved back. Symvatios did, too. Rhegorios had sharp eyes, to tell them apart so readily at such a distance. Maniakes had to squint to be sure who was who.

Standing beside Symvatios was his daughter Lysia. She also waved toward Maniakes and Rhegorios. That made Maniakes wave harder. Rhegorios, though, put his hands down by his sides. Maniakes poked him in the ribs with an elbow. "Aren't you going to welcome your sister?" he demanded.

"What, and give her the chance to put on airs?" Rhegorios said in mock horror. "She'd never let me forget it."

Maniakes snorted. He listened to the oarmaster calling the stroke and then ordering back oars as the galley came alongside a quay. Lines snaked out from the ship. Servitors ashore tied them fast. Sailors and servitors wrestled the gangplank into place.

The elder Maniakes crossed to the wharf before anyone else. Had anybody tried to precede him, his son thought he would have drawn the sword he wore on his belt and sent the presumptuous soul along the bridge it would either cross to reach Phos' heaven or fall from to descend to Skotos' ice.

With great dignity, the elder Maniakes bowed before the younger. "Your Majesty," he said, and then, with even greater pride, prostrated himself before the Avtokrator who happened to be his son.

"Get up, sir, please!" Maniakes said. This business of being Avtokrator kept having implications he didn't see till they upped and bit him. He stared around in no small alarm: what were people thinking of a father who had to perform a proskynesis before his son?

To his amazement, the servants and courtiers watching the elder Maniakes looked pleased and proud themselves. A couple softly clapped their hands at the spectacle. Whatever Maniakes had expected, that wasn't it.

Still bent on the dock, the elder Maniakes said, "Just let me finish my business here, son, if you please," and touched his forehead to the timbers. Then he did rise, grunting a little at the effort it cost him. Once he was back on his feet, he added, "Now that that's over and done, I can go back to clouting you when you do something stupid."

Where abject servility had brought nothing but approval from servitors and men of the court, that threat, obvious joke though it was, drew gasps. Maniakes rolled his eyes in wonder. Did they suppose he was going to punish his father for lese majesty?

By the way they kept staring from one of the Maniakai to the other, maybe they did. Maniakes walked over to his father, embraced him, and kissed him on both cheeks. That seemed to ease the minds of some of the spectators, but only made others more nervous.

Symvatios performed the proskynesis next. After he rose, he went on one knee before Rhegorios. "Your Highness," he said, as was proper in greeting the Sevastos of the Videssian Empire.

"Oh, Father, get up, for Phos' sake," Rhegorios said impatiently. Seeing the Sevastos imitate the Avtokrator's informality, the spectators sighed—things weren't going to be as they had been in the reign of the traditionalist Likinios. How things had been during Genesios' reign, they carefully chose not to remember.

After Symvatios had presented himself to his nephew and son, it was Lysia's turn. As before, Maniakes felt more embarrassed than exalted at having her prostrate herself. He got the strong feeling, though, that ordering her not to would have insulted her instead of making her happy. He shrugged. As he had seen with the way Triphylles lusted after an otherwise altogether unimportant title, ceremony was a strange business, almost a magic of its own.

"I'm glad you're here, cousin of mine," he said, giving Lysia a hug after she had greeted her brother. "When we left each other in Kastavala, we didn't know whether we'd ever see each other again."

"*I* knew," Lysia said, showing more confidence now than she had that day on the distant island. She said nothing about the embrace they had given each other then, though he would have bet it was in her mind as it was in his. The one they had just exchanged was decorously chaste.

The elder Maniakes said, "Son—your Majesty—have you had any word of your brothers?"

"No," Maniakes said. "It worries me. The westlands have been anything but safe for soldiers these past few years." That was an understatement. Not only had the armies of the westlands had to withstand a great onslaught from out of Makuran, they had also battered one another in endless, fruitless rounds of civil war.

"I pray the good god has not let my boys fall for nothing," the elder Maniakes said, his voice heavy with worry. "The good god grant that my line shall not fail now, at its greatest moment of triumph."

"The good god has already taken care of that, or so I hope," Maniakes replied with a grin. "We'll know for certain come spring."

"So you'll make me a grandfather, eh?" the elder Maniakes said. His chuckle was too bawdy to seem quite fitting at a ceremonial occasion. "You didn't waste much time, did you, eh? Good for you."

"Will you dine with me tonight, Father?" Maniakes said. "I shall be holding a feast in the Hall of the Nineteen Couches. Uncle, I bid you join us, too, and you, Lysia."

"The Hall of the Nineteen Couches?" The elder Maniakes rolled his eyes up toward the heavens. "We're going to have to eat reclining, aren't we? To think my own son would do such a thing to me, and at the same time make it impossible to say no."

Maniakes refused to let that half-piteous, half-sardonic appeal sway him. "If I can do it, you can do it. And if I spill fish sauce and wine down the front of my robe, with you there I'll have some reason to hope I shan't be the only one."

"See what an ungrateful child it is!" the elder Maniakes shouted out to whomever would hear him. But he spoiled the effect of his indignation by throwing back his head and laughing till he had to hold his sides.

* * *

The nineteen couches sat in a large horseshoe in the hall to which they had given their name. "Yours, of course, shall be at the center, in the keystone position, your Majesty," Kameas said, pointing to the one in question. "You shall have three times three on either side of you."

"We could invite many more than that if you'd only set out tables and chairs, the way they do it in every other dining hall in the Empire," Maniakes said testily.

"If elsewhere they forget the past, we should pity rather than emulate them," the vestiarios replied. "Here we recline, the last bastion of true elegance in a world gone shoddy and uncaring."

"I ought to start a new custom," Maniakes grumbled.

Kameas stared at him in horror that was, Maniakes realized, perfectly genuine. "No, your Majesty, I beg you!" the vestiarios cried. "In this hall, Stavrakios reclined after his great victories against Makuran, as did Yermanos before civil war tore the Empire to bits upon his death. Would you have your practices differ from theirs?"

Maniakes had his doubts about Stavrakios' reclining after his victories. From all he had ever read, the great soldier-Avtokrator had been more comfortable in the field than in the palaces. But that was not the point Kameas was trying to make. "Precedent is meant to guide, not to strangle," Maniakes said.

Kameas did not reply, not in words. He just stared at Maniakes with large, sorrowful eyes. "Your commands shall of course be obeyed, your Majesty," he said, sounding as if one of those commands were that he take poison.

Maniakes ended up eating on that central couch. He reclined on his left side, freeing his right hand for feeding himself. Not only did he find it a most awkward way to go about the business of supper, but before long his left arm, on which he leaned, seemed dead from elbow to fingertip.

Kameas beamed. So did the other servants who carried food and wine into the Hall of the Nineteen Couches and empty platters and goblets away from it. Maniakes wondered if keeping his servitors happy was worth this discomfort.

His sole consolation was that he wasn't alone in having trouble at the feast. Of all the guests there, only Kourikos, his wife Phevronia, and Triphylles seemed at ease. They had eaten this way in Likinios' day. Niphone might have been familiar with the arrangements, too, but at the moment she found facing food far more unpleasant a prospect than leaning on one elbow. If anything, for her the awkward position was an advantage: it meant she couldn't be expected to eat much.

Thrax the drungarios was the first person to dribble garum down his chin and onto his robe. He expressed his opinion of having to eat on couches so forcefully that several women turned their heads aside in embarrassment.

"Disgraceful," Niphone murmured.

A few couches down from Maniakes, Lysia giggled, then tried to pretend she hadn't. Maniakes caught her eye. She looked apprehensive till she saw him smile, but relieved after that. Moments later, Symvatios spilled sauce on himself. Lysia laughed out loud.

"Go ahead, mock your own father," Symvatios said, but his severity was as insincere as the elder Maniakes' had been earlier in the day at the harbor in the palace quarter.

After the blueberries candied in honey had been taken away, after the last toasts to the new Avtokrator and his family were drunk—mostly by the new Avtokrator and his family—the feasters began rising one by one and leaving the Hall of the Nineteen Couches. Kameas came hurrying up to Maniakes, worry on his smooth eunuch's face.

"I trust you enjoyed yourself, your Majesty?" He sounded anxious.

"More than I expected, yes," Maniakes admitted.

Kameas sketched Phos' sun-circle over his breast. "The good god be praised," he murmured to the heavens above before returning his attention to Maniakes. "Then you will not mind my scheduling further such entertainments?"

"Let's not get carried away," Maniakes said hastily. Kameas' face, which had begun to shine, crumpled again. Maniakes knew he would have to deal with a grumpy, disappointed vestiarios in the days ahead. He preferred that to the prospect of dealing with any of the nineteen couches any time soon.

One thing Maniakes hadn't anticipated before he donned the crown and the red boots: how much parchment an Avtokrator had to cope with every day. Letting clerks and logothetes take the burden could go only so far. If you didn't know what was going on inside Videssos, how could you be said to rule the Empire? To Maniakes' mind, you couldn't.

Genesios had let everything slip except matters that touched on his own hold on the throne—there he had been both wary and ruthless. But he hadn't delegated responsibility to anyone else. Things he didn't personally decide just got ignored.

"That's how Videssos got into the state it's in," Maniakes declared to anyone who would listen. Since he was Avtokrator, people had an incentive to listen to him. The flood of parchment that came to the imperial residence all but inundated him.

Most of the missives were in one way or another cries for help: towns wanting gold and artisans to rebuild walls, provinces wanting relief from taxes because their farmlands had been ravaged—he had no idea how to meet both those requests at the same time—generals wanting men and horses and weapons. He wished he had some to send them. He had managed to scrape together a couple of regiments of veteran troops, but didn't know where he could find more.

Here was a letter from another general:

Tzikas commanding west of Amorion to Maniakes Avtokrator: Greetings. I have the honor to report, your Majesty, that your brother Tatoules formerly served with my command. This past spring, the Makuraners sent a column eastward past the southern edge of the territory within my assigned area of responsibility. I dispatched a force of my own southward to attempt to check the enemy column. My move was successful but, because my colleague, the excellent Provatos, showed the spirit of a sheep and did not similarly commit a detachment of his own after promising to do so, the Makuraners were able to fall back rather than being destroyed. Our casualties were moderate, but I regret to inform you that your brother Tatoules did not return with the rest of the force. He is not certainly known to be slain. I regret I cannot convey more definite news as to his fate.

Maniakes regretted it, too; he had no way of knowing whether Tatoules was dead or alive and, if alive, whether he was wounded or in Makuraner captivity. He didn't think Sharbaraz would harm his brother if he knew he had him. They were enemies, yes, but because Makuran and Videssos were enemies. It wasn't personal, at least not as far as Maniakes was concerned. But the men of Makuran might have captured Tatoules without knowing he was brother to the Avtokrator—by all indications, he didn't know it himself. The lot of ordinary prisoners could be—too often was—harsh.

And yet that ambiguous letter from Tzikas gave him far

more knowledge of Tatoules' actions and whereabouts than he had for Parsmanios. His other brother might have been swallowed by the earth, for all the report of him that came back from the westlands.

He noted that Tzikas had done his best to raise imperial wrath against Provatos, his fellow general in the westlands. Since he didn't know the circumstances under which the two men were supposed to have cooperated, he couldn't decide which of them was in the right here. That troubled him; he knew he needed to take firmer control over his officers if the army was ever to become effective against either Makuran or Kubrat.

But he could not simply leap atop the army and ride it as if it were a placid mare. The generals, especially in the westlands, had got used to taking matters into their own hands, for the good and simple reason that Genesios had given them no choice—he led not at all. Having gained power—even if not enough to hold back Sharbaraz—they were reluctant to surrender it to Videssos the city.

"To the ice with them all," Maniakes raged to Rhegorios. "They act like a herd of virgins fit for nothing but the convent and want me to waste my time seducing them one by one."

"The truth is, they're just a pack of whores," Rhegorios said.

While Maniakes agreed with that, it didn't help him find a way to deal with his independence-minded generals. He took the question to his father. The elder Maniakes plucked at his beard and said, "Having a good-sized army under your command in the westlands will bring them to heel soon enough."

"*Would* bring them to heel, you mean," the younger Maniakes said. "As things are now, the only way I'll be able to put troops in the westlands is buying off the Kubratoi so I can free up some of the men who are trying to hold them back. I hate that, but what choice have I?"

"None I can see," his father answered. "What you have to do, though, is make sure Etzilios can't find any way to cheat you."

"I've been doing my best there. My commissioners and the khagan's cronies have been dickering for weeks about where we'll meet, who we can bring with us, and other small details." Maniakes' smile showed his sardonic streak. He went on, "The only trouble is, while we're dickering, Etzilios' men keep raiding us. As best I can tell, he thinks that's part of the way negotiating gets done."

The elder Maniakes sighed. "He has gained our attention, hasn't he? The only way I can think of to make him stop is to threaten to go to war without limit against him if he doesn't give over, and that—"

"That will just make him laugh," the younger Maniakes finished. His father nodded. He went on, "He may be a barbarian, but he's no fool, worse luck. He knows the only way we can fight a big war with him is to quit fighting Makuran, and we can't afford to do that. Even if we did, we might get another mutiny out of it—the troops remember how Likinios tried to make them winter north of the Astris and what happened afterward."

"Ah, but would they mutiny for fear of having to spend the winter on the frozen steppe, or in hope of casting you down and setting another in your place?" The elder Maniakes spread his hands. "That wasn't a question I intended you to answer, son."

"The why doesn't much matter, anyway," the younger Maniakes said. "One more civil war and we pretty much hand Videssos over to Sharbaraz, anyhow. Then he'd have to try and rule it. Seeing him struggle with that is the one reason I can think of for losing." Before his father could speak, he added quickly, "I'm joking, by the good god."

"I know you are. I wasn't going to twit you about that. But I can make a pretty good guess, I think, about when Etzilios will rein in his raiders and graciously consent to accept the gold you want to give him."

"If I have enough gold to pay the tribute," the younger Maniakes said gloomily. "All right, Father, if you feel like foretelling, tell me when Etzilios will leave us in peace."

"Right about the time the harvest is done," the elder Maniakes answered. "He'll steal all he can up till then and take away as much grain as his horses can carry. Nomads often live right on the edge of starving and make up for what they can't raise themselves by robbing their neighbors. This way, Etzilios will have our farmers working for him."

"The ones he leaves alive, anyway," the younger Maniakes said. He considered. "You may well be right. That means another couple of months of attacks, though, and not much time after the harvest season to meet with Etzilios and pay him off before the fall rains turn the roads to muck."

"Maybe we should hope they start early," his father said. "The Kubratoi won't be able to do much in fall or winter, either. Come spring, you'd be able to pay the khagan and buy peace through the campaigning season."

"I'd like that," the younger Maniakes replied. "I see only one thing wrong with it." His father waited expectantly. He explained: "It would be convenient for us, and Etzilios won't let that happen."

The elder Maniakes barked a few syllables of wheezy laughter and clapped him on the shoulder. "I wish I could say you were wrong, but I don't think you are."

Bagdasares rose from his prostration with a quizzical look on his face. "You do me great honor, your Majesty," the wizard said, speaking Videssian with the throaty Vaspurakaner accent that put Maniakes in mind of his grandparents, "but truly, the mages of the Sorcerers' Collegium can do this as well as I. Better," he added in a burst of candor that made Maniakes like him very much.

"That may be so, but you can do it well enough," Maniakes answered, "and I trust you, which is more than I can say for the sorcerers of the Collegium. They were here through Genesios' reign. Who knows what some of them may have done?"

"He used that skinny old man for the worst of his conjurations," Bagdasares said.

"So everyone tells me—and that skinny old man is now conveniently vanished," Maniakes said. "As I say, I don't know what those others did and it's too late now for me to worry about it without evidence, but if I want to find out what's likely to come of my meeting with Etzilios, I'll ask you, not them."

"Very well, your Majesty," Bagdasares said. "I shall do my best not to disappoint you, although I must say, as with any effort to look ahead to what will be, I can give you no guarantee that all will transpire as now appears most likely."

"Yes, yes, I understand that," Maniakes said impatiently. "Just get on with it, if you'd be so kind. Unless the barbarian should yet again change what passes for his mind, I'll be departing to meet him before long."

"I shall attempt to learn what may be learned," Bagdasares replied, bowing. "I should also warn you that the Kubrati shamans may cloud what I see, either because they are also peering at what may be or because they are deliberately trying to keep me from seeing ahead."

Maniakes' gesture was so peremptory, he regretted it a moment later. However rude it was, though, it got Bagdasares moving, which was what Maniakes had intended. The Vaspurakaner mage emptied out his carpetbag on the polished top of a marble table. Rummaging in the pile of oddments, he selected a small jar of wine, a mirror of polished bronze, and a tiny, intricately carved cinnabar jar that held a glob of quicksilver.

"In the mirror, we shall see what we shall see," he explained. "We can touch the future only through the law of contagion, for it is, metaphorically speaking, in contact with the present. The spirits of the wine will give us the link between present and future, while the quicksilver—" He flicked it with his finger, to break it into several shining drops. "—symbolizes the mutability of all that lies ahead and has not yet been accomplished."

"Carry on," Maniakes said. Wizardry and its techniques often fascinated him, but not today. All he cared for were results.

"As you say, your Majesty." Bagdasares spent the next couple of minutes fussily gathering back into a single globule the quicksilver he had scattered, then slid a scrap of parchment under it so he could pick it up later.

Whistling tunelessly between his teeth, he poured some of the wine into a small cup with a white, shiny glaze. He left a finger's breadth of rim showing when he set aside the wine jar. Some of that margin disappeared when he let the quicksilver fall down into the wine. A couple of wine drops splashed out of the cup and onto the table. He wiped them up with a rag.

"No one should drink of this wine," he remarked. "It's been used in these rituals before and had quicksilver in it many times. Quicksilver's not the strongest poison I know, but it's not the weakest, either. Well—"

He spread his hands over the wine cup and began a slow, sonorous chant, some of it in the Vaspurakaner tongue, the rest in Videssian so archaic that Maniakes had trouble following it. He thought he understood that Bagdasares was using the spirits in the wine to harness the quicksilver's constant changes and turn them toward what would pass from the meeting with Etzilios.

Sweat rolled down Bagdasares' forehead and across his fleshy cheeks. "This is hard," he said. "I can feel resistance between me and my goal. I shall be the stronger, though; I shall prevail—Phos surely favors a man from among his first-born." Maniakes wondered what Agathios would have to say about that. He himself, however, was more interested in what Bagdasares could tell him than in rooting out heresy wherever he found it.

When his incantation was complete, Bagdasares picked up a brightly polished silver spoon and filled it from the cup. Slowly and carefully, he brought it over to the mirror, which lay flat on the table. He poured the quicksilver-laden wine onto the smooth bronze surface. "Now you shall see what you shall see," he whispered to Maniakes.

At first, Maniakes saw only red wine spread over the surface of the mirror. Then the smeared wine became a filmy curtain and blew aside; it was as if he were peering through the mirror into infinite space filled neither with Phos' light nor Skotos' darkness. He wanted to blink—it was not something he thought man was meant to perceive—but found he could not.

After what might have been a heartbeat or some endlessly longer time, the mirror once more began to show an image. No longer did it reflect the ceiling or Maniakes' face, though. Instead, he saw the neck and head of a horse, as if he were riding on it; he thought the hands holding its reins his own. In the near distance were the walls of Videssos the city. The sun glinted from the globes of Phos' temples inside, just as it had when he approached by sea.

He wondered what lay behind him, but the image faded from his sight before he could find out. The mirror once more became its normal self. He looked away from it, scratching his head.

"Did you learn what you sought, your Majesty?" Bagdasares asked.

Maniakes glanced over to him in surprise. "Why do you ask? Didn't you see what I saw in the mirror?"

"No, your Majesty." The wizard shook his head. "The spell was created to enlighten you, not me. I know the sort of thing you experienced, as I've sometimes used that magic for my own purposes, but I did not share this particular vision with you."

"So that's the way of it, eh?" Maniakes was still bemused. "I don't know whether I saw what I needed to see or not. Your mirror showed that I will come back from my meeting with

Etzilios, which is indeed a piece of news worth having, but it did not show anything of the meeting itself."

"As I said, your Majesty, I fear I was being impeded in my efforts by the Kubrati shamans," Bagdasares answered. "Whether they were trying to hinder me or simply creating uncertainty because of their own foreseeing attempts, I cannot tell you. I will say it is not impossible, or even improbable, that I have interfered with their magic, as well."

"Good." Maniakes thought of two stones being tossed into a calm pond at the same time and of ripples spreading out from each until those ripples met each other and either flattened out or pushed each other higher. In neither case would the water be as it had been before the waves ran through it. He went on, "So Etzilios will be as much in the dark as I will over what the meeting may bring?"

"From a sorcerous point of view, yes, I think so," Bagdasares said. "Sorcery, of course, may not be a decisive factor on whatever plans he has."

"Yes, there is that." Maniakes plucked at his beard, as he often did while thinking. When he got down to it, he had very little choice. "I'll treat with the barbarian. If he and I do not come to terms, how can we wage war against Makuran?" Bagdasares did not answer. He did not have to answer. Without a truce with Kubrat, Maniakes would fight in the westlands like a man with one arm tied behind his back.

Bagdasares fished the glob of quicksilver out of the cup into which he had dropped it, then put it back in the cinnabar jar. He poured the wine back into its jar, too, and tightly stoppered it. He dried and polished the bronze mirror before returning it and the rest of his sorcerous paraphernalia to the carpetbag in which he had carried them.

"I thank you for your help," Maniakes told him. The help hadn't been as complete as he might have hoped, but the more he had to do with magic, the more he realized it was a highly ambiguous business. Attempts to foresee the future might also influence it. If that was so, would it mean that what you had seen could no longer come to pass? But if what you had seen was false, how could it influence the true future? With a deliberate effort of will, he set aside that train of thought before it made him dizzy.

After Bagdasares left the imperial residence, Maniakes wanted to talk with someone about what he had seen. He discovered his father, cousin, and uncle had gone riding into the city while he was closeted with the mage. Since he hadn't gotten into the habit of confiding in Kameas—and since he wasn't sure getting into that habit was a good idea—he went looking for Niphone.

He found her in the imperial bedchamber. She was down on all fours on the floor, throwing up into a basin. Since she was an Empress of the Videssians, the basin was of solid silver, with low-relief images of holy men and their miracles ornamenting the outside. That didn't make being sick into it any more pleasant.

Maniakes stooped beside Niphone and held her hair back from her face till she was done. "Thank you," she said in a muffled voice. "There's a jar of wine on that chest there. Could you bring me a cup and let me rinse my mouth?"

"Of course," Maniakes said. While he was pouring it, Niphone rang for a maidservant. The woman came in and carried the basin away.

After Niphone had drunk some of the wine, she said, "That's a little better. I'm so tired of throwing up every day, I don't know how to begin to tell you."

"I believe that," Maniakes said as sympathetically as he could. "I just had Alvinos here—" When talking with Niphone, he used the Videssian name the wizard had given himself; Niphone didn't care to be reminded of the Vaspurakaners as a separate people. He explained what he had seen in the mirror, and what he hadn't as well.

"So long as you come back to the city safe," Niphone said, and that was the end of her interest in Bagdasares' magic. Maniakes told himself he wouldn't have been at his best just after being violently ill. That was true, but he had the feeling she would have been as indifferent were she perfectly well. She didn't care much—no, the truth, she didn't care at all—about how the Videssian Empire was run, though she was annoyed that the running of it kept him away from her more than she would have wanted.

Seeing he might as well have been talking to the wall, he left and wandered aimlessly through the halls of the imperial residence. Had he run into Kameas, he probably would have unburdened himself to him; not only did the vestiarios' position oblige him to listen, he had a good head for detail and might have had something useful to say.

But instead of Kameas, Maniakes found Lysia. His cousin

was looking at some of the treasures stored up here. Not all of them were worth great piles of goldpieces. The battered iron helmet by which she stood, for instance, was nothing out of the ordinary to the eye. But it had once covered the head of a Makuraner King of Kings who had fallen to Videssian arms in Mashiz.

Lysia looked up at the sound of Maniakes' footsteps in the hallway and smiled to recognize him. The ceiling of the hall was set with thin alabaster panels that let in a pale, shimmering light. Lysia happened to be standing under one of them. She seemed ethereal, not quite of this world.

But there was nothing ethereal about what she said. "May you add Sharbaraz's helmet to go with the one we already have here."

"That would be fine," he said, nodding as he came up to her. "I can't even think about driving the Makuraners from our soil yet, though, let alone moving on Mashiz, not when I still have Kubrat to worry about." As he had with Niphone, he told of what Bagdasares' magic had shown him.

"You don't know what will happen before you come riding back to Videssos the city?" Lysia asked.

"No, and that's what worries me," Maniakes said. "It could be anything from the agreement I hope for to . . . just this side of being killed, I suppose."

"I don't blame you for worrying," she answered. "You ought to post troops close by, over and above the five hundred to which you've agreed, so they can come to your aid if Etzilios does prove to have treachery in mind.

"The trick of it," Lysia went on seriously, "will be finding places where they're near enough to do you some good but not so near as to make the Kubrati khagan think they endanger him—especially since he'll have his own men hanging about for the same reason."

Maniakes stared at her. "My dear cousin!" he exclaimed. "You're as clever as you are pretty, which says a good deal. Just what I aim to do, I don't think any of my generals or courtiers could have summed that up so neatly."

Under his intent gaze, Lysia looked down at the mosaicwork floor. "Your Majesty is too kind to me," she murmured.

He frowned. Along with everyone else in the Empire of Videssos, she was his subject, and protocol required that she remember it. But, as far as ceremony went, the crown still sat lightly on him, and he was used to her as a frank-spoken cousin, as near an equal as a woman was likely to become in Videssos' male-dominated society—although, from what he had seen, the Makuraners granted their women far fewer privileges than Videssians did.

He took a cousinly privilege and poked her in the ribs. She squeaked, started to poke him right back, and then checked herself. "No, you'd say I was guilty of lese majesty or some such, and cast me in a dungeon," she said, her eyes sparkling to show she was teasing him.

"Aye, no doubt, and you'd deserve it, but I need to keep you free so you can give me good advice," he answered. That could have been teasing, too, but it had enough of an earnest undercurrent to make her pause before she snapped back at him again. For that moment, at least, they liked each other very much.

VI

MANIAKES RODE AT THE HEAD OF THE PROCESSION THAT left Videssos the city through the Silver Gate, bound for the northern frontier and a meeting with Etzilios the khagan. After he had gone a couple of hundred yards, he reined in and turned to look back at everyone who was joining him in this effort to overawe the Kubrati ruler.

"We have a bit of everything here, don't we?" he said to Bagdasares, who had stopped his own horse at the same time.

"That we do, your Majesty," the wizard agreed soberly. He patted the side of his mount's neck. The mare let out a quiet, pleased snort.

Behind the Avtokrator and the mage rode the five hundred men who would serve as Maniakes' honor guard when he con- fronted Etzilios. Half of them wore blue surcoats over their chainmail, the other half gold. Blue and gold streamers flut- tered from their lances. They gave the impression of being only for show, but every one was a first-rate fighting man.

Next after them came the baggage train: horses and mules and oxen and wagons with canvas tops that could be stretched over them in case of rain. The baggage for the Avtokrator's pa- vilion was separate from the rest, marked off by blue banners with gold sunbursts on them. Kameas and other imperial servi- tors accompanied it, ready to do their best to make the Avtokrator feel as if he had never left the palaces. The treasure Maniakes would give to Etzilios was also in that part of the baggage train, guarded by half a hundred hard-faced men who made no effort to seem anything but deadly dangerous.

After the baggage train rolled wagons of a different sort:

these carried the members of a couple of the leading mime troupes in Videssos the city. The performers were veterans of many a Midwinter's Day skit in the Amphitheater, but they had never gone up before a more demanding audience. If the khagan didn't care for the shows they put on, he had blunter—or rather, sharper—ways to express his disapproval than flinging a rotten pumpkin.

"I wish we had a giant serpent to give Etzilios," Maniakes said suddenly. "I'd like to see what he'd do with one, by Phos. Give it back, unless I miss my guess—either that or feed his enemies to it."

"Such serpents seldom enough come from the Hot Lands to Videssos the city," Kameas said. "I daresay no plainsman has ever had to deal with one."

Since there were no serpents, a couple of dozen of the swiftest horses in the city followed the mime troupe's wagons. Maniakes aimed to put on horse races for the khagan. If Etzilios wanted to run his steppe ponies against these beasts, the Avtokrator wouldn't complain. And if Etzilios wanted to bet on the outcome, Maniakes figured he would win back some of the gold he was paying.

Last of all rode another fifteen hundred cavalrymen. Unlike the formal guard regiment, they lacked matching gear. If all went well, Etzilios would never see them. They accompanied the Avtokrator in case all failed to go well.

When the party—with so many noncombatants along, Maniakes had trouble thinking of it as a *force*—reached the Long Walls, the fortifications that protected the area surrounding Videssos the city from barbarian raids, he sent out his troops to check the nearby woods and copses to make sure no Kubratoi were lurking there. They found none of the nomads. That helped set Maniakes' mind at ease; Etzilios seemed to be living up to the agreements he had made.

On the road up to Imbros, Maniakes had no trouble sleeping in the elaborate pavilion of scarlet silk his servitors erected for him each night. He had had far worse beds on campaign. The servitors themselves, though, were used to life in the palaces and had trouble adjusting to being away from Videssos the city. They complained about the travel, about the food, about the noise at night, and about how drafty their tents were.

Kameas' shelter stood beside that of the Avtokrator and was the next most elaborate after it alone. Yet the vestiarios kept saying, over and over again, "Most unsatisfactory."

"What's wrong, esteemed sir?" Maniakes asked in honest bewilderment. "Seeing that we're traveling, I can't imagine doing it with any more luxury."

"It is inadequate," Kameas insisted. "The Avtokrator of the Videssians should not dine on rabbit stew, and if by chance he should, the dish should not be lacking in mushrooms to give it at least a hint of piquancy."

Maniakes ticked off points on his fingers. "First of all, I like rabbit stew. Second, I didn't so much as notice it came without mushrooms. Third, if this were a real campaign, I'd be eating out of the same pots as my men. That's the best way I know for a general to be sure their food is as good as it can be."

Kameas turned a delicate shade of green—or perhaps it was only a trick of the torchlight. "It strikes me as the best way for an Avtokrator to be sure his own food is as bad as it can be."

Barley porridge, hard rolls, onions, crumbly cheese, salted olives, garlicky smoked sausage of pork or mutton, wine sometimes halfway to vinegar . . . Maniakes decided he would be wiser not to admit a fondness for the food armies ate on the march, lest he bring a fit of apoplexy down on his vestiarios. But fond of such fare he was, no doubt because he had eaten it so often when he was young.

"How long shall we be away from the palaces, your Majesty?" Kameas asked.

"Two weeks; three at the most," Maniakes answered.

Kameas rolled his eyes, as if the Avtokrator had announced a separation of as many years. His sigh made his jowls wobble. "Perhaps we shall survive it," he said, though his tone implied he had his doubts.

Imbros was the nearest town of any size to the frontier with Kubrat, which also meant it was the town most exposed to Kubrati raiders. The farmland around it had brought in a lean harvest this year, if any.

Company by company, regiment by regiment, the extra cavalrymen Maniakes had brought with him peeled off from the main body moving toward Imbros and took up concealed positions in the woods south of the city. Riders could easily summon them to come to the Avtokrator's aid or, at need, to avenge him. Given the vision Bagdasares had shown him, Maniakes did not think it would reach that point. As the walls of Imbros came into sight, he realized he was betting his life on that vision.

Those walls had known better days. He had heard as much, but seeing it with his own eyes was a shock. The Kubratoi had torn great gaps in the stonework, not during a siege but after they got into the town. Till the fortifications were repaired, the barbarians could force their way into Imbros any time they chose. Maniakes resolved to rebuild the walls as soon as he could. How soon that would be, he couldn't guess.

A horseman on a shaggy brown plains pony approached the Avtokrator's party from the north. He carried a white-painted shield hung from the end of a lance. As he drew near, Maniakes saw he was wearing trousers of stained and faded leather, a wolfskin cap, and a jacket of marten fur unfastened to show off the cloth-of-gold beneath it: the last a sure bit of loot from Videssian soil.

Maniakes ordered his own shield of truce displayed. At that, the rider, who had reined in, came forward once more. "I, Moundioukh, greets you, your Majesty, in the names of the great and fearsome khagans of the Kubratoi, Etzilios the magnifolent," he called in understandable but mangled Videssian.

"I greet you and your khagan in return; Etzilios your ruler is indeed most magnifolent," Maniakes said gravely, holding in a smile by main force. A couple of men behind him snickered, but Moundioukh, luckily, did not notice. He sat straight in the saddle, beaming with pride to hear the Avtokrator, as he thought, honor the khagan.

"Etzilios bewaits for youse," Moundioukh said. "Where does youse wants to meets with him?"

"We need a stretch of flat, open ground," Maniakes answered, "the better to show off our mimes from the Amphitheater and the speed of our horses." He waved a hand. "Here where I am now would do well enough, if it pleases the magnifolent Etzilios." He warned himself to be careful with that, but liked it so well he had trouble heeding his own good sense.

"This should pleases him, yesly. I will takes your words his way." Moundioukh wheeled his horse and rode back toward and then past Imbros at a ground-eating trot the animal looked able to keep up all day.

Off in the distance, horns brayed like donkeys with throats of bronze, a cry more like a challenge than a fanfare. Maniakes tried making a joke of it. "Either that's Etzilios coming, or we're about to be attacked." Then he listened to himself. Just on the off chance, he made sure his sword was loose in its scabbard.

But Etzilios and his guardsmen advanced peaceably enough. Maniakes had no trouble picking out the khagan of the Kubratoi: his horse had trappings ornamented with gold, and he wore a gold circlet on his fur cap. As he got closer, Maniakes saw his sword also had a hilt covered with gold leaf.

The khagan was older than Maniakes had expected, his long, unkempt beard well on the way toward going white. He was stocky and wide-shouldered; even with those years on him, Maniakes would not have cared to meet him in a wrestling match. He had only a stump for the little finger of his left hand. His face was weathered and leathery; his nose had a list to the left.

His eyes . . . When Maniakes saw those eyes under gray, shaggy brows, he understood how Etzilios ruled his unruly people. He lacked the schooling, the formal training a man could acquire in the Empire of Videssos, but if he didn't prove one of the two or three shrewdest men Maniakes had ever seen, the Avtokrator would own himself mightily surprised. After a moment, Maniakes realized why Etzilios struck him so: the khagan put him in mind of a barbarous version of his own father.

Etzilios spoke a gruff word in his own language, then held up his right hand. The horsemen who had accompanied him halted at that word of command. He rode out alone into the open space between his party and Maniakes'. Halfway across it, he reined in and waited.

Maniakes knew a challenge when he saw one. He booted his horse in the ribs and advanced to meet the khagan. "Do you speak Videssian?" he called as he approached. "Or shall we need an interpreter?"

"I speak Videssian, so I can understand you people," Etzilios answered, using the imperial tongue far more accurately than Moundioukh had. "When I want you to understand me, I most often speak with this." His right hand covered the swordhilt.

"I know that speech, too," Maniakes said at once. He saw clearly that he dared not let Etzilios intimidate him or take advantage of him in any way, for, if the khagan ever gained an edge, he would never let it go. "You have but to begin it here and we shall go back to war. You will not find me or my men easy meat for your taking."

"I did not come here to fight," Etzilios said with the air of a man making a great concession. "You have said you will pay me gold to keep from fighting."

"That is so," Maniakes agreed. "Fear of the Kubratoi, I should tell you, is not the only reason I am taking this course. We can thrash you if we must—you did not beat Likinios' army, after all."

"And what does that have to do with the price of a good horse?" the khagan asked. "We still hold our land, and look what became of Likinios—yes, and of Genesios, too, who threw him down. The battles do not matter, Videssian Avtokrator. We won the war—otherwise, we would be paying you."

Almost, Maniakes pulled out his sword then and there and attacked Etzilios. Robbing the Kubratoi of a man of such long sight would be a great good for Videssos. But if an assassination failed, the barbarians would renew their assaults, fueled by righteous fury. Not for the first time, Maniakes regretfully set aside the thought of murder.

He said, "I have brought the forty thousand gold pieces of the first year's tribute to which you agreed with my envoy, the excellent Triphylles."

"That man talks too much and thinks too well of himself," Etzilios said.

Since Maniakes had noted both those flaws in Triphylles, he found silence on them the better part of prudence. Instead, he made a manful effort at returning to the subject at hand: "As I say, I have with me the gold I will pay you in exchange for a year's peace. I will give it to you after the entertainments I have planned in your honor."

"I'd just as soon have it now," Etzilios said. "What are these entertainments, anyhow?"

"For your enjoyment, I have brought from Videssos the city two of our leading mime troupes, whose antics will make you laugh," Maniakes said.

"People hopping around without saying anything and pretending they're funny?" Etzilios spat on the ground. "I've seen the like in towns of yours I've taken. I could live a long time without seeing it again. Why don't you just give me the gold and toss out the folderol? Then you can go home and worry about Makuran. That's what you have in mind, isn't it?"

Maniakes opened his mouth, then closed it again without saying anything. He had never heard Videssian civilization so cavalierly dismissed. And Etzilios couldn't have divined his purposes better had he been in the room when Maniakes hammered them out with Rhegorios, Triphylles, and his own father. At last, after a deep breath and a pause for thought, the Avtokrator said, "We've also brought fine horses for racing."

"You should have said that first," Etzilios told him. "I'll put up with anything to see good horses run. I'll even watch your stupid mimes, and I won't pick my nose to distract them while I'm doing it." He chuckled. Maniakes wondered if he had really done such a thing. If he had, it probably would have served its purpose.

"Let us feast together and rest this evening, your men and mine," Maniakes said, "and in the morning you can enjoy the mimes—or not—and we will hold horse races, and then, after we pray to the lord with the great and good mind to preserve the arrangement as we have made it, I will convey to you the gold and we shall be at peace."

"You pray to Phos," Etzilios answered. "Me, I worship my sword alone. It's served me better than your god ever did."

Maniakes stared at him. He had never heard the lord with the great and good mind not just rejected—the Makuraners worshiped their deity, the God, instead of Phos—but dismissed as unimportant. Etzilios was a resolute heathen, and his people with him. Most in Khatrish and Thatagush followed Phos these days, but the Kubratoi clung to the ways they had brought off the Pardrayan steppe.

"Other than on the prayers, are we agreed?" Maniakes asked.

"Oh, aye, we're agreed," Etzilios said. "If you'll hold on a bit, I'll even have my men bring your cooks some sheep they can use for the feast."

"Generous of you," Maniakes said tonelessly. He would have been more appreciative had he not been certain the sheep the Kubratoi were contributing came from Videssian flocks.

If Etzilios noticed the irony, he didn't show it. With a vague wave to Maniakes, he turned his horse and rode back toward his waiting men. Maniakes did the same. The cooks set some of his soldiers to work digging trenches and others cutting wood to fill those trenches and build racks above them for roasting meat. The cooks also broke out great tuns of fermented fish sauce and jars of peeled garlic cloves kept fresh and flavorful in olive oil. Maniakes wondered what the Kubratoi would make of the condiments. If they didn't fancy them, his own men would have more to eat. He hoped just that would happen.

As promised, the Kubratoi drove a flock of sheep to the Videssian cooks. They did indeed look like Videssian animals, but, for the sake of peace, Maniakes asked no questions. The sheep bleated in desperation as they were butchered; cattle lowed out a last futile protest. Before long, the savory smoke that rose from the cooking trenches had Maniakes' mouth watering.

He picked some of his most trusted soldiers, men who would not resent missing a chance to stuff themselves, and sent them out to form a perimeter around the camp. He also warned the goldpieces' guards to be especially wary. Then, satisfied he had done all he could to keep himself and the gold safe during the celebration, he began to hope he would enjoy himself.

He went over to the chief cook, an enormously fat man named Ostrys, and said, "Be generous with the wine you give the barbarians. The happier we make them, the more they're liable to reveal of what their master truly intends for tomorrow."

"It shall be just as you say, your Majesty," Ostrys replied, setting a pudgy finger by the side of his nose. But for his dark, heavy beard, his looks would have inclined Maniakes to guess him a eunuch: He was round enough for any two of the palace servitors. He knew, though, that Ostrys had not only a wife but several sons who looked like him and shared his nearly spherical contours.

The smell of cooking meat drew the Kubratoi in the same way it would have drawn hungry wolves from the forest. They fraternized amiably enough with their Videssian counterparts; some of them had fought one another before. Most of the nomads spoke some Videssian. Maniakes wondered how they had learned it—maybe from women they had stolen.

Priests paraded with thuribles, sending up clouds of sweet-scented incense that mingled with the odors of firewood and roasting mutton and beef to make the feast flavorful to the nose. The blue-robed clerics also sent up sonorous prayers for peace between Videssos and Kubrat, beseeching Phos to make both sides honest and righteous and to hold deceit away from them.

Maniakes glanced over to see how Etzilios would take that. The khagan's left hand twisted in a sign that looked like one of the gestures of aversion Videssian peasants used. "By the good god, they're not trying to ensorcel you," Maniakes said.

Etzilios looked down at his hand as if it had turned traitor. "I trust no magics but those of my shamans," he said, and smiled a carnivorous smile. "If they blunder, I can punish them."

Barbarian, Maniakes thought. *A clever barbarian, but a barbarian all the same. He sees what he wants now and he takes it now, without worrying about what will happen later. Later is a different world.*

What Etzilios seemed to want now was meat. He sat crosslegged on the grass, a growing pile of bones around him. He drank, too, though more moderately than Maniakes had expected; he nursed his wine well enough to wave on Videssian servitors about every other time they came by with fresh jars. That moderation did not keep him from belching cavernously. Maniakes was not offended; among the nomads, such rumblings signified approval of the fare offered.

"You Videssians should have done this years ago," Etzilios said, beaming at the feast. "But no—instead you thought to chase me, like dog after fox. But no fox am I—I am a wolf, as you have seen." He bared his teeth. They were yellow as a wolf's; in so much, if no further, he spoke the truth.

"We're making peace now. We shouldn't worry about past quarrels," Maniakes said. He wished his men were chasing the Kubratoi right now. Had he not faced war on two fronts, his men would have been doing just that. Saying as much to Etzilios struck him as unwise.

The khagan frowned, rubbed at his considerable belly. "You make this mutton too spicy, I think," he said, climbing to his feet. "My guts gripe me."

Maniakes remembered Triphylles' complaint about eating endless meals of mutton without garlic. What seemed mildly seasoned meat to a Videssian was liable to be too much for a Kubrati to appreciate. He was just glad Etzilios hadn't accused him of putting poison in the sauce.

"I will be back later," Etzilios said, and lumbered off toward a stand of elms not far away. Maniakes hadn't been sure the nomads bothered to seek privacy for performing their basic bodily functions. He hoped Etzilios had nothing worse than a bellyache. If he suddenly dropped dead now, the Kubratoi would think Maniakes had slain him—when in fact he had decided not to try.

Maniakes sipped his own wine. When he looked around at the feast, he felt reasonably pleased with himself. His men and the Kubratoi seemed to be getting along well, in spite of old enmity. Not far away, a Kubrati who didn't speak Videssian was using vivid hand gestures to show how one of his people's horses would leave all the Videssian nags in the dust. The imperials sitting by the nomad quite plainly disagreed, but nobody hauled out a sword to back up his opinion.

If Etzilios saw that, Maniakes hoped he would be pleased, too. The Avtokrator frowned. Etzilios still hadn't come back from that stand of trees. Whatever call of nature he had had to answer, he should have been done long since. Either he truly had been taken deathly ill in there, or—

A couple of couriers sat nearby. Turning to them, Maniakes said, "Mount and ride to our waiting horsemen. Tell them to be ready." The couriers got to their feet. Above the friendly din of the feast, Maniakes heard a drumroll of hoofbeats. "No, tell them to come. Run to your horses, before the Kubratoi here try to stop you."

"Is something amiss, your Majesty?" Kameas asked as the couriers dashed away. Then he heard the approaching horses, too. His face went from sallow to white. He sketched the suncircle over his heart.

"Hide!" Maniakes told him urgently. "If you can, pick someplace where they won't ever find you. Good luck, esteemed sir."

That done, Maniakes had no more time to worry about the vestiarios. He scrambled to his own feet, cursing the insistence on ceremony that had made him deck himself out in the goldencrusted imperial robe rather than chain mail. Even his sword was a ceremonial blade, not meant for real fighting.

Here came a sentry, riding as if Skotos were at his horse's heels. It wasn't the dark god, but it was the next worst thing: a whole great swarm of Kubratoi, thundering forward with gleaming scimitars upraised.

Seeing the blades gave Maniakes an instant of relief. The nomads would not loose a shower of arrows from their deadly bows, not with their own men so intermingled with his. He cherished that relief, suspecting it was all he would be able to enjoy for a long time to come.

"To arms, men of Videssos!" he shouted, as loud as he could. "We are betrayed!" He drew his ridiculous toy of a sword and slashed at a Kubrati noble sitting a few feet away.

The leather of the nomad's sleeve was enough to armor his flesh against the dull edge's bite.

In an instant, peace exploded into pandemonium. Videssians and Kubratoi who had been chatting snatched out blades and went at one another. Some of the Videssians ran for their horses, the better to resist the barbarians bearing down on them. Someone also had the presence of mind to run down the rows of the nomads' mounts, shouting, slashing tethers, and whacking the animals with his blade. Not many of the Kubratoi from among the feasters got mounted themselves.

Maniakes saw only disjointed fragments of the action. The barbarian he had tried to cut down surged to his feet and drew his own curved blade, which was no toy. Maniakes didn't want to try turning it with his gilded toothpick. He snatched up a heavy silver wine cup and dashed its contents full in the Kubrati's face. The fellow roared like a branded bull and clapped his hands to his eyes. Maniakes hit him over the head with the cup. He crumpled. Maniakes threw away his ceremonial sword and grabbed the Kubrati scimitar. Now he had a blade with which he could fight.

And none too soon. The Kubratoi were upon him and his men. He slashed at a nomad horseman, then sprang aside to keep from being trampled. Instead of going after the Kubratoi themselves, he cut at their horses all around him. His blade bit again and again. Ponies squealed in pain. That kept their riders too busy trying to keep control to have too much time to devote to murdering him.

As he fought for his life, he wondered what sort of nonsense Bagdasares had shown him in the magic mirror. How was he supposed to break free of this murderous press and get back to Videssos the city? As he dodged and ducked and cut, he knew he was lucky to be surviving from moment to moment.

A Kubrati close by snatched at an arrow that suddenly sprouted above one eye. A moment later, the nomad's hands relaxed and he slid, dead, from the saddle. Maniakes scrambled onto the little plains horse the Kubrati had been riding. Like a lot of his fellows, the Kubrati had kept his stirrup leathers very short so he could rise in the saddle to shoot. Maniakes felt as if he were trying to touch his ears with his knees.

He didn't care. On a horse, the barbarians still might slaughter him like a sheep. They couldn't mash him like a bug underfoot, though. He fought his way toward a knot of his own men who were still fighting with some kind of order. He wondered how long till his own reinforcements arrived.

Pressure on that knot of determined fighting men eased. It wasn't Videssians coming to the rescue, not yet. Some of the Kubratoi, instead of finishing their foes, were busy plundering the imperial pavilion and the rest of the camp. A separate fight broke out when they overran the guards protecting the horses that carried the tribute and started quarreling over the goldpieces like a pack of dogs over a juicy bone.

"Videssos!" he shouted, lest anyone see the pony and take him for a Kubrati. Since he was wearing the gaudy imperial robe and the red boots, that was highly unlikely, but no one can think of everything in the midst of battle.

"Your Majesty!" The soldiers toward whom he was fighting had no trouble recognizing him. When at last he joined them, he felt like a man who had managed to seize a spar after his ship sank in a sea fight.

The analogy had but one flaw: the spar he had seized was in itself in danger of sinking. The Kubratoi, both afoot and mounted, raged against their outnumbered Videssian foes. They shouted to one another in their own guttural language, captains urging their men away from the loot of the imperial tent, away from the spilled goldpieces, and into the fight. The captains were wise enough to know the time for looting was after a triumph, not before. The men were harder to convince.

Because of that, Maniakes and his guards, though beleaguered, had not been overwhelmed when horns rang out from the south. "Videssos!" This time the cry rang from hundreds of throats.

"Videssos!" Maniakes shouted again. He waved the scimitar to show he still lived. Had he been on his own horse, he would have urged it to rear. On a beast he had acquired so irregularly, though, he took no chances. As long as he was able to stay in the saddle, that sufficed.

One thing the arrival of Videssian reinforcements did: it reminded the Kubratoi they were in a fight, not just a plundering expedition. They had ignored their officers in the search for booty. Ignoring the prospect of being killed was something else again. They snatched bows from their cases and plied the oncoming imperials with arrows. The Videssians shot back. Even more than he had before, Maniakes wished he had a shield.

He waved again. "To me! To me!" he cried. If the reinforcements could reach him, what had been a chaotic struggle to keep from being ridden down and crushed could suddenly become a fight the Videssians might win ... or might still lose. Maniakes looked about worriedly. More Kubratoi were still coming down from the north. He had brought fifteen hundred men, over and above those about whom he had agreed with Etzilios. He had the bad feeling the khagan had brought more.

No help for that. He spurred southward, fighting toward the imperials as they neared him. Squeezed between two forces, the Kubratoi who tried to bar his path gave way—and, suddenly, the spar Maniakes had seized seemed a boat instead.

"Your Majesty!" the men bawled. "Here, take this!" "And this!" Someone set a helmet on his head, someone else thrust a shield at him. Since the trooper who offered it had a mailshirt while he wore no armor beneath his robes, he gladly took it. Sometimes, he thought, Phos did answer prayers.

He hadn't fought like a common trooper for years, thinking of nothing past himself and staying alive from minute to minute. He had led charges after he attained high rank, but then, even as he battled, he had had the shape of the whole fight in his mind. The struggle for survival brought him fresh awareness of what his soldiers went through. But now he had a proper battle to run. He waved men to left and right, widening his line and trying to keep the Kubratoi from outflanking the reinforcements as they had effortlessly done with his accepted force of guards.

He didn't care for the shape of this fight. Etzilios had too many men, and they were pressing too hard. Presumably Etzilios also had the priests and the mimes and the racehorses Maniakes had brought up from Videssos the city. The racehorses he would undoubtedly treat well. The Kubratoi, though, had resisted all efforts to get them to accept Phos' faith. The priests might became martyrs for the greater glory of the good god. And Phos would have to be the one who helped the mimes, too.

A rider came hurrying up to Maniakes and cried, "Your Majesty, try as we will, we can't hold them on the left. They keep overlapping us and forcing us to fall back. If we don't, they get round us, and then we are undone."

Maniakes looked that way. Sure enough, the line was sagging badly. He looked eastward, to the right. The line sagged there, too, though no one had come to tell him about it. "Blow 'retreat,' " he called to the trumpeters. "They'll surround us if we don't give ground."

The melancholy horn calls rang out. Videssian military doctrine didn't represent retreat as anything to cause shame. Realistically, no army could expect to win every fight. If you didn't win, staying to be slaughtered was stupider than drawing back, because it lowered your chances of winning the next fight.

But regardless of whether retreat was shameful, it was fraught with danger. If soldiers gave way to panic, they were just a mob, and they would be massacred as surely as if they had let the enemy surround them. "Hold together!" Maniakes shouted, over and over till his throat was raw. "If we hang together, they can't drive us like wolves after deer."

Sticking together as they drew back, as the Kubratoi poured arrows into them from both flanks and from ahead, took almost superhuman discipline. Maniakes looked around for Etzilios. If he could kill the khagan, the Kubratoi might collapse. He had had his chances earlier and passed them by. Now it was too late; Etzilios, like any sensible general, led his troops from behind. With a manifest victory developing before their eyes, they didn't need to see their ruler in action to be inspired.

More horns rang out, the braying horns of the barbarians. A quick charge at the right of Maniakes' crumbling line made him send men there to hold it. But the charge proved a feint. Screaming like fiends, the Kubratoi staged another charge into the Videssian center—and broke it.

The rout Maniakes had dreaded was on. With Kubratoi in among them as well as on their flanks, the imperials no longer even tried to hold firm. Giving up any thought of staying together, they fled southward singly and in small bands, no thought but escape in their minds. The Kubratoi pursued, baying on the chase.

Maniakes was swept along with the rest. A group of about fifty men clung together—too large for the Kubratoi to assail when so many smaller, easier targets were there for the taking. But then one of the nomads spotted the imperial raiment in among that band of Videssians, and after that they were never free of the foe again.

Had Etzilios been anywhere close by, he no doubt would have urged his men to go after the Avtokrator regardless of the casualties it cost them. But the khagan was elsewhere on the field, and none of the men dogging Maniakes thought to ride off again and ask what to do next: being barbarously self-sufficient, they believed themselves able to make their own choices.

Maniakes spied a stand of oaks ahead. "Let's ride in among them," he said.

"Aye, why not?" one of the soldiers said. "The trees will keep them from raining arrows on us the way they have been."

"We'd go faster through open country," another man said. "The closer we stick to the road, the better the time we'll make."

"How fast isn't everything," Maniakes answered. "How you go counts, too. Come on." He guided his horse toward the trees. Most of the men in the band went with him. Six or eight, though, struck off on their own in the hopes the road would give them a better chance to escape the nomads.

Once in among the trees, Maniakes brought his blowing horse to a halt and dismounted. "Here, your Majesty, you can piss later," a trooper said gruffly. Maniakes ignored him. He undid the golden belt that held his robe closed, and threw it on the ground. Then he pulled off the heavy robe with its precious metallic threads and draped it over a branch. Wearing only his thin linen undertunic and drawers, he climbed back onto the Kubrati pony. "Now they won't hound us so much," he said. "I don't look like the Avtokrator any more."

His troopers nodded approvingly. He himself felt low enough to walk under a mouse without ruffling its belly fur. What could be more dishonorable and disgraceful than abandoning the imperial raiment to escape with your hide unpunctured? Only one thing occurred to him: dying when you had a means of survival at hand. Even so, he knew he would replay this scene in his nightmares as long as he lived. Whether he would live long enough to have more nightmares remained an open question.

More than forty men emerged from the south side of the stand of oaks. Maniakes was suddenly much less conspicuous than he had been. Now the Kubratoi harassed his band no more than any other of like size. He wondered if he should also have thrown away the red boots. That would have made riding harder. Besides, keeping them on let him cling to the notion that he had salvaged something of the imperial regalia.

"Where now, your Majesty?" a trooper asked.

"Back to Videssos the city, as best we can," Maniakes answered. Bagdasares' magic—and how was Bagdasares now? and Kameas? and the servitors? and the mimes? and everyone

else Maniakes had led on this disastrous jaunt?—had shown he
would come back to the city. But it hadn't shown him safe inside the walls. Now more than ever, he wished he could have
looked back over his shoulder and seen if anyone was gaining
on him.

As the routed Videssians fled south, the pursuit grew more
distant. Maniakes wanted to draw more consolation from that
than he actually could. It wasn't so much that he and his comrades had outrun the nomads, though that was part of it. But
more, Maniakes knew all too well, was that the Kubratoi were
busy plundering not only his camp with all its riches but also
the surrounding countryside. How many Videssian peasants
would they round up and herd north to labor for them? Where
would he find other peasants to replace the ones the barbarians
were kidnapping? With the Kubratoi in the north and the
Makuraners ranging as they pleased in the westlands, Videssos
might have no people left in a few years' time.

"We have to be careful not to founder our horses,"
Maniakes warned his comrades in misfortune. "If they break
down before we get home, I expect we're done for."

His own pony, the one he had taken from the dead Kubrati,
was still working magnificently. It was an ugly little beast,
short and rough-coated, but it could run. Every so often, he
paused to let it rest and pull up some grass and weeds from the
ground. It seemed happy enough with that.

After a while, his own stomach started growling. The erup-
tion of the Kubratoi had come before he got a chance to eat
much at the feast. He rummaged in the beast's saddlebags to
see what its former owner had been carrying. The first thing he
found was a skin that, when he untied it, gave off the odor of
sour milk. He threw it away. The Kubratoi might live on such
fare, but Videssians? A moment after he had rejected the stuff,
he cursed himself for a fool. No matter how nasty it smelled,
it was food of a sort, and he was liable to be hungry by the
time he got to Videssos the city.

The nomad had also been carrying strips of sun-dried mutton and flat griddlecakes of barley. The mutton was so hard, he
could hardly bite it. As for the griddlecakes, they came as
close to having no flavor whatsoever as anything he had ever
eaten. He wolfed them down regardless. They had kept the nomad going, and they would do the same for him.

Camp that night was a cold, miserable affair. No one dared
light a fire, for fear it would draw the Kubratoi. A raw wind

blew out of the northwest. It smelled of rain, though none fell that night. Maniakes and his companions counted themselves lucky there. They had only a few blankets among them, and huddled together for warmth like the luckless sheep Maniakes' cooks had butchered for what should have been a celebration of peace with the Kubratoi.

Trying to find someplace comfortable on the ground, trying to keep the rest of the Videssians from kicking or elbowing him, Maniakes dreamed up a whole flock of grandiose vengeances to visit upon Etzilios' head. The one he liked best involved loosing Genesios' wizard, the old man who had almost killed him, against the khagan. Setting that mage, whoever and wherever he was, on the foes of Videssos for a change struck him as only fitting and proper. He fell asleep still imagining revenge.

He woke several times in the night, from people poking him or just because he was cold. At last, though the trees, he saw the gray light of false dawn. Yawning, he got to his feet. A good many other men were already awake; the morning looked as wretched as the night had been.

The soldiers shared what food they had. By the time evening came again, their supplies would be gone. The horses let out snorts of complaint as the men clambered onto them. Maniakes' steppe pony seemed fresher than most of the larger, more elegant beasts around it.

They had just left the woods when a cold rain started falling. Though it soaked him to the skin, Maniakes was not altogether unhappy to see it. "Let's see the Kubratoi try to track us when everything turns to muck," he said, and punctuated the remark with a sneeze.

The sneeze notwithstanding, that was the first even slightly optimistic thing he had said since Etzilios proved more adept at treachery than he was at preparing for it. One of the troopers promptly ruined his comment by saying, "They don't hardly need to track us. Long as they keep coming south, they're liable to run into us, and they ain't got nowheres to go but south."

Sure enough, not half an hour later they came upon a band of nomads riding on a track paralleling theirs. The Kubratoi were there in numbers about equal to those of the imperials, but did not attack them. That puzzled Maniakes, till he burst out, "They don't want to go at us sword to sword, and the rain would get their bowstrings wet." He sneezed again, this time almost cheerfully.

As gloomy day darkened toward black night, they came upon a peasant village. The farmers there gave Maniakes some baggy wool trousers and a tunic to put on instead of his soaked drawers while those dried in front of a fire, and later over them. They fed the soldiers bread and cheese and eggs, and killed a few of the chickens that pecked on the dirt floors of their homes.

When Maniakes tried to tell them who he was and to promise he would be grateful once he got back to Videssos the city, he found they didn't believe he was the Avtokrator, not even after he showed them the red boots. That touched him to the heart, at least until an old man said, "Don't matter who y'be, so long as y'got soldiers at your back. Farmers what's smart, they don't say no to soldiers."

Maniakes had enough soldiers to overawe them, but not enough to protect them if the Kubratoi attacked in any numbers. And after his band left the village on the southbound road, no one would be left to protect it at all.

As he was preparing to ride out the next morning, the old man took him aside and said, "Young feller, all that talk about bein' Avtokrator's fine and funny when you spin it afore the likes of us. But if Genesios Avtokrator ever gets wind of it, he'll have your guts for garters, likely tell. He's one hard man, Genesios is, by all they say, and not much for joking."

"I'll remember that," Maniakes said, and left it there. He wondered if any isolated villages off in the hinterlands thought Likinios was still Avtokrator. If you didn't go to town and traders didn't come to you, how would you find out what the truth was?

He and his men worked their way southward, adding other bands of fugitives as they went until, by the time they reached the Long Walls, they numbered two or three hundred. They scared off a troop of Kubratoi not far from their own size and were beginning to feel like soldiers again.

"Two more days and we're back in the city," Maniakes said, trying to hearten them further. "We'll get reinforcements and we'll have our revenge." A few of the men raised a cheer. That made Maniakes feel worse, not better. Where would he come up with reinforcements, with so much of Videssos in turmoil? If he did come up with them, where would he get the goldpieces to pay them? Those were conjurations he would gladly have assigned to the mages of the Sorcerers' Collegium, if only he had thought they had some hope of success.

Then all thoughts of what might happen and what probably wouldn't happen were swept away by a cry of despair from the rearguard: "The Kubratoi! The Kubratoi are on our heels!"

Maniakes looked back over his shoulder. He had some hope of driving the barbarians off—till he saw their numbers. Those offered but one remedy. "Fly!" he shouted. "They'll ride us into the mud if we don't." He no longer thought Etzilios was following him in particular. It seemed far more likely the Kubratoi were just taking advantage of Videssian weakness to plunder as far south, as close to the imperial city, as they could. The cause didn't matter. The result did—and it was quite as bad as deliberate pursuit.

The horses were worn to shadows of themselves. What should have been gallops were exhausted trots. Had the Kubratoi pursued harder, they might have overhauled and overwhelmed the Videssian stragglers. But their horses were frazzled, too.

It made for a strange sort of chase. Maniakes was reminded of a mime troupe he had once seen at a Midwinter's Day celebration, where everyone moved as if half frozen, drawing out each action to preposterous lengths for the sake of a laugh from the crowd. Even the memory might have been funny had he not been fleeing for his life and had he not also remembered the Kubratoi sweeping down on the two mime troupes he had brought from the capital in hopes of amusing them.

Rain started coming down again, hard and cold. Road and fields alike turned to mire, which made both pursued and pursuers slower still. Normally, the downpour would have helped Maniakes shake the Kubratoi off his trail. Now, though, they knew he was heading for Videssos the city. They didn't need to see him to follow him.

He thought about breaking off and making for some provincial town instead. But the Kubratoi had already sacked Imbros, one of the more strongly fortified cities in their path. That meant no provincial town was safe from them. If he could get behind the indomitable walls of Videssos the city, the barbarians would storm against them in vain. If—

Bagdasares' mirror had shown him approaching the imperial city. Had he not known—or at least strongly believed—he would get that far, he might have given way to despair. As it was, he kept riding, hoping to meet a rescuing force coming out of the capital and turning the tables on the nomads who pursued him.

No rescuers came forth. He was forced to conclude that he, his comrades, and, worse luck, the Kubratoi had outridden news of their coming. As far as anyone in Videssos the city knew, he had paid Etzilios his tribute and bought three years' peace in return.

"I wish I only knew as far as they did," he said when that thought crossed his mind.

At last, he and those of his fellows whom the Kubratoi had not taken came into sight of the imperial capital. The sun had come out and was shining in a watery sort of way, as if to warn that this stab at decent weather would not last long. Even watery sunlight, though, was enough to make the gilded globes that marked Phos' temples glitter and sparkle.

Here was the view the magic mirror had given him. From now on, he realized, he was on his own. Past this point, he had no guarantee of his own safety. He dug his heels into the barrel of the poor worn steppe pony. The beast snorted in exhausted protest but somehow managed to shamble on a little faster.

Maniakes and the riders with him began shouting toward the walls. "A rescue! By the good god, come to our aid!"

An arrow whined past Maniakes' head. Some of the Kubratoi still had shafts to shoot, then. Perhaps twenty feet away, a man cried out, slumped in the saddle, and slid from his horse: how cruel, to have escaped so much and yet to fall within sight of safety. Maniakes urged on his mount yet again. He was not safe himself, either.

And then, at last, a sound sweeter to him than the chorus of monks who hymned Phos' praises in the High Temple, catapults up on the wall and in the siege towers began to buck and thump, throwing darts and great stones at the Kubratoi. Chains rumbling, an iron-faced portcullis lifted. A regiment of mounted archers and javelin men rode out against the barbarians.

Resentfully, the Kubratoi withdrew, shooting over their shoulders at the Videssians who had driven them back from the walls of the capital. The imperials did not chase them far; they had a way of turning and mauling pursuers who broke ranks thinking the foe was done for.

The Videssians' commander, a handsome fellow on a handsome horse, looked down his nose at the draggled men he had rescued. "Who," he asked scornfully, "is in charge of this rag-tag and bobtail?"

"I am," Maniakes answered, weary in every pore and hardly daring to believe he had won free to the capital at last.

He had forgotten what sort of spectacle he must have seemed, filthy, dressed in ill-fitting peasant clothes, and riding a Kubrati pony on its last legs. The impressive officer set hands on hips and demanded, "And who, sirrah, are *you*?"

Worn as they were, some of the men who had come down from Imbros muttered back and forth and smiled a little, waiting to see how he would respond to that.

"I am Maniakes son on Maniakes," he said. "Who are you, excellent sir?"

The handsome officer started to laugh, but was not quite altogether a fool. He looked at Maniakes' face, then at his boots, which, however mud-spattered they had become, were undeniably red beneath the grime. "Forgive your servant Ipokasios!" he cried, suddenly solicitous rather than scornful. "I failed to recognize you, your Majesty. A thousand pardons!"

In his alarm, he grew almost as flowery as a Makuraner. Maniakes held up a hand to stem the tide of self-reproach. "Excellent Ipokasios, for driving the Kubratoi from my trail I would forgive you a great deal more than not knowing who I am, though I hope you'll greet the next ragged traveler with a touch more forbearance than you showed me."

Ipokasios hung his handsome head. "It shall be just as you say, your Majesty." Maniakes wouldn't have risked a copper to win a pile of goldpieces that it would be as he had said—he knew well-bred arrogance when he saw it—but perhaps the officer believed he was telling the truth, and was properly apologetic any which way.

From behind Ipokasios, one of his men cried, "But, your Majesty, what *happened*?"

That was the question Ipokasios should have come up with himself. Maniakes and his comrades explained: variations on the theme of treachery. The men from Videssos the city cursed to hear what had happened to the imperial camp, the priests, the mimes, and the gold.

"To say nothing of all the peasants the Kubratoi raped away from the northern marches after they routed us," Maniakes added glumly. Without enough peasants, the rest of the Empire would soon grind to a halt, though city folk had trouble remembering it.

"Peasants." Ipokasios dismissed them with a short, contemptuous wave, which proved only that he had never paused to think about where the bread he ate every day came from.

"Enough chatter," Maniakes said; making Ipokasios understand that his view of the way the Empire worked was too simple would have taken more time than Maniakes had to spare and might have taken longer than winning the war would have done. "I need to get back to the palaces as fast as I can go. I blundered into disaster; now I have to start setting it to rights."

Few people on the streets of Videssos the city recognized him as he made his way across town toward the palace quarter. That he found refreshing; being the focus of everyone's gaze had quickly come to seem a trial. Next time he achieved the present effect, though, he vowed not to use such drastic means.

Few people recognized him in the palace quarter, either. The bureaucrats who deigned to notice him did so for his ragged clothes and scruffy horse. What they were wondering, very plainly, was how such a ragged fellow had become part of a body of imperial soldiers.

At the imperial residence, guards and eunuchs likewise failed to realize what he was—until one of the latter exclaimed in high-pitched tones of horror, "Phos preserve us! It is the Avtokrator, returned in this rough guise."

The servitors fell on him like an army, crying out the virtues of soaking and steaming and hot scented oil and clean linens and silk and squab stuffed with mushrooms and fine fragrant wine. He held up a hand. "Those all sound wonderful," he said, and, as if to prove it, his belly rumbled. "First, though, I'll see my wife and my father and let them know I'm alive and what's happened to me."

"Your Majesty," one of the eunuchs quavered, "where is the esteemed Kameas?"

Maniakes grimaced, but that question, like so many others, had to be faced. "If he's lucky, prominent sir, the Kubratoi have captured him. If he's not lucky—" He didn't think he had to elaborate on that.

The eunuch looked down at the stairs of the imperial residence. "If being captured by the barbarians is good fortune, Phos ward us from the bad," he said.

After dismissing the troops who had escorted him through the city—and praising those who had fought and fled with him from just outside Imbros—Maniakes went into the imperial residence. Drawn by the commotion, Niphone waited just inside the entrance. By the expression on her face, Maniakes gauged the state of his own decrepitude.

"I'll be all right," he said. "I'm just hungry and tired and dirty and worn to a nub. I wish the rest of my news were as good as what I can say about myself." In a few gloomy sentences, he told once more of Etzilios' assault.

Niphone's finger traced the sun-circle above her heart. "So long as you are safe," she whispered.

"I'm safe," Maniakes said, and, for the first time, began to believe it himself. Every moment of every day since the Kubrati surprise had passed for him as if he were a hunted animal, with the huntsman always about to fall on him. Only luck and watchfulness had saved him, and that watchfulness had grown so ingrained in a few short days that lifting it took strong, conscious effort. After a moment, he went on, "But so much and so many have been lost: Bagdasares, Kameas, the treasure I was to give the khagan in exchange for peace, the priests who would have blessed that peace, the mimes and horses Etzilios would have marveled to see. All gone."

Niphone sketched the sun-circle again. "May the men safely walk the bridge of the separator and reach Phos' light. As for the beasts and treasure, you are the Avtokrator. Of these things you can always get more."

"Would it were so easy!" Maniakes said with a bitter laugh. "If only I could order them from a storeroom or conjure them up and have them appear when I commanded. But I cannot do those things, and I do not know where to lay my hands on more gold."

"My father is logothete of the treasury," Niphone said, as if reminding him of something he had forgotten. "Speak to him. He will get gold for you."

Maniakes had spoken with Kourikos, more than once. The main thing his father-in-law had told him was that not only the coffers but also the yearly tax revenues were disastrously low. That was hardly surprising, after years of invasion and civil war, and with the Makuraners in the westlands and the Kubratoi not only working great destruction but also keeping tax collectors from even reaching huge tracts of land. Till some of the invaders were driven out, the imperial government would have to run on shoestrings and cheese parings.

No point in burdening Niphone with any of that, though. Maniakes said, "We'll do what we can, that's all. That's all I want to do for myself right now: bathe, eat, and sleep for a week."

Rotrude would have looked at him out of the corner of her eye and said, "And then?" He could all but hear the words, and the saucy flavor her Haloga drawl would lend them. Niphone just nodded earnestly. Maniakes sighed a silent sigh. *We'll do all we can, that's all,* he thought.

Stragglers from Maniakes' journey up to Imbros kept reaching Videssos the city, sometimes by ones and twos, sometimes in larger groups. A lot of them told terrible tales about what they had seen the Kubratoi doing to the countryside as they made their way south. None of what they said surprised Maniakes, who had seen some of that for himself and owned imagination enough to guess the rest.

Five days after he returned to the capital, Bagdasares arrived aboard a horse that looked fit only for slaughter. Like Maniakes, he had trouble getting the guards to believe he was who he said he was.

"You should have turned them into toads and let them sleep stupidly in the mud at the bottom of a pond till spring," Maniakes declared when the wizard finally gained admission to his presence.

"Speak to me not of spells of changing," Bagdasares answered with a shudder. "When I saw the nomads bearing down on the feast and the encampment, I gave myself the seeming of a Kubrati. The spell was, if anything, too thorough, for not only did I look like a barbarian, I even thought like one—or rather, I thought the way I thought a Kubrati would think, which proved quite sufficiently unpleasant, I assure you."

"In that case, I expect I'm lucky you decided to make your way south instead of heading back toward the Astris with the folk you imagined to be your tribesmates," Maniakes said.

"It is no laughing matter, I assure you," Bagdasares said, though Maniakes had not laughed. "In the confusion, I got to the woods and hid there, and for the life of me I could not be sure whether I was hiding from Videssians or Kubratoi. Fear for the most part makes magic fail. My fear powered the spell to greater heights than it had any business reaching."

"How did you decide who you truly were?" Maniakes asked.

"I had to skulk among the trees for a couple of days, till I could get free and start moving south," Bagdasares answered.

"During that time, as the magic slowly waned, I began to be afraid of the nomads once more."

"I'm just glad you didn't ride off with them before your magic faded," Maniakes said.

"Not half so glad as I am," Bagdasares answered with great sincerity. "I wouldn't have cared to try to explain myself when the Kubratoi suddenly saw my true appearance rather than the seeming I had placed on myself. Mind you, I'm a much handsomer fellow than the barbarian I made myself appear to be, but there is a time and a place for everything."

The wizard's invincible self-importance made Maniakes smile, but he quickly sobered. "Magic is seldom as definite as it ought to be," he said. "I saw myself coming back to Videssos the city in your magic mirror, but I didn't see the Kubratoi riding after me, and so thought I'd concluded the treaty with them. And you wanted to seem a nomad, not to be one."

" 'Be what you wish to seem' is a good rule for life, but not for magic," Bagdasares said. "Magic confuses being and seeming too much as is."

Maniakes clapped him on the shoulder. "Well, however you got here, I'm glad you did," he said. "I'll need your help in the future, and I'd have hated to break in a new wizard."

"You're kind, your Majesty, but there are swarms of sorcerers stronger than I am." Bagdasares hung his head. "Had I been better at what I do, you might have been properly warned that Etzilios planned treachery, for instance."

"You've given me good service, and my foibles don't seem to bother you," Maniakes said. "In my ledger, those count for more than raw strength."

"Don't be absurd, your Majesty." Bagdasares raised an admonitory index finger. "Avtokrators have no foibles."

His face was perfectly straight. Maniakes stared at him, then burst out laughing. "I haven't heard anything so funny in years. Likinios was a skinflint, Genesios murdered people for the sport of it, and I—"

"Yes, your Majesty?" Bagdasares asked innocently.

"I'm trying to save the Empire. Considering the state it's in right now, if that's not a foible, to the ice with me if I know what is."

Without Kameas, the imperial household ran less smoothly than it had before. The other eunuchs were willing and gra-

cious, but the vestiarios had known how everything worked
and where everything was. No one else attained to such omni-
science. Maniakes caught a couple of servitors on the point of
coming to blows over a crimson sash each of them claimed the
other had mislaid. Such squabbles would not have happened
with Kameas supervising the staff, or, if they had, Maniakes
would never have known of them.

That the eunuchs were jockeying to be named vestiarios did
nothing to improve matters. They all tried so hard to impress
Maniakes that they ended up irking him as often as not. He
kept putting off the decision; none of them completely satisfied
him.

A couple of weeks after he returned from the north, the first
snow fell. Maniakes watched the flakes swirl in the wind with
something less than enthusiasm. When the cold froze the
ground, the Kubratoi would be able to sweep over the roads
and fields and steal whatever they had missed on earlier raids.

Sure enough, a couple of days later a band of nomads rode
down into sight of the walls of Videssos the city. Maniakes
went over to the wall to glare at them. They weren't doing
much, just sitting their horses and staring at the capital's fortifications. Maniakes understood that; the great works were
plenty to inspire awe even in a Videssian.

"Shall we drive them off, your Majesty?" Ipokasios asked.
"We have force aplenty to do it."

Maniakes was sure he wanted to perform well in front of the
Avtokrator's eye after his earlier embarrassment. But he answered, "No, let them look all they like. The more they see
about Videssos that impresses them, the more they'll come to
understand that, once our present troubles are over, we are not
to be trifled with." He almost made the sun-circle as he replied; he seemed even to himself to be speaking more in pious
hope than from any knowledge of when, if ever, Videssos'
troubles would end.

But the Kubratoi, after spending some time looking at the
wall from beyond the range of its stone- and dart-throwing engines, rode away to the north—all but one of them, who was
left behind on foot. That one started slowly walking toward the
wall. As he drew nearer, Maniakes saw he wore no beard. He
plucked at his own whiskers; he had never seen nor heard of
a clean-shaven Kubrati.

The fellow called up to the soldiers atop the wall. "Open the
gate, I pray you, that I may enter." He spoke Videssian like a

cultured man of the city. But was he a man? The voice could as easily have been contralto as tenor.

"Kameas!" Maniakes shouted. "Is it you?"

"More or less, your Majesty," the vestiarios answered. "I would be surer inside the city than I am out here. I have seen more of the wide, wild world than I ever expected to know."

"Let him in," Maniakes told the men on the wall. He hurried down a stairway at the rear of the wall and embraced Kameas when he came through the gateway they opened for him.

"Please, your Majesty, such familiarity is improper," Kameas said.

"You're not in the palaces, esteemed sir, not yet, nor in my pavilion. That means you don't tell me what to do. I tell you. And if I want to hug you, I bloody well will."

"Very well. Under these circumstances, I shall not be argumentative," Kameas said with the air of one making a great concession. Had he been his normal sprightly self, he might have given the Avtokrator more backtalk. But he was thin and worn and pale even for a eunuch, and, though the Kubratoi had dressed him in wool trousers and sheepskin jacket in place of his robes, he looked half frozen.

Concerned, Maniakes said, "Come on, esteemed sir. We'll get you back to the palaces, soak you in a warm pool, and feed you hot spiced wine and candied figs and apricots. Can you ride a horse across the city, or shall I have a litter brought for you?"

"I can ride a horse." Kameas rolled his eyes. "That is not a skill I ever thought I should acquire, but acquire it I have. From all I have seen, among the Kubratoi one either rides or is left behind for the delectation of the wolves." He shuddered. "After the journeys I have made, the trip to the palaces will be like a spring stroll through the cherry trees around the imperial residence when their blossoms fill the air with sweetness."

"I couldn't muster up that much poetry when I'm perfectly well, let alone after what you've been through," Maniakes told him. "Here, we'll get you a nice, gentle animal, not one of those steppe ponies with a mouth like iron and a will that comes straight from Skotos." He spat on the cobblestones.

"You're familiar with the breed, then," Kameas said. When Maniakes nodded, the vestiarios went on, "I did wonder if the problems I was having were entirely due to my own ineptitude.

But the Kubratoi had no trouble with their horses. I suppose they're as harsh as the beasts they ride."

He swung up onto the mare that was fetched for him—the prospect of getting him a gelding had struck the Avtokrator as being in poor taste—and seemed capable enough in the saddle, if not what Maniakes would have called comfortable there. "How did they catch you?" he asked. "What happened to you then?"

"How did they catch me?" Kameas echoed. "Your Majesty, I shall always be grateful to you for your advice to hide; had the nomads spotted me out in the open, most likely they would have ridden me down and slaughtered me. But the places for proper concealment were few. I ran into a tent, covered myself over with bedding, and hoped for the best.

"Unfortunately for me, the Kubratoi soon proceeded to loot the tents. One of the blankets under which I lay was a quilted one with a fine cover of crimson silk. A barbarian pulled it away—and discovered me."

"Did he already know you were there?" Maniakes asked delicately; the vestiarios had been considerably bulkier on the day of the Kubrati surprise.

"Well, yes, your Majesty, you might say so. He had his breeches down around his ankles when he pulled the blanket off me. I spoke none of the Kubrati language then, and have learned but few words, most of them vile, since. Still, I had no trouble figuring out his disappointment that I was not a woman. Had I been a man of the ordinary sort, I think he would have slain me out of sheer pique.

"But he did not know what to make of me, and in his curiosity decided I might be more interesting alive than dead. He fetched me out and showed me to someone of higher rank than himself, who in turn took me to a barbarian of still more exalted rank—from excellent to eminent, you might say—and, shortly thereafter, I was fetched before Etzilios.

"He had seen me attending you, your Majesty, and knew I had to be one of your eunuchs, but he did not know what a eunuch was, at least not in detail. He kept insisting they must have made me into a woman. I denied this, but refused to, ah, let him examine the evidence for himself."

"Clever," Maniakes said. "The more curious he was about you, the less likely he'd hurt you."

"I thought of that only later," Kameas said. "Your Majesty, you are a gentleman of finest quality; you have never shown any unseemly interest in the nature of my mutilation. This has not always been the case among the powerful, in my experience." The vestiarios' voice was bleak. Maniakes wondered what indignities he had suffered during Genesios' reign.

Kameas went on, "Etzilios could have forced me to expose my nakedness, of course, but having me serve him amused him more: he boasted how he'd taken everything of yours, from the imperial robe—which he wore over his furs and leathers—to the imperial eunuch. Perhaps he thought I would poison him if I was sufficiently humiliated. I wish I had indeed had the wherewithal to prove him right."

"If he wanted you to serve him, why didn't he take you back to Kubrat with him?" Maniakes asked.

"Eventually, while attending to a call of nature, I was discovered by some of the ruffians in what passes for Etzilios' court," Kameas answered. "What they saw so bemused them that they burst out of the bushes where they were hiding and dragged me forthwith before the khagan, to exhibit me to him as if I were a two-headed snake or some other freak of nature." His sallow cheeks reddened with remembered indignation.

When he did not continue, Maniakes said, "And?"

"And Etzilios, having looked his fill, immediately sent me back to you, saying you were welcome to me." Kameas sniffed. "*I* consider his judgment a vindication."

"So do I," Maniakes said, reaching out to set a hand on his shoulder. "His loss is my great gain."

"Your Majesty is gracious."

VII

ABOUT A WEEK AFTER THE MIDWINTER'S DAY FESTIVITIES
had come and gone, Kameas interrupted Maniakes as the
Avtokrator went over the accounts of revenue received from
each province. Maniakes was glad to be interrupted; the numbers added up to *not enough*. To avoid that bleak contempla-
tion, he slammed shut the register in front of him and said,
"How now, esteemed sir?"

"Your Majesty, a man awaits you at the entrance to the residence here. He claims to be your brother Parsmanios," the
vestiarios answered. "You of all people are best suited to judge
the truth of this claim."

Maniakes' heart leapt within him. He sprang to his feet, exclaiming "At last something goes my way! I'll see him at
once. And fetch my father there, too—he'll want this news no
less than I."

"It shall be as you say, your Majesty."

Heedless of his imperial dignity, Maniakes ran down the hall
toward the entrance. The closer he got, the colder the air grew.
Hypocausts—brick-lined ducts under the floor—brought
warmth from a central furnace to the rooms of the residence,
but that warmth could not compete with the winter wind whistling outside.

He didn't care. The guardsmen out there—shivering
Videssians and Halogai who looked far more comfortable now
than they did in the muggy heat of midsummer at the capital—
were keeping a wary eye on a tall dark fellow in a cavalryman's cloak and boots. One of the soldiers turned to Maniakes

and said, "Well, your Majesty, is he your brother or do we fill him full of holes?"

The last time he had seen Parsmanios, not long before he went into exile and his brother off to fight in the westlands, Parsmanios' beard had still been on the downy side, with patches where the hair grew sparsely. Now it was full and thick, with a gray streak in it that looked to follow a scar whose upper portion seamed his left cheek.

"By the good god, brother of mine, you're a man," Maniakes said.

"By the good god, brother of mine, you're Avtokrator," Parsmanios replied. "How did that happen? I heard of it by chance in a tavern out toward the border with Vaspurakan—a merchant had managed to bring in a few donkeyloads of wine. I almost fell off my chair. Many good-byes to Genesios and all, but how did you end up wearing the red boots? I suppose I should prostrate myself to you, shouldn't I?"

"If you do, I'll kick you in the ribs," Maniakes promised. He briefly told how he had come to the throne, then went on, "So what of you? You were near the border with Vaspurakan, you say? Why didn't news get there sooner? I've sent letters out after you and Tatoules, but it was like shouting into a bottomless cavern: no echo came back."

Parsmanios spread his hands. "Who brings news? Traders, soldiers—travelers, anyhow. Haven't seen many of those lately, not in the little pisspot village where I've been stuck—place called Vryetion. The princes' land is under the thumb of the King of Kings these days, and his general Abivard led an army that sliced up and cut us off from getting any word out to the east. If he'd wanted to, he could have smashed us up, but he must have figured he had bigger fish to fry. For all I know, he may have been right."

"It wouldn't surprise me," Maniakes agreed. "I got to know Abivard when we were fighting to put Sharbaraz back on his throne. He knows his business, no way around that. He'd strike toward the heart of Videssos and leave detachments behind him to wither on the vine."

Before his younger brother could answer, the elder Maniakes came out and folded Parsmanios into a bearhug. "The more of this clan we have gathered in one place," he said, "the more cause our foes have to fear."

"Any word at all of Tatoules?" Parsmanios asked.

Maniakes told him of the short, unsatisfying report he had

had from Tzikas. "I sent him a letter straightaway," he added, "but I've heard nothing further. He's been busy trying to hold Amorion against the Makuraners. If they take it, they can swarm straight down the valley of the Arandos to the sea and cut the westlands in half from west to east."

"When I got word of what had happened to you, I thought of coming here by way of Amorion and the river," Parsmanios said. "I figured I'd run into the boiler boys if I tried it, though, so I took the coast route instead. That worked well enough—I'm talking with you, anyway."

"To the ice with the boiler boys," Maniakes said, echoing his brother's use of the slangy Videssian nickname for heavy-armored Makuraner cavalry. He pointed to the doorway. "Here, come inside. We'll get some hot spiced wine inside you, make you feel like a new man."

"Hot spiced wine is good even if you feel like an old man," the elder Maniakes said.

Parsmanios laughed. "By Phos, Father, it's good to see you, and better still to hear you. If you have hot wine anywhere handy, I'll gladly drink some."

Over the wine, which was steaming and fragrant with cloves and cinnamon, the younger Maniakes said, "We'll put you up in one of the apartments in the wings off to the side of the Grand Courtroom. And—" He preened. "—you're going to be an uncle again."

"Good news," Parsmanios said, thumping him on the back. "Little by little, you're gathering in our whole clan." His face clouded. "Except Tatoules."

"We can but pray to the good god there," Maniakes said, and his brother nodded.

"If you'll recall," the elder Maniakes said to Parsmanios, "you were betrothed before you went off to the westlands. Evagria, that was the girl's name; I'm not too far into my dotage to remember it. I think Genesios took her father's head for something or other, but that's old news now, and I've forgotten what. She's still here in the city; odds are she'll be glad to see you."

Parsmanios coughed, more from discretion than catarrh. "Father, we've been based in Vryetion four or five years now. Summer before last, I wed a local girl named Zenonis. I have a baby boy myself; his name is Maniakes."

The elder Maniakes beamed. "You flatter me outrageously," he said. "As for the other, well, if you wed her, you wed her.

A settlement of gold on Evagria's family will probably make them happy enough; they've been, oh, not poor, but poorish since her father got put to the sword." He turned to the younger Maniakes. "You'll take care of that?"

"I'll take care of it some way or other," Maniakes said. "We don't have the gold for what really needs doing, let alone for smaller things like this." He frowned, first in annoyance, then in thought. At last he beamed. "I have it! I'll promote them in the nobility. Not only won't that cost me anything, I may even be able to make them pay for the privilege."

Parsmanios stared at him. The elder Maniakes laughed uproariously. "Damn me to the ice if I think you're wrong, son." He snorted, drank, and snorted again. "The good god save the poor Makuraners when we're finally able to face them. Not only will we beat 'em in the field, we'll cheat 'em out of their armor and their boots and, if they're not careful, their drawers, too."

Kameas poked his head into the study where Maniakes was trying to figure out how to stretch his gold as far as it would go or, with luck, three steps farther. "Your Majesty, the Empress has pangs she believes to be labor pains. She just asked me to send for the midwife and arrange the Red Room for the birth of, Phos willing, the heir."

"Esteemed sir, you don't need my permission to attend to such matters," Maniakes answered. "As far as birth is concerned, Niphone's serving women have made it quite clear that I am, in their words, a large, stupid man, and not to be trusted with anything of greater weight than staying out of the way and not getting underfoot."

"I was not seeking permission, your Majesty, merely informing you of what I was about to do," the vestiarios said. "This notification, I trust, will enable you to succeed at the tasks the maidservants set you."

Maniakes considered that, then said, "Have a care with that wit of yours, lest you pierce someone with it by accident."

"As always, I obey your Majesty," Kameas said. Maniakes had the satisfaction of winning a rare smile from the eunuch before Kameas hurried off to do as Niphone had asked.

The midwife was a plump, middle-aged woman named Zoïle. By the way she strode confidently through the halls of the imperial residence, she had come here before: perhaps she had helped Genesios' wife give birth, or perhaps she had aided servants at their confinements. Maniakes didn't have the nerve to ask. She was the ruler of a province where he could not go and carried herself with a ruler's pride.

"Now you just sit yourself down, your Majesty—find someplace comfortable, let them fetch you some wine, and settle yourself down to wait," she said, echoing, consciously or unconsciously, the maidservants' advice. "It may take a while, but I'll make sure you get yourself a fine baby and a healthy lady, too."

"Thank you," Maniakes said. Large, stupid man though he was, he knew Zoïle could not make the guarantee she claimed. Women died in childbirth, and afterward from fever, in spite of everything midwives could do. If fever took Niphone, he had a healer-priest ready to summon. But even healers could do only so much, and their art told cruelly on them. He prayed he would not have to make the call for which he was prepared.

After a while, Kameas came into the chamber where he sat worrying. The vestiarios said, "Under Zoïle's direction, we have transferred her majesty to the Red Room. The heir, if such the birth should produce, shall come into the world in the chamber set aside for the confinements of Empresses."

Maniakes had been born by the side of the road. So had his father; he remembered his grandmother talking about it. However steeped in ceremony Videssos was, being born in the Red Room wasn't required for imperial rank. Kameas surely knew as much. Bluntly pointing it out, however, struck Maniakes as impolitic.

The vestiarios asked, "Does your Majesty require anything?"

"Nothing I can think of, esteemed sir; thank you," Maniakes answered. "Just come in and dust me off occasionally, as you need to."

"The process should not take so long as that," Kameas said with a hint of reproof in his voice. "In my admittedly limited experience—" He left it there, undoubtedly because part of his limited experience did involve Genesios' wife, and he was too polite to make much of that in Maniakes' presence.

Periodically reports came to Maniakes of what Genesios' survivors were doing in the monastery and convents where they lived out their days. The reports always boiled down to *nothing much*. So long as they kept boiling down to that, Maniakes was content, at least there.

Kameas went off to put the finishing touches on the feast

that would celebrate the birth of Maniakes' first child. So it was described, anyhow, though the vestiarios knew he had a bastard son. He wondered how Atalarikhos was doing these days. If Niphone gave him legitimate children as fine as the son Rotrude had borne, he would be a lucky man.

With nothing to do but wait, he did that as well as he could. Every so often, his kinsfolk would come in to pat him on the shoulder and wish him and Niphone luck. "I know what you're going through, son," the elder Maniakes said. "It's never easy, though if you listen to the women, they'd gladly trade places with you."

A little while after his father left, Lysia peered into the chamber where Maniakes sat. "The good god grant everything goes well in the Red Room," she said.

He sketched the sun-circle over his heart. "May it be so," he said, and then, "She's been in there a long time, hasn't she?"

Lysia smiled at that. "It seems so to you, and no doubt it seems so to Niphone, but it's not really. These things do take a while, you know."

"I suppose so," he said vaguely. "I ought to be getting some work done, not just hiding myself away, but I've tried. I can't."

"I'd worry about you if you could," his cousin replied. "The Empire won't crumble to pieces because you're not watching it for a few hours. If you want to give the stack of parchments to Rhegorios, I'm sure he'd make short work of them." Her eyes twinkled.

"The work your brother would give them is too short to suit me," Maniakes answered with a snort. "He's a clever chap, and I'm glad to have him for my Sevastos even with Father here, but he sees the whole mosaic and doesn't pay enough attention to any one tessera in it."

"Of the two of us, I got that," Lysia's mouth twisted. "It does less good in me than it might in him, me being a woman."

"If I were to make you Sevastos, or rather Sevaste—"

"Don't mock me," Lysia said, more sharply than she was in the habit of speaking. "We both know that cannot be."

Maniakes looked at her as if he had never seen her before. "I'm sorry," he said slowly. "Till this moment, it never occurred to me that you might want the job."

"Why does that not surprise me?" she said, and then sighed. "I know why, of course. It could be worse. I know that, too. Even after I got done explaining myself, you still might not have had any idea what I was talking about. I'm glad you did figure it out, though."

"Cousin, much as I love you—" Maniakes began.

"If you loved me, you would take me seriously," Lysia broke in.

"Take you seriously? I do. I always have." Maniakes spread his hands. "If we ever find peace, maybe I'll get the chance to prove it to you. But if I'm fighting the Kubratoi and the Makuraners both, I can't set men and women in Videssos against each other, and if I appoint you to the rank you'd like—not that you wouldn't fill it well—that's what I'd do. We can't afford it. I have to find a better way."

"I know," she answered. "Realistically, I know. Sometimes, though, being kept for a brood mare and valued only for the marriage I might make and the sons I might bear is hard to stand."

"Whatever happens, you'll have a place with me," Maniakes said. "You always need to remember that."

Lysia sighed again. "You mean that well, and I thank you for it. It's far more than almost any woman in the Empire has. I hope you won't think me ungrateful if I say it's not enough." She turned and walked out before he could find an answer. He had the feeling she might have waited a long time before he came up with a good one.

But she did not have to wait now. He did. The waiting went on for what became by anyone's standards a long time. Kameas brought him supper—he ate without noticing what was on the plate in front of him—put him to bed, and then, when he woke, served him breakfast. No word came from the Red Room.

"They've been in there most of the day now," he said. "How much longer can it be?"

"I have spoken with Zoïle," the vestiarios answered. "From what she says, the lady your wife is doing as well as can be expected for a first birth, but proceeding more slowly than is often the case."

"A lot more slowly," Maniakes said. Would a midwife tell a chamberlain all she knew—or feared? Would Kameas shade whatever he did hear from the midwife? The answers that formed in Maniakes' mind were *not necessarily* and *very likely*, respectively.

When he tried to go to the door of the Red Room himself, all his servants reacted with such dismay that he never got the chance to ask any questions of Zoïle herself. "Her Majesty is very tired" was as much as anyone would tell him. Since she had been in there more than a day by then, it wasn't anything he hadn't been able to figure out for himself. He stalked down the hall, scowling at everybody he saw.

He had been worried since Niphone went into labor. It was more than worry now; it was alarm. What if he lost her? To his own embarrassment, he had never been able to call up more than a fraction of the feeling he had had for her before he was forced to sail off to Kalavria. That was a long way from saying he would have been happier without her.

He drank more wine than he should have, and felt hazy and stupid and belligerent all afternoon. He headed back to the Red Room, the wine fueling his determination to get answers one way or another.

But before he got to the door, though, a cry from within the chamber froze him in his tracks. Niphone's voice was high and thin and rather breathy; he had never imagined such a piercing sound passing her lips. He heard torment and exhaustion there, but something else, too, something he had a harder time naming. *Effort* wasn't the word he wanted, but it came closer than any other he could find.

The cry faded. Maniakes needed a moment before he could nerve himself to go on. He had just taken another step toward the closed door when Niphone cried out again. This—shriek? moan? wail?—lasted even longer than the one before it had, and sounded far more dire.

Zoïle's voice came through the door, too. He couldn't hear what the midwife said, only her tone of voice. After a moment, he recognized it: it was the same one he had used to urge on his failing Kubrati pony as it neared the walls of Videssos the city. Was Niphone failing, too? His nails bit into the palms of his hands.

Niphone let out yet another cry. It cut off in the middle. Maniakes' heart leapt into his mouth. Rotrude had never made noises like these. She had been grimly silent through the whole business of childbirth till, six or eight hours after she began, she presented him with a baby boy. Was Niphone in greater pain? Was she just more sensitive to whatever pain she felt? Or was she truly at the point of . . . failing? For fear of evil omen, Maniakes did not let *dying* cross his mind.

Silence followed. He reached for the latch. As his hand fell on it, a new cry came through the door: new in the most literal sense of the word. The high, thin wail could only have sprung from the throat of a newborn. Maniakes sagged where he stood. He had a living child. That was something. Now he needed to find out about Niphone.

The door to the Red Room opened. Zoïle came out and almost ran headlong into Maniakes. "Your Majesty!" the midwife exclaimed. She looked exhausted herself, drawn and sweaty, with dark circles under her eyes. She drew back half a pace from the Avtokrator. "Your Majesty, you have a daughter."

Bagdasares had thought it more likely he would have a son. He would twit the mage about that another time. "How is Niphone?" he demanded.

"I won't lie to you, your Majesty," Zoïle answered. "It was touch and go there for a while. I thought I might have to summon a surgeon to cut her open and try to get the baby out, aye, and a healer-priest to see if he could fix the wounds afterward before she bled to death."

"Phos!" Maniakes drew a quick sun-circle over his heart. He knew a woman lay down with death in childbed, but he had never expected to be so brutally reminded of it. Not even the luxuries of the palaces could hold all dangers at bay.

Zoïle went on, "From somewhere, though, she found enough strength to bring forth the babe at last. She has courage, your lady; I've seen women give up and die who worked less hard than she did."

"May I see her?" Maniakes asked. He didn't really want to go into the Red Room now; it had a sickroom stink of stale sweat and slops and even blood that repelled him. But after what Niphone had been through, what he wanted and what he liked seemed small things.

Still, he was not altogether sorry when Zoïle shook her head. "She wouldn't know you, your Majesty, not yet. As soon as she passed the afterbirth, she fell asleep—or passed out, whichever you'd rather. Either way, I'd sooner you let her rest." The midwife looked worried. "I hope she's not bleeding inside. I don't *think* she is—her pulse has been strong all through this—but it's hard to know for certain."

Maniakes' hands folded into fists. Even now, with the delivery done, Niphone still was not safe. He had to trust Zoïle that she would be all right—and Zoïle sounded none to sure. He found another question: "May I see my daughter?"

Now the midwife gave him a smile that pierced her worry

like a sunbeam lancing through a break in dark clouds. "That you can, your Majesty. You wait here a moment, and I'll fetch her." She opened the door to the Red Room. More of the sickroom smell wafted out. Maniakes got a glimpse of his wife lying still and pale on the bed where she had given birth. He wished he could rush to her, but sensed Zoïle was right—for now, rest would do her the most good. But standing out here alone in the hall was hard.

The midwife came out again, carrying a small, swaddled bundle. Maniakes held out his hands to take his daughter. She seemed to weigh nothing at all. Her skin was astonishingly thin and fine; not a parchment-maker in the Empire could do work like that. Her eyes, a dark blue, were open. She looked up at him—or perhaps through him. He had no idea what she was seeing.

"She looks like you, your Majesty," the midwife said.

"Does she?" Maniakes couldn't see it. To his inexperienced eyes, she looked like a baby, nothing else.

"What will you name her?" Zoïle asked.

He and Niphone hadn't talked much about names for a girl. "We'll call her Evtropia, I think," he answered, "after Niphone's grandmother." That would make her side of the family happy, and he didn't mind the name.

"Evtropia." Zoïle tasted it in her mouth and nodded. "Not bad." The midwife paused, then went on, "When she found out the baby was a girl, your Majesty, the Empress asked me to apologize to you. This was just before exhaustion took her."

Maniakes shook his head. "Foolishness. A girl baby's a long way from the end of the world. When I learned she was pregnant this time, I told her as much. We'll try again after she gets her strength back, that's all." Zoïle didn't say anything, but he saw her frown and asked, "What's wrong?"

"Your Majesty, this was a hard birth. If the Empress has another one like it ... even with a healer-priest standing by, she'd be taking a great risk, a risk of her life."

Maniakes stared, first at Zoïle and then down at his newborn daughter. Would she be the only fruit of his loins? What would happen to the throne then? Would he pass it to a son-in-law? To his brother? To a nephew? To Rhegorios or whatever heirs he might have? With a couple of sentences, the midwife had made his life more complicated.

She saw that and said, "I'm sorry, but you'd best know the truth."

"Yes." He shook his head again, this time to clear it. "Do you think her next birth would be as difficult as this one was?"

"No way to know that for certain, not till the day comes. But a woman who's had a hard time in childbed once, she's more likely to have one again. I don't think any midwife would tell you different."

"No, I suppose not." Maniakes sighed. "Thank you for your honesty. You've given me a great deal to think about." He looked down at Evtropia again. Would she be his only legitimate heir? She stared up at him, through him, past him. Her tiny features held no answers; she was trying to do nothing more than figure out the strange new world in which she found herself. At the moment, so was he.

Kourikos looked apprehensive. "Your Majesty," he said, "I am not a mage. I cannot make gold magically appear where there is none to be had."

"I understand that, eminent sir," Maniakes answered. "But without gold, the Empire is hamstrung. Soon I'll be at the point where I can't pay my soldiers—isn't that what the accountants say? If I can't pay them, either they'll mutiny, which will be a disaster—or they'll up and go home—which will be a disaster. How many more disasters do you think Videssos can stand?" He didn't expect the logothete of the treasury to give him an exact answer, but they both understood the number was not very large.

Licking his lips, Kourikos said, "Revenue enhancements from the merchants in the city and other towns could bring in a certain amount of new gold."

"Aye, but not enough," Maniakes said. "For one thing, we don't have enough merchants to let what we gain from them offset what we lose from the peasants, who are nine parts in ten, maybe nineteen parts in twenty, of all our folk. For another, thanks to all the enemy onslaughts, trade has sunk like a ship in a storm, too. The merchants can afford to give but little."

"In all this you speak truth, your Majesty," Kourikos agreed mournfully. "You have set your finger on the reasons why the treasury is in its present state."

"Knowing why is easy. Doing something about it is another matter altogether." Maniakes' voice turned pleading: "Eminent Kourikos, father-in-law of mine, how can I lay my hands on more gold? You are the acknowledged expert here; if you know no way, what am I to do?"

The logothete of the treasury licked his lips again. "One way to stretch what gold we have comes to mind." He stared down at the cup of wine on the table in front of him and said no more.

"Speak!" Maniakes urged him. "Give forth. How can I judge what you say unless you say it?"

"Very well, then." Kourikos looked like a man about to repeat an obscenity. "If we put less gold in each coin, and make up the weight with silver or copper, we can mint more goldpieces for the same amount of metal."

Maniakes stared at him. "How long has it been since an Avtokrator tampered with the currency?"

"About three hundred years, your Majesty, maybe more," Kourikos answered unhappily. "The Avtokrator Gordianos cheapened his goldpieces to help restore the Amphitheater after an earthquake."

"And you want me to break that string, eh?"

"I never stated, nor do I feel, any such desire," Kourikos said. "You asked me how gold might go further. That is one way."

Maniakes gnawed on his underlip. Videssian gold coins passed current all over the world, precisely because of their long tradition of purity. Still . . . "How much can we debase our goldpieces without drawing much notice?"

"One part in ten should cause no problem of that sort, your Majesty," the logothete of the treasury answered. Maniakes wondered what sort of experiments he had run to come back with that quick and confident reply.

"One part it is, then." Maniakes aimed a stern forefinger at Kourikos. "But only during this emergency, mind you. As soon as the worst of the crisis is past, we go back to full value for the weight. Is that understood?" His father-in-law nodded. Maniakes felt as if he had just bathed in mud—but if he didn't get the gold he needed now, having it later might do him no good. Half to himself, he went on, "One part in ten isn't enough, not when we're short by so much more than that. We don't need only to stretch the gold we have; we need more, as well. I don't know where to get it."

Kourikos coughed. "Your Majesty, I know one place where there's gold and silver aplenty, waiting to be stamped into coins."

"Aye, no doubt, and roast pigs lie around in the streets waiting to be eaten, too," Maniakes said. "If gold and silver lay ready to hand, don't you think I would have seized them?"

"That would depend on whether you saw them." Kourikos shook his head, a quick, nervous gesture. "No, not whether you saw them, for you see them every day. Say rather, on whether you realized what you saw."

"Eminent sir, don't play at riddles with me; I haven't the time for it now. If you know where I can get gold, tell me. If you don't and you're trying to show how clever you are . . . be thankful I'm married to your daughter. The state the Empire's in, even that may not save you. Speak up, if you have anything to say."

Kourikos looked as if he wished he had never raised the subject. He went to the doorway of the little chamber in the imperial residence and peered up and down the hall to make sure no servants were in earshot. When he came back, he dropped his voice to a hoarse whisper: "Your Majesty, if you need it badly enough, there is gold and silver aplenty in the temples." No sooner had the words passed his lips than he jumped up to reassure himself he hadn't been overheard.

Maniakes didn't blame him. "Rob the temples?" he exclaimed, also in a whisper. "Agathios would scream like a branded bullock, and so would every other priest and prelate in the Empire. By the good god, eminent sir, it might touch off another round of civil war on top of the Makuraners and the Kubratoi."

"I never said the gold would be easy to take," Kourikos reminded him. "I said it was there, and it is."

He was right about that. Aside from the vast sums that had gone into building the High Temple, the ornaments and the great altar at which the patriarch presided were massy lumps of precious metal. Other temples throughout Videssos, though less lavish than the chief shrine, also had riches stored away inside.

With more regret than he would have imagined a moment before, Maniakes shook his head. "Ah, eminent sir, you frustrate me worse than you know. For you're right: the gold is there, and that it's there never once crossed my mind. But I don't know if I can lay hold of it, not if I want to hold the throne, too."

"Your Majesty must be the judge of that," Kourikos said, bowing his head.

"It cannot be," Maniakes said, and then, "I don't think it can be." He could order the ecclesiastical hierarchy about as he wished, so long as he did not lapse into heresy. He could depose the ecumenical patriarch and have a synod choose a successor from among three candidates he had picked himself. But take gold from the temples? Maybe Avtokrators had dreamt of it, but no one, not even Genesios, had dared try. A man would have to be desperate even to contemplate it seriously.

Maniakes learned how desperate he was by one simple fact: The idea, once lodged in his mind, would not go away.

With a sort of cautious passion, Niphone wrapped her arms around Maniakes. It was the first time they had joined since Evtropia was born. Maniakes did his best to be gentle with her. And, remembering what Zoïle had said, when the moment came when he could hold back no more, he pulled out of her and spurted his seed onto her belly.

She stared up at him. Only one lamp was lit in the imperial bedchamber, but the dim light it threw was plenty to show her expression of rebuke. "Why did you do that?" she demanded. "How are we to get an heir if you don't make me pregnant again?"

He had never heard her speak so sharply; it was all the more surprising because her thighs still clasped him. "The midwife said you might die if you tried to bear another child," he said.

"To the ice with the midwife," Niphone said. "For one thing, how can she possibly know?"

"The time you had bearing Evtropia was warning enough for her," Maniakes said. "It ought to be warning enough for you, too."

She ignored him. From the moment Agathios wed them, she had been as modest and submissive a wife as he had ever imagined: to a fault, if anything. Now, all at once, she made a lie out of everything he had thought she was, continuing, "For another, come what may, my son will sit on the throne of the Empire of Videssos after you. Will you cheat my family of its place?"

He hadn't thought of it like that. He had plenty of relatives of one sort or another to succeed him; he would have preferred a son, certainly, but his family's line would not fail if he didn't produce one. But if a nephew or cousin or even brother of his donned the red boots, Niphone's kin would lose their place in the sun, with no way to get it back.

She went on, "My husband—your Majesty—we shall have an heir of your body, and of mine." She reached down to restore his wilted vigor, plainly intending to start trying to conceive that heir on the instant.

He took hold of her wrist. "Easy, there. I can't go again quite as fast as I could ten years ago. And even if I could, I told you already the price of a boy child is more than I care to risk."

"*You* care to risk?" Niphone said. "The risk is mine to make, not yours. Life is risk, for men and women. Men go off to war; women lie down in childbed. When men win, they bring themselves home alive, no more. But women, now, women lie down as one and get up as two. You have no right to say I may not do this."

Maniakes opened his mouth, then closed it again. If he held Parsmanios, say, out of a battle with the Makuraners for fear of what might happen to him, his brother would have reason to be furious with him. Women, though, were supposed to be protected from such risk. What if a woman didn't want to be protected? What then? Till this moment, he hadn't imagined such a thing.

He was trying to keep her alive. She should have been grateful. Since she seemed anything but, he took his most imperious and imperial tone and declared, "I am your husband. I have the right to tell you what we shall do—and what we shall not."

For a moment, he had hopes the ploy would work. Niphone was a girl conservatively reared even by the conservative standards of her family; her attitude toward her husband's decrees should have approached that of a Makuraner wife locked away in the women's quarters of her noble husband's stronghold.

Should have. Niphone looked at him. In the dim lamplight, he could not make out the expression on her face. Then she reached out and took hold of him again. She wasn't usually so bold. "One of the things that makes you my husband is *this*," she said, squeezing gently. "If you deny it to me, is that not grounds for making our marriage as if it had never been?"

The Videssian military knew retreat could be a virtue. Maniakes decided this was a time he would have to retreat—especially since, inside her hand, part of him was advancing. He took her in his arms, kissed her mouth and her neck and the hollow of her shoulder and her breasts. When the time

came for them to join, he rolled onto his back—not only was
that easier for his second round, but also for her not long out
of childbed.

She carefully lowered herself onto him. "You win," he said
in a voice that was all breath.

"No," she said, raising up and then filling herself with him
again. "We do."

Maniakes stared at the messenger who had come hotfoot
from the walls of Videssos the city. "There's a *what* out
there?" he demanded, digging a finger into his ear. "I can't
have heard you rightly."

"May it please your Majesty, you did," the messenger said.
"There's a band of Kubratoi out there, just past dart-thrower
range. The fellow who sounds like he's in charge—I misre-
member his name, but he speaks Videssian like it was an egg
he's beating in a bowl—"

"Is he called Moundioukh, by any chance?" Maniakes
asked.

"That's it, your Majesty," the messenger agreed. "You know
of him?"

"I know of him," Maniakes said grimly. "Very well, admit
him to the city. Surround his force, however large it may be,
with armed men. Be particularly careful not to give him any
promise of safe-conduct whatsoever. I will meet with him—
and him alone—in the Grand Courtroom in two hours' time.
Separate him from his men and make sure they are treated well
unless you hear otherwise from me. Have you got all that?"

"Would your Majesty be kind enough to repeat it?" the man
said. Maniakes did. The messenger gave it back to his satisfaction. Nodding, he sent the fellow back to the wall, then
shouted for Kameas.

Two hours later, he sat on the imperial throne in raiment almost as splendid as that which he had had to discard after the
Kubrati surprise. Hastily assembled dignitaries took their
places to either side of the colonnaded aisle down which
Moundioukh would walk.

But for the sounds of Moundioukh's footfalls, the Grand
Courtroom was altogether silent as the Kubrati advanced toward the throne. At the prescribed distance from it, he prostrated himself before Maniakes. With a *skreek* of gearing,
servitors behind the far wall raised the imperial throne several

feet in the air. When Moundioukh started to get up afterward, the Avtokrator snapped, "I did not give you leave to rise."

Moundioukh flattened himself against the marble once more. He turned his head to glance up at the Avtokrator. His eyes blazed; he did not seem impressed by the rising throne. "Youse gets smarts with me, your Majesties, and the magnifolent Etzilios, he will pull the Empires down around your heads," he said.

"What? Will he do worse than he has already?" Maniakes said.

"Much worser, your Majestive. There will be a slaughtering the likes of which the world has never seen the likes of," Moundioukh declared.

"Rise," Maniakes said. Moundioukh climbed to his feet, looking smug. Then he saw the expression on Maniakes' face, and his own confidence leaked away. Maniakes said, "Take this message back to Etzilios the cheat, Etzilios the robber, Etzilios the traitor: If his ravages go on, I will pull all my forces from the westlands, settle him once for all, and then go back to fighting Makuran."

"Youse is bluffing!" Moundioukh said.

"Why on earth do you think so?" Maniakes said. "The King of Kings can't hurt me worse in the west than Etzilios does in the north—and if I beat Etzilios once, he may stay beaten, while Makuran won't."

Moundioukh exclaimed, "Youse will be sorry for these!" but he sounded dismayed, not fierce and threatening. He went on, "I did not come here for insulteds. I camed to offer my magnifolent khagan's mercies to youse. Youse gives him golds, he will goes away and not bothers the towns of youse."

Maniakes laughed in his face, a long, bitter laugh. "He said that last year, and look what we got for it. Does he want me to come to Imbros again?"

"Uh, no, your Majesties." Barbarian though Moundioukh was, he did not seem immune to embarrassment.

"Well, then." Maniakes folded his arms across his chest and stared down at the Kubrati emissary. "Tell him the choice is his: he may have peace, or he may have war without limits. Videssos was here long before you Kubratoi came off the Pardrayan steppe; Videssos will be here long after you are forgotten. Look around you, Moundioukh. You are in a real city now."

Moundioukh looked, and looked uncomfortable. Phos' High

Temple would have been the best place in Videssos the city for him to see the difference between what his people could do and what the Videssians had accomplished over the centuries, but the Grand Courtroom ran a strong second.

Yet the Kubratoi had their talents, too, as he reminded Maniakes: "Youse Videssians, youse makes pretties, but youse can'ts fight for nothings. Bring on soldiers. Us slaughters they." He paused. "Unless youse pays we not to."

Maniakes did not want to pay the Kubratoi tribute. He wanted it even less now than he had when he had agreed to the three-year truce the autumn before. But he knew he could not bring the entire Videssian army—such as it was—out of the westlands. Even if he beat the Kubratoi with those forces, Makuran would make sure he got no profit from it.

Freighting his voice with all the scorn he could muster, he said, "I might give you fifteen thousand goldpieces, simply to be rid of you." They would all be cheapened ones, too, he resolved to himself.

"We takes," Moundioukh answered at once. "A one years of pieces, youse gets."

Maniakes stared at him. "You mean that," he blurted in amazement. Moundioukh nodded. Still startled, Maniakes went on, "The magnifolent Etzilios is a fool. He could have had better than three times as much for this year if he hadn't attacked me up by Imbros."

"I tells him not to does it," Moundioukh answered. "But him do not listens. Him are magnifolent, like youse says. Him listen only to himsownself. Him say, catch Avtokrators, not have tributes, have Videssos."

"He'll never get another chance," Maniakes ground out. The khagan had certainly had a point; if he had captured or killed Maniakes, all of Videssos down to the imperial city might have been his for the taking. He had done enough damage to the Empire without getting hold of the Avtokrator. Maniakes continued, "Why does Etzilios think I can trust him to keep the peace now when he broke it before? I have better things to do with my gold than throw it away for nothing."

Moundioukh let out a long, heartfelt sigh. "Him give hostages," he answered unwillingly. "Men of Kubrat, we breaks the pieces, youse does what youse wants to hostages."

"And what sort of hostages will he give?" Knowing Etzilios' wiles, Maniakes would not have been surprised to get either men of no account or outright rivals to the khagan, who would then have no trouble restraining his grief if they were executed in reprisal for his own treachery.

But, sounding unhappier still, Moundioukh answered, "Him gives I an all him send down with I. Him breaks bargains, youse breaks we."

Etzilios had used Moundioukh as an emissary before he had attacked Maniakes. That argued the khagan had a reasonably high opinion of him. "We shall see who these other men are," Maniakes said. "If they prove suitable, perhaps we have a bargain." *If I can scrape together fifteen thousand goldpieces, even cheapened ones.* He scowled down at Moundioukh. "For now, you are dismissed. This audience is ended. You will be housed as fits your station."

Moundioukh knew court etiquette; perhaps he had visited Videssos the city during Genesios' reign. He prostrated himself again, then rose and backed away from the throne till he had gone far enough to turn his back without committing lese majesty. The housing Maniakes would have liked to give him was a deep but narrow hole in the ground, but he didn't need more trouble with Etzilios than he already had.

Having Kubrati hostages went some way toward restoring his pride after the humiliation of the previous autumn. He frowned thoughtfully as the throne descended and he got down off it. His courtiers were shouting "Thou conquerest, Maniakes Avtokrator!" but he wondered whether he had gained a victory or simply given Etzilios what he wanted once more.

He shrugged. The way things were, he had very little choice but to accept the khagan's offer. He still had a long road ahead of him before he could think about having many choices when it came to dealing with the Empire's foes.

Agathios performed a proskynesis before Maniakes. "Rise, most holy sir, by all means rise," Maniakes told the ecumenical patriarch as he finished the prostration. "Here, take this couch. My vestiarios will be fetching us refreshments directly—ah, here he is now."

Right on cue, Kameas brought in a silver tray that held a jar of wine, two cups of cut and faceted crystal, and a bowl full of boiled baby squid in a sauce of wine vinegar. Agathios beamed when he saw the squid. "My favorite delicacy!" he exclaimed. "What a lucky choice, your Majesty."

"I'm fond of them, too," Maniakes said, about a two-thirds truth. To bolster it, he ate one. The choice had not been luck;

a few discreet questions from Kameas to Skombros yielded the secrets of the patriarch's taste. The synkellos knew them as well as Agathios did himself, and was not shy about telling them to the vestiarios. Had he been shy in that way, Agathios would soon have found himself with a new synkellos.

Maniakes made small talk with the ecumenical patriarch till Agathios' wine cup had been refilled once and the bowl of lightly pickled squid almost emptied. Then he said, "Most holy sir, I hope the temples have income adequate to all the tasks they undertake."

"Ah, your Majesty, we never have as much as we would like," Agathios answered solemnly. "Our charitable enterprises have stretched very thin because of the ravages of the barbarians in the north and the Makuraners in the westlands. Generous as imperial contributions have been in the past, we could always put more gold to good use."

Maniakes stifled a giggle. Agathios had come to the imperial residence ready to put the bite on him for more funds. Considering the purpose for which he had summoned the patriarch, the irony there was worth savoring.

"I'm sure you could, mostly holy sir," he said. "When the time comes that we may give you more gold from the fisc, be assured we shall gladly do so."

"Your Majesty is generous," Agathios said.

My Majesty is nothing of the sort, Maniakes thought. Aloud, he said, "The pity of it is, we can't do that now. The invaders' inroads have taken a deep bite out of the tax revenues that would normally come into the treasury."

"I sympathize with your plight," Agathios murmured.

That gave Maniakes the opening for which he had hoped. He took advantage of it, saying "I was sure you would, most holy sir. I know the temples will do everything they can to aid Videssos in our hour of need."

Had Agathios been a naively pious cleric, he would have said something like *Whatever the Empire requires, your Majesty!*—most likely in ringing tones full of self-sacrifice. He understood, though, that he was a political as well as a religious figure. Cautiously, he replied, "With our own funds strapped, as I noted, your Majesty, how could we do more?"

"I know the High Temple has vessels and censers and candelabra and other ornaments of gold and silver where bronze or glass or clay would serve as well," Maniakes said. "This is also true of other temples in Videssos the city and all around the Empire, though in lesser measure. The treasury is in desperate need of gold and silver, most holy sir. I should like to requisition some of this holy gear to aid us in our time of trouble, and pay it back weight for weight, measure for measure, when the crisis is past."

Agathios stared at him. "You would have us give up our holy vessels so the metal in them can be put to secular use? Your Majesty, forgive me, but I fear this cannot be."

"Why not?" Maniakes said; Agathios hadn't started screaming anathemas at him, as he had feared might happen. "If Videssos goes down in ruin, the temples fall with the rest. The Kubratoi are heathens; the Makuraners reverence the God, not the lord with the great and good mind."

The ecumenical patriarch *was* a political animal; his protest came out in terms of legalisms rather than theology: "But, your Majesty, such confiscations have never been heard of in all the history of the Empire. You would be setting a potentially disastrous precedent."

"Having the Empire collapse also sets a bad precedent," Maniakes pointed out, "and one much harder to mend." Emboldened by Agathios' cautious response, he went on, "Most holy sir, I regret the need that drives me to ask this of you. Without gold, without silver, we cannot pay our soldiers, and without soldiers we cannot fight either Kubrat or Makuran, let alone both. I will give you my pledge in writing to restore what we have taken as soon as we have gold from anywhere else."

"So you say now," Agathios answered suspiciously. "But what will you say come the day redemption is due?"

"I hope I'll say 'Most holy sir, here is the full weight of gold and silver the fisc borrowed from the temples. My thanks for helping Videssos get through its hour of danger,' " Maniakes told him. "If I don't say that, I expect you'll anathematize me from the pulpit of the High Temple." He had feared—he had expected—Agathios wouldn't wait so long.

The patriarch licked his lips. A bold prelate could indeed do such a thing. It was liable to touch off riots and could get a man kicked off the patriarchal throne, but it was an available weapon. Agathios had never struck Maniakes as a man overly concerned with the spiritual side of his job; administering the temples and enjoying the perquisites of office seemed to rank higher with him. The wealth the temples held, though, touched him there, and he might use the spiritual power if it was not repaid to the last silver coin.

"Let it be as you require, your Majesty," he said now, bowing his head. "I shall send the sakellarios of the High Temple to confer with the logothete of the treasury on the best way to make sure we have an exact record of how much gold and silver is borrowed from each shrine we control."

"I'm sure your treasurer and mine will quickly agree on those procedures," Maniakes said. "By giving up some of your wealth for a little while, you help preserve Phos' faith on earth."

"I hope what you say is true," Agathios answered heavily. "Should it prove otherwise, you will have a great deal for which to answer, not merely to me—I am, after all, but a man—but to the lord with the great and good mind. By your leave—" Robes swirling about him, he swept out of the imperial residence.

A couple of days later, a messenger brought Maniakes a note sealed with the treasury's signet. "Kourikos to Maniakes Avtokrator: Greetings. May your boldness against foreign foes be rewarded with victories no less splendid—and no less startling."

Maniakes read the note twice, then folded the scrap of parchment on which it was written. "If Phos grants me that," he said, "I'll take it."

"Not long after Midwinter's Day, you say?" Maniakes stared at Niphone and shook his head. "I thought you'd have more time to recover from your last birth before you had to start thinking about"—a euphemism for *worrying about*—"another one."

"It is as the good god wills." Niphone sketched the suncircle over her heart. "I am in Phos' hands now, as I have been all my life. He will do with me as he thinks best. I cannot believe he would deny you the heir Videssos needs."

"An heir is all very well," Maniakes said, "but—" He didn't go on. How were you supposed to tell your wife, *But I'm afraid this birth will be the death of you?* You couldn't. Besides, she knew the risks as well as he did. She had been the one who wanted to press ahead, where he would have protected her if she had let him.

Evtropia was almost two months old, but Niphone still looked worn from the struggle she had had bringing her daughter into the world. Could she gather enough strength to go through labor again so soon?

"We'll have a healer-priest standing by outside the Red Room," Maniakes declared. Niphone nodded obediently. *We'll have a surgeon there, too, in case we have to take the babe,* Maniakes thought. That he kept to himself.

"Everything will be all right," Niphone said, but then, as if she wasn't quite convinced of that herself, she added, "and if not, I'll dwell in Phos' eternal light forevermore."

"We'll have no more talk of that sort," Maniakes said firmly; he might have been dressing down a young soldier who wasn't shaping quite as well as he had hoped. Niphone nodded, accepting the rebuke. Maniakes hugged her to show he wasn't really angry, then walked into the hall.

He almost bumped into Rhegorios. "Have a care there, my cousin your Majesty," the Sevastos said with a grin. Then he got a look at Maniakes' face. "Oh, by the good god, what's gone wrong now?"

"Eh? Nothing. Very much the opposite, as a matter of fact." Maniakes steered Rhegorios down the hall so he could talk without his wife's overhearing. "Niphone's going to have another baby."

"That's good news, for a change," Rhegorios agreed. "Why do you look as if the Makuraners just showed up at the Cattle Crossing?" Then his eyes widened. "You're that worried about her?"

"I am," Maniakes answered. "The midwife as much as told me that if she got pregnant again—" He stopped, not wanting to speak words of evil omen, and went on at a tangent, "But Niphone was the one who wanted to try again as soon as might be, and so—" He stopped again.

Rhegorios sketched the sun-circle over his heart. "May the lord with the great and good mind look after her and the babe both. Now I understand why your face was so long."

"We'll have to see how things go, that's all." Maniakes scowled. "I wish that, somewhere in the Empire, I could make things happen, not wait for what happens and have to react to it."

"Well, if the Kubratoi stay quiet, you'll be able to take the field against the Makuraners this summer," Rhegorios said. "That looks to be fifteen thousand goldpieces well spent."

"If the Kubratoi stay quiet," Maniakes said. "And if I can find any soldiers with whom to fight Abivard and the rest of

Sharbaraz's generals. And if I can find officers who won't run away. And if I can find the money to pay them—no, robbing the temples will take care of that, I admit, but it gives me more troubles further down the line."

"Parsmanios won't run away from the Makuraners," Rhegorios said, "and he won't be sorry to get out of the city and take a command, either."

Maniakes started to answer, then paused: it was his turn to study Rhegorios' face. "You won't be sorry to see him go, will you?"

"Well, no," his cousin answered. "He's been—testy—because you didn't make him Sevastos in my place."

"I know," Maniakes said, "but I couldn't see the justice in taking you out of the post when you've done well in it. Maybe Father can make him see the sense of that. I own *I* haven't had much luck. But then, I haven't had much luck in anything since the crown landed on my head."

Rhegorios opened his mouth, probably to deny that, then stopped and thought about everything that had happened since Maniakes took the throne. What went through his mind was easy to read on his face; he hadn't fully learned the courtier's art of dissimulation. After a pause just short of awkward, he said, "The good god grant things get better."

"May it be so," Maniakes agreed. "When I meet Abivard again, I want to face him on something like even terms." He sighed. "We might be friends, he and I, did we not spring from different lands. We got on well when we worked together to put Sharbaraz back on his throne."

"Yes, and look at the gratitude he's shown since," Rhegorios said bitterly.

"He did claim to be avenging Likinios when he invaded us," Maniakes answered. "Maybe he even partway believed it at the time. Of course, he still makes the same claim now, but I don't know of anyone on either side of the border who takes it seriously these days."

"On the other hand, the border's not where it was when he started the invasions, either," Rhegorios said. "It's moved a lot farther east."

"That's one of the things I shall have to attend to—if I can." Maniakes sighed again. "The way things have gone wrong here at the Empire's heart, I sometimes wonder if I wouldn't be better off sailing away to Kastavala and carrying on the fight from a land I could really control."

Rhegorios looked alarmed. "If you're wise, my cousin your Majesty, you'll never say that where anyone but I can hear it. I can't think of a better way to start panic here, and if you don't keep a tight grip on Videssos the city, you won't hold your grip on Videssos the Empire, either."

Maniakes weighed that. "Mm, you're probably right. But I miss being able to operate from a place where I needn't fear treachery if I stir out of the imperial residence and defeat if I go beyond the city walls."

"It will get better, your Majesty," Rhegorios said loyally.

"I hope you're right," Maniakes said, "but damn me to the ice if I see how."

"Maniakes, how could you?" Lysia demanded. He could have been angry at her for forgetting protocol, but, when even his wife called him "your Majesty," he rather relished being treated like a mere human being.

"I don't know. How could I?" he asked, and then, "How could I what?"

Now his cousin hesitated: not out of deference to him, he judged, but from reluctance to mention matters out of the usual ken of unmarried Videssian women. At last, visibly gathering her nerve, she went on, "How could you get your wife with child, knowing what might happen at the end of the confinement?"

He gave her an ironic bow. "That is an excellent question, cousin of mine. As a matter of fact, I asked it of myself, and came up with no good answer."

Lysia set hands on hips. "Well, then? I thought I knew you better than to imagine you'd do such a thing."

"I wouldn't have, were it up to me alone," Maniakes answered. "As with a lot of things, though, more than one person had a say here. When Niphone insisted she wanted to take the risk, how was I to tell her no? You'd have to be wiser than I was to find a way that might work."

"She wanted to? Oh," Lysia said in a small voice. "Men being what they are, when I heard the news I assumed—" She looked down at the hunting mosaic on the floor. "I think I owe you an apology, cousin of mine."

"Maybe for that 'men being what they are,' " Maniakes said. "Have you seen me dragging serving maids off behind the cherry trees?"

Lysia looked down at the floor again; he had embarrassed

her. But she managed a mischievous smile as she answered, "No, but then I wouldn't, would I, what with them being in full leaf and flower?"

He stared at her, then started to laugh. "A point, a distinct point. But I had all winter, too, and the grove was bare then."

"So it was." Lysia dipped her head to him. "I am sorry. I thought you were more worried about the dynasty than you were about your wife."

"Niphone's the one who's more worried about the dynasty than she is about herself," Maniakes replied. "Even if I have no children, the crown will stay in my family. But if she dies without bearing an heir, her clan is cut off from the throne forever. She doesn't want that; she's made it very plain. I can't say that I blame her, and—"

"And she is your wife," Lysia finished for him. "As things are, I would have understood if you were taking up with serving maids now and again. But if Niphone is so dead set on having a boy child—" Her fingers writhed in a sign that turned aside words of evil omen.

"It will be all right," Maniakes said, as much to convince himself as to reassure her. After a moment, he went on, "I'm lucky in my family, too. You thought I was in the wrong, and you up and told me. Nice to know people still think they can tell me the truth even if I won't like it."

"But what I told you wasn't the truth," Lysia said. "I thought it was, but—"

"That's what I meant," Maniakes broke in. "Do you think anyone ever told Genesios he was making a mistake? Maybe one or two people did, right at the beginning of his reign. After their heads went up on the Milestone, do you suppose anyone had the nerve to try that again?"

"You're not Genesios," his cousin said.

"Phos be praised for that!" Maniakes exclaimed. "I'm just glad everyone understands it."

"If people didn't understand it, you would have lost the civil war," Lysia said. "Genesios had Videssos the city, he had most of the army, he had most of the fleet. But no one would fight for him, and so you won."

"And so I won." Maniakes' smile was crooked. "And so, instead of the army and the fleet against me, I have my cousin—a much more dangerous foe."

Lysia scowled at him. "I don't ever want to be your foe or a danger to you—and you ought to know that perfectly well."

He started to assure her that he did, but she overrode him: "But that doesn't mean I can't worry about what you do and why you do it. And I worry about Niphone. After so hard a time with her first birth, and then to be expecting another so soon ... Women don't have an easy time of it."

"I suppose not," Maniakes said—uneasily. Now he stared down at the shining glass tiles set into the floor. "But for all of me, you may ask Niphone if this wasn't her idea, and none of mine."

"How would I say such a thing?" Lysia put up her hands, as if to push away the very idea. "And why would I? I believe you, even if I think she's foolish. But if—Phos prevent it—all should not go as she hopes, what would you do? She links our clan to the bureaucratic families of the city. We need their support."

"We need them quiet, at any rate," Maniakes said. "One thing about having so many enemies outside the Empire: sometimes it keeps even Videssians from fighting among themselves."

"And sometimes it doesn't, if you'll remember what happened all through Genesios' reign," Lysia retorted.

"True." Maniakes sighed. "Too true. These Videssians—" He started to laugh. He was of pure Vaspurakaner blood, but his parents had been born in the Empire and he himself thought more like a Videssian than like a man newly come from the princes' land. He might say *these Videssians*, but he felt at home among them.

"What *would* you do?" Lysia said. "I mean, if—" She didn't go on, but she didn't need to, either.

She had a point. What with Zoïle's warnings, Niphone's health was something about which he did have to worry. Thinking aloud, he said, "I suppose I could bring Rotrude here from Kalavria—"

Lysia's lip curled. Again, she didn't say anything. Again, she didn't need to. He couldn't marry Rotrude, not as Avtokrator; she not only too obviously wasn't of Videssian blood, but she also didn't—and didn't want to—think like a Videssian. He would have a hard time legitimating Atalarikhos, too, for the same reasons. If he did make his bastard son legitimate, the boy would be a weak heir, open to challenge from ambitious generals and the men of his own clan both. Better Atalarikhos stayed far from the city.

Maniakes spread his hands. "What would you have me do,

then?" he said. "Marry only for the sake of the girl's family, and not care whether I feel anything for her? I've done that once, by the good god, and once is plenty. Or maybe I should put on a blue robe with the red boots, and be Avtokrator and monk at the same time? I haven't the temper for that, I fear."

"Please," Lysia whispered.

"I'm sorry," he answered. "I shouldn't say those things. I shouldn't even think them. I know that. I should be thinking everything with Niphone will be fine: Phos grant it be so. That's what you get for being my dear cousin, you know. I'm used to talking things over with you, and when you ask me a question, I do my best to answer it."

"It's all right," Lysia said, and might halfway have meant it. "It's just that you startled me—I hadn't expected so much to come welling up. Even if you wear the red boots, you're still a man; you need someplace to go with your troubles. If I can help there, I'm glad to do it."

"You did," Maniakes said, and slipped an arm around her shoulder for a moment. In a musing voice, more to himself than to her, he went on, "You know, should the occasion arise—which Phos prevent, as we both said—I could do much worse for myself than to marry you."

"Our fathers are brothers," she said. He cocked his head to one side, trying to make sure of her tone of voice. He didn't think she sounded shocked, as she very well might have. It was, he thought, more as if she was reminding him of a certain practical difficulty that would have to be met.

He was shocked himself, but less than he might have been. He and Lysia had always got on well, and he thought the spark of something more might be there. He had felt it when they said farewell back at Kastavala, and he thought she had, too.

His laugh sounded nervous, even to himself. "I can't think of a better way to make the most holy ecumenical patriarch Agathios have kittens." Then he laughed again, this time with real humor. "No, I take that back. Borrowing gold from the temples probably outraged him more than anything two people, even two cousins, could do."

"Don't be too sure," Lysia answered. "If we weren't cousins—" She shook her head and didn't go on.

Just as well, Maniakes thought. "All this is moonshine and foolishness, anyhow. Zoïle is a good midwife, none better; she'll bring Niphone through without any trouble. And if there is trouble, she'll have a healer-priest standing by. She's said as much. With any luck at all, we'll have an heir. If Phos is kind, he'll live to grow up and come after me, and the two of us can forget what we've said here. No, not forget, but pretend it didn't happen."

"That may be the wisest thing to do." Lysia turned and walked down the hall. He watched her go, and wondered: was he relieved or disappointed or both at once? He sketched Phos' sun-circle above his heart. If the good god was kind, he would never have to find out.

VIII

WHEN AN AVTOKRATOR SAILED OVER THE NARROW STRAIT of the Cattle Crossing to campaign against the King of Kings of Makuran, it was often an occasion of great ceremony. The patriarch would bless the Emperor and the grand and glorious host he had with him. The people of Videssos the city would cheer the soldiers as they filed onto the troopships. In flush times, palace servitors would hand out largess to the crowd. Sometimes, as Kameas reminded Maniakes, a chorus would sing of the victories the great Stavrakios had won in the west, to inspire those who came after him to do likewise.

But for having Agathios the patriarch present when he sailed, Maniakes broke with most of those traditions. He was leading only a couple of regiments out from the capital: if he was to keep the walls garrisoned, he had no more to lead. He did not want the people of the city to gawp at his little force, lest the Makuraners learn how small it was. He couldn't afford to dole out largess; he could barely afford to pay his troops. As for the triumphal chorus, Videssian soldiers had gained so little glory against the armies of the King of Kings lately that he feared they would take Stavrakios' triumphs more as reproach than inspiration.

Agathios spat on the planks of the pier in rejection of Skotos, then raised his hands toward Phos' sun as he said, "May the lord with the great and good mind bless our armament here and instill in Maniakes Avtokrator, his viceregent on earth, the courage and steadfastness to persist even in the face of the many troubles that lie before us. May he keep our brave men safe from harm, and may they restore the Empire and its temples to the grandeur that once was theirs. So may it be."

"So may it be." The response went up from Maniakes, from his brother Parsmanios, and from the men who would accompany them into the west.

Maniakes tried to ignore the sour look Agathios sent him. When the ecumenical patriarch talked about restoring the temples to the grandeur that once was theirs, he meant not only liberating those in land under Makuraner occupation. He also had in mind getting back the gold and silver that had gone from the temples to the imperial mints.

"Thank you for the prayer wishing us success, most holy sir," Maniakes said. "You're wise to pray for our victory, for, if we fail, you assuredly shall not not be repaid."

"I promise you, your Majesty, such mundane considerations were far from my thoughts," Agathios murmured. He sounded most sincere, but sounding sincere was part of the patriarch's job.

Maniakes wondered how Agathios would have sounded had he mentioned that he and his first cousin were drawn to each other. No doubt his outraged indignation would have been . . . most sincere.

In lieu of that confrontation—one that he hoped never to have to bring up—Maniakes turned to his father and Rhegorios. "I'm going to trust the two of you not to give this half of the Empire to Etzilios while I'm busy in the westlands," he said. He intended it as a joke, but it came out sounding more like a plea.

"He seems quiet now," the elder Maniakes said. "Phos grant that he stay so."

Rhegorios added, "Have a care in the westlands, too, my cousin your Majesty. Remember, don't get too bold too fast. The Makuraners have been winning for a long time, and our side losing. Don't take on a lot of battles you haven't much chance of winning, or you'll give our men the notion they can't beat Makuran no matter what."

"I'll remember that," Maniakes answered. If headstrong Rhegorios was advising him to be careful, he had to think that was a good idea. And yet, if he did not go out and try to drive the armies of the King of Kings from the westlands, he might as well hand them over to Makuran.

"You'll have to remember it, son," the elder Maniakes said.

"You haven't any large army here, and the ones in the west-lands have been battered to bits in the past six—no, seven now—years. If you want to do anything worthwhile, you'll have to train up some soldiers who aren't used to getting trounced."

"That's one of the things I intend to do," Maniakes said, nodding. Then he grimaced. "Of course, what I intend to do and what Abivard lets me do aren't likely to be one and the same thing."

On that imperfectly optimistic note, he embraced first the elder Maniakes and then his cousin. That done, he boarded the *Renewal* for the short trip over the Cattle Crossing.

The suburb on the western shore of the strait was simply called Across, in reference to its position in relation to that of Videssos the city. The *Renewal* beached there, the rowers driving it well up onto the sand. Sailors let down the gangplank so Maniakes could descend first. He had thought about making a speech pointing out his presence in the westlands; Genesios hadn't fared forth to fight the Makuraners in all his years on the throne, while Likinios, though far more able an Avtokrator than the man who had stolen his throne, had not been a soldier and seldom took the field at the head of his own troops.

In the end, though, Maniakes said, "Let's go," and let it go at that. Speeches a long way from the battlefield did nothing to win wars, and making great claims after suffering great defeats struck him as an easy way to get a name as either a brainless braggart or a desperate man.

He *was* a desperate man, but didn't care to advertise it.

The rest of the fleet beached itself. Videssian law banned the suburbs of the imperial capital from improving their harbors with docks, assuring that the greatest proportion of commerce went through Videssos the city.

Sailors, troopers, and grooms coaxed horses off bulky, beamy transports. The animals kicked up sand on the beach, obviously glad to be off the rolling, shifting sea. Maniakes had seen that with every sea journey a cavalry force had ever undertaken. Horses were marvelous beasts on dry land but hated travel by water.

Maniakes turned to Parsmanios, who had descended from the *Renewal* after him. "You'll head up our vanguard," he said. "You've been through this country more recently than anyone else here; I expect you'll know where we can safely go and where we'd best avoid."

"I hope so," his brother answered. "When I was making my way to the city, Tzikas still held Amorion, which meant the whole valley of the Arandos was under our sway. If Amorion falls—"

"We're in even more trouble than we thought we were," Maniakes finished for him. "By the good god, we're in so much already, how much harm could a little more do?" He laughed. Parsmanios gave him an odd look. If you were Avtokrator, though, not even your brother could get away with telling the world at large you had softening of the brain.

Forming up on the beach, helmets and javelin points glittering in the morning sun, baggy surcoats flapping in the breeze, the regiments Maniakes had brought with him from Videssos the city made a fine martial display. He had no doubt they could crush an equal number of Makuraners. The trouble was, far more Makuraners than two regiments could hope to handle were loose in the westlands.

Parsmanios went up to take his place at the van. Maniakes looked around for someone with whom he could talk. He waved to Bagdasares. "Joining up with whatever forces we already have here won't be enough. We'll have to form a whole new army if we expect to beat back the Makuraners."

"That won't be easy, your Majesty, not with the enemy roaming as he would through the countryside," the wizard answered. "We're liable to be too busy fighting to do much in the way of recruiting."

"The same thought's running through my mind, and I'm not what you'd call happy with it, either," Maniakes said gloomily. "But if we don't have enough veteran troops and we can't raise new ones, what does that leave us? Not much I can see— outside of losing the war, I mean."

"Your reasoning is so straightforward, only a lawyer or a theologian could be displeased with it," Bagdasares said, which drew a snort from his sovereign. "Still, if the Arandos valley remains in our hands, it should prove a fertile recruiting ground in more ways than one."

Maniakes snorted again. "I wish that were true, but it's not. It might be, if we'd won a few victories. As is, though, the only thing men of fighting age will have heard for the past seven years is how the Makuraner heavy cavalry has chewed to rags everything we've sent against it. Hardly anyone volunteers for the privilege of dying messily in a losing war."

Bagdasares dipped his head. "Your Majesty is wiser than I."

"Really? If I'm so clever, why did I want to be Avtokrator in the first place?" Maniakes rolled his eyes. "What wearing the red boots will do to you is make you distrust every noble-sounding scheme you've ever heard from anyone. You start wondering what the fellow thinks he stands to gain from it."

"If you keep looking at the world that way, you'll—" Bagdasares stopped talking. If the Avtokrator learned cynicism, those around him learned caution.

"Say it, whatever it is," Maniakes said; he knew that too well. "If I don't know what people are thinking, I'm going to make more mistakes than I would otherwise. Whatever you were going to tell me, I want to hear it."

"Of course I obey your Majesty," the mage said with a sigh that argued he was unhappy about said obedience. "I was going to say, if you look for the worst in people, you'll surely find it, and end up as sour as poor dead Likinios."

"Mm," Maniakes said judiciously. "I remember the way Likinios was toward the end of his reign—wouldn't trust his own shadow if it got behind his back where he couldn't watch it. No, I don't care to have that happen to me, but I don't care to ignore trouble ahead, either."

"You walk a fine line," Bagdasares said.

And so do all the people around me, Maniakes thought. *They've seen I'm not a brainless bloodthirsty beast like Genesios, which has to ease their minds, but they have to wonder if I'll turn cold and distant the way Likinios did. I wonder about that myself.*

To keep from having to think about it, Maniakes walked over to the nearest transport that was unloading horses. He climbed aboard the black gelding he had been riding since he returned from the disastrous meeting with Etzilios. Since he had got back to Videssos the city, he hadn't been on the steppe pony he had managed to seize in the fighting. He was thinking about breeding it to some of the mares in the imperial stables, in the hopes of adding its phenomenal endurance to the blood-lines of his beasts.

Looking at the ugly, rough-coated little animal, his grooms had been uniformly aghast at the idea. He hadn't had time to persuade them before he set out on campaign. After he got back, if he remembered . . .

Despite the ruin that had overtaken so much of the west-lands, the farmers of the coastal lowlands still lived contented, almost untroubled lives. The warm, moist air and rich soil let them bring in two crops a year, and left them enough after they paid their taxes that famine was no more to be imagined than, say, an invasion from the armies of the King of Kings.

Men dressed in no more than loincloths and women in calf-length shifts of thin linen, the farmers labored in green fields and black earth. The soldiers making their way down the paths through those fields might have come from another world, one that did not impinge on the peasants.

Maniakes sent riders ahead of his little army and off to either side of its route, crying out for men to join the struggle and help cast the invaders from the Empire of Videssos. Only a tiny trickle of would-be warriors presented themselves at each night's campsite, though. Maniakes had horses, weapons, and armor for all of them, and would have had mounts and gear for five times their number.

On the third night out from Videssos the city, he looked at the latest handful of new recruits and asked, "If I sent you men back to your villages to bring in your fellows, do you think you could do a better job of it than my troopers have managed?" As he spoke, he sent up a silent prayer to Phos that the answer would be yes.

But, to a man, the new soldiers shook their heads. One of them slapped his belly and said, "Begging your pardon, your Majesty, but we eat well in these parts. Most of your soldiers, now, they're hungry men."

That was true. Maniakes had seen it often enough: the men likeliest to take up fighting for their trade were those whose farms had failed or who hadn't managed to make a go of it for themselves in the city. He spoke to the fellow who had answered him. "If you have a full stomach, what are you doing here?"

"If I don't fight the Makuraners somewheres else, looks like I'd have to fight 'em on my own land," the farmer told him. "Trouble is, most people, they can't see far enough to worry that kind of way."

"You don't know how right you are," Maniakes said feelingly. "What I ought to do is, I ought to send you back to Videssos the city and make you into a logothete. I have the feeling you'd be wasted as a common soldier. What's your name?"

"I'm Himerios, your Majesty," the peasant said, his eyes

wide. "D'you really mean that? Have to tell you, in case you do, I can't read nor write my name."

"That would help, I admit," Maniakes said. "You'd best stay in the army after all, Himerios. I will keep my eye on you, though. I just wish you—and all your comrades here—had brought your brothers and cousins with you when you decided to join us."

"My cousin said good riddance, is what he said," Himerios answered, spitting on the ground to show what he thought of that. "He's got an eye on my plot of ground, he does. His'd be better if he took more time tending it, the fat, lazy son of a donkey." He chuckled. "He's on my mother's side of the family, you gather."

One of the men who evidently knew Himerios dug an elbow into his ribs and said, "Hey, if you could fight as good as you talk, the Makuraners, they'd be running back to their own country already."

Amid general laughter, Himerios cursed his friend up and down, back and forth, inside and out. Maniakes laughed, too, but the mirth slipped from his face after he left the campfire around which the new recruits sat. Better than having Himerios fight like five men would have been his bringing five men with him. That hadn't happened. Because it hadn't, Maniakes would have an even harder time against the Makuraners than he had expected.

The Arandos flowed lazily through the coastal lowlands, its waters turbid with sediment and, downstream from villages, sometimes foul-smelling from the wastes dumped into it. Maniakes made it a point never to camp where the water did smell bad. He had seen armies melt away like snow in the early days of spring when a flux of the bowels ran through them. Some men died, some who didn't got too sick to be worth anything as fighters, and some who got only a touch of the disease took off for home anyhow.

To Parsmanios, he said, "If men start coming down with the flux, we're ruined, because it'll spread faster than the healer-priests can hope to stop it."

"You're not telling me anything I don't know, brother of mine—er, your Majesty," Parsmanios answered. "The one good thing I can say about Vryetion, where I was stuck for so long, is that the water was always pure there. Now that I think on it, it's likely one of the reasons we based ourselves there."

"The one good thing you can say about the town?"
Maniakes asked slyly. "I'll have to remember that, come the
day I meet your wife. I wonder what she'd have to say about
it."

"Something interesting and memorable, I have no doubt,"
Parsmanios answered. "No one ever wonders where Zenonis
stands about anything."

"She'd need to be headstrong, to stay with one of us,"
Maniakes said. "Anyone who thinks our clan shy and retiring
hasn't met us yet." He spoke with more than a little pride; having a reputation for being cantankerous wasn't the worst thing
in the world.

Parsmanios smiled and nodded, but then said, "What of
Niphone? Not that I know her well, but she seems quiet
enough, willing to stand in your shadow."

"You probably know better than I that what outsiders see of
husband and wife isn't everything that's there," Maniakes answered. His brother nodded again. He didn't go on to explain
that, had Niphone truly been as modest and self-effacing as she
seemed, she wouldn't have had a new baby growing in her
belly now.

Parsmanios said, "And what of our cousin, Rhegorios?
When do you aim to marry him off?" He spoke carefully,
doing his best to conceal his resentment at the place Rhegorios
held at court.

"His own father will have a good deal to say about that,"
Maniakes answered. "Uncle Symvatios is hardly one to curl up
and pretend he's not there, either, though he is better-natured
about going after what he wants than some blood kin I could
name."

If Parsmanios thought that applied to him, he didn't show it.
"The final word will be yours, of course," he said, in his per-
sistence unwittingly proving his brother's point. "You're the
Avtokrator, after all. I suppose you'll settle on a girl from one
of the high bureaucratic families, to bind it to us. You won't
want to pick anyone from too prominent a clan, though, or
with backing like that Rhegorios might decide to see how his
feet look in the red boots."

"If you already know all the answers, brother of mine, why
ask the questions?" Maniakes said. "Actually, I don't worry
too much about Rhegorios' trying to steal the throne. This past
year, he's seen how much the Avtokrator has to do. By all the
signs, it's more than he cares for."

"Maybe so," Parsmanios said darkly, "but you never can tell." Since Videssos' recent history proved how true that was—who would have expected a no-account captain like Genesios to murder his way to the throne?—Maniakes had to nod. Parsmanios went on, "And you'll be thinking about the same sorts of things for Lysia, no doubt. Whoever marries her may get ideas because he's so close to the throne. You'll have to keep an eye on that."

"So I will." Thinking about a husband for Lysia made Maniakes uncomfortable. Recognizing that made him even more uncomfortable. He breathed a silent prayer that Niphone would be safely delivered of a son.

Parsmanios didn't notice the short reply. He was building a chain of logic, and as intent on his work as any shaven-skulled theologian. "She'd long since have been wed if the lot of you hadn't been sent to Kalavria," he said. "I don't suppose our uncle was able to find a suitable match for her there."

"Well, no, he couldn't," Maniakes said, and then changed the subject by main force: "We'll be getting into Kyzikos tomorrow, I expect. I'll want you to use some of the vanguard—men you can count on, mind you—to surround the mint there and make sure it's not plundered. I don't know how much gold we'll be able to draw from it, but the one thing we can't do is get in arrears on the soldiers' pay."

"I shall attend to it," Parsmanios promised. "I'll speak to my captains tonight, let them help me pick out a good, reliable company."

Maniakes frowned. His brother should already have had a good idea of which companies under his command were good ones, which not so good. Till he came to Videssos the city, he hadn't enjoyed high rank. If you were to deserve high rank, though, you couldn't just enjoy it; you also had to meet the demands it set on you. Maniakes hoped Parsmanios would learn that. He didn't have much time.

As Maniakes' little force headed west along the north bank of the Arandos, the land began to rise toward the central plateau, at first so slowly it was hard to notice, then more rapidly. The Arandos itself seemed to shake off age as the Avtokrator moved farther from its mouth. It flowed more rapidly and in a straighter course, giving up on looping back on itself as it bumped over a series of rapids as the plateau drew near.

Garsavra lay at the very edge of the westlands' central plateau, at the confluence of the Arandos and the Eriza, which came down from the north. Had it not been for the rapids that hindered trade coming up from the east, Garsavra might have grown into a great city. Even as things stood, it was the chief trading town for the eastern part of the plateau.

It also had stout fortifications in excellent repair. When the hypasteos, a plump, important-looking little fellow named Rhousas, came out of the city to prostrate himself before Maniakes, the Avtokrator complimented him on that.

"Oh, I thank you very much, your Majesty," Rhousas answered as he rose. "I do my best to keep this city ready to hold out as long as may be against the attacks of the fearsome Makuraners, who know not Phos." By the way he strutted in place, he might have been personally responsible for every stone that had gone into the wall.

Maniakes had heard that sort of self-aggrandizement too often in his nearly a year on the throne to let it impress him. "I suppose your garrison commander had nothing to do with getting your city ready to defend itself."

He had seen officials deflate like popped pigs' bladders when he made that sort of remark to them. He glanced over to the garrison commander, a gray-bearded, weatherbeaten man who seemed half asleep. Rhousas said, "Oh, yes, the excellent Byzakios did lend a hand. But the garrison numbers only a couple of hundred, and he was so busy seeking to form a city militia that he and his men played but a small role in the recent reconstruction."

"A couple of hundred? For a town this large and important, in a time when we're invaded?" Maniakes turned to Byzakios. "Surely you had more men once. What happened to the rest of them?"

" 'Bout what you'd expect, your Majesty," Byzakios answered, his voice full of an upcountry twang. "Some of 'em got killed in this fight or that. And others, well, they were just stolen, you ask me. Every time a rebel came through, he'd pull away a few more. I sent Tzikas a draft of three hundred; I reckoned he'd need 'em worse'n I did."

"I think you're right," Maniakes answered. "I think you did very well indeed to train up a militia to take the place of your departed soldiers, too. In a pinch, will they fight?"

"You never know till the day comes," Byzakios said. "Maybe so, maybe not. Best guess is, they'll do all right up on the wall, but Phos' light take their souls if the Makuraners break in despite 'em."

"Aye, that sounds likely," Maniakes agreed. "When amateurs like that get into hand-to-hand with professional soldiers, they'll come off second best every time." He sighed. "You're stripped down to a couple of hundred regulars? I can't take many away from you, then."

"May I talk frank, your Majesty?" Byzakios asked. When Maniakes nodded, the commandant studied him, then muttered, half to himself, "Well, he *was* a soldier his own self." To Maniakes, he said, "You better not take any, not if you want this town to have any chance of holding. You want my head because the mouth in it's too big, you've got your excuse to take it."

"It seems to be doing a good enough job up there on your shoulders, excellent sir," Maniakes said. "We'll leave it there for now."

A look passed between Byzakios and Rhousas. Maniakes had seen that look before when he dealt for the first time with officials who didn't know him personally. It said, *He's not Genesios,* and pleased and saddened him at the same time. True, it was a compliment, but one that should have been superfluous. Genesios had a great deal for which to answer; Maniakes suspected he would be answering to Skotos for all eternity.

Rhousas said, "I am sorry, your Majesty, but we have little revenue for the fisc. Commerce these past few years has been very bad. Goods come in down the Arandos and the Eriza, but not much goes out, especially to westward. In good years, we'd send caravan after caravan to the *panegyris,* the trade fair, at Amorion. This year—" He spread his hands in regret.

"Not much point going on to Amorion when you know you can't go further without likely getting robbed and murdered," Byzakios said.

"Too true," Maniakes said mournfully. "For that matter, there's the risk of getting robbed and murdered *inside* Amorion. What news have you from there? Are the Makuraners pressing against the city, and what force has Tzikas inside it to hold them at bay?"

"They are moving, there west of Amorion," Byzakios answered. "We don't know all we ought to from out there: Have to rely on spies and such in what by rights is our very own land." He shook his head indignantly. "Terrible thing. Anyways, Tzikas has several thousand soldiers, along with whatever he's done about getting the townsfolk ready to fight. They'll fight hard, I reckon. They know nothing good'll happen to 'em if they yield themselves up, that's sure: prisoners go to digging underground, it's said."

"Can Tzikas hold, if Abivard throws everything he has against the place?" Maniakes asked.

Byzakios and Rhousas looked at each other again. This time, the unspoken question was, *How much truth can we tell?* At last, Byzakios answered a question with another question: "Your Majesty, when the Makuraners throw everything these days, what holds?"

"Something had better start holding," Maniakes said, kicking at the dirt, "or the whole Empire will come crashing down. Curse it, we can beat the Makuraners in battle. My father and I did it at the end of Likinios' reign. By the good god, Stavrakios sacked Mashiz."

"Ah, your Majesty, but that was a long time ago," Rhousas answered sadly. Maniakes couldn't tell whether the city governor meant Stavrakios' exploits or his own.

Garsavra gave every sign of being a town with a prosperous history. The local shrine, like a lot of such centers all through the Empire, was modeled after the High Temple in Videssos the city. A lot of such imitations deserved the name more by intent than by its execution, but from Garsavra's shrine one could get at least a feeling for what the original was like.

The local temple fronted on the market square in the center of town. That expanse of cobbles was almost as big as the plaza of Palamas back in the capital. Everyone from Rhousas down to the apprentice grooms in the stables spoke of how that square had been packed with merchants from the capital, from Opsikion and even Kalavria in the east, from Amorion and Vaspurakan and Mashiz in the west.

It was not packed now. A couple of potters had set up forlorn booths in one corner, displaying earthenware made from the grayish-yellow local clay. A herder had half a dozen lambs to sell. A couple of weavers displayed bolts of wool. At a portable desk, a scribe wrote a letter for a patron who could not. Over most of the square, though, pigeons strutted in search of crumbs, with scrawny cats prowling after them.

When Maniakes came out of the hypasteos' residence to walk across to the temple to pray, the merchants abandoned their stalls and ran up to him, crying, "Mercy, your Majesty!" "How can we pay the hearth tax and the head tax, let alone that on our profits?" "We have no profits, by the good god!" "Mercy, mercy!"

He wondered how many merchants in how many cities would have sung the same tune had he appeared before them. Too many; he knew that much. "I'll do what I can for you," he said, and felt how inadequate the words were. The best thing he could do to help the merchants—the best thing he could do to help the Empire—would be to drive the Makuraners out of Videssian territory once and for all. He had never had any trouble figuring out what wanted doing. How to do it was something else again.

After a couple of days' rest and resupply, Maniakes and his little army made for Amorion. Once they were up on the plateau, the weather got less muggy, though it continued blazing hot. Grain and fruit trees grew close by the Arandos and along the banks of its small tributaries. Away from water, the land was baked dusty, with only scrubby grass and brush growing on it. Cattle and sheep grazed on the scrub.

"We'll be able to keep the army fed and watered, even if the supply lines fail," Parsmanios observed at camp one evening. "My little force in Vryetion lived off the local herds a good deal of the time."

"I'd like to be able to pay for any animals I end up having to take," Maniakes said. "Of course, what I'd like to do and what I can do are liable to be two different beasts. Wearing the red boots has taught me that."

"Any command will," Parsmanios agreed. "The bigger the command, I suppose, the harder the lesson."

Maniakes listened carefully to his brother's tone. Another thing sitting on the imperial throne had taught him was that you couldn't trust anybody. He hated having to try to gauge how sour Parsmanios sounded at any given moment, but couldn't see what choice he had.

He said, "Another three or four days and we'll be in Amorion. Then we can stop worrying about our supply lines for a while—and start worrying about whether Abivard is going to try storming the place with us inside it." His laugh was anything but jolly. "Another thing you learn is that you're always worrying about something. The day you think everything is fine is the day you haven't noticed the plot against you just starting to bubble."

"I expect you're right." Parsmanios rose and sketched a salute. "I'm going to see to my men and then turn in."

"Good enough, brother of mine." Maniakes liked the way Parsmanios assumed the responsibility that went with commanding the vanguard. It was a far bigger command than he had ever had before, but he was shaping well in it—Maniakes had not had any complaints about his diligence since that evening outside of Kyzikos. If he ever scraped together enough troops to operate with two armies at the same time, Parsmanios might well make a capable commander for one of them. The Avtokrator rubbed his chin. Tzikas was already commanding an army, and had been doing so as a virtually independent lord for several years now. Promoting Parsmanios over his head would not please him. Would it touch off a revolt? Maniakes would have to think about that, too.

"Wearing the red boots also teaches you life is much more complicated than you'd ever imagined," he told the silk walls of his tent. Unlike his livelier subjects, they did not argue with him.

The scout who came galloping back to Maniakes kicked up a plume of dust. Maniakes spied it long before the scout himself became visible. The fellow reined in; his horse was lathered and blowing. After saluting Maniakes with clenched right fist over his heart, he said, "We've spotted dust ahead, your Majesty—lots of it, and getting closer fast."

Maniakes frowned. "Any idea who's kicking it up?"

"No, your Majesty," the scout said.

"Could be reinforcements," Maniakes said hopefully. But even he didn't think that was likely. "Reinforcements hereabouts should be heading straight for Amorion, not for us."

"That's so, your Majesty," the rider agreed. "Whatever that is, it's heading dead away from Amorion, no two ways about it."

"No." Maniakes shaded his eyes with his left hand and peered westward. He clicked his tongue between his teeth. "I don't see anything—yet. But if a lot of men are coming from Amorion, odds are they're either our troopers fleeing the place—or Makuraners who've taken it. Ride back to your place; be ready if Parsmanios needs you to carry more messages."

"Aye." The horseman saluted again and set spurs to his mount, urging the animal up into a gallop as fast as he could.

Maniakes turned to the trumpeters who were never far from his person on campaign. "Order the army into battle array," he said. The musicians saluted, raised the long, straight brass horns to their lips, and blared out the signal that would take Maniakes' little force out of column and into line. "We'll anchor our left on the Arandos," he shouted.

Each regiment broke in two. Half of one regiment stayed back to protect the baggage train and form a reserve. The other half and the whole regiment deployed in three elements, the center one—the one Maniakes led—forward. It was a flexible formation, well prepared to deal with anything . . . except overwhelming numbers.

The force had practiced going from column into line of battle many times and moved now without undue fuss or wasted motion. Even so, by the time they were ready to fight, Maniakes could clearly see the dust the men of the vanguard had already spotted. He clamped his jaw down hard to help keep from showing his worry. As the scout had said, somebody out there was kicking up a *lot* of dust.

Then horsemen in mail shirts emerged from out of the dust. He recognized some of their surcoats and banners—his own vanguard was mixed in among them. A shout rose above the drumming of the horses' hooves: "Amorion is fallen!"

When he understood that cry, he grunted as if he had taken a blow to the belly. In truth, the Empire of Videssos had taken the blow. For years, the fortress at Amorion had kept the Makuraners from overrunning the Arandos valley and perhaps from reaching the Sailors' Sea. If Abivard had at last forced his way into Amorion—

"You, there!" Maniakes shouted, pointing to a fleeing horseman who did not belong to his own vanguard. "Tell me at once what happened off to the west."

For a moment, he thought the soldier would ride on by without stopping or answering. He hadn't been part of a rout till Etzilios ambushed him outside Imbros, but now he knew how to recognize one. At the last instant, though, the fellow reined in and shouted, "Amorion is fallen!"

It might have been a cry of lamentation like those in Phos' sacred scriptures, wherein the lord with the great and good mind nearly despaired over the wicked way of mankind. The fugitives took it up again and again: "Amorion is fallen!" "—is fallen!" "—is fallen!" "—is fallen!"

As the cry echoed and reechoed, Maniakes' men cried out,

too, in anger and alarm. They knew—he had taken pains to impress upon them—how important the city at the west end of the Arandos was. And, unschooled in formal logic though they were, they could reason out the misfortune its fall implied.

"Does Tzikas still live?" Maniakes called to the man who had stopped.

"Aye, so he does," the cavalryman answered, and then, recognizing Maniakes' regalia, added, "your Majesty." He wiped sweat from his forehead with the sleeve of his surcoat before going on. "He commands the rear guards; Phos bless him and keep him safe, he's still trying to hold the boiler boys away from the rest of us."

"Get into line with us," Maniakes said, not just to him but to all the fugitives within earshot. "We'll ride forward to Tzikas' aid and, the good god willing, surprise the Makuraners and steal a victory from them."

His calm and the good order of the force he led persuaded some of the soldiers who had abandoned Amorion to try fighting again. Others, though, kept on going, thinking flight their only refuge. Maniakes did not have enough men to hold them in line by force. And their fear infected some of the warriors who had been with him since Videssos the city, so that they wheeled their horses and fled with the fugitives. Their companions tried to stop them, but too often in vain.

Another scout rode back to Maniakes from the vanguard. Saluting, the fellow said, "Your Majesty, the most eminent sir your brother bids me warn you his force is cracking to pieces like the ice on a stream at the start of springtime. His very words."

"Tell him he may fall back on the main body here, but—" Maniakes waved an arm to show the chaos all around him. "—we're in the same boat, and I fear the boat is sinking." The scout saluted and rode back toward the vanguard. The scores of men coming the other way stared at him and shouted out warnings. One or two took courage from his example and stayed to fight alongside the Avtokrator. Most, though, just shook their heads and kept on fleeing.

Along with the vanguard Parsmanios commanded, a new group of warriors approached Maniakes and his men. Among them was a standard bearer still holding the Videssian banner, gold sunburst on blue, on high. Next to him rode a gray-bearded fellow in gilded chain mail on a fine gray horse.

"Eminent Tzikas!" Maniakes shouted, loud as he could.

The gray-bearded man's head came up. Maniakes waved to him. He started to wave back, then seemed to recognize Maniakes and changed the gesture to a salute. "Your Majesty!" he called, and rode toward the Avtokrator.

Maniakes waved at the chaos all around them. "What happened?" he asked. "After holding so long—"

Tzikas shrugged, as if to deny that any of the sorry spectacle was his fault. "We lost, your Majesty," he answered. "That's what happens when every Makuraner in the world comes at you, when none of the other generals in the westlands will lend you a counterfeit copper's worth of aid, when all we hear from Videssos the city is that there's no help to be had there, either, or else that your head is forfeit if you ever take a pace away from the soldiers who protect you—" He made a disgusted gesture. "I could go on, but what's the use? To the ice with it. To the ice with everything."

"Amorion's gone to the ice, seems like," Maniakes said. He remembered that Tzikas had blamed the failings of one of his fellow generals for the defeat in which Tatoules disappeared, and wondered if the man knew how to take responsibility for his own actions.

"Do you think you'd have done better, your Majesty?" Tzikas growled—almost the same question Genesios had put to Maniakes when he was captured.

"Who can say?" Maniakes looked Tzikas up and down. "Splendid footgear you have there, eminent sir," he remarked. But for a couple of narrow black stripes, Tzikas' boots were of imperial crimson. At any distance, they would have looked like the red boots reserved for the Avtokrator alone.

The general shrugged again. "The way things have been, all the Videssian authority around these parts has been invested in me—nothing much coming from the capital but trouble, as I said. I thought I ought to look the part, or come as close to it as I could in law and custom."

He was on this side of both law and custom—barely on this side, but inarguably so. Maniakes wondered if, one fine day, he might have pulled on boots without any black stripes. The Avtokrator wouldn't have been a bit surprised. Taking Tzikas to task, though, would have to wait. "Are you pursued?" he asked the ever-so-punctilious general.

"We're not riding east to settle our supper, your Majesty," Tzikas answered. "Aye, the boiler boys are on our trail, great droves of 'em." He peered north, then south, gauging the forces Maniakes had with him. "No point even standing in their way. They'll go through you like a knife through fat bacon."

"Mm, not necessarily," Maniakes answered after a moment's thought. "They're chasing what they think is a broken band of fugitives, after all. If we hit the ones out in front of the pursuit and hit them hard, we may be able to knock their whole army back on its heels. Phos willing, we'll save the Arandos valley for this year, or most of it, anyhow."

Tzikas' face was pinched and narrow, not one for showing joy under the best of circumstances. Now that circumstances were far from the best, he all but radiated gloom. "Your Majesty, if you press forward and see the numbers arrayed against us, you will know resistance is hopeless."

"Until I see them for myself, I don't know anything of the kind," Maniakes answered. "Eminent sir, if you and as many of your men as you can bring want to ride with us, you'll be welcome and you can give useful aid. If not, then kindly keep running east; don't stay around infecting us with the notion that everything is lost."

He waited to see how Tzikas would take that. The general scowled; he wasn't used to taking orders or to being dismissed so peremptorily. After a moment, he said, "You are the Avtokrator; it shall be as you command." His voice was flat, empty of any feeling whatsoever, for good or ill.

Maniakes could not fault him when he started shouting to his men to rally. He had a bigger voice than his slim frame suggested, and used it to good effect. Some of the horsemen fleeing the fall of Amorion kept right on fleeing, but others reined in and began adding themselves to Maniakes' regiments. Maniakes' troopers seemed to gain fresh heart, too, seeing that not everything was falling to pieces before their eyes.

"Forward!" Maniakes shouted. The trumpeters sent the command to the whole force, as if the men were ships spread across the sea. They advanced at a trot they could quickly kick up to a gallop at need.

Here and there, they passed Videssians leading lame horses and men on foot whose horses must have foundered altogether or been killed. Those soldiers stared in disbelief at the spectacle of a strong force from their own side heading toward the oncoming Makuraners rather than away from them.

They also passed dead horses and dead men—freshly dead, not yet bloated and stinking. Those would have been wounded

when they fled Amorion and its environs, but they hadn't
made it to safety. Maniakes' mouth was a thin, bitter line. So
many men thrown away these past seven years. Genesios
couldn't have done a better job of gutting the Empire if he had
set out to accomplish exactly that.

Then Maniakes spied another body of soldiery riding east.
At first, from a distance, he thought they were more imperials
trying to break free from the Makuraners. After a moment, he
realized they were the Makuraners from whom the garrison at
Amorion had been trying to get free.

They rode big, strong horses. With their style of fighting,
they needed such sturdy beasts, too. The riders wore full armor
of chain and splints, with lamellae protecting their arms and
legs. Chainmail veils of iron rings hung from their helmets to
ward their face. Only their eyes and hands showed, and iron
half-gauntlets held weapons away from the backs of those
hands.

Even their horses wore iron scales mounted on leather, an
armor that reached back to the animals' flanks. The riders carried long, heavy spears, with swords slung in scabbards on
their left sides so they could protect themselves if their
spearshafts broke in battle.

"Ply them with arrows!" Maniakes shouted. "Stay at long
range and scattered—don't come to close quarters with them."
Those were standard tactics for Videssians fighting their western neighbors. Videssian cavalrymen wore mail shirt and helmet only, and never rode armored horses. The Makuraner
horsemen and their mounts had to be sweltering in the heat,
which was why the Videssians had given them the scornful
"boiler boy" nickname.

The Makuraners' lances came down to point straight at their
foes; the sun sparkled off sharp-edged iron. "Sharbaraz King
of Kings!" the heavy-armored cavalrymen shouted in their own
language. Maniakes spoke it, not with any great fluency but
enough to make himself understood. The Makuraners had other
cries, too: "Abivard!" and "Hosios Avtokrator!"

Maniakes looked around for Abivard but did not see him.
The enemy who had been his friend must not have been with
his foremost troops. His own men yelled "Videssos!" and
"Maniakes Avtokrator!" back at the Makuraners. A few
Videssians also yelled "Tzikas!" They all sounded fierce and
spirited, which made Maniakes' heart leap. Videssians had lost

so many fights lately that any show of courage had to come as a surprise to their foes.

His troopers reached back over their shoulders to pluck arrows from their quivers, then nocked them, drew bows back to their eyes, and let fly. A couple of hundred years before, such horse archery would have been much more difficult, but stirrups let a rider control his mount well enough that he could without hesitation use both hands to shoot. Stirrups also let the Makuraners charge with the lance without fear of being unseated: Videssos and Makuran had taken the same notion and gone in different directions with it.

Not all of Maniakes' troops were archers. For closer-in work, javelin men nipped toward the enemy, flung their darts, and then tried to make off before the Makuraners could draw near enough to spear them out of the saddle. Not all of them escaped as they would have hoped. At close quarters, an armored Makuraner boiler boy was more than a match for any one Videssian horseman.

The trick, though, was not to let the Makuraners use their superior power to full advantage. Maniakes' men outnumbered their foes. No armor covered every part of a man's body; no armor kept every shaft from penetrating. After a short, sharp combat, the Makuraners broke off and tried to escape.

That wasn't easy. Their horses still had to carry the extra weight of iron they bore. And the horses wore no armor behind. The Videssians plied their vulnerable haunches with arrows. The horses screamed in pain and terror. Their harassed riders fought hard to master them.

Maniakes' troopers cheered like wild men at the startling sight of Makuraners showing their backs. They galloped after the boiler boys with more spirit and excitement than Videssian troops had shown in the westlands for years.

"How far will you let them go?" Tzikas asked, adding "your Majesty" half a beat late. "Before long, either the Makuraners will rally or they'll find more of their kind and punish us for our presumption."

He was very possibly right. Biting his lip, Maniakes acknowledged that with a grudged nod. But, with fussy caution such as Tzikas had shown, no wonder the Makuraners had run wild through the westlands. If you assumed taking the initiative against them was presumption, you wouldn't take the initiative. Tzikas might well be a genius of a defensive fighter; he probably was, to have held Amorion so long. Still, while lack of defense could make you lose a war, having it was no guarantee you would win.

Maniakes realized he hadn't answered the general's question, which, phrased differently, had also been in his own mind. "We'll go a little farther," he said. "Having the men know they can beat the boiler boys may be worth more to us than goldpieces."

"Having them think they can beat the Makuraners only to discover they're wrong may cost us more than goldpieces," Tzikas answered dolorously.

Again, Maniakes nodded. He waved on his horsemen nonetheless. It occurred to him that he might need to worry less than he had thought about Tzikas' trying to usurp the throne. By all signs, the man was too cautious to go squat behind a bush at night without shining a torch there to make sure he wouldn't meet a bear.

Maniakes drew his sword. So did Tzikas. His face stayed set in disapproving lines, but he did not lack animal courage. Together, they joined the Videssian cavalry in pursuit of the Makuraners.

The leaders from among Maniakes' men had got well ahead of the Avtokrator and the general. Maniakes urged his gelding after them. Just before he caught them up, fresh horn calls came up ahead, horn calls different from those Videssos used. "Straighten up, there!" Maniakes shouted to the horsemen in front of him. "Form line of battle. Don't pelt after them like a herd of sheep gone mad on crazyweed."

"There are a lot of Makuraners up there," Tzikas remarked. It wasn't *I told you so*, but it might as well have been.

Along with the horn calls, shouts and screams rang out. All at once, Maniakes'. horsemen were no longer pursuers but pursued. They came galloping back toward him, riding harder than they had after the fleeing Makuraner heavy cavalry. Horses' barrels ran with blood from frantic spurring; animals' flanks showed lines from the whip.

Close behind them, in no better order, coursed more Makuraner riders. These were not boiler boys, but the light cavalry the King of Kings used to bulk up his forces. They were armed with bows and swords, and armored for the most part with nothing more than iron pots for their heads and heavy leather jerkins. Maniakes knew their kind: wild and fierce when they had the advantage, and as quick to panic if things went wrong or they were checked.

But how to check them? "Stand fast!" Maniakes cried; individually, his men enjoyed the same advantage over the Makuraner light horsemen as the heavy cavalry did over the Videssians. But the imperials would not stand fast, not when they saw enemy horsemen sliding round their flanks.

In a fury, Maniakes spurred toward the Makuraners. They scattered before him; they had no taste for hand-to-hand combat with a man both well protected and bold. Tzikas stayed at his right hand, slashing with his sword. A few other imperials rode with them, doing their best to stem the building rout.

Maniakes traded sword strokes with a Makuraner too hemmed in to evade him. Whatever words the fellow shouted were lost in the general din of combat. Sweat carved canyons through the pale dust covering the soldier's swarthy skin. His face was long, rectangular, solemn, with large, dark, deep-set eyes that could show soulful seriousness but now blazed with blood lust.

With a cunning stroke, Maniakes knocked the sword from his hand. It flew spinning into the dirt. But, before the Avtokrator could finish him, another Makuraner made straight for him. He had to twist awkwardly to meet the new onslaught, and knew a moment's stark fear that he would not be able to twist in time.

Then Tzikas attacked the oncoming horseman, forcing him to sheer off before he could strike at the Avtokrator. "My thanks," Maniakes said. He turned back toward the Makuraner he had disarmed, but the fellow had taken advantage of his moment of distraction to get away.

"I am privileged to serve your Majesty," Tzikas said. Maniakes had trouble reading anything into his tone. Was that simple statement of fact, submissiveness, or irony? The Avtokrator could not tell.

He got no time to worry about it, either. More Makuraner horns were winded. He had a brief glimpse of more horsemen riding to the growing fight from out of the west. Grimacing, he nodded toward Tzikas. "Seems you were right, eminent sir," he said. "Now let's see how we can get ourselves out of this mess."

"Aye, your Majesty." Tzikas hesitated, then went on, "Do you know, neither Likinios nor Genesios, so far as I remember, ever admitted he was wrong."

"Maybe I'm just new on the throne," Maniakes said, his voice dry. Tzikas sent him a sharp look, then decided it was a joke and laughed. Maniakes continued, "Admitting I made the mistake doesn't much help me put it to rights now."

"No, not this time," Tzikas agreed. "But that may not be so on some other occasion—provided we live to see other occasions."

"Yes, provided," Maniakes said. Given the number of Makuraners who swarmed forward to shoot arrows at his men, that was by no means obvious. The tactical solution presenting itself—that was all too obvious, with headlong retreat the only possible choice to escape catastrophe.

Though Videssian doctrine dealt matter-of-factly with retreat, Maniakes bared his teeth in an anguished scowl. His own willingness to push forward to meet Etzilios had led to disaster outside of Imbros. Now he had been impetuous again, and was again paying the price for it.

"I wish I were a turtle," he said to no one in particular. "I'd go into my shell and never come out."

"This can have its advantages," Tzikas said with a grave nod. "Thus Amorion remained in our hands throughout Genesios' unhappy reign."

"And thus it was lost in mine," Maniakes answered. "A proud record, isn't it? But you may be right more often than not—you certainly are this time. I can't help thinking, though, that sometimes the cure for too much boldness is more, not less."

Tzikas' dark, mournful eyes did all the contradicting he couldn't speak aloud. For now, though, boldness in attack was simply out of the question. Avtokrator and general rode side by side, fighting when they had to and doing their best to hold the retreat in check.

"Rally! Rally!" someone cried in Videssian: Parsmanios. When he spied his brother, he said, "Here's a fine mixed-up day, where the leader of the main force gets ahead of the leader of the van."

"Here's a fine dreadful day," Maniakes said. Then he added his own voice to Parsmanios', trying to persuade his cavalrymen and those who had originally ridden with Tzikas to hold fast. Now and again, he thought he would succeed. But then either more Makuraners would come up or the Videssians would begin to melt away, and he would have to fall back and try again.

At last, not long before sunset, his forces succeeded not in halting the Makuraners but in breaking free of them and being able to set up camp without getting attacked while they were going about it. A miserable camp it was, too. Wounded men groaned and cursed. Here and there, healer-priests labored to bring forth their curative magic and restore to health some warriors who had been grievously wounded.

As always, Maniakes watched the blue-robes with more than a little awe. When one of them laid hands on a man, even someone as blind to magic as the Avtokrator could sense the current of healing passing to the one who was hurt. And, when the priest took his hands away, the healed wound would look as if it had been suffered years before.

But the cost on the healer-priests was high. After each man they treated, they would emerge from their healing trance like men awakening from some killing labor after not enough rest. They would gulp food and swill down wine, then lurch on to the next desperate case. And, after they had healed two or perhaps three men each, they would fall asleep so deeply that even kicking at them did no more than make them stir and mutter.

Men whose hurts were not bad enough to require such drastic intervention made do with surgeons who drew arrows and sewed up gashes and poured wine over wounds to keep them from rotting. So the surgeons said, at any rate. Maniakes often wondered if they helped as many men as they hurt.

He strode through the camp, doing his best to keep up the soldiers' spirits. He found Bagdasares sitting on the ground with his head in his hands, as if afraid it would fall off if he didn't keep tight hold on it. "Magical sir, have you any skill in healing?" Maniakes asked.

Bagdasares looked up. "What's that?" he said blankly. "Oh, your Majesty. No, I'm sorry, I fear I have none whatever. Even among mages, healers are a special breed. Their gift can be trained if it is present, but it must be inborn; I know of no man without that innate talent who ever succeeded in relieving another's misery."

Maniakes sighed. "I thought you would say something of the sort, else you would have been laboring with the priests as best you could. By the good god, though, I wish it were otherwise. If you cannot heal, what can you accomplish for us in this joyless place?"

"Not even as much as a fighting man could," Bagdasares answered with a guilty frown. "All I'm good for is eating up food that might instead go to someone who has a chance of keeping both himself and me alive."

"How do we change that in the future?" Maniakes asked. "Wizards should not have so many limits on their sorcerous powers."

"We do better than we once did," Bagdasares said. "In the days of Stavrakios the Great, the healing art was but newly born, and as likely to kill a healer-priest as to cure the poor chap he was trying to save."

"We know more of other arts than they did in his day, too," Maniakes said. "I was thinking about that not so long ago— you read the accounts of his campaigns and you'll see he and his followers didn't know the use of stirrups. I wouldn't like to try riding without them, I tell you that."

He rubbed his chin, thinking how strange it was to be talking about changes from long-ago days after a lost battle. Even thinking about changes from long-ago days felt strange. He hadn't noted any changes in the way he lived through his whole lifetime, save those that went with his own change in age and station. He didn't ever remember his father talking about such changes, either; if they had gone on, they had done so at a pace too slow for any one man to notice.

But go on they had. A river would eventually shift its bed with the passing years. So, too, when you looked far enough, the course of human knowledge and endeavor shifted. He supposed that accumulation of slow, steady, but in the end significant changes had been growing since the day when Phos created Vaspur, firstborn of all mankind.

He let out a snort. If he was to be properly orthodox by Videssian standards, he could not let himself believe in the tale of Vaspur and other doctrinal matters the most holy Agathios would no doubt term heretical. He shook his head. No—he could not let himself be seen to believe in the tale of Vaspur and the rest.

"Your Majesty?" Bagdasares asked, wondering what the snort and the headshake meant.

"Never mind," Maniakes said. "Fuzz on the brain, that's all. Amazing, the notions I can come up with to keep from thinking about the mess we're in."

"Ah, yes," Bagdasares answered. "The mess we're in. What do we do about it? What *can* we do about it?"

"Nothing I can see," Maniakes said, the words bitter as alum in his mouth. "Come morning, the Makuraners are going to attack us again. They'll have more men than we will, and they'll have their peckers up because they've beaten us once."

"They've beaten us more than once," Bagdasares said incautiously.

"Too true," Maniakes said. "So long as they keep it in mind—as we have to as well—it'll be worth extra men to their side . . . not that they'll need extra men tomorrow. They'll attack us, they'll beat us, and we'll have to retreat again. Pretty soon we'll be back in Garsavra, at the edge of the plateau." He scowled. "By the good god, pretty soon we'll be back in Videssos the city, with all the westlands lost."

"Surely it won't be so bad as that," Bagdasares said.

"You're right," Maniakes said glumly. "It's liable to be worse."

Scouts from the rear guard came galloping into Maniakes' miserable camp not long after dawn began painting the eastern sky with pink and gold. "The Makuraners are moving!" they shouted in tones that could have been no more horror-stricken were they announcing the end of the world.

As far as the Empire of Videssos went, they might as well have been announcing the end of the world.

Maniakes had hoped to mount a defense, maybe even a counterattack, against the men from Makuran. One look at his army's reaction to the news that the enemy was on the way drove that thought from his head. Men cried out in alarm. Some fled on foot; others made as if to rush the guards who were keeping watch on the long lines of tethered horses. No one showed the slightest eagerness to fight.

"What now, your Majesty?" Tzikas asked. He still wasn't saying *I told you so*, but by his expression he was thinking it very loudly now.

"We fall back," Maniakes answered bleakly. "What else can we do?" While Videssian military doctrine did not necessarily condemn retreat, after a while you got to the point where you had no room left in which to retreat. His situation in the westlands was rapidly approaching that point.

Tzikas sighed with more resignation than Maniakes could make himself feel. "Ah, well, your Majesty," he said, evidently trying to console, "had we not run into them yesterday, they would have come upon us in short order."

"Which doesn't make our predicament here any better."

Maniakes raised his voice to a shout that carried through the camp: "Parsmanios!"

His brother hurried up to his tent a couple of minutes later. "Aye, your Majesty?" he asked, as formally polite as if unrelated to the Avtokrator.

"You'll go from vanguard commander to rear guard today," Maniakes said. "I don't expect miracles; just try to keep 'em off us as best you can."

"I'll do whatever I'm able to," Parsmanios answered. He hurried away.

"Command me, your Majesty," Tzikas said.

Maniakes was reluctant to do that; he gauged Tzikas' obedience as springing more from policy than from conviction. But, without any choice, he said, "Stay by me. We'll fight side by side, as we did yesterday."

"Let it be as you say," Tzikas replied. Even as he spoke, the sound of Makuraner horns blown in excitement and triumph came faintly to Maniakes' ear across a rapidly shrinking stretch of ground.

"Fall back!" the Avtokrator ordered, and his own hornplayers relayed the dolorous call to everyone within earshot.

It wasn't a complete rout, not quite. Maniakes' soldiers hung together as a unit instead of wildly riding off every which way in search of safety. Maniakes hoped that was because of the discipline he had helped instill in them on their way to the encounter with the Makuraners. He was, however, realistic enough to suspect that the troopers stuck together only because they thought they were likelier to survive by doing so.

The running fight lasted from dawn till late afternoon. Then Maniakes set an ambush in a grove of almond trees not far from the Arandos. The only way he could get his men to stay there and await the Makuraners was to lead the ambush party himself. Even then, he had to growl at one nervous horseman: "You try and run off on me and I'll kill you myself."

Before long, the Makuraners came up, a few boiler boys mixed with a larger band of light horsemen. They rode in loose order, laughing and joking and plainly not looking for any trouble. *Why should they?* Maniakes thought bitterly. *We haven't given them any up till now.*

He drew his sword. "Videssos!" he shouted, and spurred his horse out of its hiding place.

For a hideous instant, he thought the men he had gathered would let him ride to his doom all alone. Then more shouts of

"Videssos!" and some of "Maniakes!" split the air. The thunder of hoofbeats behind him was some of the sweetest music he had ever heard.

The Makuraners looked almost comically horrified as he and his men barreled toward them. The fight was over bare moments after it began. The Videssians rode through and over their foes, plying bow, javelin, and sword with a will. A few Makuraners managed to break out of the engagement, their cries of terror loud and lovely in Maniakes' ears. More, though, either died at once or were overtaken and slain from behind.

"A victory! A great victory!" yelled the man Maniakes had threatened to kill. He was bold now, even if he hadn't been then, and the Avtokrator did not begrudge him his sudden access of spirit. Seeing Maniakes, he asked, "What does our victory bring us, your Majesty?"

Maniakes wished he would have picked almost any other question. He didn't answer aloud, but all he had won by routing the Makuraners' advance party was the chance to camp for the night without being attacked and then, when morning came, to resume the retreat.

Tzikas undoubtedly would have thought he was lucky to get even that much. Maybe Tzikas was right; in his stand at Amorion, he had shown himself a master of defensive fighting. But Maniakes remained convinced he could not win by merely defending. As soon as he could, he aimed to take the offensive.

As soon as he could, though, wouldn't be any time soon. And, moreover— "Take the offensive where?" he said. Try as he would, he found no answer.

IX

From the little harbor in the palace quarter, Maniakes glumly peered west over the Cattle Crossing at the smoke rising in great fat columns above the suburb called Across. Only that narrow stretch of water—and the dromons that unceasingly patrolled it—held the armies of the King of Kings away from Videssos the city.

"In all the wars we've ever fought with the Makuraners, they've never reached the Cattle Crossing before," he said morosely.

His father sighed and clapped him on the shoulder. "So long as they don't get across the strait, you still have the chance to go down in history as the great hero who drove them back from the very brink of victory," the elder Maniakes said.

"What brink?" Maniakes said. "They have their victory, right there. And how am I supposed to drive them back? They've cut me off from the westlands, and we draw most of our tax revenues from that part of the Empire. How will I pay my soldiers? Phos, Father, they aren't even ravaging Across and letting it go at that. From what the sailors say, they're settling in to winter there."

"I would, in their sandals," the elder Maniakes answered calmly. "Still, just because they're at Across doesn't mean they hold all the westlands."

"I know that," Maniakes said. "We're still strong in the hill country of the southeast, and not far from the border with Vaspurakan, and we still hold a good many towns. But with Abivard's army plugging the way against us, we can't do much to support the forces we still have there, and we can't do anything at all to get revenue out of the western provinces."

"I wish I could tell you you're wrong," his father said, "but you're not. One good thing I can see is that Abivard's men have done such a fine job burning out the croplands all around Across that they'll have a hard time keeping themselves fed through the winter, especially if our horsemen can nip in and pinch off their supply lines."

Maniakes grunted. When you had to look at the worst part of a disaster and figure out how it might—eventually—redound to your advantage, you were hard up indeed. As a matter of fact, the Empire of Videssos *was* hard up indeed.

The wind began to rise. It had a nip to it; before long, the fall rains would start, and then the winter snows. He couldn't do anything much about solving the Empire's problems now, no matter how much he wanted to. Come spring, if he was wise enough—and lucky enough—he might improve the situation.

"Niphone seems to be doing well," the elder Maniakes said, sketching the sun-sign to take his words straight up to Phos. "And your daughter has a squawk that would make her a fine herald if she were a man."

"All very well," Maniakes answered, "and the lord with the great and good mind knows I'm grateful for what he chooses to give me. But when set against *that*—" He waved toward the Makuraners on the far side of the Cattle Crossing. "—my personal affairs seem like coppers set against goldpieces."

His father shook his head. "Never belittle your personal affairs. If you're miserable at home, you'll go and do stupid things when you take the field. More stupid things than you would otherwise, I mean."

"Ha!" Maniakes clapped a hand to his forehead. "I was enough of an idiot out there for any eight miserable men you could name. Do you know what Genesios asked me just before I cut off his head? He asked if I'd rule the Empire any better than he had. From what happened my first year, I'd have to say the answer is no."

"Don't take it too much to heart," the elder Maniakes said. "You're still trying to muck out the stables he left you—and he left a lot of muck in them, too."

"Oh, by the good god, didn't he!" Maniakes sighed. "You make me feel better—a little better. But even if the muck isn't all my fault, I can still smell its stink. We'll have to move it farther from the castle." He gestured again toward the smoke rising from Across.

"They can't spend the winter there," his father said. "They can't. After a while, they'll see they can't cross the strait to menace the city, either, and they'll pull back."

But the Makuraners didn't.

Kameas came into the chamber where Maniakes was fighting a losing battle against the provincial tax registers. If no gold came in, how was he supposed to keep doling it out? Could he rob—or, to put it more politely, borrow from—the temples again? Did they have enough gold and silver left to make that worthwhile?

He looked up, in the hope the vestiarios would bear news interesting enough to distract him from his worries. Kameas did: "May it please your Majesty, a messenger has come from the palace harbor. He reports that the Makuraner general Abivard, over in Across, has sent word to one of your ship captains that he would have speech with you."

"Would he?" Maniakes' eyebrows shot up.

"Aye, your Majesty, he would," answered Kameas, who could be quite literal-minded. He went on, "Further, he pledges your safe return if you go over the Cattle Crossing to Across."

Maniakes laughed long and bitterly at that. "Does he indeed? Etzilios made me the same pledge, and see how well that turned out. I may be a fool, but I *can* learn. No matter how generous Abivard is with pledges, I shall not put my head inside the Makuraners' jaws and invite them to bite down."

"Then you will not meet with him?" The vestiarios sounded disappointed, which made Maniakes thoughtful. Kameas went on, "Any chance to compose our differences—"

"Is most unlikely," Maniakes interrupted. Kameas looked as if the Avtokrator had just kicked his puppy. Maniakes held out a hand. "You needn't pout, esteemed sir. I'll talk with him, if he wants to talk with me. But I don't expect miracles. And we're hardly in a position to demand concessions from Abivard, are we?"

"No, your Majesty, though I wish we were," Kameas said. "I shall convey your words to the messenger, who in turn can pass them on to the Makuraner general."

"Thank you, esteemed sir. Tell the messenger to tell Abivard that I will meet with him at the fourth hour of the day tomorrow." Videssos—and Makuran, too—divided day and night into twelve hours each, beginning at sunrise and sunset, respectively. "Let him put his standard on the shore, and I will come and speak to him from a boat. My war galleys will be close by, to prevent any treachery."

"It shall be as you say," Kameas answered, and waddled out to pass on the conditions to the messenger. Maniakes lowered his eyes to the cadaster he had been studying when the vestiarios came in. The numbers refused to mean anything to him. He shut the tax register and thought about seeing Abivard again. As he had told Kameas, it wasn't likely anything would come of talking with him. But hope, like any other hearty weed, was hard to root out altogether.

"There, your Majesty." The officer in command of the boat in which Maniakes rode pointed. "You see the red lion banner flapping on the beach."

"Aye, I see it," Maniakes answered. "By the good god, I hope it's never seen on a Videssian beach again." He glanced back over his shoulder. There on the eastern shore of the Cattle Crossing, he was still Avtokrator, his word obeyed—by those outside his immediate household—as if he were incarnate law. In the land he was approaching, though, Sharbaraz's word, not his, was law.

There beside the Makuraner banner stood a tall man in a fancy striped caftan of fine, soft wool; the fellow wore a sword on his belt and a conical helmet with a feathered crest and a bar nasal on his head. At first Maniakes did not think he could be Abivard, for he had streaks of gray in his beard. As the boat drew closer, though, Maniakes recognized the grandee who had stayed with Sharbaraz even when his cause looked blackest.

He waved. Abivard waved back. "Take us well inside arrow range," Maniakes told the boat captain. "I want to be able to talk without screaming my lungs out."

The fellow gave him a dubious look. "Very well, your Majesty," he said at last, but warned the rowers, "Be ready to get us out of here as fast as you can work the oars." Since Maniakes found that a sensible precaution, he nodded without comment.

In the Makuraner language, Abivard called, "I greet you, Maniakes." No respectful title went with the name; the men of Makuran did not recognize Maniakes as legitimate Avtokrator of the Videssians.

"I greet you, Abivard," Maniakes replied in Videssian. Abivard had mastered some of the Empire's tongue when he and Maniakes campaigned together against Smerdis the Makuraner usurper. Since he had spent so much time in Videssian territory since those days, he probably had more now.

Maniakes expected him either to get on with what he had come to say or to launch into a florid Makuraner harangue about Videssian iniquity. He did neither. Instead, he said, "Have you or your guardsmen any silver shields?"

"Is he daft?" the captain of the small boat murmured.

"I don't know," Maniakes murmured back. By Abivard's intense tone, by the way he stared intently across the water at Maniakes, he meant the question to be taken seriously. Maniakes raised his voice. "No, Abivard. Silver shields are not part of my guards' ceremonial dress, nor of my own. Why do you ask?"

The *no* made Abivard's shoulder slump; Maniakes could see as much, even across the water that separated them. But the Makuraner general rallied and said, "Maniakes, the King of Kings and the Avtokrator should not be at odds with each other, but should govern their states like true brothers. For there is no other empire like these."

"Abivard, I would better like hearing that from you if we were not at war, and if you called me 'Majesty' instead of the fraud and pretender whom Sharbaraz King of Kings—you see, I recognize him; he would not be King of Kings if Videssos had not recognized him—raised up in my place. Sharbaraz wants to be Videssos' big brother, to watch over us and tell us what to do. If you speak of brotherhood, go back to your proper border and do it there, not here at the Cattle Crossing."

"If you will come to an understanding with Sharbaraz King of Kings, may his years be many and his realm increase, the states of Makuran and Videssos will not let their thoughts drift apart from each other. They should be eager to become friendly and to agree," Abivard answered.

Florid Makuraner harangue, indeed, Maniakes thought. Aloud, he replied, "When you say we should become friendly and agree, you mean I should become Sharbaraz's slave."

"If you acknowledge his supremacy, he will grant you a treaty admitting your place on the Videssian throne," Abivard said. "So he has told me, swearing by the God and the Four Prophets. The greatness of this treaty will endure, for when goodwill and friendship toward each other prevail by our using concern and good counsel, it would be unholy to raise arms against each other and unjustly distress and harass our subjects."

"Does that mean you'll be leaving Across this afternoon, or will you wait till tomorrow?" Maniakes asked sweetly.

Abivard ignored him. He had his speech set and he was going to finish it: "What will come of this? If you acknowledge the authority of Sharbaraz King of Kings, may his years be many and his realm increase, you will be more fortunate than other men, and throughout your life you will be admirable and deserve emulation. But if you let this chance go and decline to make a great and good peace—if you do not figure out what is to your advantage—you will see instead hostility and enmity. You will cause all-out, discordant, impossible warfare, and it is only too likely that you will be choosing great toil and exertion, and will spend many lives. You will spend your treasures but will create only the maximum of destruction. In general, the war's end will result only in great evil for you. You can see this from what has happened since I invaded Videssian territory, and from the terrible things it has seen and suffered. But with peace, the condition of your state will stop being so very pitiful and wretched."

"Frankly, Abivard, I don't believe a word of it," Maniakes said. "If you want peace, if Sharbaraz King of Kings wants peace, you may have it any time you like. All you need do is pack up your soldiers and go back to Makuran. Leave Videssian soil and we shall have peace."

Abivard shook his head. Maniakes would have been astonished had he done anything else. The Makuraner general said, "Peace can be yours, if you want it. Send envoys dealing with that matter to Sharbaraz King of Kings. He will be persuaded by me, I am sure, and will come around to your point of view. Make peace now, secure and pure for all time to come."

In and of itself, that was more of a concession than Maniakes had thought to get from Abivard. But he answered, "From all I have seen, Sharbaraz King of Kings is persuaded by no man these days. He does as he pleases, and if it pleases him to outrage my envoys, he will, with no one to let or hinder him."

"His principal wife is my sister," Abivard said, speaking with rather than at Maniakes for the first time since his odd question about silver shields. "If he heeds anyone, he heeds me."

Maniakes studied him. "How often does he heed anyone? But seldom, or I miss my guess."

"The King of Kings is his own judge, as a man who calls himself Avtokrator should know," Abivard said.

"That is true, but a man who listens only to himself will sooner or later hear the words of a fool, with no one to tell him so," Maniakes answered. "How can you weigh the proper course when you don't know all the choices?"

"Consider where we are talking, Maniakes," Abivard said, "and think whether this King of Kings or the Avtokrator has planned more wisely. If we were speaking outside Mashiz, I might think your point better taken."

"I said, 'sooner or later,' " Maniakes replied. "That something has not happened yet doesn't mean it can never happen. Do you play at dice?" He waited for Abivard's nod before going on, "Then you know that just because no one has rolled the double ones of Phos' little suns for a long time doesn't mean they can't come up on the next throw."

"With us, a double two is the winning throw—we call it 'the Prophets Four,' " Abivard said. "One and three ranks next; some of us call that 'Fraortish and the rest,' others 'the lady Shivini and the men.' " He kicked at the sand of the beach. "But I did not ask you here to talk about dice. I take it you will not yield even if reason calls on you to do so?"

"I will not. I cannot," Maniakes said. "Stavrakios took Mashiz, but you Makuraners went on, and now you have won a triumph. You will not take Videssos the city, and we, too, shall rise from the ruins."

"Videssos the city cries out to be sacked," Abivard said. "It may yet happen, Maniakes, and sooner than you think."

"Say what you will," Maniakes answered, "but if you so much as dip a toe into the waters of the Cattle Crossing, a dromon will row up and slice it off."

Abivard scowled. Maniakes knew he had angered him. That bothered the Avtokrator not at all. The Makuraners were fine horsemen and clever artificers; in close combat on land and in siege operations they were a match for their Videssian neighbors. One thing they were not, though, was sailors. They could look over the Cattle Crossing at Videssos the city, but the imperial navy kept them from getting to the other side of that little strip of water.

"I have no more to say to you, Maniakes," Abivard said. "When we meet again, we shall be at war once more."

"Be it so, then." Maniakes turned to the captain of the light boat. "It is over. It accomplished nothing. Take me back to the docks in the palace quarter."

"As you say, your Majesty," the officer answered, and gave the oarsmen their orders. The light boat pulled away from the beach by Across. Maniakes looked back over his shoulder. Abivard stood on the sand, watching him go. The Makuraner general took a couple of steps toward the Cattle Crossing, but did not try to get his feet wet.

Alvinos Bagdasares plucked at his thick black beard. "Let me make sure I understand you correctly, your Majesty," he said. "You want me to learn why Abivard was so interested in finding out whether you or your retinue had along a silver shield when you spoke with him the other day?"

"That's right," Maniakes said. "It meant something important to him, and he was disappointed when I told him no. If I know why, it may tell me something I can use to help drive the Makuraners back where they belong. Can you learn for me what it is?"

"I don't know," Bagdasares answered. "If the answer is in some way connected with sorcery, other sorcery may be able to uncover it. But if it springs from something that happened to Abivard on campaign, say, odds are long against our ever knowing what was in his question."

"Do everything you can," Maniakes said. "If you don't find the answer, we're no worse off than we would have been had you not tried."

"This is not something I can accomplish overnight," the wizard warned him. "It will take research into the spell most likely to be effective, and more time, perhaps, to gather the materials to complement the symbolic portion of the enchantment."

"Take your time." Maniakes' mouth twisted. "Why not? By all the signs, Abivard is going to winter in Across after all. I don't know what he gains by it except humiliating us, but he certainly does that. Still, it's not as if we haven't been humiliated enough other ways lately."

"I'm sure it could be worse, your Majesty," Bagdasares said.

Maniakes fixed him with a baleful glare. "Really, sorcerous sir? How?"

He gave Bagdasares credit; instead of mumbling an apology, the mage quite visibly thought about how things might be worse. At last he said, "Well, the Makuraners and Kubratoi could make common cause against us."

"Phos forbid it!" Maniakes burst out, appalled. "You're right. That would be worse. The good god grant Sharbaraz never thinks of it. It wouldn't be easy to arrange; not with our war galleys holding Abivard off in the westlands. A good thing they are, too—otherwise I'd have something new and dreadful to worry about, alongside all the old dreadful things on my mind now."

Bagdasares bowed. "I did not mean to trouble you, your Majesty. I sought but to obey."

"You succeeded all too well," Maniakes said. "Go on, now; see how to go about finding what was in Abivard's mind. And I—" He sighed and reached for a cadaster from the westlands. He knew what revenues would be recorded inside: none. "I shall set about making bronze without tin—and without copper, too, come to that."

After a little while, Maniakes' interest in seeing how little the Empire would be able to spend in the year to come palled. He got up from the table where he had been depressing himself and went wandering through the halls of the imperial residence. Those halls were chilly; winter would soon be at hand. Maniakes glanced west; he could not see the Makuraners lording it over the suburbs of the imperial capital, but he felt their presence. The humiliation of which he had spoken to Bagdasares burned at him like vinegar poured onto a wound.

The hallways of the residence held mementos of Avtokrators past. Genesios, fortunately, had not tried to immortalize himself in that particular way. If he had, Maniakes would have thrown whatever he had left behind onto the rubbish heap. The best memorial Genesios could have had was the pretense that he had never existed.

Not wanting to think about Genesios, Maniakes paused awhile in front of a portrait of Stavrakios. The Avtokrator of old wore the red boots, the heavy crown, and the gilded chainmail that went with his office, but in spite of those trappings resembled a veteran underofficer much more than anyone's expectations of what an Emperor should look like. He was painted as squat and muscular, with blunt, battered features, dark pouches under his eyes, and an expression that warned the whole world to get out of his way. Not all of the world had listened, so Stavrakios spent most of his long reign forcibly moving it aside.

Maniakes, who now needed to salute no living man—no matter what Sharbaraz had demanded of him—gave Stavrakios a formal salute, clenched right fist over his heart. "If you could beat the Makuraners, no reason I can't," he said.

The old picture, of course, didn't answer. If it had, Maniakes would have suspected either that he was losing his wits or that Bagdasares was playing a sorcerous joke on him. All the same, he could almost hear what the great Avtokrator of days gone by was thinking: *Well, if you're going to, what are you waiting for?* In his mind's ear, Stavrakios sounded a lot like his own father.

He studied the portrait a while longer, wondering how Stavrakios would have got out of this predicament—or how he would have kept from getting into it in the first place. The best answer Maniakes could come up with was that Stavrakios wouldn't have gone into anything with an inadequate force. Maniakes had done that twice now, first against the Kubratoi—he had anticipated treachery there, but not on the scale Etzilios had planned—and then against the Makuraners. Again, that hadn't been altogether his fault—how could he have anticipated Amorion falling just before he got to it?—but the results had been disastrously similar.

He nodded to Stavrakios. "All right, sir, I was stupid twice, which is once more than I'm entitled to, but I promise you this: next time I put troops into battle, the numbers will be on my side."

"They'd better be."

For a moment, Maniakes thought he was again imagining Stavrakios' reply. Then he realized he really had heard the words, and whirled around in surprise. His father grinned at him. "Sorry to break in like that, son—your Majesty—but you'd just said something that makes a good deal of sense. I wanted to make sure you'd remember it."

"You managed that, by the good god," Maniakes said. Now he set the palm of his hand over his heart, which was still pounding in his chest. "To say nothing of scaring me out of six months' growth."

His father's grin got wider, and rather unpleasant. "Fair enough—we'll say nothing of that. But what you said was wise: if you're going to hit the other fellow, make sure you hit him so hard he can't get back up. Try and do things by halves and you'll just end up throwing both halves away."

"Yes, I've seen that," Maniakes agreed. "But the goldpiece has two faces. If I charge ahead on one course with everything I have, it had better be the right one, or else I only make my mistake larger and juicier than it would have been."

"Juicier, eh? I like that." The elder Maniakes let out a wheezing chuckle. "Well, son, you're right—no two faces on the goldpiece there. You'd better be right for Videssos' sake, too. We're at the point now where being even a little wrong could sink us. Even bad luck might. Do you know that, when I was a boy, old men would talk about one year when they were children that was so cold, the Cattle Crossing froze from here all the way over to Across, and you could go to and from the westlands dryshod? If we get that kind of winter again—"

"Our dromons won't be able to patrol the strait, and the Makuraners will be able to cross from the westlands and lay siege to us," Maniakes finished for him. "You do so relieve my mind. Every time it snows this winter now, I'll be looking up and wondering how long it will last and how bad it will be. As if I didn't have enough things to worry about."

The elder Maniakes chuckled again. "Maybe now you understand why, when the eminent Kourikos tried to put the red boots on me, I turned him down flat."

Niphone got up out of bed to use the chamber pot. The cold air that got in when she lifted up the quilts and sheepskins that held winter at bay woke Maniakes. He grunted and stretched.

"I'm sorry," Niphone said. "I didn't mean to bother you."

"It's all right," Maniakes said as she slid back into bed. "There's already the beginning of light in the east, so it can't be too early. In fact, since today's Midwinter's Day, it's getting light as late as it does any time during the year."

"That's true." Niphone cocked her head, listening. "I think the snow's given way to rain." She shivered. "I'd rather have snow. The rain will turn to ice as soon as it touches the ground, and people and horses will be sliding everywhere."

"It won't freeze on the Cattle Crossing, which is all that matters to me . . . almost all," Maniakes amended, slipping a hand up under her wool nightdress so that his palm rested on her bulging belly. As if to oblige him, the baby she was carrying kicked. He laughed in delight.

"This one kicks harder than Evtropia did, I think," Niphone said. "Maybe that means it will be a boy."

"Maybe it does," Maniakes said. "Bagdasares thinks it will be a boy—but then, he thought Evtropia would be a boy, too. He's not always as smart as he thinks he is."

That was one reason Maniakes had not asked his wizard to try to learn how Niphone would fare in her confinement. Another was that Bagdasares hadn't yet figured out why Abivard had been interested in a silver shield. He had warned that would take time, but Maniakes hadn't expected it to stretch into months. And if he couldn't manage the one, how could the Avtokrator rely on his answer to the other?

"When does the mime show at the Amphitheater begin today?" Niphone asked.

"We've spread word through the city that it will start in the third hour," Maniakes answered. "Any which way, though, it won't start till we're there."

"We don't want to make the people angry," Niphone said, "nor to anger the lord with the great and good mind, either." The covers shifted as she sketched Phos' sun-sign above her heart.

He nodded. "No, not this year." Midwinter's Day marked the time when the sun was at its lowest ebb in the sky, when Skotos snatched most strongly at it, trying to steal its light and leave the world in eternal frozen darkness. As the days went by, the sun would rise ever higher, escaping the evil god's clutches. But, after this year of disasters, did Phos still care about Videssos? Would the sun move higher in the sky once more? Priests and wizards would watch anxiously till they learned the answer.

Niphone rode to the Amphitheater in a litter borne by stalwart guardsmen. Maniakes walked alongside, with more guardsmen to protect him from assassins and to force a way through the crowds that packed the plaza of Palamas. A dozen parasol-bearers carrying bright silk canopies proclaimed his imperial status to the people.

Bonfires blazed here and there across the square. Men and women queued up to leap over them, shouting, "Burn, ill-luck!" as they jumped. Maniakes broke away from his guards to join one of the lines. People greeted him by name and slapped him on the back, as if he were a pig butcher popular with his neighbors. On any other day of the year, that would have been lese majesty. Today, almost anything went.

Maniakes reached the head of the line. He ran, jumped, and shouted. When he landed on the far side of the fire, he stumbled as his booted foot hit a slushy bit of ground. Somebody grabbed his elbow to keep him from falling. "Thanks," he gasped.

"Any time," his benefactor said. "Here, why don't you stay and see if you can't catch somebody, too? It'd make a man's day, or a lady's even more." The fellow winked at him. "And they do say anything can happen on Midwinter's Day."

Because they said that, if babies born about the time of the autumnal equinox didn't happen to look a great deal like their mothers' husbands, few people raised eyebrows. One day of license a year helped keep you to the straight and narrow the rest of the time.

The next few people in the queue sailed over the bonfires without difficulty. Then a woman leapt short and almost landed in the flames. Maniakes ran forward to drag her away. "Niphone!" he exclaimed. "What were you doing, jumping there?"

"The same thing you were," his wife answered, defiantly lifting her chin. "Making sure I start the new year without the bad luck piled up from the old one."

Maniakes exhaled through his nose, trying to hold on to patience. "I put you in the litter so you wouldn't tire yourself out walking or go into labor sooner than you should, and you go and run and jump?"

"Yes, I do, and what are you going to do about it?" Niphone said. "This is Midwinter's Day, when everyone does as he—or she—pleases."

Faced by open mutiny, Maniakes did the only thing he could: he cut his losses. "Now that you have jumped, will you please get back into the litter so we can go on to the Amphitheater?"

"Of course, your Majesty." Niphone demurely cast her eyes down to the cobbles of the plaza of Palamas. "I obey you in all things." She walked back toward the bearers and other guardsmen, leaving him staring after her. *I obey you in all things,* his mind translated, *except when I don't feel like it.*

When the parasol-bearers emerged through the Avtokrator's private entrance, waves of cheers and clapping rolled down on Maniakes like surf from a stormy sea. He raised a hand to acknowledge them, knowing they weren't for him in particular but in anticipation of the mime show that now would soon begin.

He took his seat at the center of the long spine that ran down the middle of the Amphitheater's floor. Most days, the enormous structure was used for horse races; the spine defined the inner margin of the course. Today, though—

Today Maniakes said, "People of Videssos—" and the crowd quieted at once. A magic, not of sorcery but of architecture, let everyone in the Amphitheater hear his voice when he spoke from that one spot. "People of Videssos," he repeated, and then went on, "May Phos be with you—may Phos be with us—all through the coming year. As the sun rises higher in the sky from this day forward, so may the fortunes of the Empire of Videssos rise from the low estate in which they now find themselves."

"So may it be!" the multitude cried with one voice. Maniakes thought the top of his head would come off. Not only could everyone in the Amphitheater hear him when he spoke from that one spot, as long as he stayed there all the noise in the great tureen of a building poured right down on him.

He gestured to Agathios, who sat not far away. The ecumenical patriarch led the tens of thousands of spectators in Phos' creed. Again the noise of the response dinned in the Avtokrator's ears.

Maniakes said, "To sweeten the year to come, I give you the mime troupes of Videssos the city!"

Applause rocked him once more. He sat down, leaned back in the throne set on the spine for him, and prepared to enjoy the mimes as best he could—and to endure what he could not enjoy. Everything save Phos himself was fair game on Midwinter's Day; an Avtokrator who could not take what the mimes dished out lost favor with the fickle populace of the city.

Leaning over to Agathios, Maniakes asked, "Did Genesios let himself be lampooned here?"

"He did, your Majesty," the patriarch answered. "The one year he tried to check the mime troupes, the people rioted and his guardsmen looked likely to go over to them instead of keeping them in check. After that, he sat quiet and did his best to pretend nothing was happening."

"What a pity," Maniakes said. "I was hoping he would give me a precedent for massacring any troupe that didn't strike my fancy." Agathios stared at him, then decided he was joking and started to laugh.

Maniakes was joking—after a fashion. But worries about offending the Avtokrator went out the window on Midwinter's Day along with everything else. Mime troupes were supposed to mock the man who held the throne—and he was supposed to take it in good part, no matter how much he wanted to set his guardsmen on the impudent actors.

Out came the first troupe. Most of them were dressed up as extravagant caricatures of Makuraner boiler boys, though they weren't mounted. One fellow, though, wore an even more exaggerated likeness of the imperial regalia Maniakes had on. The troupe's act was of the utmost simplicity: the boiler boys chased the fellow playing Maniakes around and around the racetrack. The crowd thought that was very funny. Had he been sitting up near the top of the Amphitheater, with no concerns past his own belly and perhaps his family, Maniakes might have found it funny, too. As it was, he smiled and clapped his hands and did his best to hold his temper.

He had a long morning ahead of him. One troupe had him and Parsmanios out looking for Tatoules, and finding a horse apple instead. Another had made a huge parchment map of the Empire of Videssos—it must have cost them a good many goldpieces—and proceeded to tear it in half and burn up the part that held the westlands. Still another had him running from first the Kubratoi and then the Makuraners, and the two sets of Videssos' foes colliding with each other and getting into a brawl.

Maniakes really did clap over that one. Then he realized that, if the Kubratoi and Makuraners really did meet, they would of necessity do so over the corpse of the Empire. He wondered if the mimes—or the audience—fully understood that. He hoped not.

At last the show ended. Maniakes rose and led the audience in a cheer for the performers who had entertained them—and embarrassed him. He hadn't been the least bit sorry when rotten fruit greeted a couple of troupes that lacked the saving grace of being funny. Had he had a basket of rotten apples at his feet, he would have pelted most of the mimes. As it was, he took the mockery as best he could.

People filed out of the Amphitheater, off to revel through the rest of the short day and the long night. Maniakes walked back to the imperial residence beside Niphone's litter; this time, the Empress stayed inside. That relieved him as much as having the mime shows end.

No sooner had he returned to the residence, though, than Kameas came up to him and said, "Your Majesty, the wizard Alvinos waits at the southern entrance. He would have speech with you, if you care to receive him."

For a moment, Maniakes failed to recognize the Videssian-sounding name Bagdasares sometimes used. When he did, he said, "Thank you, esteemed sir. Yes, I'll see him. Perhaps he's had some success with his magic after all. That would be a pleasant change."

Bagdasares prostrated himself before Maniakes. The Avtokrator hadn't always made him bother with a full proskynesis, but did today: he was less than pleased with the mage, and wanted him to know it. Bagdasares did; when Maniakes finally gave him leave to rise, he said, "Your Majesty, I apologize for the long delay in learning what you required of me—"

"Quite all right, magical sir," Maniakes answered. "No doubt you had a more important client with more pressing business."

Bagdasares stared, then chuckled uneasily. "Your Majesty is pleased to jest with me."

"I do wish I'd heard more from you sooner, and that's a fact," Maniakes said. "Here it is Midwinter's Day, by the good god, and I set you the problem a few days after I met with Abivard. When I told you to take your time, I own I didn't expect you to take *all* of it."

"Your Majesty, sometimes seeing the problem is easier than seeing the answer to it," Bagdasares replied. "I'm still not sure I have that answer, only a way toward it. But this is Midwinter's Day, as you said. If you have it in mind to revel rather than worry about such things, tell me and I shall return tomorrow."

"No, no, never mind that," Maniakes said impatiently. He could see all the problems Genesios had left him, but, as Bagdasares had said, seeing how to surmount them was another matter. "It's possible I owe you an apology. Say on, sorcerous sir."

"Learning why someone does something is always tricky, your Majesty," the wizard said. "Sometimes even he does not know, and sometimes the reasons he thinks he has are not the ones truly in his heart. Finding those reasons is like listening to the howl of yesterday's wind."

"As you say," Maniakes answered. "And have you managed to capture the sound of yesterday's wind for today's ears?"

"I shall make the attempt to capture it, at any rate," Bagdasares said. "I have tried this before, with uniform lack of success, but in my previous conjurations I always assumed Abivard's question arose from some connection with Sharbaraz King of Kings or with some mage from Mashiz or both. Failure has forced me to abandon this belief, however."

Maniakes wondered if Bagdasares was wrong or merely lacked the strength and skill to prove himself right. He did not say that; making a mage question his own ability weakened him further. Instead he asked, "What assumption do you set in its place, then?"

"That Abivard acquired this concern independently of the King of Kings, perhaps in opposition to him—would it not be fine to see Mashiz rather than Videssos engulfed in civil strife?—or perhaps from before the time when he made Sharbaraz's acquaintance."

"Mm, it could be so," Maniakes admitted. "If it is, how do you go about demonstrating it?"

"You have indeed set your finger on the problem, your Majesty," Bagdasares said, bowing. "Recapturing ephemera, especially long-vanished ephemera, is difficult in the extreme, not least because the application of the laws of similarity and contagion often seems irrelevant."

"Seems irrelevant, you say?" Maniakes' ear had been sensitized to subtle shades of meaning by more than a year on the throne. "You want me to understand that you have found a way around this difficulty."

"I think I have, at any rate," Bagdasares said. "I've not yet tested it; I thought you might care to be present."

"So I can see how clever you've been, you mean," Maniakes said. Bagdasares looked injured, but the Avtokrator spoke without much malice. He went on, "By all means, sorcerous sir, dazzle me with your brilliance."

"If I can but give satisfaction, your Majesty, that will be enough and to spare," the mage answered. He was not usually so self-effacing, but he didn't usually keep the Avtokrator waiting a couple of months for a response, either. Now he was all briskness. "If I may proceed, your Majesty?"

Without waiting for Maniakes' consent, he drew from his

carpetbag a lamp, a clay jar—at the moment tightly stoppered—and a silver disk about as wide as the palm of his hand. A rawhide cord ran from one side of the disk to the other, to symbolize the support by which a soldier carried a shield.

Bagdasares worked the stopper from the jar and poured water in a narrow stream on a tabletop. "This is seawater, taken from the Cattle Crossing," he said. He set the silver disk close by it, then made a few quick passes over the lamp. Not only did it light, but with a flame far more brilliant than the usual, so that Maniakes had to squint and shield his eyes against it.

"It's as if you brought the summer sun into the imperial residence," he said.

"The effect does not last long, but will be useful here," Bagdasares answered. He picked up the disk and used it to reflect the sorcerously enhanced light into Maniakes' face. The Avtokrator blinked and squinted again. Nodding in satisfaction, Bagdasares said, "Here we have a silver shield shining across a narrow sea, not so?"

"Exactly so," Maniakes agreed.

"Now to uncover the origins of the phrase," Bagdasares said, and began to chant not in Videssian but in the throaty Vaspurakaner language. After a moment, Maniakes recognized what he was chanting: the story of how Phos had created Vaspur, firstborn of all mankind. Between verses, the mage murmured, "Thus do we approach the problem of origins." Then he was chanting again—verses Agathios would surely have condemned as heretical. Agathios, however, wasn't here. Maniakes had grown up with these verses. They didn't bother him.

Suddenly, out of the air, a deep, rich voice spoke. Maniakes habitually thought in Videssian. He had just been listening to a chant in the Vaspurakaner tongue. Now he quickly had to adjust to yet another language, for the words, wherever they came from—and he could see no source for them—were in Makuraner: "Son of the *dihqan*, I see a broad field that is not a field, a tower on a hill where honor shall be won and lost, and a silver shield shining across a narrow sea."

Maniakes cocked his head to one side, wondering if more would come, but found only silence. Bagdasares, his broad forehead glistening with sweat despite the chill of Midwinter's Day, staggered and almost fell. He looked worn to exhaustion, and sounded it, too, saying "Did you understand that, your Majesty? It was not in a tongue I know."

"I understood it, yes," Maniakes answered, and did his best to render it into Videssian for the mage. He went on, "It sounds to me as if you called back into being a prophecy from long ago."

"So it would seem, indeed." Shoulders bent, gait halting, Bagdasares hobbled over to a chair and sank into it. "Might I trouble you for some wine? I find myself fordone."

Maniakes called for a servitor. Response came slowly; like so many others throughout Videssos the city, most of his household staff were out reveling on the holiday. Presently, though, a serving woman brought in a jar of wine and two cups. Bagdasares spat on the floor in rejection of Skotos, then drank down what the servant had poured him.

After a couple of slower sips of his own, Maniakes said, "When I campaigned with Abivard and Sharbaraz against Smerdis the usurper, Abivard had with him a soothsayer named . . ." He hesitated, trying to dredge up the memory. "Tanshar, that's what he called himself."

"Was it his voice we heard, then?" Bagdasares asked.

"I'd not have thought so, though I had scant dealings with him myself," Maniakes answered. "His beard was white, not gray. I can hardly imagine him sounding as . . . as virile as did that voice you summoned from the deep."

"If he was the one who gave the prophecy I recalled here, who can say what power was speaking through him?" Bagdasares sketched the sun-sign. "Not all such powers conform to our usual notions of fitness, that much I can tell you."

"I'd like to be surer than 'Well, this is possible,' " Maniakes said. He ruefully shook his head. "What I'd like and what I get are apt to be two different things. You needn't remind me of that, magical sir, for I've already learned it for myself. Still and all, though, Abivard was responding to something in his past he reckoned important. 'A broad field that is not a field'—I wonder what that meant, other than that the soothsayer had a gift for obscurity."

"Abivard could tell us—provided the prophecy came true," Bagdasares said. "But then, if some of it hadn't come true, I don't suppose Abivard would have been worrying about the rest—and I don't suppose we could have reconstructed it so readily. My magic, I think, responded to magic already in the prophecy."

"That sounds reasonable, sorcerous sir," Maniakes agreed. "So now we have the answer to the question that's been troubling us since I met with Abivard. But, even knowing the answer, we still don't know why Abivard wanted to see, or would see, that shining silver shield. What conclusions do you draw from that?"

"Two possibilities occur to me," Bagdasares answered. "One is that we were simply asking the wrong question. The other is that the question was indeed the right one, but the fullness of time for the answer has not yet come round."

Maniakes nodded. "And there's no way to know which until the fullness of time does come round—if it ever does." He sighed. "Thank you, sorcerous sir—I think."

Triphylles puffed a little as he rose from his proskynesis. "Your Majesty, you honor me beyond my worth by summoning me before your august presence this day. How may I serve you? Command me." His rather doughy face took on an expression intended to convey stern devotion to duty.

The last time Maniakes had commanded him—to fare north as envoy to the Kubratoi—he had also had to cajole him with the promise of a boost in rank. He couldn't do that again; *eminent* was the highest rung on the ladder. He had to hope Triphylles really did own a living, breathing sense of duty. "Eminent sir, no doubt you will recall that last fall I met with the Makuraner warlord Abivard, whose forces, worse luck for us, still occupy Across."

"Of course, your Majesty." Triphylles looked westward, though all he saw in that direction was a wall of the chamber in which Maniakes had received him. "The smoke from their burnings is a stench in the nostrils of every right-thinking man of Videssian blood."

"So it is," Maniakes said hastily; Triphylles looked set to launch into an oration. The Avtokrator went on, "Abivard suggested that one way in which the Makuraners might possibly be persuaded to withdraw was through the good offices of an embassy sent to Sharbaraz King of Kings."

He got no further than that. In a baritone scream, Triphylles bellowed, "And you want me to be that embassy? Your Majesty, how have I offended you to the point where you keep sending me off to loathsome places in the confident expectation I shall be killed?"

"There, there," Maniakes said, as soothingly as he could.

"Mashiz is not a loathsome place; I've been there myself. And Sharbaraz isn't the cheerful sort of murderer Etzilios is, either—or at least he wasn't back in the days when I knew him, at any rate."

"You will, I trust, forgive me for reminding you that in the years since then his disposition does not seem to have changed for the better?" Triphylles was not normally a man of inspired sarcasm; *amazing what being a little bit unhappy can do*, Maniakes thought.

Aloud, he said, "You will be an embassy, eminent sir, and the law of nations prohibits such from being assaulted in any way."

"Oh, indeed, your Majesty, just as the law of nations prevented Etzilios from assailing you at what was claimed to be a peace party." Triphylles still looked frightened and defiant, and was upset enough to be more imaginatively sardonic than Maniakes had thought possible for him.

The Avtokrator said, "I didn't have any reason to want to be rid of you, eminent sir, but you'll give me one if you keep on with your complaints."

"A paradox worthy of a theologian," Triphylles exclaimed. "If I am silent, you'll send me away, thinking I consent, whereas if I tell you I don't consent, that will give you what you reckon good cause to send me away."

Maniakes tried again: "I want to send you to speak to Sharbaraz because I think you are the man best suited to the task. You've shown yourself a gifted speaker again and again—not least here today."

"If I truly were gifted, I would have talked you out of sending me to Etzilios," Triphylles said darkly. "And now Mashiz? No seafood, date wine, women locked away as if they were prisoners—"

"Less so than they were before Sharbaraz took the throne," Maniakes interrupted. "The King of Kings and Abivard both have strong-willed wives—Sharbaraz is married to Abivard's sister, as a matter of fact."

"And to a good many others, by all accounts," Triphylles said. "But I was simply using that as an example of the reasons I shall be most distressed to travel to a far land yet again."

You had to listen carefully with Triphylles, as with most Videssian courtiers. He had said *shall*, not *should*. He didn't do such things by accident; he meant he had resigned himself to going. Maniakes said, "Thank you, eminent sir. I promise, you won't be sorry when you return from Mashiz."

"A good thing, too, for I shall certainly be sorry on the journey thither and while I'm there—very likely on the way back, too," Triphylles said. "But if I must leave the queen of cities, what am I to say to the King of Kings when I am ushered into his gloomy presence?"

"One of the reasons I send you forth is my confidence that you will know what to tell Sharbaraz and how to say it when the time comes," Maniakes answered. "You know what Videssos needs from him: that he recognize me as Avtokrator and pension off his false Hosios, and that his troops leave the westlands as soon as may be." He scowled. "I will pay him tribute for as long as five years, much as I hate doing it, to give us the chance to get back on our feet."

"How much per year will you give him?" Despite complaints, Triphylles turned businesslike.

Maniakes sighed. "Whatever he demands, more or less. We're in a worse position for hard bargaining than we were with Etzilios."

"Indeed, and look what I won for you with that negotiation," Triphylles said. "The chance to be captured and just as nearly killed."

"Ah, but now you've had practice," Maniakes said blandly. "I'm sure you'll do much better with Sharbaraz. I *am* sure you'll do better, eminent sir, else I'd not send you out."

"You flatter me beyond my worth," Triphylles said, and what was usually a polite disclaimer and nothing more now sounded sour in his mouth. He sighed, too, hard enough to make a lamp flicker. "Very well, your Majesty, I obey, but by the good god I wish you'd picked another man. When do you aim to send me off into the Makuraner's maw?"

"As soon as may be."

"I might have known."

Maniakes went on as if Triphylles had not spoken: "You make your preparations as quickly as you can. I'll arrange a safe-conduct for you with Abivard, and perhaps an escort of Makuraner horsemen, as well, to keep you safe on the road to Mashiz." He smacked a frustrated fist into his open palm. "Eminent sir, you have no notion how much it galls me to have to say that, but I will do it, for your sake and for the sake of your mission."

"Your Majesty is gracious," Triphylles said. Maniakes

thought he would leave it at that, but he evidently took courage from having spoken freely before without anything dreadful happening to him, so he added, "You might as well be honest and put the mission ahead of me, as you surely do in your own mind."

If he hadn't been dead right, Maniakes would have felt insulted.

South and east of the wall of Videssos the city lay a broad meadow on which soldiers were in the habit of exercising. Maniakes drilled his troops there all through the winter, except on days when it was raining or snowing too hard for them to go out.

Some of the men grumbled at having to work so hard. When they did, the Avtokrator pointed west over the Cattle Crossing. "The smoke that goes up from Across comes from the Makuraners," he said. "How many of you have your homes in the westlands?" He waited for some of the troopers to nod, then told them, "If you ever want to see those homes again, we'll have to drive the Makuraners out of them. We can't do that by fighting the way we have the past few years. And so—we drill."

That didn't stop the grumbling—soldiers wouldn't have been soldiers if they didn't complain. But it did ease things, which was what Maniakes had intended.

Along with his father and Rhegorios, Parsmanios, and Tzikas, he worked hard to make the exercises as realistic as he could, to give the men the taste of battle without actual danger—or with as little as possible, at any rate. They fought with sticks instead of swords, with pointless javelins, with arrows that had round wooden balls at their heads instead of sharp iron.

Everyone went back to the barracks covered with bruises, but only a few men got hurt worse than that: one luckless fellow lost an eye when an arrow struck him just wrong. He was only a trooper, but Maniakes promised him a captain's pension. You had to know when to spend what gold you had.

Sometimes, when the exercises were done, Maniakes would ride up to the edge of the Cattle Crossing and peer west at Across. Every now and then, when the day was sunny, he saw moving glints he thought were Makuraners in their heavy armor. They, too, were readying themselves for the day when their army and his would come to grips with each other again.

"I wish it weren't so built up over there," he complained to Rhegorios one day. "We'd have a better idea of what they were up to."

"That's what we get for raising a city there," his cousin answered with an impudent grin. Then, growing thoughtful, Rhegorios waved back to the Videssians' practice field. "Not much cover here. If they have men with sharp eyes down by the shore, they shouldn't have much trouble figuring out what we do."

"True enough," Maniakes said. "But that shouldn't be any great surprise to them, anyhow. They must know we have to ready ourselves to fight them as best we can. Whether it will be good enough—" He set his jaw. "These past seven years, it hasn't been."

"The lord with the great and good mind bless our fleets," Rhegorios observed. "They can't fight our battles for us, but they keep the Makuraners from setting all the terms for the war."

"It's always a good idea to go on campaign with a shield," Maniakes agreed. "It will help keep you safe. But if you go with only a shield, you won't win your war. You need a sword to strike with as well as the shield for protection."

"The fleet could ascend a fair number of rivers in the westlands a good distance," Rhegorios said in the tones of a man thinking aloud.

"That doesn't do us as much good as we'd like, though," Maniakes said. "The dromons can't interdict rivers the way they can the Cattle Crossing. For one thing, we don't have enough of them for that. For another, the rivers in the westlands are too narrow to keep the Makuraners from bombarding them with catapults from the shore."

Approaching hoofbeats made him look up. The rider wasn't one of his troopers, but a messenger. "News from the north, your Majesty," he called, holding out a boiled-leather message tube to Maniakes.

The Avtokrator and Rhegorios looked at each other in alarm. Urgent news from the north was liable to be bad news: Etzilios on the move was the first thing that crossed Maniakes' mind. While he would have taken a certain grim pleasure in separating Moundioukh's head from his shoulders, that alone would not have compensated him for the damage a large-scale Kubrati raid would cause. Trapped between the steppe nomads and the Makuraners, the Empire of Videssos held little territory it could call its own these days.

Maniakes unsealed the message tube with more than a little trepidation. "Tarasios hypasteos of Varna to Maniakes Avtokrator: Greetings." Maniakes had to pause a moment to remember where Varna was: a coastal town, northwest of Imbros. His eyes swept down the parchment.

Tarasios continued, "I regret to have to inform your Majesty that the Kubratoi raided our harbor two days before my writing of this dispatch. They came by sea, in the *monoxyla* they habitually use for such incursions: boats made by hollowing out single large logs through fire, and then equipping them with rowers, low masts, and leather sails. Such vessels cannot challenge dromons, of course, but are more formidable than the description would suggest, not least because they are capable of accommodating a dismaying number of armed men.

"Varna, unfortunately, had no dromons present when the raiders descended upon us. They plundered a couple of merchantmen tied up at the quays, then threw fire onto those quays, the merchantmen, and the fishing boats nearby. But the fire did not spread from the harbor to the town, and the garrison repelled the barbarians upon their attempt to force entry into Varna by scaling the sea wall. That effort failing, they returned to their *monoxyla* and sailed away northward."

The hypasteos went on to request aid for his beleaguered city from the imperial fisc. The fisc was at least as beleaguered as Varna, but perhaps Tarasios didn't know that. Maniakes resolved to do something for him, although he knew that something wouldn't be much.

Rhegorios said, "Well, my cousin your Majesty, who's gone and pissed in the soup pot now?"

"How do you think Moundioukh's head would look hanging from the Milestone?" Maniakes asked dreamily. "The Kubratoi have violated the truce I bought, so I have the right to take it." He passed his cousin the message from Tarasios.

Rhegorios went through it, lips moving as he read. "Isn't that peculiar?" he said when he was through. "It doesn't sound like a big raid. I wonder if it wasn't some of the Kubratoi going off on their own to see what they could steal, maybe without Etzilios' even knowing about it."

"It could be so," Maniakes agreed. "My guess is that Etzilios will say it's so, whether it is or whether it isn't. I won't take Moundioukh's head right away, however much I think he'd be improved without it. What I will do is send a message straight to Etzilios, asking him what's going on here. If I don't get an answer I like, that will be time enough to settle with Moundioukh."

The messenger bearing Maniakes' query left Videssos the city the next day. Two weeks after that, he returned in the company of a small troop of Kubratoi who rode under shield of truce. The Avtokrator met their leader, a bearded barbarian named Ghizat, in the Grand Courtroom.

Ghizat approached the throne with a large leather sack under one arm. He set it down beside him while he performed a proskynesis. "Rise," Maniakes said in a voice colder than the chilly air outside. "Has your khagan forgotten the truce he made with us?"

"No, him not forgets, youse Majesty," said Ghizat, who seemed to have learned his Videssian from Moundioukh. "Him sended I down to these city with presents about you."

"What sort of present?" Maniakes asked. The size and shape of the leather sack made him hope he knew the answer, but Etzilios had taught him never to rely too much on hope.

Ghizat fumbled with the rawhide lashing that held the mouth of the sack closed. He turned it upside down and dumped a severed head out onto the polished marble floor of the courtroom. In violation of every canon of court etiquette, exclamations of shock and horror rose from the assembled bureaucrats and courtiers.

"This thing," Ghizat said, spurning the head with his foot, "this thing once upon a time it belongs to Paghan. This here Paghan, him leads *monoxyla* fleets what sails up along Varna. Etzilios the magnumperous, him not knows nothing about this fleets till too late."

The late Paghan stared up toward Maniakes with dull, dead eyes. The weather had remained wintry, so his mortal fragment was neither badly bloated nor stinking. Maniakes said, "How do I know he's not some no-account Kubrati sacrificed to let your khagan claim he's keeping the peace?"

"Couple kinds way," Ghizat answered. "First kind ways is, we Kubratoi never does nothing like these, no ways, nohow. Second kind ways is, Moundioukh and them other hostages personages, them knows Paghan, them tells youse what him are. Them knows other six headses us brings, too, know they when they still on bodies, yes sir."

Maniakes clicked his tongue between his teeth. He could

indeed check that. He wouldn't know for certain whether these particular barbarians had in fact led the attack on Varna, but he could learn whether they were prominent among their people.

"Fair enough," he said. "Give me the names and stations of these men whose heads you've brought. If Moundioukh's account of them tallies with yours, I shall accept that Etzilios is not to blame for this raid."

"Youse Majesty, the bargains you have," Ghizat said, and told him the names of the other nomads now shorter by a head. "You does what you wants over they. Put headses up on big pointy stone prick—what you call it?"

"The Milestone," Maniakes answered dryly. A couple of courtiers tittered and then did their best to pretend they hadn't: it was a pretty good description. "I'll do that with some, I think, and send the rest to Varna so the people there know the raiders have been punished."

"Howsomever. They yourses now," Ghizat said. He prostrated himself again, to show he had said everything he intended to say.

"You will stay in the city until Moundioukh confirms what you and Etzilios have told me," Maniakes said; Ghizat knocked his head against the stone to show he understood. Maniakes turned to Kameas. He pointed to Paghan's head. "Take charge of that, eminent sir. Convey it first to Moundioukh with the others and then to the Milestone."

"Er—yes, your Majesty." Looking anything but delighted, the vestiarios approached the head and picked it up by the very tip of its tangled beard with his thumb and forefinger. If his expression was any guide, he would sooner have handled it with a long pair of smith's tongs. He carried it away.

Ghizat rose, backed away from the throne till he had reached the distance protocol prescribed, and then turned and left the Grand Courtroom. From behind, his bowlegged swagger was amusing to watch.

After the audience ended, Maniakes returned to the imperial residence. Kameas, looking a bit green, presently reported to him: "Your Majesty, Moundioukh applies the same names to the Kubratoi—or rather, the abridged selection from the Kubratoi—as Ghizat gave them. The distinguished barbarous gentleman expressed forceful if ungrammatical surprise at discovering these individuals in their present state."

"Did he?" Maniakes said. "Well, by the good god, that's something. I take it to mean Etzilios will likely look for more tribute this year, and also to mean he'll keep his men quiet if we pay him enough."

"May it be so." Kameas hesitated, then decided to go on: "And, may it please your Majesty, I should be indebted to you if I were spared such, ah, grisly duties in the future. Most, ah, disturbing."

Maniakes reminded himself that the vestiarios' sole experience of war and battle had been Etzilios' assault on the imperial camp by Imbros. "I'll do what I can to oblige you, eminent sir. I must remind you, though, that life comes with no guarantee."

"I am aware of that, your Majesty, I assure you," Kameas answered tonelessly. Maniakes' cheeks heated. A eunuch was aware of it in ways no entire man ever could be.

Feeling foolish and flustered, Maniakes dismissed the vestiarios. He hoped Kameas would go have a mug of wine, or maybe several. If he ordered him to do something like that, though, Kameas was liable to be touchy enough to disobey because he had just been commanded to do something else he didn't care for. Sometimes you got better results with a loose rein.

Sometimes, of course, you didn't. The Makuraners were not going to leave the westlands unless Videssos drove them out, not unless Triphylles worked a miracle bigger than most of the ones accomplished through thaumaturgy. Keeping peace with the Kubratoi would help with the fight against Makuran, but, as he had told Kameas, life came with no guarantee. Pretty soon, Niphone would bear their second child. If it was a boy, he would become heir to the throne. Maniakes wanted to be sure he had an Empire left to inherit.

X

THE SOUP WAS RICH WITH MUSSELS, TUNNY, CRAB MEAT, mushrooms, and onions. Niphone paused with silver spoon halfway to her mouth. "I don't think I'd better eat any more," she said in a thoughtful voice.

Maniakes stared across the table at her. She sat some distance back from it; her bulging belly made sure she could come no closer. "Do you mean what I think you mean?" he asked.

He had spoken quietly. She didn't answer for a little while, so he wondered if she had heard him. Her gaze was searching, inward. But then she nodded with abrupt decision, as if she were a captain ordering troops forward into a breach in enemy lines. "Yes, there's another pang," she said. "Once you've known labor once, you don't confuse it with the tightenings you feel all through the last part of your confinement. This baby will be born tonight or tomorrow."

"We're ready," Maniakes said. "Everything will go exactly as it should, Phos willing." He sketched the sun-circle over his heart, a shorthand prayer to the lord with the great and good mind. Then, raising his voice, he called for Kameas. When the vestiarios came into the dining room, he spoke one word: "Now."

Kameas' eyes widened. As Maniakes had before him, he drew the sun-circle above his left breast. "I shall send for the lady Zoïle directly," he declared, "and make all other necessary preparations as well."

Those necessary preparations had nothing to do with the Red Room; the imperial birthing chamber had been ready for months. What Kameas meant was that he would summon, along with Zoïle, a healer-priest from the Sorcerers' Collegium and a surgeon. Coming out and saying that in front of Niphone would have reminded her of the risks she took; Maniakes was grateful for the vestiarios' tact.

Kameas bowed and hurried away. Maniakes got up from his seat, went around the table, and set his hands on Niphone's shoulders. "Everything will go perfectly," he repeated, as if saying it could make it so.

"Of course it will," his wife answered. "Why—" She paused as another labor pain came and went. "—shouldn't it?"

"No reason at all," Maniakes said heartily. "We'll have ourselves a fine boy by this time tomorrow." He hesitated. "Are the pains bad yet?"

"No, not yet," Niphone said, "but I know what lies ahead." She shrugged. "I endured it once. I can do it again."

Maniakes waited nervously for Zoïle to arrive. When Kameas escorted her into the dining room, she did not bother prostrating herself before the Avtokrator: She ruled the domain Niphone was reentering. She went over to the Empress, looked into her eyes, felt her pulse, and finally nodded.

"How does she seem?" Maniakes asked.

"Pregnant," Zoïle snapped, whereupon the Avtokrator shut up. The midwife gave her attention back to Niphone. Solicitude returned to her voice. "Can you walk, your Majesty?"

"Of course I can," Niphone said indignantly. To prove it, she got to her feet.

Zoïle beamed at her. "In that case, your Majesty, why don't you take yourself to the Red Room, and get as comfortable as you can? I'll be along shortly; as you'll remember, much of the first part of labor can be boring."

"I remember what comes afterward, too," Niphone said, the first sign of apprehension she had shown in all her pregnancy. She turned back to Maniakes. "I will give you a son."

"Come through safe, that's all," he told her. He might as well not have spoken. Her head held high, she waddled out through the door and down the hall toward the chamber where legitimate Emperors who were the sons of Emperors came into the world: where dynasties, in other words, were born along with babies.

Zoïle looked out the door to see how far Niphone had gone. Far enough, evidently, for Zoïle turned back to Maniakes and said, "Aye, she's pregnant again, your Majesty, and by the good god I wish she weren't."

Maniakes had no trouble interpreting the glare in the midwife's black eyes. *Men*, it said. In a hurt voice, he remarked, "Why does everyone think this is my fault?"

"Are you telling me you're *not* the father?" Zoïle asked sweetly, at which point the Avtokrator threw his hands in the air and gave up on convincing her he wasn't a stupid, lecherous brute. If she wanted to think that, she would, and he didn't seem able to do anything about it.

"Do the best you can for her," he said.

"I would anyhow, your Majesty, for my own sake," the midwife replied with quiet pride. Her mouth thinned into a bloodless line. "And if I can't, Phos willing the healer and the surgeon can. You've sent for them?"

"Yes," Maniakes said. "I don't want them to come into the residence, though, till Niphone goes inside the Red Room and you close the door. If she saw them, it would just make her worry more."

Zoïle considered that, tasting the words one by one. "Maybe there's hope for you yet," she said, and went down the hallway after the Empress before Maniakes could think of any fit reply.

A couple of minutes later, Kameas led two men into the dining room. "Your Majesty, I present to you the healer-priest Philetos and the surgeon Osrhoenes." Both men prostrated themselves before Maniakes. Philetos was tall and lean, with a lined face, dark freckles on his shaven crown, and a beard white as clean snow. He wore a plain blue robe, its only ornamentation the cloth-of-gold circle on his left breast that symbolized Phos' sun.

Osrhoenes was also tall, but heavyset. He was some years younger than Philetos; gray rested lightly in his hair and beard. He wore a black robe; Maniakes peered closely at it, trying to see whether the somber color masked old bloodstains. He couldn't tell. Osrhoenes carried a small leather case, also black. Maniakes tried not to think about the sharp blades inside.

To Osrhoenes he said, "Sir," and to Philetos, "Holy sir," then went on to both of them together: "I trust you will forgive me when I say I hope your services won't be needed here today, though of course I shall pay you for your time regardless."

"Part of the gold you give me shall go to the sakellarios at the High Temple so as to swell the ecclesiastical treasure, the rest to the upkeep of the Sorcerers' Collegium," Philetos said;

healers, like other priests, were constrained by vows of poverty.

Osrhoenes merely bowed to Maniakes. He was a secular man; the fee he got from Maniakes would go into his own belt pouch.

To Kameas the Avtokrator said, "If you would be so kind, escort these gentlemen to their place opposite the doorway to the Red Room. Perhaps you will find them chairs, so they may wait comfortably. If they want food or wine or anything else, see that they have it."

"Certainly, your Majesty," Kameas said. Maniakes was certain his instructions had been unnecessary; to the vestiarios, perfect service was a matter not only of pride but also of routine. Fortunately, that perfect service included not showing up the Avtokrator. If Maniakes was too nervous to let Kameas do what was required without nagging, Kameas would condescend not to notice.

The eunuch led Philetos and Osrhoenes away. That left Maniakes alone with his worries, which he would rather not have been. Zoïle's warnings after Niphone's last confinement, the midwife's worried look now, Niphone's insistence on bearing an heir or dying in the attempt, his own fear over his wife's safety . . . Mixed together, they made a corrosive brew that griped his belly and made his heart pound as it would have before combat.

He jumped and spun around when someone tapped on the doorframe. "I didn't mean to startle you," Lysia said. "I just wanted to tell you that I pray the lord with the great and good mind will grant you a son and heir—and that the Empress comes through safe."

"Thank you, cousin of mine," Maniakes said. "My prayers ride along the same path. May Phos heed them all." As he had so often lately, he sketched the sun-circle over his heart. So did Lysia.

He waited for her to reassure him that everything would surely be all right. Instead, she said, "I didn't think you'd want to be here by yourself, fretting because you can't do anything but fret."

"Thank you," he said. "That was kind." He made himself produce something that sounded a little like a laugh. "Now I can be here with you, fretting because I can't do anything but fret."

Lysia smiled. "Yes, I suppose you will be, but maybe not as

much. Shall I call one of the servants and have him bring you a jar of wine? That might take the edge off your worry."

"Another kind thought, but no," Maniakes answered. "If I started drinking wine now, I don't think I'd stop till I was sodden. And that wouldn't do when Niphone or the midwife hands me the baby, and it won't do now. Nothing wrong with being worried when you have something to worry about. Before too long, the reason will go away and everything will be fine."

"Phos grant it be so." Lysia took a breath, as if to add something else, then looked away and shook her head. "Phos grant it be so," she repeated softly. Maniakes thought about asking her what she had been on the point of saying, then decided he would probably be better off not knowing.

He made awkward small talk for a couple of minutes. Then his father came into the chamber. The elder Maniakes seemed not in the least surprised to find Lysia there before him. "I remember waiting and pacing while *you* were being born," he told the Avtokrator. "I thought it was taking forever, though I daresay your mother thought it was taking a good deal longer than that." He sighed. "Nobody can tell me that was more than two or three years ago, and look at you!"

Rhegorios joined them a little later, and Symvatios moments after his son. Parsmanios did not make his quarters in the imperial residence, so he took longer to arrive. Kourikos' home was outside the palace quarter altogether; close to two hours went by before he and Phevronia came to join the wait for their second grandchild from Niphone.

By then, Maniakes had long since called for the wine he had turned down when Lysia suggested it. He even sipped at a cup, nursing it, savoring the flavor, but not drinking enough to let it affect him much. Having family around him did make things easier to bear—but the burden remained on him . . . and on his wife.

Parsmanios thumped him on the shoulder. "It takes time, brother of mine. Nothing to be done but wait."

"I know," Maniakes replied abstractedly. It had taken a very long time when Evtropia was born. He had hoped it would go faster this time; women's second labors, from what he had heard, often did. The sooner Niphone gave birth and began to recover, the happier he would be.

But no word came from the Red Room. Leaving his relatives behind, he walked down the hall to the birthing chamber.

Philetos and Osrhoenes sat in their chairs, a board for the war game set on a little table between them. A quick glance showed Maniakes that the healer-priest had the surgeon on the run.

Inside the Red Room, Niphone groaned. The sound made Maniakes flinch. "Do you know how she fares?" he asked the two men. "Has Zoïle come out?"

Almost in unison, the two men shook their heads. "No, your Majesty," they said together. Philetos went on, "One lesson I have learned as a healer-priest, and that is never to joggle a midwife's elbow." The expression of most unclerical rue that passed over his face suggested he had learned the lesson the hard way. By the way Osrhoenes rolled his eyes, he had had the same lesson, and maybe the same teacher.

Niphone groaned again—or perhaps this cry was closer to a scream. It wasn't quite like any of the sounds of agony Maniakes had heard on the battlefield, so he had trouble assigning it a proper name. That didn't make it any less appalling, especially since it came not from a wounded soldier but from his wife.

But while he winced, Osrhoenes and Philetos went back to studying the game board—covertly, because he still stood by them, but unmistakably. He took that to mean they had heard such cries before, which meant—which he hoped meant—such cries were a normal part of giving birth. All the same, he could not bear to listen to them. He retreated back up the hall. When he looked over his shoulder, he saw that the physician and healer-priest had returned to their game.

His father clucked sympathetically on seeing his face. "Going to be a while yet, eh?" the elder Maniakes said.

"Looks that way," the Avtokrator said. He wore the red boots that marked him as ruler of all Videssos, but some things not even a ruler could command. Niphone's cries painfully reminded him of the limits to his power.

He waited ... endlessly. He made small talk, and forgot what he had said the moment the words passed his lips. Kameas brought in a meal. Maniakes ate without tasting what was set before him. It got dark outside. Servitors lit lamps. Presently Kameas brought in more food, and Maniakes realized it was long enough since the last time for him to be hungry again.

By then, Parsmanios had fallen asleep in his chair and begun to snore. Symvatios' face, usually jolly, was full of shadow-filled lines and wrinkles. "Hard," he said to Maniakes, who nodded.

Kameas came into the chamber. "Can I bring you anything, your Majesty?" he asked, his voice low so as not to disturb Parsmanios—or Rhegorios, who was also dozing. The vestiarios' face, though smoother than Symvatios', showed no less concern.

"Esteemed sir, what I want now you can't bring me," Maniakes answered.

"That is so," Kameas said gravely. "May the good god grant that you receive it nonetheless." He dipped his head and slipped out of the room. His soft-soled shoes flapped against the marble and tile of the floor.

Lysia got up, walked over to Maniakes, and set a hand on his shoulder without saying anything. Gratefully he put his own hand on top of hers. Symvatios' head bobbed up and down like a fishing float in choppy water. The elder Maniakes' face was shadowed; the Avtokrator could not make out his father's expression.

Someone—not Kameas—came running up the corridor. "Your Majesty, your Majesty!" Zoïle was shouting.

Parsmanios awoke with a start. Rhegorios jerked out of his light sleep, too. "I don't fancy the sound of that," he said, rubbing at his eyes.

Maniakes didn't fancy it, either. He stepped out into the hallway—and recoiled in dismay at the sight of the midwife. Zoïle's arms were red to the elbows with blood; it soaked the front of her robe and dripped from her hands to the colored tiles of the floor mosaic.

"Come quick, your Majesty," she said, reaching out to grab at Maniakes' sleeve in spite of her gory fingers. "There's no hope to stop the bleeding—I've tried, Philetos has tried, and it's beyond what we can do. But we still may get the baby out of her alive, and with that done, the healer-priest may yet have another chance, a tiny one, to save your lady's life."

The hot-iron stink of blood filled the corridor. It made thinking straighter all the harder for Maniakes, arousing as it did the panic of the battlefield. At last, he managed, "Do as you must, of course, but why do you need me?"

Zoïle looked at him as if he were an idiot. "Why, to give the knife into Osrhoenes' hands and show your assent to his cutting. It would be for your lady, but she's too far gone to do it."

Seeing the state the midwife was in should have told Maniakes as much. Maybe he was an idiot. He also realized that, if Niphone was in such desperate straits, Philetos' chances of saving her after the surgeon had done his work were forlorn indeed. He moaned and shook his head, wishing he could have kept the illusion of hope.

No time for that now. No time for anything now. He trotted down the hall toward the Red Room, Zoïle at his elbow. Osrhoenes stood waiting outside the door. Seeing Maniakes, he reached into his bag and drew out a lancet. The keen blade glittered in the lamplight. Had any of the Avtokrator's guardsmen seen him, he might have died in the next instant for daring to draw a weapon in the presence of the Emperor.

Maniakes thought of that only later. When Osrhoenes held out the lancet to him, it was not a threat but a gesture as formal as a proskynesis. Maniakes took the knife, held it a moment, and returned it to the surgeon. "Do what you can," he said. "You shall not be blamed, come what may."

Osrhoenes bowed to him, then turned and went into the Red Room. Zoïle followed him. Maniakes had a brief glimpse of Niphone lying motionless on a bed in the center of the chamber, her face slack and pale as death. Philetos, his shoulders slumped, stood beside her. The midwife closed the door and he saw no more.

Nails biting into his palm, he waited for Niphone's shriek as the knife laid her belly open. No shriek came. For a moment, he was relieved, but then his heart sank further: if she was silent, it could only be because she was too nearly gone to feel anything.

He feared he would hear no sound from the Red Room but the frantic, muffled talk from Zoïle, Osrhoenes, and Philetos that leaked through the thick doors of the chamber. That would mean everything had been too late, that the baby was gone along with its mother.

He tried to figure out what that would mean for Videssos, what he would have to do next if it was so. He found his mind utterly stunned and blank. He tried to flog it into action, but had no luck. Past *my wife is dead, and my baby, too,* nothing meant anything.

Then, after what seemed an eternity but could not have been more than a handful of minutes, a newborn's angry, indignant wail pierced the portal of the Red Room. Maniakes needed a moment to recognize the sound for what it was. He had been so certain he would not hear it, he had trouble believing it when it came.

He stood rigid, leaning toward the Red Room. Of itself, his right hand sketched the sun-sign above his heart. If the baby lived, why not Niphone, too? "Please, Phos," he whispered.

When Zoïle came out, she carried a tiny bundle, tightly swaddled in a lambswool blanket. "You have a son, your Majesty," she said.

Instead of being joyful, her voice was numb with fatigue and grief. She had torn the neck opening of her robe, too, a sign of mourning. Maniakes asked the question anyhow. "Niphone?"

Tears ran down the midwife's cheeks. She bowed her head. "They—we—all of us—did everything we could to save her, your Majesty, but even to get the babe out alive and well . . . I think we thank the lord with the great and good mind for that much. I wouldn't have guessed Osrhoenes could do it, and I've never seen anyone faster with a knife than he is."

"Give me the boy," Maniakes said. He undid the blanket enough to make sure the baby had the proper number of fingers on each hand and toes on each foot and that it was indeed a boy child. No doubt there; its private parts were out of proportion to the rest of it. "Are they supposed to be like that?" Maniakes asked, pointing.

"That they are, your Majesty," Zoïle answered, seeming glad to talk about the baby rather than its mother. "Every boy comes into the world so." He would have guessed she followed that with a ribald joke after most births. Not tonight, not here.

He wrapped his son in the blanket once more. As he had when he had lost the fight east of Amorion, he made himself go on even in defeat. "Philetos couldn't save her after the cuts?" he asked, still trying to find out what had gone wrong.

"It's not like that, not Philetos' fault," Zoïle said. "A surgeon doesn't try to take a babe out of a mother unless she's on the point of dying anyhow. The ones the healers save after that are the special miracles, the ones priests talk of from before the altar to point out how we should never give up striving and hoping for the good. But most of the time, we lose the mother when the surgeon cuts."

"What do I do now?" Maniakes asked. He wasn't really talking to the midwife. Maybe he wasn't talking to anyone, maybe he spoke to Phos, maybe to himself. The good god did not swoop miraculously out of the sky with answers. If there were any, he would have to find them.

Zoïlc said, "The baby is all he should be, your Majesty. He turned pink nice as you please when Osrhoenes drew him forth and cut the cord. Phos willing, he'll do well. Have you chosen a name for him?"

"We were going to call him Likarios," Maniakes answered. "We—" He stopped. *We* didn't mean anything, not any more. Tears rolled down his cheeks. He might not have loved Niphone with the passion he had felt for her after they were first betrothed, but he cared for her, admired her bravery, and mourned her loss. It left an empty place in his life, and a bigger one than he had imagined till this moment when the event made imagination real.

"We'll tend to things here, your Majesty, prepare the body for the funeral," Zoïle said gently. Maniakes' head bobbed up and down, as if on a spring; he hadn't even thought about the funeral yet. Having a son and suddenly not having a wife had been all he could take in. The midwife, no doubt, had seen that before. She reminded him of what needed doing next. "Why don't you take your son—take Likarios—and show him to your kinsfolk? They'll be worried; they'll need to know what's happened here."

"Yes, of course," Maniakes said; it all seemed very easy, once someone took charge of you.

He started up the hallway toward the chamber where his relatives waited. He thought he was doing fine till he walked past the corridor on which he was supposed to turn. Shaking his head, he went back and did it right.

No one had presumed to come after him. His father and Lysia waited outside the chamber from which he had been summoned. Rhegorios stood inside, but had his head out the door. Maniakes didn't see anyone else. *The rest of them must be inside,* he thought, pleased with his talent for logical deduction.

In his arms, Likarios twitched and began to cry. He rocked the baby back and forth. He had had some practice doing that with Evtropia before he had gone out on campaign the summer before. She was bigger when he had gotten back; holding her didn't feel the same any more. *They grow. You stay the same from one day to the next—or you think you do. With them, there's no room to think that.*

"Is it a boy you're holding there?" the elder Maniakes called.

At the same time, Lysia asked, "Niphone—how is she?"

"Aye, Father, a boy," Maniakes replied. When he didn't answer Lysia, she groaned and covered her face with her hands: She knew what that had to mean.

So did the elder Maniakes. He stepped forward to fold the Avtokrator into an embrace—an awkward one, because Maniakes still held his newborn son in the crook of his elbow. "Ah, lad," the elder Maniakes said, his voice heavy with grief, "I lost your mother in childbed. I never dreamed the same ill-luck would strike you and your lady, too."

"I feared it," Maniakes said dully. "After she bore Evtropia, the midwife warned her—warned me—she shouldn't have another. I would have been content to see the throne come down to a brother or a cousin or a nephew, but Niphone insisted that she try to bear a son to succeed me. And so she did, but the price—"

Kourikos and Phevronia came out into the hallway. The face of the logothete of the treasury was even more pinched and drawn than usual; Phevronia, her hair all unpinned, looked haggard and frightened. Kourikos stammered slightly as he spoke, as if the words did not want to pass his lips: "Your Majesty, I pray you, tell me I have misunderstood your words to your father."

Maniakes could hardly blame him. "Behold your grandson, father-in-law of mine," he said, and held Likarios out to Kourikos. The logothete took the baby with a sure touch that said he hadn't forgotten everything he had once known about children. Maniakes went on, "More than anything, I wish I could tell you—tell you and your lady—that you have misunderstood me. The truth is, I cannot; you have not. Niphone . . . your daughter . . . my wife—" He looked down at the floor. The hunting mosaic blurred as his eyes filled with tears.

Phevronia wailed. Kourikos put his free arm around her. She buried her face in his shoulder and wept like a soul damned to the eternal ice.

Gravely Kameas said, "I share your sorrow, your Majesty. I shall set in train arrangements for care of the young Majesty here and, with your permission, shall also begin preparations for the Empress' funeral obsequies. The weather remains cool, so the matter is not so urgent as it might otherwise be, but nevertheless—"

Phevronia wept harder yet. Kourikos started to bristle at the vestiarios' suggestion, then seemed to slump in on himself. He nodded jerkily. So did Maniakes. *You have to go on,* he told himself, and wondered how to make himself believe it.

As with anything else connected with the imperial household, the funeral carried a heavy weight of ceremonial, in this case melancholy ceremonial. The limestone sarcophagus in which Niphone was laid to rest bore carved scenes showing the bridge of the separator, the narrow passage souls walked after death. Demons snatched those who failed Phos' stern judgment and fell from the bridge, dragging them down to Skotos' ice. The last panel of the relief, though, showed one soul, intended to represent Niphone, winging upward toward Phos' eternal light.

Deceased Avtokrators and their kinsfolk were by ancient tradition interred beneath a temple in the western part of Videssos the city, not far from the Forum of the Ox, the capital's ancient cattle market. The temple, dedicated to the memory of the holy Phravitas, an ecumenical patriarch from before the days of Stavrakios, was ancient, too, though not so ancient as the Forum of the Ox.

Kameas produced for Maniakes a robe of black silk shot through with silver threads. The Avtokrator had no idea of where the robe came from; it certainly did not hang in the closet adjoining the imperial bedchamber. It smelled strongly of camphor, and its wrinkles and creases were as firmly set as if it were made of metal rather than fabric.

"Be gentle with it, your Majesty," Kameas said. "The cloth is fragile these days."

"As you say," Maniakes answered. "How old is it, anyhow?"

The vestiarios' shrug made his several chins wobble. "I apologize, your Majesty, but I cannot tell you. My predecessor at this post, the esteemed Isoes, was himself ignorant of that, and told me his predecessor did not know the answer, either. I also cannot tell you how long the answer has been lost. That might have happened in the days of Isoes' predecessor, or it might have been a hundred years before his time."

Maniakes fingered the silk. He doubted the mourning robe had been new in his grandfather's days, but had no way to prove that. Kameas also brought him polished black leather covers for his boots. Strips cut in them let a little of the imperial crimson shine through; even in mourning, the Avtokrator remained the Avtokrator. But, looking down at himself, Maniakes saw that he made a somber spectacle indeed.

The other mourners in the funeral party—Kourikos and Phevronia, the elder Maniakes, Parsmanios, Rhegorios, Lysia, and Symvatios—wore unrelieved black. The horses drawing the wagon on which the sarcophagus lay were also black—though Maniakes knew a groom of the imperial stables had carefully painted over a white blaze on one of the animals.

Also in black surcoats, with black streamers hanging from their spears, were the guardsmen who marched with the mourners and the funeral wagon. For the day, the parasol-bearers who preceded the Avtokrator in all his public appearances carried black canopies rather than their usual colorful ones.

As the funeral party approached the plaza of Palamas, Maniakes saw it was packed with people; the folk of Videssos the city were eager for any spectacle, no matter how sorrowful. Some of the people wore black to show their sympathy for the Avtokrator. Others had dressed in their holiday best: for them, one show was as good as another.

At the edge of the plaza nearest the palace quarter waited the ecumenical patriarch Agathios. His regalia had not changed; he still wore the blue boots and a cloth-of-gold robe encrusted with pearls and gems, as he would have at a wedding or any joyous occasion. But his face was somber as he prostrated himself before Maniakes. "Your Majesty, I beg you to accept my condolences for your tragic loss."

"Thank you, most holy sir," Maniakes answered. "Let's get on with it, shall we?" As soon as the words were out of his mouth, he regretted them; Agathios looked scandalized. Maniakes had not meant anything more than wanting to have the funeral over so he could grieve in private, but anything an Avtokrator said that could be misinterpreted probably would be, and he knew too well he had left himself open to such misinterpretation.

Without a word to Maniakes, Agathios turned away and took his place at the head of the mournful procession. He called in a great voice to the crowds filling the plaza of Palamas. "Stand aside, people of Videssos! Make way for the last journey of Niphone, once Empress of the Videssians, now bathed in Phos' eternal light."

"May it be so," the people answered, their voices rising and falling like the surf that beat against the seawall. As best they could, they did clear a path through the plaza. Where their own efforts were not enough, the guards moved them aside with their spearshafts.

Even as the people moved back to make way for the funeral procession, they also pushed forward to speak a word of consolation to Maniakes or to his family. Some of them also pressed forward to get a glimpse of Niphone, who lay pale and still and forever unmoving inside the sarcophagus.

"I pray she knew she gave you a son," a man said to Maniakes. He nodded, though Niphone had known nothing of the sort.

A few of the folk in the plaza kept their hands at the hems of their tunics, ready to use the garments to help catch any largess the Avtokrator might choose to dispense. That thought had never entered his mind, not for today's occasion. He shook his head, bemused at the vagaries of human nature to which his position exposed him.

Though the plaza of Palamas was far wider than Middle Street, the procession had better going on the capital's main thoroughfare. The crowds there stayed off the street itself and under the covered colonnades to either side. When Maniakes glanced up, he saw a goodly number of people atop the colonnades as well, peering down at him and at the woman who had given him two children in just over a year and a half and now would give no more ever again.

Maniakes slowly walked past the government office buildings. Faces stared out at him from almost every window as clerks and bureaucrats escaped their scrolls and counting boards for a little while. The farther he went, the harder keeping up a dignified front before the people became.

In the Forum of the Ox, the crowds grew thick and hard to manage once more. The forum had once been the chief marketplace of Videssos the city for cattle and all other goods, a position long since usurped by the plaza of Palamas. Now most of what was bought and sold here was not fine enough to succeed in the newer square close by the palaces. The Forum of the Ox, even packed as it was now, seemed tired and sad and shabby and rundown.

Again the ecumenical patriarch appealed to the crowd to stand back and let the funeral procession pass. The people responded more slowly than they had in the plaza of Palamas. That was partly because the Forum of the Ox was even more crowded than the plaza had been, and partly because the people who crowded it looked to be less inclined to listen to requests from anyone than were the more prosperous Videssians who frequented the plaza of Palamas.

Little by little, the procession inched its way across the square and back onto Middle Street. After a couple of short blocks, the parasol-bearers followed Agathios south down a narrow, twisting lane that led toward the temple dedicated to the memory of the holy Phravitas.

As was true on a lot of such lanes, second- and third-story balconies grew close to each other above the street until they all but cut off light and air from it. Maniakes remembered thinking when he first came back to Videssos the city that the ordinance mandating balconies to keep a proper distance from one another had not been enforced during Genesios' reign. It didn't look as if building inspectors were doing much better now that he wore the red boots. He exhaled through his nose. He had had a few more immediately urgent things to worry about than whether balconies conformed to law in all particulars.

Legal or not, the balconies were jammed full of people. When Maniakes looked up to the narrow strip of sky between them, he saw dozens of faces staring down at him. One of those faces, a woman's, up on a third-floor balcony, was not only staring but deathly pale, pale as Niphone, pale enough to draw Maniakes' notice even in the midst of the crowd, even in the midst of his sorrow.

The woman leaned over the wooden rail of the balcony. Her mouth opened wide. Maniakes thought she meant to call something to him, although he would have had trouble hearing her through the noise of the crowd. Perhaps that was what she intended, but it was not what happened. She choked and gagged and vomited down onto the funeral procession.

The stinking stuff splashed the sarcophagus, the funeral wagon, and one of the guardsmen. He leapt aside with a cry of disgust. Maniakes pointed a furious finger up at the woman. Afterward, he regretted showing his anger so openly, but that was afterward.

The guard's was not the only disgusted cry to go up. Other cries rose, too, cries of "Shame!" and "Sacrilege!" and "Profanation!" and, inevitably, "Blasphemy!" Those cries rang loudest from the balconies, and loudest of all from the balcony where the luckless woman stood. Other people standing there with her seized her, lifted her, and, while she screamed, flung her down to the cobbles below. The scream abruptly cut off.

Maniakes whirled and stared in horror at the body of the woman who sprawled only a few feet behind him. By the unnatural angle at which her head joined her body, her neck was broken. She would never rise from the street again. Maniakes' hand drew the sun-sign over his heart. "By the lord with the great and good mind," he cried, his voice full of anguish, "must even the funeral of my wife grow wrong?"

But other shouts went up from the crowd, shouts of fierce exhilaration: "Death to defilers!" "She got what she deserved!" "We avenge you, Niphone!" and even, "Thou conquerest, Empress Niphone!"

Far from being ashamed at what they had done, the men who had thrown the woman to her death raised their arms in triumph, clenched fists pumping the air. The cheers that echoed up and down the narrow street said not just they but also the city mob thought of them as heroes.

Maniakes looked helplessly toward his father. The elder Maniakes spread his hands, as if to ask *What can you do?* The Avtokrator knew the answer to that only too well: *not much.* If he sent his guardsmen into that building after the killers, they would have to fight through the crowd to get inside, fight their way upstairs, and then come down with their prisoners to face the wrath of the mob again. Having the capital erupt in riots was not something he could afford, not with all the other bitter troubles the Empire had these days.

"Forward!" he shouted, and then again: "Forward! Let us grant Niphone such dignity as we can, such dignity as she deserves."

That reached the crowd. Their baying, which had reminded him of nothing so much as a pack of wolves in full cry on a winter's night, eased. Still shaking his head in amazement and disbelief, he hurried on toward the temple dedicated to the memory of the holy Phravitas.

If that temple wasn't the oldest building in Videssos the city, it was among them. In the High Temple and shrines modeled after it, the altar stood under a dome at the center of the worship area, with pews approaching it from each of the cardinal directions. The temple of the holy Phravitas conformed to a more antique pattern. It was a rectangular building of red brick, the bricks themselves darkened and smoothed by age. Its entrance was at the west side; all seats faced the east, the direction from which Phos' sun rose each day.

Agathios strode to the altar, his gleaming robes swirling about him. The senior priest normally responsible for the temple bowed low to his ecclesiastical superior and kissed his outstretched hand in token of submission. Maniakes' guardsmen lifted Niphone's sarcophagus off the wagon that had borne it hither and carried it to a black-draped bier by the side of the altar.

Maniakes and his family took their places in the pews nearest the holy table. When other mourners, some nobles, some simply townsfolk, had filled the rest of the seats, Agathios raised his hands to the heavens, not in triumph but in supplication. That was the signal for those in the temple to rise once more.

"We bless thee, Phos, lord with the great and good mind," Agathios intoned, "by thy grace our protector, watchful beforehand that the great test of life may be decided in our favor."

By its very familiarity, repeating the creed helped steady Maniakes: Not that his grief diminished, but it was channeled into pathways where his mind regularly traveled. The ecumenical patriarch gestured. Maniakes and his companions sat back down. Being in a temple—even if not the one where he usually prayed—and listening to the patriarch also helped transmute anguish into routine, which was easier for the mind to grasp and deal with.

Agathios said, "We are gathered here today to commend to Phos and his eternal light the soul of our sister Niphone, who died in the most noble way given to a woman: that is to say, in bringing new life into our world."

Phevronia sobbed noisily. Kourikos patted his wife's shoulder, doing his best to comfort her. His best struck Maniakes as ineffectual, but then, Phevronia had a right to her sorrow. Losing parents was hard. Losing a spouse was harder. Losing a child, especially a child in what should have been the prime of life, turned the natural order of things on its head.

Maniakes wondered if he ought to be angry with Niphone's mother and father for making her feel she had to bear him a son so as to keep alive her family's influence over the imperial line. He had tried calling up that anger; it would have made his grief easier to bear. He hadn't managed it, though. Many would have taken the same risk Niphone had, and she had done it of her own free will.

"Surely the good god will demonstrate his bounteous compassion and will suffer our sister Niphone to cross the bridge of the separator unharried by the demons who mount up from the eternal ice," Agathios said. "Surely she shall have no part of Skotos and his devices." The ecumenical patriarch spat in rejection of the dark god. Maniakes and the other mourners imitated him.

Agathios went on for some time, describing Niphone's manifest virtues. He had spoken with Maniakes about those, and with Kourikos and Phevronia, and with Nikaia, the abbess of the convent dedicated to the memory of the holy Phostina. So far as Maniakes could tell, every word he said was true.

If Niphone had all those virtues, why did she have to die so young? That was a silent scream inside Maniakes, the way, no doubt, it had been a silent scream in every generation of mankind all the way back to Vaspur the Firstborn—of whom Agathios did not think in those terms. If the ecumenical patriarch had any new light to shed on the question, he did not show it to Maniakes.

After praising Niphone and reassuring everyone who heard him that Phos had indeed taken her soul into the realm of eternal light, after leading his listeners in Phos' creed once more, Agathios said, "And now let her discarded earthly remains be consigned to their final resting place."

That was the signal for Maniakes, Kourikos, and Phevronia to come forward and stand by the sarcophagus. Before the guardsmen lifted it from the bier, Maniakes looked into it one last time. Niphone seemed at peace. He had seen too many dead men on the battlefield to lie to himself by thinking she merely looked asleep, but he could hope she had indeed passed over the bridge of the separator.

The priest who normally presided at the temple dedicated to the memory of the holy Phravitas handed Agathios a lighted torch, murmuring, "The lamps in the memorial chamber below have been kindled, most holy sir."

"Thank you, holy sir," the patriarch answered. He gathered up Niphone's closest survivors and the guardsmen by eye, then went down a stone staircase to the chamber below the temple.

When Genesios toppled Likinios, he had thrown the dead Avtokrator's body and those of his sons into the sea and sent their heads far and wide to prove they were dead. After Maniakes cast down Genesios in turn, the tyrant's head had gone up on the Milestone and his body was burned. The imperial tombs, then, had not had anyone inhumed in them for some years.

The chamber was very quiet. The thick, still air seemed to swallow the sound of footsteps. Lamplight played off marble and cast flickering shadows on inscriptions and reliefs of Avtokrators and Empresses who had been dead for decades, centuries, even a millennium. On some of the oldest inscriptions, the Videssian was of so antique a mode that Maniakes could hardly read it.

Amid all the whiteness of the marble, one space in the back of the chamber gaped black. Quietly grunting with the effort, the guardsmen slid Niphone's sarcophagus into it. Agathios said, "In a year's time, your Majesty, you or the Empress' sadly bereaved parents may set a memorial tablet here, one properly describing her courage and virtues. Please know that I share your sorrow and offer you my deepest and most sincere sympathy."

"Thank you, most holy sir," Maniakes answered. Kourikos and Phevronia echoed him. Even as he spoke, though, the Avtokrator wondered how sincere Agathios truly was. He had said all the proper things, but said them in a way that suggested duty more than piety. Maniakes sighed. The patriarch was at least as much a political creature as he was a holy man.

"It's over," Phevronia said in a dazed, wondering voice. "It's over, and there's nothing left of her, not any more, not ever again."

She was right. It was over. Nothing was left. Feeling altogether empty inside, Maniakes started back toward the stairs. Agathios hurried to get in front of him, to lead the upward-bound procession as he had the one going down. The guardsmen came next. More slowly, Kourikos and Phevronia followed, leaving the chamber under the temple dedicated to the memory of the holy Phravitas empty until the next time someone from the royal house died.

Kameas said, "May it please your Majesty, a messenger has just come bearing word from Abivard the Makuraner general."

"What can he want of us now?" Maniakes wondered. He had trouble concentrating on the affairs of Videssos; he had laid Niphone to rest only a few days before. Gamely he tried to bring his mind to the business at hand. "Have him enter, esteemed sir."

The messenger prostrated himself, then handed Maniakes a

rolled parchment sealed with ribbon and wax. As he broke the seal, he wondered if he would be able to make sense of the letter inside. He spoke Makuraner fairly well but didn't read it.

Abivard, though, must have had a local translate his thoughts for him, for the missive was written in Videssian: "Abivard the general serving the mighty Sharbaraz King of Kings, may his years be many and his realm increase, to Maniakes styling himself Avtokrator: Greetings. I learn with sadness of the death of your wife. Accept, please, my condolences on this, your personal loss; may the Prophets Four guide her to union with the God."

Maniakes turned to Kameas. "Bring me sealing wax, please, esteemed sir." As the vestiarios hurried off to get it, Maniakes inked a reed pen and wrote rapidly on a sheet of parchment: "Maniakes Avtokrator to the Makuraner general Abivard: Greetings. My thanks for your kind personal wishes. My own wish is that you and your army would withdraw from lands to which you have no right. I speak there both as Avtokrator of the Videssians and in my own person. It was for that purpose that I sent the eminent Triphylles as ambassador to Sharbaraz King of Kings. Have you yet any word of the progress of his embassy?"

He rolled up the parchment and tied it with one of the ribbons he normally used for decrees. Kameas returned with a stick of the crimson sealing wax reserved for the Avtokrator alone. The eunuch handed the wax to him, then picked up a lamp. Maniakes held the lamp to the flame. Several drops fell onto the ribbon and parchment. While they were still soft, Maniakes pressed his sunburst signet into them. He withdrew the ring, waved the sealed letter in the air to make sure it hardened properly, and gave it to the messenger. "Be sure this reaches Abivard, by whatever means you have of arranging such things." He didn't need to know the details, and so did not inquire after them.

The messenger took the parchment, stuffed it into a waterproof tube of boiled, waxed leather, and, after prostrating himself to Maniakes once more, hurried out of the imperial residence. "May I see what the Makuraner general wrote, your Majesty?" Kameas asked.

"Yes, go ahead," Maniakes answered. Maybe Stavrakios had been bold enough to keep his vestiarios from knowing everything that happened to him. Few Avtokrators since had been. Maniakes certainly was not.

Kameas said, "He speaks you fair, no doubt of that. One thing the Makuraners have shown, though, is that their deeds don't commonly live up to the words they use to cloak them."

"Too true," Maniakes said. "The same holds true for the Kubratoi. The same held true for Videssos, too, during the reign of my late and unlamented predecessor. I, of course, am the very Milestone of truthfulness."

"Of course, your Majesty," Kameas said, so seriously that Maniakes doubted whether he had caught the intended irony. Then the vestiarios let out the smallest, most discreet snort imaginable.

"Go on, esteemed sir," Maniakes told him, starting to laugh. "Take yourself elsewhere."

"Yes, your Majesty," the vestiarios replied. "The good god grant that Abivard give you good news concerning the eminent Triphylles."

He turned and swept away, leaving Maniakes staring after him in astonishment. He hadn't seen what the Avtokrator had written; he hadn't been in the chamber then. "How did you know?" Maniakes asked. But by then Kameas was a long way down the hall. If he heard, he gave no sign.

Great pillars of smoke rose from Across, as they had when Abivard's forces entered the suburb the autumn before. Now they were leaving, giving Maniakes easy access to the westlands if he wanted to try conclusions with the Makuraners again this summer.

Wondering whether he did was only part of what worried him. He turned and put the other part to Rhegorios: "If he's leaving there, where in Phos' holy name is he going?"

"My cousin your Majesty, damn me to the ice if I know." Rhegorios spat on the ground in rejection of Skotos. "All I can say is, he's likely headed where he thinks he can do us the most harm."

"He could have done worse staying right where he was," Maniakes said, discontent in his voice. "Across was like the stopper in the jar; his holding it kept us out of the westlands. Now we can go back, if we dare. But what will happen to us if we do?"

"Can't tell that till we try it—if we try it," Rhegorios answered. "But I can tell you what happens if we don't: the Makuraners get to keep the countryside for another year and make it even harder for us to get it back when we do finally work up the nerve to try."

Maniakes grimaced. That his cousin was blunt did not mean he was wrong. Maniakes said, "I wish I thought our army was in better shape. We've worked hard this winter, but . . ." He let that hang.

"You could take Tzikas' advice," Rhegorios said with a curl of his lip. "If you stay right here in Videssos the city, you know, and only wait long enough, why, eventually every single fellow who opposes you now will die of old age, and then Videssos will be free to take back its own."

"Ha-ha," Maniakes said in a hollow voice. His cousin exaggerated Tzikas' cautious approach to war, but only slightly. "We have to fight the Makuraners, we have to do it in the westlands, and we have to do it on our own terms. We can't afford any more fiascoes like the one last summer. If we aren't in a position to go out there and win, we shouldn't fight."

"How do you propose to guarantee that?" Rhegorios asked. "Just about every time there's a battle, the bastards on the other side have a nasty habit of fighting back. You can't simply count on them to lie down and die, no matter how much you wish they would."

"To the ice with you," Maniakes said, laughing in spite of himself. "You know what I mean, no matter how clumsily I say it. I can't let myself get lured into situations where I don't have the advantage. The more of what's ours we take, the more men and resources we gather for the next step."

"If we can start by taking back Across, that will be something," Rhegorios said.

Take it back they did, after the dromons on endless patrol in the Cattle Crossing reported that Abivard and his horsemen had indeed abandoned the suburb. Soon after imperial soldiers reentered Across, Maniakes sailed over the strait to the westlands to see what the Makuraners had done to it.

His first impression was that what his men had taken was not worth having and that the Makuraners had abandoned it only because nothing was left to wreck. Most of what could burn had been burned; what hadn't been burned had been torn apart to get fuel for the fires made of the rest.

In ever-growing streams, people emerged from the ruins to spin him tales of woe and horror. He listened to them sympathetically but without much surprise; he knew how armies treated a countryside populated by enemies. The Makuraners had done nothing out of the ordinary. Robberies and rapes were part of the long, sad litany of man's inhumanity to man—and to woman.

"But, your Majesty," said an aggrieved merchant whose stock of fine boots now adorned Makuraner feet, "aren't you going to chase after those thieving heathens and make 'em pay for what they done?" By his tone, he expected Maniakes to set a properly itemized bill before Abivard the next time he saw him.

"I'll do everything I can," Maniakes said evasively; he didn't care to answer that just being in the westlands this year was as much as he had hoped for. "Consolidating my position here comes first, though. After all, we don't want the Makuraners back, do we?"

"What we want and what we get aren't always the same thing," the merchant answered, his voice sour. Only after the words were out of his mouth did he seem to realize they might be taken as criticism of Maniakes. A moment after that, he had made himself scarce. Maniakes ruefully shook his head. It wasn't as if the same thought hadn't crossed his mind a time or twelve.

Engineers surveyed the ground west of Across, seeking the best line on which to establish field fortifications. The suburbs on the far side of the Cattle Crossing from Videssos the city had been unwalled for hundreds upon hundreds of years. Who could have imagined an enemy dangerous enough to penetrate to the very heart of the Empire? Imagined or not, the Makuraners had been here; the evidence of that was only too obvious.

The chief engineer, a stocky, dour man named Stotzas, said, "I can lay you out the sites for some fine works, your Majesty. I see one trouble, though—no, two." He was the sort who saw more troubles the longer he looked at something.

Maniakes had no trouble seeing these for himself. He held up his thumb. "Where am I going to find the men to build the works you lay out?" He stuck up his index finger beside thumb. "Where am I going to find soldiers to put in the works even if you do manage to build them?"

"You've just rolled Phos' little suns," Stotzas said. His big, blunt-featured head bobbed up and down as he nodded. "Mind you, your Majesty, I'll do everything I can for you, but . . ." His voice trailed away. He didn't flee, as the merchant had, but he didn't look delighted about speaking the whole truth, either.

"But there's liable not to be much you can do, what with manpower being the way it is," Maniakes suggested.

Stotzas nodded, glad for the respite. He said, "At that, I've got it easy. Brick and stone don't argue back. The lord with the great and good mind may know what to do about the mess with the temples, but I'm bound for the ice if I do."

"Nor I," Maniakes answered, feeling a good deal less than impudent. "Whoever came up with the idea of forcing priests in places the Makuraners hold to adapt Vaspurakaner usages was a fiendishly clever man. Some of the priests will have done it sincerely, others to curry favor with the invaders, others just to survive. Sorting out who did what for which reasons is liable to take years, especially when everybody's busy calling everybody else a liar."

"Like I said, bricks and stone, they keep quiet," Stotzas replied. "Shave a man's head and put a blue robe on him and it doesn't seem like he'll ever shut up."

That wasn't altogether fair. A great deal of the monastic life, for instance, was passed in prayerful silence. But the chief engineer had a point. In defending themselves and accusing their neighbors, the clerics who jostled for audience with Maniakes did the reputation of the temples no good.

After listening to one set of denunciations and counter-denunciations, all of them backed with documents—each side insisting the documents of the other were forgeries—Maniakes burst out, "A pox take the lot of you, holy sirs!" That wasn't the way a good and pious ruler was supposed to address his clerics, but he was too fed up to care. "You may send this whole great mound of tripe to the most holy Agathios, to let him deal with it as he will. Until such times as he decides the case, I command you to live at peace with one another and to respect one another as orthodox, regardless of who may have done what to whom while the Makuraners were here."

"But, your Majesty," one blue-robe cried, "these wretches reveled in their lapse into heresy, glorying in the chance to bring the temples into disrepute."

A priest of the other faction shouted, "You're the ones who dragged the good name of the temples through the wineshops and bathhouses with your shameless pandering to the invaders."

The two sides started calling each other liars and apostates again, just as they had when they first came before Maniakes. He slammed his open palm down on the table in front of him.

The small thunderclap of noise made clerics from both sides momentarily fall silent in surprise.

"Perhaps you misunderstood me, holy sirs," Maniakes said into that brief silence. "You may respect one another as orthodox until the ecumenical patriarch renders his decision on your cases, or you may call one another heretics to your heart's content—in gaol. Which will it be?"

The clerics weren't screaming at one another when they left his presence, which represented progress of a sort. When they were gone, he slumped back in his chair and covered his face with his hands. Rhegorios came over and thumped him on the shoulder. "Cheer up, my cousin your Majesty. You'll have cases like that in every town we reconquer from the Makuraners."

"No, I won't, by the good god," Maniakes burst out. "Agathios will, and we'll find out what—if anything—the most holy sir is made of and what he's good for." Given what he had seen of Agathios, that wasn't apt to be much. He screwed his face up, as if he had tasted wine gone into vinegar. "You've given me the first decent argument I've heard for letting the Makuraners keep the westlands."

Rhegorios laughed, as if he had made a joke.

From Across, Videssian forces cautiously pushed south and west. It was by no means a reconquest of the westlands but a slow, wary reoccupation of territory Abivard had, for the time being, abandoned. In somewhat bolder style, Maniakes ordered a few bands of horsemen deeper into the westlands to see if they could nip in behind big Makuraner forces and wreck the supply columns that kept them stocked with arrows and spearpoints and iron splints for their cuirasses.

He ordered his men not to attack the Makuraner field armies. "Not this year," he said. "First we learn to hurt them in other ways. Once we know we can do that, we think about facing them in open battle again. Meanwhile, let's see how they like moving through a hostile countryside."

The short answer was, the Makuraners didn't like it. They started burning villages to show they didn't like it. Maniakes didn't know whether to mourn or cheer when he got that news. It would depend on whether the Makuraners cowed the westlands or infuriated them.

In response, he sent for more raiding parties, many of them aboard ship to go to the northern and southern coasts of the westlands and strike inland from there. "Maybe, just maybe," he told his father, "we'll be able to force the boiler boys off balance for a change. The one place where they can't match us is on the sea."

"That's so," the elder Maniakes agreed. He plucked a long white hair from his beard and held it out at arm's length so he could see it clearly. After he let it fall to the ground, he looked sidelong at his son and asked, "Have you got a naval captain whose head you wouldn't mind seeing up on the block?"

"I could probably come up with one," Maniakes allowed. "Why would I want to, though?"

His father's eyes twinkled. "The Kubratoi can't match us on the sea, either. Those *monoxyla* of theirs are all very well— until they run up against a dromon. After that, they're wreckage with butchered meat inside. I was just thinking you could send a captain up along the coast of Kubrat to raid and then, when Etzilios screamed blue murder, send him the fellow's head and say it was his idea all along."

Maniakes gaped, then laughed till the tears came. "By the good god, Father, now you've gone and tempted me. Every time I look north, I'm going to think of doing just what you said. It might not even make the khagan go back to war with us; he's clever enough, curse him, to see the joke."

"If you weren't at war with Makuran . . ." the elder Maniakes said.

"And if I had a ship's captain I really wanted to be rid of," the Avtokrator added. "It would hardly be fair to an up-and-coming officer."

"That's true," the elder Maniakes said. "He wouldn't be up-and-coming afterward; he'd be down-and-going, or rather gone."

They both laughed then, long and hard enough that Kameas stuck his head into the chamber to find out what was going on. After they had explained—each more sheepish than the other—the vestiarios said, "In times like these, any cause for mirth, no matter how foolish, is to be cherished."

"He's right," Maniakes said after Kameas left. "Between the way the war is going and losing Niphone, the imperial residence has been a gloomy place."

"A man who's happy without reason is likely either a fool or a drunk, or else both," his father answered. "We'll get back down to business soon enough. I'm sure of that."

His prophecy was fulfilled a couple of days later, when a

messenger delivered a dispatch from Abivard, brought to Videssian-held territory behind a shield of truce. Maniakes drew it out of its boiled-leather tube. Like the one the Makuraner general had sent before, it was written in Videssian, though not in the same hand as the earlier missive had been:

Abivard general to Sharbaraz King of Kings, may his years be many and his realm increase, to Maniakes styling himself Avtokrator of the Videssians: Greetings. In reply to your recent communication regarding the status of the man Triphylles whom you sent as embassy to the good, pacific, and benevolent Sharbaraz, favorite of the God, beloved of the Prophets Four, I am bidden by his puissant majesty to inform you that the aforesaid man Triphylles, in just punishment for his intolerable insolence, has been confined to prison outside Mashiz to ponder his folly.

The message stopped there. Maniakes' eyes kept going for a couple of lines' worth of blank parchment, as if to force more meaning from the sheet he held. "He can't do that," the Avtokrator exclaimed—to whom, he could not have said.

"Your Majesty?" The messenger hadn't the slightest idea what Maniakes was talking about.

"He can't do that," Maniakes repeated. "Sharbaraz can't just throw an ambassador into jail because he doesn't fancy the way he talks." If that were the only criterion, Moundioukh, for instance, would never see the outside of a cell again. Maniakes went on, "It violates every law of civilized conduct between empires."

"Why should Sharbaraz care a fig about anything like that?" the messenger said. "For one thing, he's a cursed Makuraner. For another, he's winning the war, so who's going to stop him from doing whatever he pleases?"

Maniakes stared at him without answering. The fellow was right, of course. Who would—who could—stop Sharbaraz King of Kings from doing whatever he pleased? Maniakes had proved singularly unable to pull off the trick.

"Is there a reply, your Majesty?" the messenger asked.

"Yes, by the good god." Maniakes dipped a pen in a pot of ink and began to write on a sheet of parchment he had been about to use to authorize more expenditures for repairing the walls of Imbros. This was more urgent—unless, of course,

Etzilios decided to break the truce for whose extension Maniakes had just paid.

"Maniakes Avtokrator of the Videssians to Abivard general of Makuran: Greetings." The pen scratched gently as it raced over the writing surface. "I am shocked and dismayed to learn that Sharbaraz King of Kings would so forget the law of nations as to imprison my ambassador, the eminent Triphylles. I demand his immediate release." *How? On pain of war?* his mind jeered. *You're already at war—and losing.* "I further demand proper compensation for the outrage he has suffered, and his immediate return to Videssos the city, where he may recuperate from his travail. I do not judge you guilty in this matter. Pass my letter on to your sovereign, that he may act on it in all possible haste."

He called for sealing wax from Kameas and closed the letter in on itself before giving it to the messenger. "How much good this will do, Phos alone knows," the Avtokrator said, "but Phos also knows no good at all can come unless I do protest."

After the messenger departed, Maniakes spent a little while calling curses down on Abivard's head. Had the Makuraner general not urged the course upon him, he never would have sent Triphylles off to Sharbaraz. He had assumed the King of Kings would not mistreat an envoy, and also that Sharbaraz would be interested in extracting tribute money from Videssos.

But Sharbaraz was already extracting money from Videssos. With enough plunder coming in, he cared nothing for tribute. Maniakes kicked at the floor. For an angry moment, he wished Kourikos and Triphylles had never come to Kastavala. Niphone would still be alive if they had stayed in Videssos the city, and it was hard to see how the empire could have been in worse shape under Genesios than it was now under his own rule. And he himself would still have been back on the island of Kalavria with his mistress and his bastard son, and none of the catastrophes befalling his homeland would have been his fault.

He sighed. "Some people are meant to start fires, some are meant to put them out," he said, though no one was there to hear him. "Genesios started this one, and somehow or other I have to figure out how to pour water on it."

He sat down and thought hard. Things were better now than they had been the year before. Then he had tried to match the Makuraners at their own game. It hadn't worked; Videssos had been—and remained—in too much chaos for that. Now he was trying something new. He didn't know how well his strategy of raids and pinpricks would work, but it could hardly fare worse than what had gone before it. With luck, it would rock Abivard back on his heels. The Makuraners in the westlands hadn't had even that much happen to them for a long time.

"Even if it works, it's not enough," he muttered. Harassing Abivard's forces wouldn't drive them off Videssian soil. He couldn't think of anything within the Empire's capacity that would.

XI

M<small>ANIAKES</small> <small>THRUST A PARCHMENT AT</small> T<small>ZIKAS</small>. H<small>E</small> <small>WISHED HE</small> had the leather tube in which the message had reached Videssos the city; he would have hit his gloomy general over the head with it. "Here, eminent sir, read this," he said. "Do you see?"

Tzikas took his own sweet time unrolling the parchment and scanning its contents. "Any good news is always welcome, your Majesty," he said, politely—and infuriatingly—unimpressed, "but destroying a few Makuraner wagons west of Amorion doesn't strike me as reason enough for Agathios to declare a day of thanksgiving."

By his tone, he would not have been impressed had the message reported the capture of Mashiz. Nothing Maniakes could do would satisfy him, save possibly to hand him the red boots. Had he not been such a good general, Maniakes would have had no qualms about forcing him into retirement—but his being such a good general was precisely what made him a threat now.

Keeping a tight rein on his temper, Maniakes said, "Eminent sir, destroying the wagons is not the point. The point is that we have warriors raiding deep into territory the Makuraners have held since the early days of Genesios' reign—and coming out safe again to tell the tale."

More than your warriors in Amorion did, he thought, all the while knowing that was unfair. Tzikas had done well to hold out in the garrison town for as long as he had. Expecting him to have hit back, too, was asking too much.

The general handed the note back to him. "May we have

many more such glorious successes, your Majesty." Was that sarcasm? Luckily for Tzikas, Maniakes couldn't quite be sure.

"May we indeed," he answered, taking the comment at face value. "If we can't win large fights, by all means let us win the small ones. If we win enough small ones, perhaps the Makuraners will have suffered too much damage to engage us in so many of the large ones."

"Did it come to pass, that would be very good," Tzikas agreed. "But, your Majesty—and I hope you will forgive me for speaking so plainly—I don't see it as likely. They have too strong a grip on the westlands for even a swarm of fleabites to drive them out."

"Eminent sir, if neither large fights nor small ones will get the Makuraners out of the westlands, isn't that the same as saying the westlands by rights belong to them these days?"

"I wouldn't go quite that far, your Majesty," Tzikas said, cautious as usual. Maniakes, by now, had the distinct impression Tzikas wouldn't go very far for anything—a more relentlessly moderate man would have been hard to imagine. In a way, that was a relief, for Maniakes could hope it meant Tzikas wouldn't go far in trying to overthrow him, either.

But it limited what he could do with the general. Send Tzikas to lead what should have been a dashing cavalry pursuit and you would find he had decorously ridden after the foe for a few miles before deciding he had done enough for the day and breaking off. No doubt he was a clever, resourceful defensive strategist, but a soldier who wouldn't go out and fight was worth less than he might have been otherwise.

Maniakes gave it up and went to see how his children were doing. Evtropia greeted him with a squeal of glee and came toddling over to wrap her arms around his leg. "Papapapa," she said. "Good!" She talked much more than he remembered Atalarikhos doing at the same age. All the serving women maintained she was astonishingly precocious. Since she seemed a clever child to him, too, he dared hope that wasn't the usual flattery an Avtokrator heard.

A wet nurse was feeding Likarios. Nodding to Maniakes, she said, "He is a hungry one, your Majesty. Odds are that means he'll be a big man when he comes into his full growth."

"We'll have to wait and see," Maniakes answered. That *was* flattery, nothing else but.

"He quite favors you, I think," the wet nurse said, trying again. Maniakes shrugged. Whenever he looked at his infant son, he saw Niphone's still, pale face in the sarcophagus. It wasn't as if the baby had done that deliberately, nor even that he felt anger at his son because of what had happened to Niphone. But the association would not go away.

Maniakes walked over to look down at the boy. Likarios recognized him and tried to smile with the wet nurse's nipple still in his mouth. Milk dribbled down his chin. The wet nurse laughed. So did Maniakes, in spite of everything—his son looked very foolish.

"He's a fine baby, your Majesty," the wet nurse said. "He eats and eats and eats and hardly ever fusses. He smiles almost all the time."

"That's good," Maniakes said. Hearing his voice, Likarios did smile again. Maniakes found himself smiling back. He remembered Evtropia from the fall before, when she had been a few months older than her little brother was now. She had thrown her whole body into a smile, wiggling and thrashing from sheer glee. She hadn't cared then—she still didn't care—that the Makuraners had conquered the westlands and were sitting in Across. As long as someone had been there to smile at her, she had stayed happy. He envied that.

The wet nurse stuck a cloth up on her shoulder and transferred Likarios from her breast. She patted him on the back till he produced a belch and a little sour milk. "That's a good boy!" she said, and then, to Maniakes, "He's a healthy baby, too." She quickly sketched the sun-circle over her still-bare left breast. "He hasn't had many fevers or fluxes or anything of the sort. He just goes on about his business, is what he does."

"That's what he's supposed to do," Maniakes answered, also sketching the sun-sign. "Nice to see someone doing what he's supposed to do and not fouling up the job."

"Your Majesty?" the wet nurse said. Politics wasn't her first worry, either. Whatever happened outside her immediate circle of attention could have been off beyond Makuran, as far as she was concerned. Maniakes wished he could view matters the same way. Unfortunately, he knew too well that what happened far away now could matter in Videssos the city later. If he and his father hadn't helped restore Sharbaraz to his throne, the westlands likely would have remained in Videssian hands to this day.

"Papapapa!" Evtropia wasn't going to let her brother keep all his attention. She came over to Maniakes and demanded, "Pick up me."

"How smart she is," the wet nurse said as Maniakes obeyed his daughter. "Hardly any children that little make real sentences."

Evtropia squealed with glee while Maniakes swung her through the air. Then she got bored and said, "Put down me," so he did that. She went off to play with a doll stuffed with feathers.

The wet nurse made no effort to put her dress to rights. Maniakes wondered whether that was because she thought Likarios would want more to eat or so she could display herself for him. Even if he slept with her only once, she could expect rich presents. If he made her pregnant, she would never want for anything. And if, as in a romance, she swept him off his feet and he married her . . .

But he didn't want to marry her, or even to take her to bed. After a while, she must have realized that, for she slipped her arm back into the left sleeve of the dress. The baby had fallen asleep. She got up and put him in his cradle.

Maniakes played with Evtropia for a while. Then she started to get cranky. One of the serving women said, "It will be time for her nap soon, your Majesty."

"No nap," Evtropia said. *"No nap!"* The second repetition was loud enough to make everyone in the room flinch—except her brother; he never stirred. Even as she screamed, though, Evtropia betrayed herself with a yawn. Maniakes and the serving woman exchanged knowing glances. It wouldn't be long.

The Avtokrator felt better after he left his children. Unlike most of the Empire, they were doing well. *Yes, and look at the price you paid.* But he hadn't paid the price. Poor Niphone had.

He missed her more than he had thought he would: not just waking up alone in the large bed in the imperial bedchamber but talking with her. She had never been afraid to tell him what she thought. For an Avtokrator, that was precious. Most people told him what they thought he wanted to hear, nothing more. Only among his own blood kin could he hope to find honesty now.

Slowly he walked down the hallway and out of the imperial residence. The guards on the low, broad stairs stiffened to attention. He nodded to them—letting your bodyguards think you took them for granted wasn't smart. His real attention, though, was on the westlands.

Rebuilding in Across went on by fits and starts. A few of

the burned temples there had been restored; the gilded domes
that topped their spires glinted in the sunlight. The Makuraner
army that had held the suburb was now ravaging its way
across the westlands. Despite Maniakes' pinpricks, he could
not keep that army from going where it would, wrecking what
it would.

And if, as they might, Abivard and his men chose to winter
in Across yet again? Could he hope to hold them away from
the nearest approach to the capital? He wondered whether he
could get away with telling himself what he wanted to hear:
that the reconstituted Videssian forces would surely drive the
invaders far, far away.

"The only problem being, it's not true," he muttered. If
Abivard decided to come back to Across, he could, and all the
hopeful restorations would go up in flames like the buildings
they were replacing.

He wondered if it was worthwhile to go out and fight the
Makuraners west or south of Across. Regretfully, he concluded
it wasn't, not till he could fight with some hope of winning.
Videssos couldn't afford to throw men away in losing fights,
not any more. Yes, the Makuraners would go on ravaging the
countryside if he didn't fight them, but if he did, they would
smash up his army and then go on ravaging the countryside.

"To the ice with choices between bad and worse," he said,
but he had no means to consign those choices there.

Summer advanced, hot and muggy. Maniakes let Moundioukh and his fellow hostages ride north from Videssos the
city toward Kubrat, not so much because he was convinced of
Etzilios' goodwill as because holding hostages indefinitely was
bad form and could create ill-will even if none had existed before.

"Youse not regrets thises, majesties," Moundioukh assured
him. Maniakes already regretted it, but found it impolitic to
say so.

Over in the westlands, Abivard took enough raids from the
southeastern hill country that he finally hurled his mobile force
against it, to try to end the annoyance once and for all. When
word of that came to Videssos the city, Maniakes felt like cele-
brating.

So did his father. With an evil chuckle, the elder Maniakes
said, "I don't think he knows what he's getting into. That
country is almost as hard for a big force to operate in as

Vaspurakan: it's all cut up into dales and valleys and badlands, and if you take one of them, that helps you not a bit with the next one just over the ridge."

"With a little luck, he may get stuck there like a fly in a spiderweb," Maniakes said. "That would be lovely, wouldn't it? We'd have a chance to get back real chunks of the westlands then."

"Don't count your flies till you've sucked them dry," his father warned. "Going into the southeast was a mistake; getting stuck there would be a worse one. From what I recall of Abivard, we're lucky he's made one mistake, but we'd be fools to count on two."

"Have to take all the advantage we can of the one," Maniakes said. "In a lot of places in the coastal lowlands, they bring in two crops a year. If Abivard stays busy in the southeast, we might even see a bit of revenue from them." He scowled. "I wish I could lay siege to some of the towns he's garrisoned, but I can't think of anything that would make him bring his main force back faster. I'd sooner let him play his own games down there for as long as he likes."

"Yes, that's wise." The elder Maniakes nodded. "We didn't get into this mess in one campaigning season, and we won't get out of it in one, either." He coughed, then wiped his mouth on his sleeve. "Anybody who thinks there are quick, easy answers to hard questions is a fool."

"I suppose so." Maniakes let out a wistful sigh. "What do you call somebody who *wishes* there were quick, easy answers to hard questions?"

His father rumbled laughter. "I don't know, boy. A human being, maybe?"

As the weeks passed, some revenue did reach Videssos the city from the nearer regions of the westlands. Maniakes had to fight the temptation to tax them till their eyes popped, just for the sake of immediate gold. If you flayed the hide off the sheep this year, what would you do for wool the next?

Kourikos said, "But, your Majesty, without significant revenue enhancements, how can we continue our necessary activities?"

"To the ice with me if I know," Maniakes answered with what he hoped wasn't deathbed cheeriness. "As I read the numbers, though, eminent sir, with this new gold coming in, why, we're almost back to bankrupt. We haven't been that well off since Likinios was still wearing his head."

The logothete of the treasury studied him. He watched Kourikos trying to decide whether he was serious—and not having the nerve to come right out and ask. He hadn't seen a funnier spectacle since Midwinter's Day.

"Joke, eminent sir," he said at last, to put the logothete out of his misery.

Kourikos tried a smile on for size. It didn't fit well; he hadn't smiled much since he had lost his daughter. "It might as easily have been simply a vivid metaphor for our present predicament."

Maniakes thought that was what a joke was, but knew he lacked the erudition to get into a literary discussion with Kourikos. "I haven't seen Makuraners or even Kubratoi swarming over the walls of the city, eminent sir. Until I do, I'm going to try to keep believing we have hope."

"Very well, your Majesty," Kourikos replied. "I have heard the patriarch say despair is the one sin that admits of no forgiveness."

"Have you?" Maniakes looked at him in no small surprise. "I wouldn't have thought the most holy sir had so much wisdom hidden in him."

Now Kourikos looked thoroughly scandalized, which was the very thing the Avtokrator had in mind.

Maniakes had hoped that, when Abivard decided he had had enough of grinding his army to bits in the hills and valleys and badlands of the southeastern part of the westlands, he would pull back into the central plateau and rest and recuperate there. He rejoiced when dispatch riders brought word that Abivard had apparently had enough of the southeast. Hard on the heels of those men, though, came other riders warning that the Makuraners, instead of drawing back to lick their wounds, were heading north with a large force.

"North through the lowlands?" Maniakes asked in dismay. He clung to disbelief as long as he could, which wasn't long: by the way Abivard was moving, he did intend to pass the winter just over the Cattle Crossing from Videssos the city, as he had the year before. Maniakes examined a parchment map of the westlands, hoping to find something different on it from what he had seen earlier in the year. "Any chance of holding them at the line of the Arandos?"

"There would be, if we had a real army to match his instead of a scant few regiments we can count on not to run screaming the first time they set eyes on a boiler boy," Rhegorios answered glumly.

The Avtokrator let out a long sigh. If Rhegorios, aggressive as he was, didn't think the Makuraners could be held at the river, then they couldn't be. "If we had forces south of the river to slow them down, we might get more men into place to stop them," he said, and then sighed again. The only forces Videssos had south of the Arandos were the hillmen of the southeast. They were fine, fighting where the terrain favored them. But they lacked both numbers and skill to confront the Makuraners on the flat ground of the lowlands, and they wouldn't just be pursuing Abivard's army, they would have to get in front of it. Thinking with his head rather than his heart, Maniakes knew the thing couldn't be done.

Rhegorios said, "At least we have forces down almost as far as the Arandos. Considering where we were last year after Amorion fell, that's progress of a sort. We haven't written off the whole of the westlands, as I'd feared we might."

"Haven't we?" Maniakes asked, his voice bitter. "If Abivard can travel through them as he pleases and the most we can do is bother him a bit now and then, do they belong to us or to him? It was generous of him to let us use some of them a bit this summer, but you can't say he's given them back."

"You can pray for miracles, your Majesty cousin of mine, but that doesn't always mean Phos will grant them," Rhegorios said. "If the good god did grant them all the time, they wouldn't be miracles any more, would they?"

One of Maniakes' eyebrows quirked upward. "Shall we send for Agathios to shave your head and give you a blue robe? You argue like a priest."

"I haven't it in me to be a priest," Rhegorios answered, his eyes twinkling. "I like pretty girls too well, and I'd sooner have it in them." When Maniakes made as if to throw a punch at him, he skipped back with a laugh, but persisted. "Was I right or wrong, eh?"

"What, about miracles or about pretty girls?" Just making the quip sobered Maniakes. He had bedded a couple of serving maids since Niphone died. He had been ashamed after each time but, like his cousin, found himself even more miserable as a celibate. Somberly, he went on, "Yes, you're right about miracles. Shall I go on and give the rest of your speech for you?"

"No, as long as I'm here, I may as well do it," Rhegorios said; try as you would, you couldn't keep him serious for long.

"Given the mess Genesios left you, doing anything worth speaking of in the first couple of years of your reign would have taken a miracle. Phos didn't give you one. So what?"

"Now you sound like my father," Maniakes replied. "But if the Makuraners were shipbuilders, the Empire probably would go under: that's so what. The best we could hope for would be to stand siege here."

"Videssos the city will never fall to a siege," Rhegorios said confidently.

"You're right; it would probably take a miracle to make that happen—but suppose the God doled one out to the Makuraners?" Maniakes said, deadpan.

Rhegorios started to answer, stopped, stared at the Avtokrator, then tried again: "You almost caught me there, do you know that? For one thing, the God is only a figment of the Makuraners' imaginations. And for another, I don't think we've been quite sinful enough for Skotos to rise up and smite us that particular way. If the sun turned north again after last Midwinter's Day, we're good for a while longer, or I miss my guess."

Maniakes sketched the sun-circle over his heart. "May you prove right." He studied the map some more. "If we can't hold them at the Arandos, we certainly can't hold them anywhere between there and Across. Can we hold them with the new works we've built outside Across?"

He wasn't asking Rhegorios the question; he was asking himself. His cousin assumed the burden of answering it, though: "Doesn't seem likely, does it?"

"No," Maniakes said, and the word tasted like death in his mouth. "Why did we waste our time and substance rebuilding, then?" But it wasn't *we*. He had given the orders. He slammed his fist against the map. Pain shot up his arm. "I made the same mistake I've been making ever since I put on the red boots: I thought we were stronger than we are."

"It's done now," Rhegorios said, an epitaph for any number of unfortunate occurrences. "Are you going to send an army into the westlands to try to defend what we've rebuilt?"

"You're trying to find out if I'll make the same mistake one more time even now, aren't you?" Maniakes asked.

Rhegorios grinned at him, utterly unabashed. "Now that you mention it, yes."

"You're as bad as my father," Maniakes said. "He's had all those years land on him to make him so warped and devious;

what's your excuse? . . . But I haven't answered your question, have I? No, I'm not going to send an army over to Across. If Abivard wants it so badly, he can have it."

Rhegorios nodded, gave the map a thoughtful tap, and left the chamber where it hung. Maniakes stared at the inked lines on the parchment: provinces and roads where his word did not run. All at once, he strode to the door, shouting for wine. He got very drunk.

The *Renewal* bounced in the chop of the Cattle Crossing. Makuraners stood on the western shore, jeering at the dromon and calling in bad Videssian for it to come beach itself on the golden, inviting sand. "We hello you, oh yes," one of them shouted. "You never forget you meet us, not never so long as you live." His teeth flashed white in the midst of his black beard.

Maniakes turned to Thrax. "Hurl a couple of darts at them," he said. "We'll see if they jeer out of the other side of their mouths."

"Aye, your Majesty," the drungarios of the fleet replied. He turned to his sailors. One of them set an iron-headed dart, its shaft as long as an arm and thicker than a stout man's middle finger, in the trough of the catapult. Others turned windlasses to draw back the engine's casting arms, which creaked and groaned under the strain. Thrax called orders to the oarsmen, who turned the *Renewal* so it bore on the knot of Makuraners. "Loose!" the drungarios shouted as a wave lifted the bow slightly.

The catapult snapped and bucked like a wild ass. The dart hurtled across the water. A scream went up from the shore—it had skewered someone. Yelling with glee, the catapult crew loaded another missile into the engine and began readying it to shoot again.

Maniakes had expected the Makuraners to disperse. Instead, all of them with bows shot back at the *Renewal*. Their arrows raised little splashes as they plinked into the water well short of their target. The sailors laughed at the foe.

"Loose!" Thrax cried again. Another dart leapt forth. This time the sailors—and Maniakes with them—cursed and groaned, for it hit no one. But the Makuraners scattered like frightened birds even so. That changed Maniakes' curses into cries of delight. Soldier against soldier, the boiler boys were still more than the Videssians could face with any hope of victory. But, when they came up against the imperial fleet, the Makuraners found foes they could not withstand.

"We rule the westlands!" Maniakes shouted, making the sailors stare at him before he added, "Or as much of them as isn't more than two bowshots from shore."

The sailors laughed, which was what he had had in mind. Thrax, earnest and serious as usual, said, "If it please your Majesty, I'll order the dromons in close to shore so they can shoot at clumps of the enemy who have come down too close to the sea."

"Yes, do that," Maniakes said. "It will remind them we don't tamely yield our land to Abivard and the King of Kings. It may even do the Makuraners a little real harm, too, which wouldn't be the worst thing in the world."

Maniakes hoped darts flying at them from beyond bow range would convince the Makuraners to stay away from the seaside, which might have let him land raiders with impunity. Instead, Abivard's men set up catapults of their own, close by the edge of the sea. Some of them threw stones big and heavy enough to sink a dromon if they hit it square. But they didn't—they couldn't—and in a few days the engines vanished from the beaches. The Makuraner engineers weren't used to turning their machines to aim at a target more mobile than a wall, and especially weren't used to shifting them to hit a target that was not only moving but doing its best not to get hit.

And the Videssian sailors, who compensated for wave action whenever they used their dart-throwers and who practiced hitting land targets, had a fine time shooting at catapults that had to stay in one place and take it. They damaged several and killed a fair number of the engineers who served them before Abivard figured out he was involved in a losing game and pulled back his machines.

A few days later, the first snow fell. Maniakes hoped Abivard's men would freeze inside Across, yet at the same time could not wish for too savage a winter. If the Cattle Crossing iced up, Abivard might have his revenge for the little wounds the catapult crews on the dromons had inflicted on his force. Maniakes wished his father hadn't told him the story of that dreadful winter.

He went back to drilling his soldiers on the practice field out by the southern end of the city wall. As they had the winter before, the Makuraners sometimes came out to see what they could see. Sometimes, now, a dromon would chase them away from the beach of Across. Maniakes took considerable satisfaction whenever he saw that happen.

No less an authority than Tzikas said, "Your Majesty, they look more like fighting men than they did a year ago—and you have more of them now, too." He tempered that by adding, "Whether you have enough men, whether they'll be good enough: those are different questions."

"So they are." Maniakes shaded his eyes with his hand and peered west over the Cattle Crossing. He saw no Makuraners today; a dromon slid smoothly through the channel, not pausing to harass any of Abivard's men. But Maniakes knew they were there, whether he could see them or not. Not all the smoke that rose above Across came from cookfires. The Makuraners were busy wrecking the suburb all over again.

"Come the spring, I expect you will put them to the test." By the way Tzikas sounded, that was more a judgment against Maniakes' character than an expression of hope for victory.

"Spring feels a million years, a million miles away." Maniakes kicked at the yellow-brown dead grass under his boots. Frustration gnawed at him like an ulcer that would not heal. "I want to go against them now, to drive them off Videssian soil with a great swift blow."

"You tried that once, your Majesty. The results were imperfectly salubrious, from our point of view." Tzikas might have been a litterateur criticizing a bad piece of poetry rather than a general commenting on a campaign.

Maniakes regarded him with reluctant respect. That he criticized his sovereign at all bespoke a certain courage and integrity—or perhaps such a perfect confidence in his own rightness as to blind him to any offense he might give.

Either way, he also seemed blind to how much Maniakes hated acknowledging himself unable to strike back at Abivard's army. He was glad to get back inside the walls of Videssos the city. In there, try as he would, he could not see the Cattle Crossing, let alone the land on the western shore. He could try to pretend all of it still yielded up taxes to the fisc, still recognized him as its ruler.

Before he had gone far into the city, he discovered—not for the first time—he was no good at fooling himself. When he got to the palace quarter, he could distinguish once more the smoke, rising from Across, from that coming off the myriad fires within Videssos the city. Even had his pretense survived so long, that would have killed it.

Oblivious to his worries, Rhegorios said, "To the ice with Tzikas; he's the sort who'd order up a lemon for his sweet." That was true, but did little to lift Maniakes' spirits. When he didn't answer, Rhegorios let out an indignant sniff. At the imperial residence, he went off in a huff.

"Wine, your Majesty?" Kameas asked. The only reply he got was a shake of the head. He was trained not to show annoyance, and very emphatically didn't show it. Maniakes wondered if the night's supper would suffer on account of that. No, he decided. Kameas also had great pride in service.

"Nice to know someone has pride in something," Maniakes muttered. Everything he had spent so much time and effort and gold rebuilding in the spring and summer had fallen to pieces in a few weeks as fall approached. Maybe things would get better when spring came once more ... or maybe the good weather would just lead to yet another round of catastrophes.

He went into the chamber where he was in the habit of trying to match the dribbles of revenue that came into the fisc with the unending flood of gold that poured out of it. He had had a new, slender trickle of gold coming in from those parts of the westlands closest to Videssos the city, but he couldn't rob—or even borrow from—the temples nearly so much this year: they didn't have much, either. That meant he had to pay out less or cheapen the currency again, which amounted to the same thing.

If he stopped paying everyone but the soldiers ... he wouldn't have any bureaucrats to collect next year's taxes. If he put more copper in the goldpieces, people would start hoarding good money, traders would stop doing business ... and he wouldn't have much in the way of taxes to collect next year.

Someone rapped on the door. "Go away," he growled without looking up, assuming it was Kameas coming to try to make him feel better.

But the voice that said "Very well" didn't belong to Kameas: it was Lysia's. Maniakes' head came up with a jerk. There weren't many people in the city he didn't want to irk, but she was one of them.

"I'm sorry," he said. "I thought you were someone else. Please come in." She had already started to turn away. For a moment, he thought she would ignore the invitation; stubbornness ran all through his family. He said, "If you don't come in here this instant, cousin of mine, I'll call you up before the

Avtokrator on a charge of lese majesty through wanton and willful disobedience."

He hoped that would amuse her instead of making her angry, and it did. "Not that!" she cried. "Anything but that! I abase myself before your Majesty."

She really did start a proskynesis. "Never mind that, by the good god," Maniakes exclaimed. They both started to laugh, then looked warily at each other. Since Niphone died, they had been cautious when they were together, and they hadn't been together much. Maniakes sighed, scowled, and shook his head. "I think back on how things were at Kastavala, and do you know what, cousin of mine? They don't look so bad. I didn't have to look over my shoulder whenever I wanted to talk to you, and I didn't have to worry about peering over the water and seeing the Makuraners wrecking everything in sight." He sighed again. "It might even be better back there now, come to think of it."

"Don't let your father hear you say that," Lysia warned. "He'd box your ears for you, whether you wear the red boots or no. I can't say I'd blame him, either. How could you fight the Makuraners in the westlands if you were back on Kalavria?"

"How can I fight them now?" he asked. "I was watching their smoke rise up from Across while I was out with the troops at the practice field. There they sit, right at the very heart of the Empire, and I dare not do anything more against them than the little pinprick raids we tried this summer."

"They aren't at the heart of the Empire," Lysia said. "We are, here at Videssos the city. As long as we hold the heart, we can bring the rest back to life one day, no matter how bad things are in the westlands."

"So everyone says. So I've thought," Maniakes answered. "I really do wonder if it's true, though." Suddenly the notion of sailing back to Kalavria, leaving behind the hateful reminders of how weak the Empire of Videssos had grown, seemed sweeter than honey to him. Back at the old fortress above Kastavala, he could think of the Empire as it had always been, not in its present mutilated state, and could rule it without worrying so much about the day-to-day emergencies that made life here in the capital feel so difficult.

But, before he could make clear to Lysia his vision of the benefits abandoning Videssos the city might bring, she said, "Of course it's true. There's never been a fortress, never been a port, like this one in the history of the world. And if you give up on Videssos the city, why shouldn't the people here give up on you?"

He paused thoughtfully. She had a point. She had a couple of points, in fact. If the fickle city mob raised up a new Avtokrator, that man, whoever he was, would gain a tincture of legitimacy because he held Videssos the city. He would also gain its walls, its dromons . . . and even Genesios the unspeakable had reigned half a dozen years with those advantages.

And so, keeping his longing for Kalavria to himself, he said, "Maybe you're right. I told you once you had the wit to be Sevastos. I know you got angry at me then—"

"And if you tell me again, I'll get angry at you now," Lysia said. By the way her nostrils flared, she *was* angry. "The city mob wouldn't let me do that any more than they'd let you sail away. And," she added grudgingly, "my brother has shaped well in the job."

Maniakes got up from the table piled high with receipts and registers and requests for gold he did not have. Any excuse for escaping from those requests was a good one, as far as he was concerned. He walked over to Lysia and set his hands on her shoulders. "I am sorry, cousin of mine," he said. "It just seems as if everything has gone to the ice since we came to Videssos the city. I should never have named my flagship the *Renewal*. Every time I board it, that strikes me as a cruel joke—maybe on myself, maybe on the Empire."

"It'll come right in the end," she said, hugging him. In the sea fights before he took Videssos the city, he had watched floundering men find floating planks and cling to them as if they were life itself. That was how he clung to Lysia now. She still had faith in him, no matter how much trouble he had holding onto faith in himself.

He was also acutely aware of holding a woman in his arms. After a little while, she could hardly have failed to notice his body responding to hers. He never was sure whether she first raised her head or he lowered his. When their lips met, it was with as much desperation as passion—but the passion was there.

At last they drew back, just a little. "Are you sure?" Lysia said softly.

He didn't need to ask what she meant. His laugh rang harsh. "I'm not sure of anything any more," he said. "But—" He went to the door of the chamber and closed it. Before he let the bar fall, he said, "You can still go out if you like. We've talked about this before, after all. If we go on from here, it will complicate both our lives more than either of us can guess now, and I have no idea whether it will come right in the end, whether it will turn out to be worth it."

"Neither do I," Lysia said, still in a low voice. She didn't leave. She urged no course on him. He stood a moment, irresolute. Then, very carefully, he set the bar in its bracket. He took a step toward her. She met him halfway.

It was chilly and awkward and they had no comfortable place in the room—and none of that mattered. Their two robes and their drawers on the mosaic floor did well enough. Maniakes expected to find her a maiden, and he did. Past that, everything was a surprise.

He had thought to be slow and gentle, as he had been with Niphone their first night together, bare hours after Agathios set the imperial crown on his head. Lysia did grimace and stiffen for a moment when he entered her to the hilt, but she startled him by taking pleasure afterward. She had no practiced skill at what they did, but enthusiasm made up for a great deal.

She exclaimed in surprise and delight a moment before he could hold back no longer. Even as he spent, he thought of pulling free of her and spurting his seed onto her belly, as he had that once with Niphone. But he discovered that thinking of a thing and being able to do it were not one and the same: even as the idea skittered over the topmost part of his mind, his body drove ever deeper into hers and, for a little while, all thought went away.

It returned too quickly, as thought has a way of doing at such times. "Now what?" he murmured, his face scant inches from hers. He wasn't really talking to her, or to anyone.

She answered with a woman's practicality. "Now let me breathe, please."

"I'm sorry," Maniakes said, and got off her. She had a sunburst print between her breasts from the amulet Bagdasares had given him.

Sliding away from him, she started to dress. When she got a look at her drawers, she clucked to herself. "There won't be any hiding this from the serving women." Her mouth twisted in wry amusement. "Not that I'd bet anything above a worn copper that the servants don't already know."

Maniakes glanced toward the barred door that had given them privacy—or its illusion. "I wouldn't be surprised if you're right." He put on his clothes a little faster than he would have without her words. After running his fingers through his hair, he said "Now what?" again.

"Easiest, maybe, would be to pretend this never happened," Lysia answered. She paused, then shook her head. "No, not easiest. Most convenient, I should say."

"To the ice with convenience," Maniakes burst out. "Besides, you just said the servants will know, and you're right. And what the servants know today is gossip in the plaza of Palamas day after tomorrow."

"That's true." Lysia cocked her head to one side and studied him. "What then, my cousin your Majesty?"

"I know what I'd do if you weren't my cousin," Maniakes said. "If you weren't my cousin, I expect we'd have married years ago, out on Kalavria."

"You're probably right." Lysia hesitated, then went on, "I hope you won't be angry if I tell you there were times when I was very jealous of Rotrude."

"Angry?" Maniakes shook his head. "No, of course not. I—had feelings for you that way. I didn't think you had them, too, not till I was about to sail off to see if I could overthrow Genesios."

"And you were sailing to Niphone," Lysia added. "What was I supposed to do then? I did what I thought I had to do. But now? Whatever we do now, we're going to make a scandal."

"I know," Maniakes said. They also took the chance of having the scandal become all too dreadfully obvious in nine months' time—although actually, if that befell, it would become obvious rather sooner. With that worry in mind, he went on, "The best way I can think of to deal with this is for me to marry you now, in spite of everything . . . if that's what you want to do, of course."

"It's what I'd like," she said, nodding. "But will a priest marry us? If he does, will Agathios anathematize him? And what will our families say?"

"I'm sure I can find a priest who will do as I tell him," Maniakes answered. "What Agathios will do . . . I don't know. He's a political beast, but this— We'll just have to find out." If Agathios thundered of sin, the city mob was liable to erupt. "We'll have to find out about our fathers, too, and our brothers." He had known this would complicate his life. Maybe he hadn't let himself think about how much.

And maybe the same thoughts were running through Lysia's mind. She said, "It really might be easiest to pretend this didn't—" She stopped and shook her head. Plainly, she didn't want to do that.

Neither did Maniakes. He said, "I've loved you as a cousin for as long as I can remember, and I've always thought a lot of your good sense. And now, with this—" Even after they had made love, he hesitated about openly saying so. "—I can't imagine wanting anyone else as my wife." He went over to her and took her in his arms. She clung to him, nodding against his chest.

"We'll just have to get through it, that's all," she said, her voice muffled.

"So we will," Maniakes said. "Maybe it won't be so hard."

After squeezing her once more, he went to the door and unbarred it. Then he opened it and looked up and down the corridor. He saw no one, heard no one. For a moment, he was relieved; *we got away with it* ran through his mind. Then he thought about how seldom the corridors of the imperial residence were so eerily quiet and deserted. Odds were that the servants were deliberately avoiding going anywhere near that door he had just unlocked.

He clicked his tongue between his teeth. A serving maid wouldn't have to see Lysia's drawers. The secret was already out.

The elder Maniakes took a long swallow of wine. He peered down into the depths of the silver cup, as if he were Bagdasares, using it as a scrying tool. "You aim to do what?" he rumbled.

"To marry my cousin," Maniakes answered. "We love each other, she has the best head on her shoulders of anyone in the family except maybe you, and ... we love each other." His ears heated at the repetition, but it was done.

His father raised the cup again, draining it this time. He was careless when he set it down on the table, and it fell over, ringing sweetly as a goldpiece. He muttered to himself as he straightened it. To Maniakes' amazement, he started to laugh. "It does keep things in the family, doesn't it?"

"Is that all you have to say?" Maniakes demanded.

"No, not by a long shot," the elder Maniakes said. "Phos only knows what my brother will do—is Lysia telling him?" He waited for Maniakes to nod before continuing, "The patriarch will scream 'Incest!' at the top of his lungs, you know. Have you thought about that?"

Maniakes nodded again. "Oh, yes." Part of him was screaming the same thing. He was doing his best not to listen to it. The same probably held true for Lysia. That was one more complication he hadn't thoroughly thought through. And yet—"It didn't just . . . happen out of the blue, you know."

"Oh, yes, I do know that," his father answered. "One day back on Kalavria when Rotrude was pregnant with your boy—" He put one hand out in front of his own considerable belly. "—she told me she'd stick a knife in you if she ever caught you in bed with your cousin."

"Did she?" Maniakes said, amazed. He was, in fact, amazed for a couple of reasons. "I would have guessed she'd tell me that, not you."

"So would I," the elder Maniakes said. "I think being with child might have had something to do with her acting so weak and womanish." He rolled his eyes to show he did not intend that to be taken seriously. "But the point of it is, she'd noticed the two of you. I had, too, but I wasn't so sure. I'd known the both of you longer than she had, of course, and I knew you'd always been friendly. She was the one who saw it was something more than that."

"Rotrude always knew me pretty well," Maniakes said soberly. "Seems she knew me better than I knew myself there." He walked over to the pitcher of wine, which had on it a low relief of a fat old man drunkenly chasing a maiden who was neither fat nor old nor overburdened with clothing. After pouring his own cup full, he raised it to his lips and drank it down without drawing breath. Then he filled it again. "But, Father, what am I going to do?"

"Eh?" The elder Maniakes dug a finger in his ear. "You told me what you were going to do. You're going to marry her, aren't you? What do you expect me to do about it? Tell you I think you're a fool? I do think you're a fool—a couple of fools, I gather. But am I going to take a leather strap and turn your arse red? Send you to your room without supper? By the good god, son, you're a man now, and entitled to your choices, no matter how stupid I think they are. And you're the Avtokrator. I've read the chronicles, I have. Avtokrators' fathers who try giving them orders have a curious way of ending up shorter by a head."

Maniakes stared at him in genuine horror. "If you think I'd do such a thing, I'd better take off the red boots and shave my own head for a monk."

"No, son, the monastery is the other place for fathers who make their imperial sons unhappy," the elder Maniakes said. He studied the Avtokrator. "Are you sure this can't be settled somewhere short of marriage?"

"You mean, by keeping her as mistress?" Maniakes asked. His father nodded. He shook his head. "I wouldn't take honor away from her." His laugh held irony. "Some would say falling in love with her did that, wouldn't they? Well, let them. But that's not the only problem I see. Suppose we don't wed, but I do take another wife one day. What would she and her family think about the arrangement Lysia and I have?"

"Nothing good, I've no doubt," the elder Maniakes said. "Suppose instead that you put your cousin aside now? What then?"

"Then my life looks cold and empty and dark as Skotos' icy hell," Maniakes answered, spitting on the floor in rejection of the dark god. "When I look out at the Empire, gloom is all I see. Must I see the same when I look here at the imperial residence?"

"I told you, son, you're a man grown," his father answered. "If this is what you want and what my niece wants—" He coughed a little at that, but went on gamely enough. "—then it's what you will have. Where we go from there is any man's guess, but I expect we'll find out before long."

Kameas said, "Your Majesty, the most holy ecumenical patriarch Agathios has arrived at the residence in response to your summons."

"Good." Maniakes' stomach knotted within him at the prospect of the meeting that lay ahead, but he did not show it. "Bring him to me. Full formality throughout here, mind you; he is not summoned for a friendly chat."

"I shall observe your Majesty's requirements in all particulars," the vestiarios replied with dignity. He swept away. The tiny, mincing steps he took under his long robe made him seem to float as he moved, like a ship running before the wind.

"Your Majesty," Agathios said at the doorway after Kameas announced him. He went down to his knees and then to his belly in full proskynesis. When he started to get up before

Maniakes had given him leave, the Avtokrator coughed sharply. Agathios bent his back once more, touching his forehead to the marble floor.

"Rise, most holy sir," Maniakes said after a wait he judged suitable. "You may take a seat."

"Er—thank you, your Majesty." Warily, the patriarch sat down. He suited his tone to the one Maniakes had taken: "In what way may I be of service to your Majesty this morning?"

"We have thought the time ripe to abandon the single life and choose for ourself another bride," Maniakes answered. He couldn't remember the last time he had bothered with the imperial *we*, but he would try anything to overawe Agathios today, which was why he had summoned the patriarch to the palace quarter rather than visiting him at his own residence next to the High Temple.

"I rejoice at the news and wish you joy, your Majesty," Agathios said, fulsomely if without any great warmth. He hesitated, then asked, "And to whom have you chosen to yoke yourself for what I pray will be many happy and fruitful years?"

Maniakes didn't miss that hesitation. He wondered what sort of rumors the ecumenical patriarch had heard. None had got back to him yet from the plaza of Palamas, which did not mean they were not there. Carefully, he said, "We have chosen to wed Lysia the daughter of the most noble Symvatios." He made no mention of Lysia's relationship to him; if anyone was going to raise that issue, it would have to be Agathios.

The patriarch did raise it, in a sidelong manner. "Has the most noble Symvatios given this union his approval?"

"Yes, most holy sir, he has," Maniakes answered. "You may ask this of him yourself if you doubt me." He had spoken the truth; his uncle hadn't said no. But if Symvatios had been enthusiastic at the prospect of his daughter's becoming Empress, he had concealed that enthusiasm very well.

"Of course I rely on your Majesty's assurance." Agathios hesitated again, coughed, and looked this way and that. Maniakes sat silent, willing him to keep quiet. Here in the imperial residence, Agathios, a malleable soul if ever there was one, would surely be too intimidated to argue from a doctrinal standpoint . . . wouldn't he? After that long, long pause, the ecumenical patriarch resumed: "Be that as it may, however, I must bring it to your Majesty's attention that the bride you propose to wed is, ah, within the prohibited degrees of relationship long established in canon law and also forbidden under all imperial law codes."

He hadn't screamed *incest* at the top of his lungs, but that was what his polite, nervous phrases amounted to. And what he would do back at the High Temple was anyone's guess. Maniakes said, "Most holy sir, what pleases the Avtokrator has the force of law in Videssos, as you know. In this particular case, it pleases us to exempt ourself from the secular laws you mention. That is within our power. Similarly, it is within your power to grant us a dispensation from the strictures of canon law. So we ask and so we instruct you do to."

Agathios looked unhappy. In his boots, Maniakes would have looked unhappy, too. Had the patriarch had a little less backbone, he would have yielded, and that would have been that. As it was, he said, "Let me remind your Majesty of the pledge he gave on entering Videssos the city to assume the imperial dignity, wherein he promised he would make no alterations in the faith we have received from our fathers."

"We do not seek to alter the faith, only to be dispensed from one small provision of it," Maniakes answered. "Surely there is precedent for such."

"A man who lives by precedent alone can, should he search, find justification for almost anything," Agathios said. "Whether the results of breaking justify one doing so is, you will forgive me, debatable."

Maniakes glared at him. "Most holy sir, do you tell me straight out that you will not do as I instruct you?" He kicked at the floor in annoyance—he had fallen out of the imperial *we*.

Agathios looked even unhappier. "May it please your Majesty—"

"It pleases me not at all," Maniakes snapped.

"May it please your Majesty," the patriarch repeated, "I must in this matter, however much I regret doing so, heed the dictates of my conscience and of anciently established canon law."

"However much you regret it now, you'll regret it more later," Maniakes said. "I daresay I can find another patriarch, one willing to listen to common sense."

"Avtokrators have indeed cast patriarchs down from their seats in the past," Agathios agreed gravely. "Should your Majesty undertake to do so in this instance, however, and for this cause, my opinion is that he will bring to birth a schism among the priests and prelates of the holy temples."

Maniakes bit into that one like a man stubbing his tooth on an unseen bone in his meat. "The Empire cannot afford such a schism, not now."

"Far be it from me to disagree with what is so self-evidently true," Agathios said.

"Then you will do my bidding and marry me to the woman I love," Maniakes said.

"She is your first cousin, your Majesty. She is within the degrees of relationship prohibited for marriage," the patriarch said, as he had before. "If I were to perform such a marriage in the High Temple, the temples throughout the Empire would likely see schism. If you oust me, rigorists would rebel against whatever pliant prelate you put in my place. If I acceded to your demands, those same rigorists would rebel against me."

Knowing the temper of Videssian priests, Maniakes judged that all too likely. "I do not wish to have to live with Lysia without the sanction of marriage," he said, "nor she with me. If you will not perform the ceremony in the High Temple, most holy sir, will you let it be done here at the small temple in the palace quarter by some priest who does not find the notion as abominable as you seem to?" He had yielded ground to Etzilios. He had yielded ground to Abivard. Now he found himself yielding ground to Agathios. He stood straighter. A private wedding was the only concession he would so much as consider.

With what looked like genuine regret, Agathios shook his head. "You ask me to designate someone else to commit what I still reckon to be a sin. I am sorry, your Majesty, but the matter admits of no such facile compromise."

Maniakes let out a long, unhappy breath. He didn't want to dismiss the ecumenical patriarch. Sure as sure, that would start a tempest in the temples, and Videssos might fall apart under such stress.

Agathios might have been reading his thoughts. "Since affairs of state have come to such a pass of hardship and difficulty," the patriarch said, "I urge you to incline toward putting your own affairs in good order. Do not contemplate this lawless action rejected by the statutes of Videssos, nor transgress decency with your cousin."

"You have said what you think good," Maniakes answered,

"but you do not persuade me. I shall act as I think best, and
the consequences of my action shall rest on me alone."

"So they shall, your Majesty," Agathios said sadly. "So they
shall."

Some of Maniakes' bodyguards entered the High Temple
with him. Others, the big fair men from Halogaland who did
not follow Phos, waited outside. One of them yawned. "I hope
your head priest will not talk long today," he said in slow
Videssian. "Too nice the day for standing about."

Maniakes thought it was chilly and raw, but Halogaland rou-
tinely knew winters like the one of which his father had spoken in horror. "However long he speaks, I'll hear him out," he
said. The tall, blond Haloga dipped his head in resigned acqui-
escence.

In the exonarthex, priests bowed low to Maniakes. They did
not prostrate themselves, not here. In the High Temple, Phos'
authority was highest, that of the Avtokrator lowest, of anywhere in the Empire.

A small opening in a side wall gave onto a stairway leading
up to the small chamber reserved for the imperial family.
Maniakes climbed those stairs. His Videssian guards mounted
them with him. A couple of men stopped just out of sight of
the bottom of the stairway; the rest accompanied him to the
chamber and posted themselves outside the door.

As Maniakes peered out through the filigree grillwork that
gave Avtokrators and their families privacy when they cared to
have it, he saw one of the blue-robed priests who had greeted
him hurry down the aisle and speak to Agathios, who was
standing by the altar in the center of the temple.

Agathios heard him out, then nodded. His gaze went to the
grill. From times when he had worshiped in the public area of
the High Temple, Maniakes knew he was effectively invisible
behind it. All the same, for a moment he and the patriarch
seemed to lock eyes.

Then Agathios looked away from him and up toward the
great dome that was the architectural centerpiece of the High
Temple. Maniakes' eyes traveled up to the dome, too, and to
the mosaic of Phos in stern judgment covering its inner surface. The good god's eyes seemed to look into his, as they
would have had he been anywhere in the High Temple. The
Phos in the dome there was the model for depictions of the
good god in temples throughout the Empire. Some of the pro-

vincial imitations looked even fiercer than the original, but none could approach it for awe-inspiring majesty. You would have to think twice before contemplating sin under that gaze.

Try as he would, though, Maniakes had trouble seeing the desire to marry his cousin as something for which the lord with the great and good mind would condemn him to the eternal ice. In his time on the throne, he had seen the difference between rules in place because they made sense and those in place because they were in place. He reckoned the prohibition that so exercised Agathios one of the latter.

The patriarch kept looking up into the dome. His back was straighter when at last he gave his attention to the growing number of worshipers filing into the pews that led up to the altar. Presently Maniakes heard and felt priests shutting the doors down below him.

Agathios lifted up his hands. The congregants rose. Behind the filigree screen, Maniakes stood with everyone else, though no one except that Phos brooding in righteousness could have seen him had he stayed seated. Along with the rest of the worshipers, he followed the patriarch's lead in reciting Phos' creed, then sat once more as a chorus of priests sang the good god's praises.

Going through the infinitely familiar liturgy, rising and sitting, praying and chanting, cleansed Maniakes' spirit of some of the worry with which he had entered the High Temple. It served to unite him to the good god and also to unite the people of the Empire with one another. Wherever Videssos' dominions ran, men and women prayed in the same way and acknowledged the same clerical hierarchy. A schism would shatter that unity hardly less than the Makuraner occupation of the westlands had.

Following Agathios' lead, the worshipers stood for a last time, repeated Phos' creed, and then sat back down to hear the ecumenical patriarch's sermon. That, of course, varied from day to day, from week to week, and from temple to temple. Maniakes leaned forward and put his ear close to the grillwork so as to miss nothing. It was principally for the sermon he had come, not for the liturgy, comforting though that was.

"May the lord with the great and good mind look down kindly upon Videssos and ensure that we pass through the present crisis unharmed," Agathios said. Small murmurs of "So may it be" floated up to Maniakes from the pews; a good half the congregants sketched the sun-circle over their hearts. Maniakes traced a quick sun-circle himself.

The patriarch went on, "May the lord with the great and good mind also instill piety and wisdom into the heart of the Avtokrator. The course he presently contemplates would make it difficult for Phos to grant his blessings to him in particular and to the Empire as a whole. While I grieve with his Majesty and sympathize with the loneliness now engulfing him, I must respectfully remind you all that the laws of the temples are not a bill of fare at an eatery, wherefrom a man may choose those courses pleasing to him while paying no heed to the rest. They form a seamless garment, which will fall to rags if any one of them be torn from it."

He looked up toward the grillwork behind which Maniakes sat. "The Avtokrator is of course Phos' viceregent on earth, and heads the Empire consecrated to the good god's true and holy faith. He is at the same time a man, far from being the good god's son or any other such outlandish notion, and is subject to the same fleshly temptations as other men. Such temptations are lures of Skotos, to be resisted with all the power a man shall have."

Agathios went on in that vein for some time. He was polite, reasonable; he did not shout about incest or urge the people of Videssos either to rise against their Avtokrator or risk the imperilment of their souls. As Maniakes had seen, Agathios enjoyed being patriarch and wanted to hold the job. He was giving Maniakes as little excuse to oust him as he could—but he also was not retreating from the position he had set forth in the imperial residence.

It was, in its own way, a masterful performance. In the abstract, Maniakes admired it. He was, however, not much given to abstraction at the moment.

As Agathios dismissed the congregants from the liturgy, Maniakes rose from his seat and left the private imperial box. The guards nodded to him as he came out. One asked, "Did the sermon please you, your Majesty?"

He didn't mean anything by it: by his tone, it was just a question for the sake of casual conversation. But it was not the question Maniakes wanted to hear then. "No," he snapped.

"Will you sack him then, your Majesty?" the guard asked eagerly. The eyes of all his companions lit up. Doctrinal controversy was meat and drink to anyone who lived in Videssos the city.

"I hope not," Maniakes answered, visibly disappointing the soldiers. They were still trying to get more out of him when he left the temple and came out to where the Halogai waited.

The northerners found Videssian theological squabbles inordinately complex. "This stupid priest does not do what you want, your Majesty, you put his head up on the Milestone," one of them said. "The next chief priest you pick, he do what you tell him." He hefted his axe. By the look of him, he was ready to carry out the sentence he had passed on Agathios.

"It's not that simple," Maniakes said with a regretful sigh. The Halogai all laughed. In their bloodthirsty code, everything was simple.

Despite more prodding from the Videssian guards, Maniakes stayed quiet and thoughtful all the way back to the imperial residence. When he got there, he called for Kameas. "How may I serve you, your Majesty?" the vestiarios asked.

"Summon me the healer-priest Philetos," Maniakes answered.

"Of course, your Majesty." Kameas' smooth, beardless face twisted in concern. "Is your Majesty ill?"

"No," Maniakes said, but then amended that: "I'm sick to death of Agathios, I'll tell you so much."

"I . . . see," Kameas said slowly. In a speculative tone of voice, he went on, "The holy Philetos, being so much concerned with his healing researches, is apt to be of less certain obedience to the most holy ecumenical patriarch than a good many others from the ecclesiastical hierarchy whose names spring to mind."

"Really?" Maniakes said in mock surprise. "How on earth can you suppose such a consideration might matter to me?"

"It is my duty to serve your Majesty in every possible way," Kameas answered; it was not quite responsive, but informative enough in its way. The vestiarios went on, "I shall summon the holy sir directly."

"Good," Maniakes said.

After Philetos had prostrated himself before the Avtokrator, he asked, "How may I serve your Majesty?" He sounded genuinely curious, which Maniakes took as a sign that he was too busy with his research to care about what was going on in the wider world around him.

"I want you to perform the ceremony of marriage for me," the Avtokrator said, coming straight to the point. If Agathios wouldn't ask a cooperative priest to tend to that, he would do it himself.

Philetos' gray eyebrows rose. "Of course I shall obey, and I—I am honored that you should think of me," he stammered, "but I can't imagine why you have chosen me rather than the ecumenical patriarch. And—er, forgive me, but to whom would you have me join you in marriage?"

He *was* naive. Again, Maniakes answered directly. "To my cousin Lysia." He did not waste time skirting the relationship, as he had with Agathios.

If Philetos had been surprised before, he was astonished now. "She is your first cousin, is she not, your Majesty?" he asked, and then answered his own question: "Yes, of course she is. Have you a dispensation from the patriarch for this union?"

"No," Maniakes said. "I ask it of you even so."

Philetos stared at him. "Your Majesty, you put me in a difficult position. If I obey you, I suffer the wrath of my ecclesiastical superior, while if I disobey—" He spread his hands. He knew under whose wrath he fell if he disobeyed the Avtokrator.

"That is the choice you must make, and you must make it now," Maniakes said.

"Your Majesty, I have never performed the ceremony of marriage in all my days in the priesthood," Philetos said. "My interest has centered on applying Phos' goodness and mercy to broken and infirm bodies, and I took my priestly vows for that purpose alone. I—"

Maniakes cut him off. "You are not prevented from serving the part of a priest with less abstruse concerns, are you?"

"Well, no, but—" Philetos began.

"Very well, then," Maniakes broke in again. "Your answer, holy sir."

Philetos looked trapped. He was trapped, as Maniakes knew very well. The Avtokrator thought about pledging some large sum of gold to the Sorcerers' Collegium after the ceremony was done, but found a couple of reasons not to do so. Such promises were as likely to offend as to accomplish their purpose. Even more to the point, he couldn't lay his hands on any large sum of gold for the Collegium.

"Very well, your Majesty," Philetos said at last. "I shall do as you say, but I warn you that trouble is likelier than joy to spring from your decision."

"Oh, I know it will cause trouble." Maniakes' laugh held scant humor. "But I have so much trouble already, what's some more? And wedding Lysia will bring me joy. I know that, too. Aren't I entitled to a little now and then?"

"Joy is every man's portion from Phos," Philetos answered gravely. Maniakes suddenly wondered if he was yielding because he felt guilty over having failed to save Niphone and was seeking this way to make amends. He didn't ask. He didn't want to know, not for certain; finding out would make him feel guilty in turn. Philetos went on, "When would you like the ceremony celebrated?"

"At once," Maniakes said. *I don't want to give you the chance to change your mind.* He called for Kameas. When the vestiarios came in, he said, "Gather together Lysia, my father, her father, and Rhegorios. The wedding will go forward."

"Your Majesty, when you bade me summon the holy sir here, I took the liberty of alerting the people whom you mention to that possibility," Kameas replied. "They are all in readiness."

"That's—most efficient of you," Maniakes said. "I suppose I shouldn't be surprised at such things anymore, but every once in a while I still am."

"I aim to be taken for granted, your Majesty," Kameas said.

While Maniakes was still trying to figure out how to reply to that, Philetos asked, "Where will the wedding take place, your Majesty? I gather you do not care to draw a great deal of attention to it—"

"You gather correctly, holy sir," Maniakes answered. "I had in mind the small temple here in the palace compound. It may be in something less than perfect repair, as it's not been used a great deal by the past few Avtokrators, but I did think it would serve."

Kameas coughed. "Again anticipating your Majesty, I have sent a crew of cleaners to that small temple, to make such efforts as they can toward improving its appearance and comfort."

Maniakes stared at him. "Esteemed sir, you *are* a marvel."

"Your Majesty," Kameas said with considerable dignity, "if something is to be done, it is to be done properly."

XII

Parsmanios scowled at Maniakes. "Brother of mine, you didn't do that properly, not even close to it. The whole city's buzzing now that word's seeped out."

"Yes, the people are buzzing," Maniakes admitted. "They aren't screaming, though, the way I was afraid they would. With luck the buzz will die down and I'll be able to go on about my business."

His brother continued as if he hadn't spoken: "And I don't much fancy you going and tying yourself to Symvatios and Rhegorios, either, let me tell you that. You treat them better than you do your own flesh and blood, and there's a fact."

"There's your problem, brother of mine," Maniakes said. "You're not jealous of Lysia; you're jealous of Rhegorios."

"And why shouldn't I be?" Parsmanios retorted. "If you're Avtokrator, he has the place that should be mine by right. You had no business naming a cousin Sevastos when you had a brother ready to hand."

Maniakes exhaled through his nose. "First of all, you weren't 'ready to hand' when I needed a Sevastos. You were off in your piddlepot little town. You hadn't been my right arm all the way through the war with Genesios, and Rhegorios had. And ever since I gave him the post, he's done a first-rate job with it. We've been over this ground before, brother of mine. Why do you want to walk down the track again?"

"Because I didn't think you'd be stupid enough to commit in—" Parsmanios stopped, not quite soon enough.

"You are dismissed from our presence." Maniakes' voice went cold as a winter storm. "You have incurred our displea-

sure. We do not care to speak with you again until you have
expiated your offense against us. Go." He hadn't used the imperial *we* half a dozen times since he had become Avtokrator,
and now twice inside a few days. It seemed a better way to
show his anger than shouting for the guards to fling
Parsmanios in the gaol that lay under the government office
building on Middle Street.

Parsmanios stalked away. Not two minutes later, Rhegorios
rapped on the door jamb. "My cousin your brother looked imperfectly delighted with the world when he walked out of the
residence here," he remarked.

"Your cousin my brother will look even less delighted if he
tries to set foot in the residence any time soon," Maniakes answered, still fuming.

"Let me guess," Rhegorios said. "If it takes more than one,
go get yourself someone with a working set of wits and put
him in my place."

"You're in no danger there." Maniakes kicked at the floor.
If he did it often enough, he might tear loose a couple of tiles
from the mosaic there. That would give him the feeling he had
accomplished something and vex Kameas when he noticed,
which he would in a matter of hours. Kicking again, Maniakes
went on, "When even my own brother shouts *incest* at me—"

"I wouldn't lose any sleep over it, my cousin your Majesty
brother-in-law of mine." Rhegorios grinned at the clumsy collection of titles he had used to label Maniakes. "Forgive my
bluntness, but I have trouble seeing Parsmanios leading rioters
baying for your head."

"Now that you mention it, so do I." Maniakes came over to
slap Rhegorios on the shoulder. "If you were leading the rioters, now—"

"They'd be laughing, not baying," Rhegorios said. "Most of
the time, I just amuse people." Despite that claim, his face was
serious. "But I might have been out there trying to make the
mob howl, you know."

Maniakes gave him a pained look. "Not you, too? You
never let on . . . and if you had, I don't see how Lysia and I
could have gone on."

"I might have been out there, I said. Before I did anything,
though, I went and talked with my sister. For some reason or
other, marrying you was what she wanted to do, and I've come
to have a great deal of respect for Lysia's good sense. If you
have any sense of your own, you'll pay attention to her, too."

"I intend to," Maniakes answered. "If I didn't think I wanted to listen to her when she told me something, this would have happened differently."

"Yes, I can see how it might have." Rhegorios thought for a moment. "Better this way." He nodded judiciously. So did the Avtokrator.

Maniakes looked forward to Midwinter's Day with the same eager anticipation a little unwalled town in the westlands felt on the approach of Abivard's army. He could not hold back the passing days, though, and avoiding the Amphitheater would have been an unthinkable confession of weakness. When the festival came, he and Lysia went out across the plaza of Palamas to the great stone bowl where, he confidently expected, they would be mocked without mercy.

A few of the people in the plaza made a point of turning away from the Avtokrator and his new bride. More, though, treated them with the casual equality that was everyone's due on Midwinter's Day. The two of them leapt over a fire hand in hand, shouting, "Burn, ill-luck!"

Inside the Amphitheater, some catcalls and hisses greeted Maniakes and Lysia. He pretended not to hear them and squeezed Lysia's hand. She squeezed back, hard; she was not used to public abuse.

The elder Maniakes and her own father and brother greeted her warmly when she and the Avtokrator ascended to the spine of the Amphitheater. So did Tzikas, who looked splendid in a gilded chain-mail coat. Parsmanios tried to make his nods to her and Maniakes civil, but did not succeed well. The elder Maniakes scowled at him. Afterward, Parsmanios worked harder at acting friendly, but managed only to pour honey on top of vinegar.

Agathios the patriarch made no effort to be friendly. As far as he was concerned, Maniakes and Lysia might as well not have existed. He did recite the creed to begin the day's events, but even that felt perfunctory.

After the patriarch sat down once more, Maniakes took his place at the spot from which he could speak to the whole Amphitheater. "People of Videssos the city," he said, "people of the Empire of Videssos, we have all of us had another hard year. The lord with the great and good mind willing, when we gather here for the next Midwinter's Day, we shall have passed through sorrow into happiness. So may it be."

"So may it be," the people echoed, the acoustics of the Amphitheater making their voices din in his ears.

"Now let the revelry begin!" Maniakes shouted, and sat down to make as if he enjoyed the lampoons the mimes were going to aim at him. *Anything can happen on Midwinter's Day*: so the saying went. Usually that meant something like finding an unexpected love affair. But it could have other, more sinister meanings as well.

To the Avtokrator's relief, the first mime troupe mocked only his failure to regain the westlands. He had seen himself portrayed as running away from anything in Makuraner armor—even if it was an old man on a swaybacked mule—and as fouling his robes while he ran: mimes had been making those jokes about him since he took the throne. If he had managed to smile for them before, he could do it again without straining himself unduly.

When the troupe trooped off, he glanced over to Lysia. She smiled back and mouthed, "So far, so good." He nodded; he had been thinking the same thing.

It didn't stay good for long. The very next troupe of mimes had a fellow dressed in gaudy robes and wearing a crown of gilded parchment sniffing lasciviously after a band of pretty little girls played by pretty little boys in wigs and dresses. When he found one who wore a dress much like his robe and a scarf much like his crown, he slung her over his shoulder and carried her away with a lecherous smirk on his face.

The crowd roared laughter. It dinned in Maniakes' ears. He had to sit there and pretend to be amused. As he had warned her to do, Lysia also feigned a smile. But, through that false expression, she said, "What a filthy lie! I'm not that far from your own age, and anyone who knows anything about us knows it."

But most of the people in the city didn't really know anything about Maniakes and Lysia. That was the point. The city mob formed its opinions from things like mime shows and seventh-hand gossip.

Some people who did know Maniakes and Lysia were laughing, too. Parsmanios, for instance, was on the far side of a polite show of mirth. So was Kourikos, who sat farther down the spine among the high-ranking bureaucrats. Not far away from him, Tzikas, glittering in that mail shirt, sat quiet, sedate, and discreet. So did Agathios. The ecumenical patriarch continued to walk his fine line, disapproving of the

Avtokrator's conduct but not seeking to inflame the city by his own.

Maybe I should have sent him as envoy to Sharbaraz, Maniakes thought, wondering what had happened to poor Triphylles.

Another troupe came out. This one lampooned Niphone's funeral, with people throwing up all along the route. It was in extremely bad taste, which meant the crowd ate it up. Maniakes bared his teeth, curled the corners of his mouth upward, and endured.

The next skit had Lysia chasing Maniakes rather than the other way round. Lysia had no trouble bearing up under it, but it infuriated Maniakes. "I wish Genesios hadn't tried to put down the mimes and failed," he said. "I don't want to imitate him at all, but I could try suppressing the troupes myself if only he hadn't had a go at them."

"It's all right," Lysia answered. "We pay one day a year to have peace the rest of the time."

"That's usually a good bargain," Maniakes said, "but what the people see here today will color the way they look at us for the rest of the year, and for a long time after that, too."

The next troupe came out. What the people saw was another variation on the same theme: this one had Rhegorios pushing Lysia at Maniakes. Rhegorios laughed at that one. It angered both Maniakes and Lysia. Having to keep his face twisted into the semblance of a smile was making Maniakes' cheeks hurt. He glanced over at his guardsmen. Loosing them on the mimes would have turned his smile broad and genuine. Instead of slaughtering the troupes, though, he had to pay them for entertaining the people.

They certainly were entertaining Parsmanios. His brother laughed long and hard until the elder Maniakes leaned over and said something to him in a low voice. Parsmanios sobered after that, but the sullen looks he sent his father said his mind had not been changed. No one spoke to Kourikos. Maniakes' former father-in-law showed more enjoyment of the mimes' crude jokes than seemed quite fitting in such a normally humorless man.

One troupe's lampoon was of the patriarch Agathios, for being too spineless to do a proper job of condemning Maniakes and Lysia. The fellow playing him raised an angry hand, drew it back in fright, raised it, drew it back. Finally, a man dressed in an ordinary priest's robe gave him a kick in the fundament that sent him leaping high in the air.

Tzikas guffawed at that skit. Agathios assumed what was probably meant to be an expression of grave dignity, but looked more as if he had been sucking on a lemon.

At last, the ordeal ended. The crowd in the Amphitheater didn't hiss and scream curses at Maniakes when he rose to dismiss them. Not too many of them laughed at him. He considered that a major triumph.

When he and Lysia got back to the imperial residence, it was as still and quiet as it ever got: most of the servants and several members of his family were off reveling in Videssos the city. Lysia looked down the empty corridors and said, "Well, we got through it and we don't have to worry about it for another year. The good god willing, the mime troupes will have something besides us to give them ideas by then."

Maniakes caught her to him. "Have I told you anytime lately that I like the way you think?"

"Yes," she answered, "but I always like to hear it."

"A message from Abivard, you say?" Maniakes asked Kameas. "By all means, let's have it. If it's word Triphylles has been released, that'll be news good enough to warm this miserably cold day."

"True, your Majesty," the vestiarios said. "The servitors are stoking the furnace and the hot air is going through the hypocausts, but sometimes—" He shrugged. "—the weather defeats us in spite of all we can do."

"A lot of things lately have defeated us in spite of all we can do," Maniakes said wearily. "Sooner or later, the weather will get better. So will the rest—I hope. Send in the messenger."

After the fellow had prostrated himself, and while he was gratefully sipping at a steaming cup of wine spiced with cinnamon and myrrh, Maniakes opened the leather message tube he had given him. The Avtokrator was becoming all too familiar with the lion of Makuran on scarlet wax that Abivard used to seal his messages. He broke the wax, unrolled the parchment, and read the letter his foe had commanded some poor Videssian to write for him:

Abivard general to Sharbaraz King of Kings, may his years be many and his realm increase, to Maniakes styling himself Avtokrator of the Videssians: Greetings. I regret to inform you that the man Triphylles, whom you sent as an envoy to the glorious court of Sharbaraz King of Kings, and who was subsequently imprisoned as just and fit punishment for undue and intolerable insolence before his majesty, has suffered the common ultimate fate of all mankind. I pray the God shall accept his spirit with compassion. In lieu of returning his corpse to you, Sharbaraz King of Kings ordered it cremated, which was of course accomplished before word of these events reached me so that I might transmit them to you.

Maniakes read through the missive twice. He still could not—and did not—believe Triphylles had acted insolently enough for any prince to find reason to cast him into prison. The noble had begged not to be sent to the Makuraner court at Mashiz, but Maniakes had overborne his objections. He had been confident Sharbaraz adhered to civilized standards of conduct. And now Triphylles was dead after a long spell in gaol, and who was to blame for that? Sharbaraz, certainly, but also Maniakes.

"Fetch me sealing wax and a lamp," he said to Kameas. As the eunuch hurried away, Maniakes inked a pen and wrote his answer. "Maniakes Avtokrator of the Videssians to Abivard slave to Sharbaraz Liar of Liars, Killer of Killers: Greetings. I have received your word of the mistreatment and tragic death of my emissary, the eminent Triphylles. Tell your master one thing from me, and one thing only: he shall be avenged."

When Kameas returned with the stick of wax and a lighted lamp, he took one look at Maniakes' face and said, "A misfortune has befallen the eminent Triphylles." He sketched the sun-sign above his plump breast.

"It has indeed: a mortal misfortune," Maniakes answered grimly. He tied his letter with ribbon and pressed his sunburst signet into hot wax. Then he popped it into the tube and gave it to the messenger. "Deliver this into Abivard's hands, or into those of his servants."

"I shall do as you say, of course, your Majesty." The messenger saluted with clenched right fist laid over his heart.

"Very well." Maniakes shook his head in sad bewilderment. "When I fought alongside them, Abivard and Sharbaraz seemed decent enough fellows." He plucked at his beard. "For that matter, Abivard still seems decent enough. War is a nasty business, no doubt of that, but he hasn't made it any filthier than it has to be—no great massacres in the towns he's taken, nothing of the sort. But Sharbaraz, now . . . Sitting on the throne of Mashiz has gone to his head, unless I'm sadly wrong."

The messenger stood mute. Quietly, Kameas said, "We have seen that in Videssos the city, too, your Majesty. Likinios came to think that anything could be so, simply because he ordered it; Genesios spilled an ocean of blood for the sport of it—and because he was afraid of his own shadow—"

"And the more blood he spilled, the more reason he had to be afraid," Maniakes broke in.

"That is nothing less than the truth, your Majesty," Kameas agreed. "We find ourselves fortunate with you."

The vestiarios did not lay flattery on with a trowel, as if it were cement—not with Maniakes, at any rate, no matter what he might have done for Genesios. He had seen the present wearer of the red boots did not care for such things. Now Maniakes had a disheartening thought: he imagined all his servants watching him, wondering if and how he would turn into a monster. So far, Kameas, at least, seemed satisfied he hadn't. That was something.

He waved to the messenger. The man nodded and hurried off to do his bidding. He would have been astonished and angry had the fellow done anything else. If you expected absolute obedience all the time, who would warn you when you started giving orders that did not deserve to be obeyed? If someone did warn you, what were you liable to do to him?

Would you do what Genesios had done to anyone upon whom his suspicions fell—had he had cloudbursts of suspicions? What Sharbaraz had done to Triphylles when the envoy said something wrong—or when the King of Kings imagined he had said something wrong?

How *did* you keep from becoming a monster? Maniakes didn't know, but hoped that over the years he would find out.

The broad lawns of the palace quarter, so inviting and green in spring and summer, were nothing but snowfields now. When the snow was fresh and the sun sparkled off it, it was pretty in a frigid way. Today, gray clouds filled the sky and the snow was gray, too, gray with the soot from the thousands of braziers and hearths and cook fires of Videssos the city. Looking out at it through the bare-branched trees surrounding the imperial residence, Maniakes screwed his mouth into a thin, tight line. The gloomy scene matched his mood.

A servant walking along a paved path slipped on a patch of ice and landed heavily on his backside. Maniakes faintly heard the angry curse the fellow shouted. He got to his feet and, limping a little, went on his way.

Maniakes' eyes went back down to the petition for clemency he was reading. A prosperous farmer named Bizoulinos had started pasturing his sheep on a field that belonged to a widow who lived nearby. When her son went to his house to protest, Bizoulinos and his own sons had set upon him with clubs and beaten him to death. The local governor had sentenced them to meet the executioner, but, as was their right, they had sent an appeal to the Avtokrator.

After reviewing the evidence, he did not find them in the least appealing. He inked a pen and wrote on the petition: "Let the sentence be carried out. Had they observed the law as carefully before their arrest as they did afterward, they and everyone else would have been better off." He signed the document and impressed his signet ring into hot wax below it. Bizoulinos and his sons would keep their appointments with the headsman.

Maniakes rose and stretched. Condemning men to death gave him no pleasure, even when they had earned it. Better by far if people lived at peace with one another. Better by far if nations lived at peace with one another, too, or so he thought. The Makuraners, perhaps understandably given their successes, seemed to feel otherwise.

A flash of color through the screen of cherry tree trunks drew his eye. A couple of men in the bright robes of the upper nobility were walking along not far from the Grand Courtroom. Even at that distance, he recognized one of them as Parsmanios. The set of his brother's wide shoulders, the way he gestured as he spoke, made him unmistakable for Maniakes.

The man with whom he was talking was smaller, slighter, older than he. Maniakes squinted, trying to make out more than that. Was it Kourikos? He couldn't be sure. His hands closed into angry fists just the same. His brother had no business associating with someone who so vehemently disapproved of his marriage to Lysia.

His scowl deepened. Parsmanios disapproved of that marriage, too, and hadn't been shy about saying so. He hadn't said so in an effort to change Maniakes' mind, either. He had just been out to wound—and wound he had, metaphorically anyhow.

Who was the fellow beside him? Maniakes could not make him out, though he brought his eyelids so close together that he was peering through a screen of his lashes. If that was Kourikos, he and Parsmanios could cook up a great deal of mischief together.

Whoever they were, the two men went into the Grand Courtroom together. "They're plotting something," Maniakes muttered. "By the good god, I'll put a stop to that."

He listened in his mind's ear to what he had just said and was appalled. He didn't know with whom Parsmanios had been talking, or what he had been talking about. This had to be how Genesios had started: seeing something innocent, assuming the worst, and acting on that assumption. Two men together? Obviously a plot! Stick their heads up on the Milestone to warn others not to be so foolish.

Acting without evidence led to monsterdom. Ignoring evidence, on the other hand, led to danger. But would his brother, *could* his brother, betray him? The clan had always been close-knit. Until he had evidence, he wouldn't believe it. He wished he and Parsmanios were boys again, so their father could solve their differences with a clout to the head. That wouldn't work now, even should Parsmanios deserve it. *Too bad*, Maniakes thought.

One thing Maniakes found: he was far happier wed to Lysia than he had been before they married. Had he not been so worried about the state of the Empire, he would have said he had never been so happy in his life. That came as a considerable relief to him, and something of a surprise, as well. He had done the honorable thing with her after they found themselves in each other's arms, but hadn't guessed the honorable would prove so enjoyable.

Lysia had always been a companion, a sounding board, someone who could laugh with him or, when he deserved it, at him. He still sometimes found himself bemused to be waking up in the same big bed with her. "I was afraid," he said one morning, "we wouldn't stay friends once we were lovers. Good to see I was wrong."

She nodded. "I had the same fear. But if we can't rely on each other, who's left?"

"No one," Maniakes said as they got out of bed. Then he

backtracked. "That's not quite true. My father, and yours, and Rhegorios—" He started to name Parsmanios, but he couldn't. How sad, not to be able to count on your own brother.

In any case, Lysia shook her head, then brushed the shiny black curls back from her face. "It isn't the same," she said. After a moment, he had to nod. She frowned thoughtfully, looking for the right words with which to continue. At last, she found them: "What we have is ... deeper somehow." She flushed beneath her swarthy skin. "And don't you dare make the joke I know you're thinking. That's not what I meant."

"I wasn't going to make the joke." Maniakes did not deny it had crossed his mind. "I think you're right."

"Good," Lysia said. She seemed happy, too, which eased Maniakes' mind. He reached for the bell pull that summoned Kameas, who slept in the room next to the imperial bedchamber. Lysia went on, "As well it's winter, and I'm in a woolen gown. I wouldn't want the vestiarios to come in after I'd got out of bed bare, the way I do when the weather is hot and sticky."

"Yes, Niphone was modest about him at first, too, but she got used to it," Maniakes said.

"I wasn't thinking of that," Lysia answered. "What would it do to him to see me naked? He's not a man in his body, poor fellow, but does he think a man's thoughts even if they do him no good?"

"I don't know," Maniakes admitted. "I wouldn't have the nerve to ask, either. I suspect you're right, though. That sort of consideration couldn't hurt, anyhow." He clicked his tongue between his teeth. If you did have a man's urges all those years, and were utterly unable to do anything about them— How could you go on living? He thought it would have driven him mad. For Kameas' sake, he hoped the eunuch was as sexless as his voice.

When he did summon Kameas, the vestiarios went through the robes in the closet with a critical eye. At last, he said, "Does the leek-green wool suit your Majesty this morning?"

"Yes, that should do." Maniakes felt of it. "Good thick cloth. This one would keep me warm in a blizzard."

He threw off his sleeping robe and was about to let Kameas vest him in the formal one for daily wear when he felt a warmth that had nothing to do with thick, soft wool. His hand went to the amulet Bagdasares had given him back in Opsikion, when he was still trying to overthrow Genesios. The gold-and-hematite charm was almost hot enough to burn his chest, almost hot enough to burn his palm and fingers as they closed on it.

For a moment, he simply stood there in surprise. Then he remembered the wizard's warning: if the amulet grew hot, that meant he was under magical attack. He also remembered Bagdasares warning him that it could not long withstand such an attack.

Clad only in drawers and the amulet, he ran out of the imperial bedchamber and down the halls of the residence. Behind him, Lysia and Kameas both cried out in surprise. He didn't take the time to answer them—at every step, the amulet felt hotter.

He pounded on the door to Bagdasares' room, then tried the latch. Bagdasares hadn't barred the door. He burst in. The wizard was sitting up in bed, looking bleary and astonished. Beside him, with the same mix of expressions, was one of Lysia's serving women. Neither of them seemed to wear even as much as the Avtokrator did.

"Magic!" Maniakes said, clutching the amulet.

Intelligence lit in Bagdasares' fleshy features. He bounded out of bed, making the sun-sign as he did so. He *was* nude. By the way she squeaked and clutched the bedclothes to herself, so was the maidservant.

Maniakes felt as if something was squeezing him, inside his skin. However much good the amulet was doing, it wasn't altogether keeping the hostile spell from having its way with him. He yawned, as if trying to clear his head while he had a cold. That did nothing to relieve the oppressive sensation slowly building inside him.

Bagdasares kept his case of sorcerous supplies by his bedside. Reaching into it, he pulled out a ball of twine and a knife whose white bone handle had a golden sunburst set into it. He used the knife to cut off a good length of twine, then began tying the ends together in an elaborate knot.

"Whatever you're doing there, please hurry," Maniakes said. He felt something wet on his upper lip. Reaching up to touch it, he found his nose was bleeding. Worse was that he thought a nosebleed the least of what the magic would do to him when it fully defeated the power of the amulet.

"Your Majesty, this must be done *right*," Bagdasares answered. "If I make a mistake, I might as well not have done it at all." Easy for him to say—his head wasn't being turned to pulp from the inside out. Maniakes stood still and hoped he wouldn't die before Bagdasares got through doing things right.

The mage finished the knot at last. When Maniakes looked at it, his eyes didn't want to follow its convolutions. Bagdasares grunted in absentminded satisfaction and began to chant in the Vaspurakaner language, running his hands along the circle of twine as he did so.

It wasn't just pressure inside Maniakes' head now—it was pain. He tasted blood; it dropped onto the floor of Bagdasares' room. By the expression on the maidservant's face, he wasn't a pretty sight. And if Bagdasares didn't hurry up, he was going to find out that being a slow wizard was one way of being a bad one.

Bagdasares cried out to Phos and to Vaspur the Firstborn, then passed the circle of twine over Maniakes' head and slowly down to his feet. It began to glow, much as had the lines of power from his protective spell back in Opsikion. The wizard invoked the good god and the eponymous ancestor of his people once more when the circle of twine touched the ground. He was careful to make sure it surrounded the blood Maniakes had lost.

What color was the enchanted cord? Gold? Blue? Orange? Purple? Red? It flickered back and forth among them faster than Maniakes' eyes could follow. After a moment, he didn't care. The heat from the amulet began to fade against the skin of his chest, and his head no longer felt as if the walls of his skull were going to squeeze together, crushing everything between them.

"Better," Maniakes whispered. Still in her nightdress, Lysia appeared in the doorway, her eyes wide and frightened. Kameas was right behind her. Maybe Bagdasares' magic hadn't been so slow after all, if they were just now getting here. It certainly had seemed slow.

With his head no longer feeling as if it were about to cave in on itself, he was able to pay more attention to the shifting colors of the twine. They changed ever more slowly. Red . . . gold . . . blue . . . and all at once, the twine was just twine again. "What does that mean?" Lysia asked, before Maniakes could.

"It means the assault against his Majesty is over," Bagdasares answered. "He may leave the circle now, if he so desires." Maniakes had wondered how long he would have to stay in there. Even so, he hesitated before stepping out beyond the confines of the cord. If by any chance Bagdasares was wrong—

Maniakes didn't let himself think about that. He stepped over the cord. If he had felt in the least peculiar, he would have jumped back into the circle. Nothing untoward happened. He glanced over at Kameas. "I'm glad I hadn't put on that leek-green robe, esteemed sir," he said. "I would have bled all over it, and that's very fine wool."

"To the ice with the wool," Kameas said, unwontedly emphatic. "I am glad your Majesty is safe."

"Safe?" Maniakes said. "An Avtokrator isn't safe from the day he dons the red boots to the one when he gets shoved into a niche under the temple dedicated to the holy Phravitas. Nobody's trying to kill me right now, though. A few minutes ago—" He shivered as he realized what a narrow escape he had had.

Lysia seemed to have understood that all along. Turning to Bagdasares, she said, "Can you find out who did this, sorcerous sir? No. Let me ask it another way: can you find out who was behind the attempt? If the mage escapes, that's one thing. But if whoever paid him to try to slay the Avtokrator stays free, he will surely try again."

Bagdasares' frown brought his heavy eyebrows together. "Finding out who did the deed or planned it will not be easy, not in the abstract. I think I could determine, on a yes-or-no basis, whether any particular individual was involved in the attack."

"That should do the job," Maniakes said. "I can think of most of the people who might want to be rid of me, I expect. What would you need from them for your sorcery? Whatever it is, I'll arrange it, I promise you that."

"I shouldn't require much, your Majesty," Bagdasares answered. "Something that belongs to one of the individuals you suspect would suffice. A sample of his writing, for instance, would be excellent."

"I'll have trouble taking care of that for Abivard, I fear— maybe I promised too readily." Maniakes paused. "Or maybe not. Would a fragment of the wax he used to seal a letter he dictated do the job?"

"It should, your Majesty. A man's seal is almost as much uniquely his own as his script." Bagdasares ran a hand through his tousled hair. "And whom else shall I examine?"

Lysia and Kameas both flicked a glance toward the serving

maid who shared the wizard's bed. Maniakes didn't need that hint. He had thought of her, too. But, while he did aim to thwart gossip or warnings, he didn't want to hurt her feelings. He said, "Let's not think of that while we're all so disheveled." Kameas wasn't disheveled, but then Kameas, as best Maniakes could tell, was never disheveled. He finished, "After breakfast is time enough."

After breakfast, the four of them gathered in a small reception chamber and considered who was liable to want Maniakes off the throne. Kourikos' name quickly came up. So did that of Phevronia, his wife. "She is liable to resent your marriage to me even more than her husband does," Lysia said quietly.

"I might not have thought of that for myself," Maniakes said. "Thank you."

"I have good reasons—many good reasons—to want you on the throne for a very long time," Lysia answered.

"Speaking of reasons, Agathios has—or thinks he has— reasons to want you deposed, your Majesty," Bagdasares said.

"So he does," Maniakes agreed. "Well, the most holy ecumenical patriarch is prolix with his pen. We'll have no trouble getting a writing sample from him."

"The eminent Tzikas," Kameas said.

"We'll check him," Maniakes said, nodding. "I'd be surprised if he proves to have anything to do with this, though. He may want the throne, but I think he'd like to see it drop into his lap."

"He is not aboveboard in what he does," Kameas insisted. "Such men earn close scrutiny, and deserve it." Eunuchs had a reputation for deviousness. Maybe they got suspicious when they sensed it in others.

"The drungarios," Bagdasares said. "Thrax."

Maniakes had all he could do to keep from bursting out laughing. If ever there was a man who wasn't devious, Thrax was the one. But he nodded again even so. Straightforward men got ambitious, too.

"The eminent Triphylles will have kin who may resent his passing in a foreign land," Kameas said. Maniakes hardly knew Triphylles' kin, but that was a possibility.

"Genesios' widow, too," he observed thoughtfully. "She may be mured up in a convent, but nothing is ever sealed as tight as you wish it was. Messages can go in, messages can come out."

After that, a silence fell. "Have we no more candidates?"

Bagdasares asked. "If not, let us be about the business of obtaining samples of these person's writings or other articles closely associated with them."

"One more person comes to mind," Maniakes said, and then paused. He glanced over to Lysia. "Your brother would name the name if we failed to, and he would be right. Come to that, so would my father, I think."

"Parsmanios, do you mean?" she asked, naming Maniakes' brother to keep him from having to do it.

He sighed. "Aye. After we quarreled, I saw him—not so long ago—deep in conversation with someone who I think was Kourikos, though I would not take oath to that on Phos' holy scriptures. Bagdasares, we'll need to be extra careful in getting a sample from him, and you'll need to be discreet in and after your test of that sample. If he learns I suspected him, he may become willing to conspire against me even if he wasn't before."

"Your Majesty, a mage who gossips is soon a mage without clients," Bagdasares answered. "As you command, though, I shall exercise particular care here. That same care should be applied, as you say, in obtaining writings from him."

"We should have in the archives orders he wrote for the vanguard as we advanced toward Amorion," Maniakes said. "We can get some of those without his being any the wiser, I should think."

"That would be excellent, your Majesty," Bagdasares said with a nod. "As soon as you convey to me the necessary documents, I shall begin examining them to see if their owners were involved in this wicked effort against you."

"I'm sure I have here at the residence parchments written by Kourikos and Agathios," Maniakes said. "You can start on those right away. I also have the letters from Abivard here, so you'll be able to do whatever you aim to do with the bits of wax from his seal."

Kameas said, "It might be instructive to go out and ask the guards whether anyone came wandering by a little while ago, inquiring after your Majesty's well-being. You or I would not be so foolish, but few people find themselves at a disadvantage by underestimating the stupidity even of seemingly clever people."

No one who had held the imperial throne for a while would have presumed to disagree with that. Hoping the case would unravel like the sleeve of a cheap robe when the first thread pulled lose, Maniakes walked out to the entrance. No one, though, had come round to see if he was still intact. He sighed. Since the day he had donned the red boots, nothing had been easy. He didn't suppose he ought to expect anything different now.

When he turned back to deliver the negative news, he found his father coming up the hall toward him. "Are you all right, son?" the elder Maniakes asked. "The servants are telling all sorts of ghastly tales."

"I shouldn't be surprised, but yes, I'm fine." Maniakes explained what had happened.

His father's face darkened with anger. Sketching Phos' sun-sign above his left breast, he growled. "To the ice with whoever would try such a thing. Worse than hiring an assassin, if your ask me: a mage doesn't have to get close to try to slay you. Who's on your list?"

Maniakes named names. His father nodded at each one in turn. Then the Avtokrator named Parsmanios. The elder Maniakes' eyes closed in pain for a moment. At last, with a sign, he nodded again. "Aye, you'll have to look into that, won't you? He was away from us for a long time, and he hasn't been happy with his circumstances since he came to Videssos the city. But by the good god, how I hope you're wrong."

"So do I," Maniakes answered. "As you say, there's not been a lot of love lost between us, but he is my brother."

"If you don't remember that, you're a long step closer to the ice right there," the elder Maniakes said. "Bagdasares is finding out what you need to know, is he? How soon will he have any idea of what's toward?"

"Where we have specimens, he's already started work," Maniakes answered. "For some of the people who might have done it, we'll either have to pull samples out of the archives or else get them to give us new ones. We should have something from Parsmanios in the files."

The elder Maniakes sighed once more. "You have to do it, but this is a filthy business. I wonder if we wouldn't have been better off staying on Kalavria in spite of all the tears and speeches the nobles gave."

"I've thought the same thing," the Avtokrator said. Now he sighed in turn. "Going back wouldn't be easy, not what with everything that's happened since. But heading for a place where no one's plotting against you has its temptations."

"If we did go back, someone might start plotting against you," his father said. He named no names, but Rotrude sprang into the Avtokrator's mind. She hadn't married since he had left, she would be jealous of Lysia, and she would want to advance Atalarikhos' fortunes. The Haloga style in such matters was liable to include good old straightforward murder. Maniakes felt like jumping into the sea. Only the fish would bother him there.

Kameas stood in the doorway, waiting to be noticed. "Yes, esteemed sir?" Maniakes asked.

"The excellent Bagdasares has tested writings from the most holy Agathios and the fragments of Abivard's seal, your Majesty," the vestiarios replied. "He reports that neither man was involved in the attack on you. He is about to evaluate writings from the eminent Kourikos, and wonders if you might be interested in observing the process, as you expressed the belief that he may well be one of the guilty parties."

"Yes, I'll come," Maniakes said, glad not to have to gauge the odds of Rotrude's turning against him. "What about you, Father?"

"Thank you; I'll stay here," the elder Maniakes said. "What wizards do can be useful. How they do it never much interested me, because I have no hope of doing it myself."

The Avtokrator knew he would never make a wizard, either, but found what they did intriguing even so. When he walked into the chamber where Bagdasares was working, the mage showed him a piece of parchment with crabbed notations complaining about a lack of funds. "This is indeed written in the hand of the eminent Kourikos?" Bagdasares asked. Maniakes nodded.

Whistling softly between his teeth, Bagdasares set the parchment on a table. He poured wine from one jar and vinegar from another together into a cup. "They symbolize what is and what shall be," he said, "and this chunk of hematite—" He held it up. "—is by the law of similarity attuned to the piece of the same mineral in the amulet that protected you and allowed you to reach me. Now—"

He dipped a glass rod into the cup that held the mixed wine and vinegar, then dabbed several drops of the mixture onto the parchment. The letters and numbers there smeared as they got wet. Chanting, Bagdasares touched the wet places with the lump of hematite. "If the eminent Kourikos was involved with the magic, your Majesty, we should see those areas begin to glow as my sorcery exposes the connection."

Maniakes waited. Nothing happened. After a couple of minutes, he asked, "Has it done everything it's going to do?"

"Er—yes, your Majesty," Bagdasares answered. "It would appear that the eminent Kourikos was in fact not one of those who so wickedly plotted against you."

Pointing out to an Avtokrator that he was wrong could be a risky business. Maniakes, however, greeted the wizard's words with a shrug, and Bagdasares relaxed. Maniakes was just as well pleased not to have the logothete of the treasury under suspicion, for his innocence made Parsmanios' more likely. Maniakes wished he could have been positive it was Kourikos he had seen with his brother, but he couldn't, and no help for it.

Doing his best to make life difficult, Bagdasares said, "We do, of course, still have to test the script of the logothete's wife."

"I'm sure you'll attend to that in due course," Maniakes said. He supposed Kourikos could have been a go-between for Phevronia and Parsmanios without directly doing business with the mage who had tried to kill him, but it didn't strike him as probable. He rubbed his chin. "I don't think I have a handwriting specimen from the eminent Tzikas here. I'll send him a note and get one back in return."

As if on cue, Kameas stuck his head into Bagdasares' makeshift thaumaturgical laboratory and said, "Your Majesty, a clerk has fetched writings hither from the government offices." The vestiarios had discretion and to spare; he never mentioned Parsmanios' name.

"Let him come in, eminent sir," Maniakes said. The clerk, a weedy little man in a robe of wool homespun, prostrated himself and then gave the Avtokrator a sheet of parchment tied into a cylinder with a ribbon. When Maniakes slid off the ribbon, he saw it was indeed one of Parsmanios' orders of the day for the vanguard of an army now long defeated.

The clerk disappeared, presumably to return to the hordes of pigeonholes where such documents slept against the unlikely chance that they, like this one, might eventually need to be revived. Maniakes forgot about him the moment he was gone. His attention swung back to Bagdasares, who was preparing the document for the same treatment he had given the one written by Kourikos.

The mage sprinkled the marching order with his mix of wine and vinegar. He began his chant once more and touched the piece of hematite to the parchment. Immediately it was suffused in a soft nimbus of blue-violet light. "The test has found an affirmative, your Majesty," Bagdasares said. Like Kameas, he did not speak Parsmanios' name.

A crushing weight of sorrow descended on Maniakes. "Are you certain, sorcerous sir?" he asked. "No doubt or possible misinterpretation?"

"No, your Majesty," Bagdasares said sadly but without hesitation. "I regret being the agent who—"

"It's not your fault," Maniakes said. "It's my brother's fault." He walked down the hall to the room where he had left his father. He looked in. "Parsmanios," he said. The elder Maniakes grimaced but nodded. The Avtokrator walked out to the guards who stood on the steps. He divided them in two and told one group, "Go find Parsmanios. He'll probably be in one of the wings of the Grand Courtroom at this time of day. Whatever he's doing, fetch him here at once."

The guards asked no questions, but hurried off to do his bidding. When he went back into the imperial residence, he found his father standing near the entrance. "What will you do with him? To him, I should say?" the elder Maniakes asked.

"Hear him out," Maniakes answered wearily. "Then have him tonsured and send him into exile in the monastery at Prista, up on the northern shore of the Videssian Sea. It's either that or take his head."

"I know." The elder Maniakes clapped the younger on the back. "It's a good choice." He scowled. "No. It's the best choice you could make. I never dreamed I'd have to thank you for sparing your brother's life, but I do."

Maniakes did not feel magnanimous. He felt empty, betrayed. A messenger arrived with Tzikas' reply to his note. He didn't even look at it, but sent the fellow straight on to Bagdasares. Then he went out and stared east through the cherry trees toward the Grand Courtroom.

Before long, the guards headed back to the residence, Parsmanios in their midst. He was complaining volubly: "This is an outrage, I tell you! When the Avtokrator hears of how you high-handedly jerked me out of that meeting with the eminent Themistios, logothete of petitions, and how he stared as you did so, his Majesty will—"

"Commend his men for carrying out his orders," Maniakes

interrupted. He spoke to the guards: "Make sure he has no weapons." Despite Parsmanios' protests, the soldiers removed his belt knife and, after some searching, a slim holdout dagger he wore in his left boot. That done, they escorted him to the chamber to which his father had returned.

"Why, son?" the elder Maniakes asked, beating the Avtokrator to the question.

"Why what?" Parsmanios began. Then he looked from his father to his brother and saw that wouldn't get him anywhere. From assumed innocence sprang fury. "Why do you think, the ice take you? You shut me away from everything you did, you gave Rhegorios the spot that should have been mine—"

"I didn't know you were alive when Rhegorios got the Sevastos' spot," Maniakes said. "How many times must I tell you?"

Parsmanios went on as if he hadn't spoken. "And as if that wasn't enough, you started swiving his sister. Why didn't you just take him to bed? Incest with one wouldn't be any worse than incest with the other."

"Son, you would be wiser to have a care in what you say," the elder Maniakes said. "You would have been wiser to have a care in what you did, too."

"Better you should tell that to *him*," Parsmanios said, pointing to his brother. "But no, you don't care what he does. You never cared what he did. He was your eldest, so it had to be right."

"My backside says you're a liar," Maniakes said, "not that you haven't shown that already."

"Say whatever you want," Parsmanios said. "It doesn't matter now. I failed, and you'll take my head, and that will be the end of it."

"I had in mind taking your hair, not your head," Maniakes said, "but listening to the swill you spew tempts me to give you what most traitors get." He shook his head. "Exile to Prista will do." He paused, wondering how best to put his next question. At last, he said, "Shall we send anyone into exile with you?"

Parsmanios stood mute. Maniakes thought of turning him over to the torturers to see what they could wring out of him, but couldn't make himself do it. He called the guards, saying "My brother is a proved traitor. I want him kept in a constantly guarded chamber here in the residence for the time being. Later, until he is sent off into exile, we'll move him to a cell under the government office building." Some of the guardsmen looked astonished, but they saluted to show they understood before leading Parsmanios away.

Maniakes looked up toward the ceiling. "Every time I think it can't possibly get any worse, can't possibly get any harder, it does."

"You did that as well as you could, son," the elder Maniakes told him. "Better than I would have managed it, and that's a fact."

"I never should have had to do it in the first place." Maniakes sat down and rested his chin on the knuckles of one hand. "My idiot brother—" He would have gone on, but Kameas paused in the doorway, waiting to be acknowledged. "Phos, what now?" Maniakes cried.

The vestiarios flinched, then gathered himself. "Your Majesty, the mage Alvinos requests your presence." He used Bagdasares' Videssian-sounding name more often than almost anyone else, perhaps because it fit in with his notions of what was proper. Vaspurakaners had played a major role in Videssian life for centuries, but Videssians seldom admitted or even noticed how large it was.

Bagdasares bowed when Maniakes came into the chamber where he labored. "I have here something I had not thought possible, your Majesty: an ambiguous result on my test of this writing from Tzikas. I do not know whether he was involved in the sorcerous attempt on your life or he was not." He wiped his forehead with the back of his hand. "It is a puzzlement."

"Show me what you mean by an ambiguous result," Maniakes said.

"Certainly." Bagdasares walked over to the parchment lying on the table. "As the ritual required, I sprinkled it with my mixture of wine and vinegar, then added the spiritual element of the spell and used the hematite. You see for yourself."

See Maniakes did. Most of the drops of the mixture had fallen on the writing, where they had had no effect save to blur it. But one or two had splashed down by the edge of the parchment. After Bagdasares touched his hematite to them, they had begun to glow like the entire document Parsmanios had written.

"It's almost as if Tzikas was in contact with the parchment without having written what purports to be his reply," Bagdasares said. "And yet the message is—or rather was, before it was smeared—addressed directly from him to you."

Suspicion flared in Maniakes. Tzikas was subtle, a master of defense. "I wonder if he took alarm at getting a message from me just after he tried to do me in and had someone else write a reply." He glanced at Bagdasares. "Will my looking at it or touching it do any harm?"

"No, your Majesty," the mage answered.

The Avtokrator stepped up to the makeshift worktable. As Bagdasares had said, the mixture of wine and vinegar had smeared much of the writing on the parchment. (It had also left the scraped sheepskin tangy to the nose.) Maniakes bent to examine those few words he could still make out.

"This isn't Tzikas' hand," he said after a moment. "I've seen his script often enough to recognize it, by the good god. I don't know who wrote this, but he didn't. If he took the note afterward, though—"

"That would account for the positive reaction at the edges of the sheet, where he would have touched it before returning it to your messenger," Bagdasares finished for him. "If that fellow didn't see with his own eyes Tzikas doing the writing, I think we can be confident enough in our evaluation to summon the eminent general to give an accounting of himself."

"We'll find out," Maniakes said. He called Kameas, who arranged to have the messenger return to the imperial residence.

"No, your Majesty, I didn't see him write it," the man said. "He stepped inside for a bit, then came back out. Nobody told me I was supposed to watch him do the writing." He looked anxious.

"It's all right," Maniakes said. "No blame for you." He went out to the guards. "I now require the immediate presence of the eminent Tzikas."

As they had when he had ordered them to fetch Parsmanios, they came to stiff attention. "Busy day around here," one of them observed as they went off to do his bidding. Maniakes let that go with a nod. Bringing in Parsmanios had been easy. If Tzikas didn't feel like coming, he had men loyal to him who might fight. Maniakes scowled and shook his head at the idea of a new round of civil war breaking out in Videssos the city.

He waited. The guardsmen were gone a long time. When they came back, they did not have Tzikas with them. Apprehension on his face, their leader said, "Your Majesty, we've searched everywhere the eminent Tzikas is likely to be, and we spoke with several men who know him. No one has seen him since shortly after he gave your messenger some sort of note."

"I don't fancy the sound of that," Maniakes said. "Go to the guard barracks, rout out the off-duty men, and make a proper search, crying his name through the streets and especially searching all the harbor districts."

"Aye, your Majesty," the guard captain said. "The harbor districts, eh? You fear he may try to flee to the Makuraners in Across?"

"No," Maniakes answered. "I fear he's already done it."

He went back into the imperial residence to report that dispiriting news to his father. The elder Maniakes made a sour face. "These things happen," he said. "He's no fool. The note must have put his wind up, and as soon as he gave it to you, he lit out for parts unknown—or parts known too well. What will you do now?"

"See how much Parsmanios will admit, then get him tonsured and send him into exile," the Avtokrator said. He again thought of giving his brother over to the torturers and again couldn't make himself do it. He doubted whether Parsmanios would have had the same compunctions about him.

Parsmanios scowled at him when he walked into the chamber where his brother was being held under guard. "Come to gloat, have you?" the younger man said bitterly.

"No, just to let you know your comrade Tzikas has run off to the Makuraners," Maniakes answered. "I wonder if he'll get a better bargain from them than he would have from me. I wouldn't have sent him to the chopper, not when I was leaving you alive: no justice to that. You could have gone off to Prista together."

"How wonderful," Parsmanios said. "How generous."

Maniakes wondered if his brother was trying to provoke him to take his head instead of exiling him. He ignored that, asking "So he was your comrade?"

"If you already know, why bother asking?" Parsmanios replied.

"Who was the wizard?" Maniakes persisted. "Who hired him?"

"I don't know his name," Parsmanios answered. "Bring on the needles and the red-hot pincers if you like, but I never heard it. Tzikas and I met him in an old house not far from the Forum of the Ox. I don't think the house was his. I think he just—infested it. Tzikas got him. He'd known him, I guess, but said having me there would help make the magic stronger.

Maybe it did, but it still wasn't strong enough, worse luck for me."

Even if true, none of that was very informative. No doubt that was deliberate on Parsmanios' part. Keeping his voice as light as he could, Maniakes asked, "What did the wizard look like?"

His brother said, "A man. Maybe your age, maybe a little older. Not fat, not thin. Kind of a long nose. He spoke like someone with an education, but a mage would, wouldn't he?"

"I suppose so," Maniakes answered absently. He knew considerable relief that the sorcerer Tzikas had found was not the horrible old man Genesios had employed. That old man had almost slain him across half the breadth of the Empire. Maniakes would have been happiest if he stayed lost forever. Against any ordinary mage, Bagdasares and the wizards of the Sorcerers' Collegium were protection aplenty.

Parsmanios said, "If you ever pluck my wife and son out of the provinces, don't blame them for anything I've done."

"You're in no position to ask favors, brother of mine," Maniakes said. Parsmanios stared at him, stared through him. He softened his words a little: "I wouldn't do anything to them because of you. As you say, they had nothing to do with your stupidity."

"I'm not the one who was stupid," Parsmanios answered—he had his own measure of the clan's stubbornness. "So many women all through the Empire would drop their drawers if you lifted a finger, and you had to go and wallow in filth instead. Even if I failed, Skotos waits for you."

Maniakes spat on the floor to avert the evil omen. "She's not my sister and she's not ten years old," he said in exasperation, but saw he might as well have been talking to the wall. He threw his hands in the air. "Fine, Parsmanios. Have the last word. Enjoy it all the way to Prista." He walked out of the chamber that confined his brother, and did not look back.

A blizzard blew in the next day. Maniakes had planned to send Parsmanios into exile on the instant, but realized that might well entail losing not only his brother, whom he would not have missed, but also a ship and its crew—the Videssian Sea was a bad risk in wintertime. He transferred Parsmanios to the prison under the government offices, with instructions to the gaoler to keep him apart from the other prisoners. When good weather arrived, Parsmanios would depart.

After the blizzard eased, a fellow with a message from Abivard came down to the shore at Across carrying a shield of truce. Upon his being conveyed to the palaces, Maniakes was less than delighted but also less than surprised to see him. The Avtokrator turned to Kameas, who had announced the messenger's arrival. "Would you care to place a small wager on the contents of that tube, esteemed sir?"

"Thank you, your Majesty, but no," the vestiarios replied. "I have a more pressing need for every goldpiece currently in my possession." He probably had a good many of them in his possession, too. Maniakes wondered how far confiscating his property would go toward making the Empire solvent. He shook his head, annoyed at himself. He wasn't that desperate—he hoped.

He popped the lid off the message tube, drew out the parchment inside, unrolled it, and began to read aloud: "Abivard general to Sharbaraz King of Kings, may his years be many and his realm increase, to Maniakes falsely styling himself Avtokrator of the Videssians: Greetings."

"He hasn't said '*falsely* styling himself Avtokrator' in a while," Kameas observed.

"So he hasn't," Maniakes said, and then, "Well, I insulted him and Sharbaraz in my last letter." He coughed. "I read on: 'Whereas the eminent general Tzikas, who in former days misguidedly gave allegiance to you, has now recognized his earlier errors, he bids me inform you that he acknowledges the sovereignty over the Empire of Videssos of Hosios Avtokrator son of Likinios Avtokrator, and rejects your regime as the vile, vain, illegitimate, and void usurpation it is universally known to be, and bids all Videssians to do likewise, seeing that only in this way shall peace be restored to your land.' "

Kameas pursed his lips as he considered the message. At last, he delivered his verdict: "The content, your Majesty, can hardly be reckoned surprising. As for the style, I must say I confess to a certain admiration; not everyone could have packed so much information into a single, grammatically proper, sentence."

"If I want literary criticism, esteemed sir, rest assured I shall ask for it," Maniakes said.

"Of course, your Majesty," the vestiarios said. "Are you then seeking advice as to your proper conduct in response?"

"Oh, no, not this time." Maniakes turned to the messenger, who looked miserably cold in a Makuraner caftan. "You speak

Videssian?" When the fellow nodded, the Avtokrator went on, "I have no written reply for you. But tell Abivard he's welcome to keep Tzikas or kill him, however he pleases, but if he does decide to keep him, he'd better not turn his back. Have you got that?"

"Yes, your Majesty," the messenger answered, his accent strong but understandable. He repeated Maniakes' words back to him.

Maniakes spoke to Kameas: "Have him taken west over the Cattle Crossing. If Abivard doesn't worry about Tzikas more now then while he was holed up in Amorion, he's a fool." That would get back to Abivard, too. Maniakes couldn't do anything about his rebellious general's flight, not now. With a little luck, though, he could keep Abivard from taking full advantage of Tzikas. And if Abivard chose to ignore his warnings, which were, of course, hardly disinterested, the Makuraner general stood an excellent chance of falling victim to the refugee about whose presence he now boasted.

Kameas escorted the messenger out of Maniakes' presence. When he came back, he found the Avtokrator sitting with his elbows on his knees, his face buried in his hands. "Are you all right, your Majesty?" the vestiarios asked anxiously.

"To the ice with me if I know," Maniakes answered, weary beyond anything sleep could cure. "Phos! I didn't think Tzikas had the nerve to betray me, and he went and did it anyhow. Who knows what will come crashing down on me—and down on Videssos—next?"

"Your Majesty, that is as the author of our fate, the lord with the great and good mind, shall decree," Kameas said. "Whatever it may be, I am sure you will meet it with your customary resourcefulness."

"Resourcefulness is all very well, but without resources even resourcefulness struggles in vain," Maniakes said. "And Genesios, curse him, was right to ask if I'd do any better than he at holding back the Empire's foes. So far, the answer looks to be no."

"You've done far better at everything else, though," Kameas said. "Videssians no longer war with Videssians and, the present unpleasantness aside, we've not had a single pretender rise against you. The Empire stands united behind you, waiting for our luck to turn."

"Except for the people—my brother, for instance—who stand behind me so I won't see the knife till it goes into my back, and the ones who think I'm an incestuous sinner who ought to be cast into the outer darkness of excommunication and anathema."

Kameas bowed. "As your Majesty appears more inclined today to contemplate darkness than light, I shall make no further effort to inject with any undue optimism." He glided away.

Maniakes stared after him, then started to laugh. The vestiarios had a knack for puncturing his pretensions. This time, he had managed to pack a warning in with his jibe. A man who contemplated darkness rather than light was liable to end up contemplating Skotos rather than Phos. As he had when questioning Parsmanios, Maniakes spat on the floor in rejection of the evil god.

Someone tapped on the door: Lysia. "I have news, I think," she said. Maniakes raised an eyebrow, waiting for her to go on. She did, a little hesitantly: "I—I think I'm with child. I would have waited longer to say anything, because it's early to be quite sure, but—" Her words poured out in a rush. "—you could use good news today."

"Oh, by Phos, that is the truth!" Maniakes caught her in his arms. "May it be so." Likarios remained his heir, but another baby, especially one that was his and Lysia's, would be welcome. He resolved, as he had more than once before, to pay more attention to the children he had already fathered.

He studied Lysia with some concern. Niphone had been thin and frail, while his cousin whom he had wed was almost stocky and in full, vigorous health. Nevertheless . . .

"It will be all right," she said, as if plucking the alarm from his mind. "It will be fine."

"Of course it will," he said, knowing it was not *of course*. "Even so, you'll see Zoïle as soon as may be; no point waiting." Lysia might have started to say something. Whatever it was, she thought better of it and contented herself with a nod.

XIII

SPRING CAME. FOR MANIAKES, IT WAS NOT ONLY A SEASON of new leaf and new life. As soon as he was reasonably confident no storm would send a ship to the bottom, he took Parsmanios from the prison under the government offices and sent him off to exile in Prista, where watching the Khamorth travel back and forth with their flocks over the Pardrayan steppe was the most exciting sport the locals had.

Maniakes, on the other hand, watched Lysia. She was indeed pregnant, and proved it by vomiting once every morning, whereupon she would be fine . . . till the next day. Any little thing could touch off the fit. One day, Kameas proudly fetched in a pair of poached eggs. Lysia started to eat them, but bolted for the basin before she took a bite.

"They were looking at me," she said darkly, after rinsing her mouth out with wine. Later, she broke her fast on plain bread.

Dromons continually patrolled the Cattle Crossing. Maniakes watched Abivard as well as Lysia. This spring, the Makuraner general gave no immediate sign of pulling back from Across. Maniakes worried over that, and pondered how to cut Abivard's long supply lines through the westlands to get him to withdraw.

But, when the blow fell, Abivard did not strike it. Etzilios did. A ship brought the unwelcome news to Videssos the city. "The Kubratoi came past Varna and they're heading south," the captain of the merchantman, a stocky, sunburned fellow named Spiridion, told Maniakes after rising from a clumsy proskynesis.

"Oh, a pestilence!" the Avtokrator burst out. He pointed a

finger at Spiridion. "Have they come down in their *monoxyla* again? If they have, our war galleys will make them sorry."

But the ship captain shook his head. "No, your Majesty, this isn't like that last raid. I heard about that. But the beggars are on horseback this time, and looking to steal what's not spiked down and to burn what is."

"When I beat Etzilios, I'll pack his head in salt and send it round to every city in the Empire, so people can see I've done it," Maniakes growled, down deep in his throat. All at once, thinking of how fine he would feel to do that to the Kubrati khagan, he understood what must have gone through Genesios' vicious mind after disposing of an enemy—or of someone he imagined to be an enemy, at any rate. The comparison was sobering.

Spiridion seemed oblivious to his distress. "We'd be well rid of that khagan, yes we would. But you've got all these soldiers sitting around eating like there's no tomorrow and pinching the tavern girls. Isn't it time you got some use from 'em? Don't mean to speak too bold, but—"

"Oh, yes, we'll fight them," Maniakes said. "But if they're already down past Varna, we'll have a busy time pushing them back where they belong."

Where they really belonged was north of the Astris, not on any territory that had ever belonged to Videssos. Likinios had tried pushing them back onto the eastern edge of the steppe, and what had it got him? Mutiny and death, nothing better. And now the Kubratoi, like wolves that scented meat, were sharp-nosing their way down toward the suburbs of Videssos the city.

Maniakes rewarded Spiridion with gold he could not afford to spend and sent him on his way. That done, he knew he ought to have ordered a force out to meet Etzilios' raiders, but hadn't the will to do it on the instant. After Parsmanios and Tzikas had conspired against him, he had asked the lord with the great and good mind what could possibly go wrong next. By now, he told himself bitterly, he should have known better than to send forth such questions. All too often, they had answers.

A couple of minutes after Spiridion left, Lysia came into the chamber where Maniakes sat shrouded in gloom. "The servants say—" she began hesitantly.

He might have known that the servants *would* say. Trying to keep anything secret in the imperial residence was like trying to carry water in a sieve. Everything leaked. "It's true," he answered. "The Kubratoi are riding again. The good god only knows how we'll be able to stop them, too."

"Send out the troops," Lysia said, as if he had complained about a hole in his boot and she had suggested he take it to a cobbler.

"Oh, I will," he said with a long sigh. "And then I'll have the delight of seeing them flee back here to the city with their tails between their legs. I've seen that before, too many times." He sighed again. "I've seen everything before, too many times. It wouldn't take more than a couple of coppers to get me to sail off for Kalavria and never come back."

He had said that before when things looked bleak. Now, all at once, the idea caught fire within him. He could see the mansion up above Kastavala, could hear the gulls squealing as they whirled overhead—oh, gulls squealed above Videssos the city, too, but somehow in a much less pleasant tone of voice—could remember riding to the eastern edge of the island and looking out at the Sailors' Sea going on forever.

The idea of the sea's going on forever had a strong appeal for him now. If there was no land on the far side of the Sailor's Sea—for no one who had ever sailed across it had found any, no one, that is, who had ever come back—he would actually have found one direction from which enemies could not come at him. From his present perch in embattled Videssos the city, the concept struck him as miraculous.

He took Lysia's hands in his. "By the good god, *let's* go back to Kastavala. Things here will sort themselves out one way or another, and right now I don't much care which. All I want to do is get free of this place."

"Do you really think it's the best thing you could do?" Lysia said. "We've talked of this before, and—"

"I don't care what I said before," Maniakes broke in. "The more I think of leaving Videssos the city now, the better I like it. The fleet will hold Abivard away from the city come what may, and I can command it as well from Kastavala as I can right here where I stand now."

"What will your father say?" Lysia asked.

"He'll say 'Yes, your Majesty,' " Maniakes answered. His father would probably say several other things, too, most of them pungent. He would certainly have something to say about Rotrude. *I'll have to deal with her,* Maniakes thought. He was surprised Lysia hadn't mentioned her, and mentally thanked her for her restraint. Aloud, he went on, "What's the point of being Avtokrator if you can't do what you think best?"

"Can you be Avtokrator if you don't hold Videssos the city?" Lysia said.

That had brought him up short the last time he had thought of removing to Kastavala. Now, though, he said, "Who says I wouldn't hold the city? An Avtokrator on campaign isn't here, but no one rebels against him because of that—well, not usually, anyhow. And the bureaucrats would stay right where they are." He laughed sardonically. "They don't think they need me to run the Empire, anyhow. They'll be glad for the chance to show they're right."

"Do you truly think this is best?" Lysia asked again.

"If you want to know the truth, dear, I just don't know," Maniakes said. "This much I'll tell you, though: I don't see how going to Kalavria could make things much worse than they are now. Do you?"

"Put that way, maybe not." Lysia made a wry face that, for once, had nothing to do with the uncertain stomach her pregnancy had given her. "It shows what a state we've come, to, though, when we have to put things that way. It isn't your fault," she added hastily. "Genesios left the Empire with too many burdens and not enough of anything with which to lessen them."

"And I've made mistakes of my own," Maniakes said. "I trusted Etzilios—or didn't mistrust him enough, however you like. I tried to do too much too soon against the Makuraners. I've been hasty, that's what I've been. If I'm operating out of Kastavala, I won't be able to be hasty. News will get to me more slowly, and the orders I send will take their time moving, too. By all the signs, that would make things work better than they do now."

Lysia said, "Well, perhaps it will be all right." With that ringing endorsement, Maniakes got ready to announce his decision to the wider world.

Themistios, the logothete in charge of petitions to the Avtokrator, was a stout, placid fellow. Most of the time, his was a small bureaucratic domain, dealing with matters like disputed tax assessments and appeals such as the one the now probably late Bizoulinos had submitted. Now he presented Maniakes with an enormous leather sack full of sheets of parchment.

"Here's another load, your Majesty," he said. "They'll be coming into my offices by the dozens every hour, too, that they will."

"This is the third batch you've given me today, eminent sir," Maniakes said.

"So it is," Themistios agreed. "People are upset, your Majesty. That's something you need to know."

"I already had an inkling, thanks," Maniakes said dryly. What Themistios meant, at least in part, was that he was upset himself and making no effort to do anything about the flood of petitions begging Maniakes to stay in Videssos the city except passing them straight on to the Avtokrator.

Themistios coughed. "Forgive me for being so frank, your Majesty, but I fear civil unrest may erupt should you in fact implement your decision."

"Eminent sir, I have no intention of taking all my soldiers with me when I go," Maniakes answered. "If civil unrest does pop up, I think the garrison will be able to put it down again."

"Possibly so, your Majesty," the logothete said, "but then again, possibly not." He tapped the pile of petitions. "As is my duty, I have acquainted myself with these, and I tell you that a surprising number of them come from soldiers of the garrison. They feel your departure abandons them to the none too tender mercies of the men of Makuran."

"That's absurd," Maniakes said. "The boiler boys can no more get over the Cattle Crossing than they can fly."

"Your Majesty is a master of strategy," Themistios said. Maniakes looked sharply at him; given the number of defeats he had suffered, he suspected sarcasm. But the logothete seemed sincere. He went on, "Simple soldiers will not realize what is obvious to you. And, if their courage should fail them, what they fear may follow and become fact."

"I shall take that chance, eminent sir," Maniakes replied. "Thank you for presenting these petitions to me. My preparations for the return to Kastavala shall go forward nonetheless."

Themistios muttered something under his breath. Maniakes waited to see if he would say it out loud and force him to notice it. The logothete didn't. Shaking his head, he left the imperial residence.

The next day, Kourikos presented himself to the Avtokrator. After he had risen from his prostration and been granted leave to speak, he said, "Your Majesty, it has come to my attention that you are removing large sums of money in gold, silver, and precious stones from a treasury that, as you must be aware, is painfully low on all such riches."

"Yes, I am, eminent sir," Maniakes said. "If I'm going to center the administration at Kastavala, I'll need money to meet my ends."

"But, your Majesty, you'll leave too little for Videssos the city," Kourikos exclaimed in dismay.

"Why should I care about Videssos the city?" Maniakes demanded. The logothete of the treasury stared at him; that question had never entered Kourikos' mind. For him, Videssos the city was and always would be the center of the universe, as if Phos had so ordained in his holy scriptures. Maniakes went on, "What have I ever had here except grief and trouble?—from you not least, eminent sir. I shall be glad to see the last of the city, and of you. I tell you to your face, I thought the one who conspired with my brother was you, not Tzikas."

"N-not I, your Majesty," Kourikos stammered. He was suddenly seeing that having a family connection to the Avtokrator could bring danger as well as advantage. "I—I do not agree with what you have done, but I do not seek to harm you or plot against you. You are father to my grandchildren, after all."

"That's fair enough, eminent sir." Maniakes laughed ruefully. "It's better than I've had from almost anyone else, as a matter of fact."

Emboldened, Kourikos said, "Then you will abandon your unfortunate plan for taking yourself and so much of the Empire's wealth back to that provincial hinterland whence you came here?"

"Eh? No, I won't do anything of the sort, eminent sir," Maniakes said. "I've had more of Videssos the city than I want. Nothing anyone has told me has given my any reason to change my mind."

"It sounds to me, your Majesty, as if it would take a miracle vouchsafed by the lord with the great and good mind to accomplish that," Kourikos said.

"Yes, that might do it," Maniakes agreed. "I can't think of much less that would."

Kameas pursed his lips. "Your Majesty, this is the third time this past week that the most holy ecumenical patriarch Agathios has requested an audience with you. Do you not think you would be wise to confer with him? True, you are

Phos' viceregent on earth, but he heads the holy hierarchy of the temples. His words are not to be despised."

"He won't sanction my marriage, and he wants to keep me from sailing off to Kalavria," Maniakes answered. "There. Now I've said what he'll have to say, and I've saved myself the time he'd take."

Kameas glowered at him. "There is a time for all things. This does not strike me as the time for uncouth levity."

Maniakes sighed. He had seen enough on the throne to know that, when the vestiarios was blunt enough to use a word like *uncouth*, he needed to be taken seriously. "Very well, esteemed sir, I'll see him. But he used to be a flexible man. If he's just going to repeat himself, he won't get far."

"I shall convey that warning to Skombros, his synkellos," Kameas answered. And Skombros, Maniakes had no doubt, would convey it to Agathios. The Avtokrator got the idea that Kameas and Skombros probably complemented one another well. Neither had much formal power; each had influence that made his formal insignificance irrelevant.

When Agathios came to the imperial residence a few days later, he did not wear the blue boots and pearl-encrusted cloth-of-gold vestments to which his rank entitled him. To take their place, he had on a black robe of mourning and left his feet bare. After he rose from his proskynesis, he cried, "Your Majesty, I beg of you, do not leave the imperial city, the queen of cities, a widow by withdrawing the light of your countenance from her!"

"That's very pretty, most holy sir, but you may bawl like a branded calf as much as your heart desires without convincing me I ought to stay," Maniakes said.

"Your Majesty!" Agathios gave him a hurt look. "I am utterly convinced that this move will prove disastrous not only for the city but also for the Empire. Never has an Avtokrator abandoned the capital in time of crisis. What necessity is there for such a move, when we shelter behind our impregnable walls, safe from any foe—"

"Any foe who has no siege engines," Maniakes interrupted. "If the Makuraners were on this side of the Cattle Crossing instead of the other one, we'd be fighting for our lives right now. About the only two peaceful stretches of the Empire I can think of are Prista on the one hand—which is not a place I want to go myself—and Kalavria on the other."

"Your Majesty, is this justice?" Agathios said. "You have

borrowed from the temples large sums of gold for the suste-
nance and defense of the Empire, and now you seek to abandon Videssos' beating heart?" He sketched the sun-circle above
his own heart. "What more concessions could we possibly offer you to persuade you to change your mind and return to the
course dictated by prudence and reason?"

For a moment, Maniakes took that as nothing but more rhetoric of the kind the patriarch had already aimed at him. Then
he wondered whether Agathios meant what he said. Only one
way to find out: "I don't know, most holy sir. What do you offer?"

When he had first come into Videssos the city, he had
watched Agathios go from thundering theologian to practical
politician in the space of a couple of breaths. The shift had bemused him then and bemused him again now. Cautiously, the
ecumenical patriarch said, "You have already taken so many of
our treasures that I tremble to offer more, your Majesty, but, if
our gold would make you remain in the city, I might reckon it
well spent."

"I appreciate that," Maniakes said, on the whole sincerely.
"It's not lack of gold that drives me out of Videssos the city,
though."

"What then?" Agathios asked, spreading his hands. "Gold is
the chief secular advantage I can confer upon you—"

They looked at each other. The patriarch started to raise an
admonitory hand. Before he could, Maniakes said, "Not all advantages are secular, most holy sir. If they were, we'd have no
temples."

"You swore to me when you took the throne that you would
make no innovations in the faith," Agathios protested.

"I've never said a word about innovations," Maniakes answered. "A dispensation, though, is something else again."

"Your Majesty, we have been over this ground before,"
Agathios said. "I have explained to you why granting a dispensation for your conduct in regard to this marriage is impracti-
cable."

"That's true, most holy sir, and I've explained to you why
I'm leaving Videssos the city for Kalavria," Maniakes answered.

"But, your Majesty, the cases are not comparable," the ecumenical patriarch said. "I am in conformity with canon law
and with long-standing custom, while you set established practice on its ear." Maniakes didn't say anything. Agathios

coughed a couple of times. Hesitantly, he asked, "Are you tell-ing me you might be willing to remain in Videssos the city and administer the Empire from here, following ancient usage, should you receive this dispensation?"

"I'm not suggesting anything." Maniakes stroked his chin. "It would give me ecclesiastical peace, though, wouldn't it? That's worth something. To the ice with me if I know whether it's worth staying here in Videssos the city, though. One more Midwinter's Day like the last couple I've had to endure and I'd be tempted to climb up to the top of the Milestone and jump off."

"I, too, have suffered the jibes of the falsely clever and the smilingly insolent on Midwinter's Day," Agathios said. "Per-haps you will forgive me for reminding you that, should your disagreement with the temples be resolved, one potential source of satire for the mime troupes would be eliminated, thus making Midwinter's Day shows less likely to distress you."

"Yes, that is possible," the Avtokrator admitted. "Since you've said no dispensation is possible, though, the discussion has little point—wouldn't you agree, most holy sir?"

Agathios drew himself up to his full if unimpressive height. "I have the authority to go outside normal forms and proce-dures if by so doing I can effect some greater good, as you know, your Majesty. Should I—and I speak hypothetically at the moment, you must understand—dispense you from the usual strictures pertaining to consanguinity, would you in turn swear a binding oath similar to the one you gave me at the outset of your reign, this one pledging never to abandon Videssos the city as the imperial capital?"

Maniakes thought, then shook his head. "Saying I'd never do something puts chains around me, chains I don't care to wear. I would swear never to abandon the city save as a last resort, but the definition of what constitutes a last resort would have to remain in my hands, no one else's."

Now the patriarch plucked at his bushy beard as he consid-ered. "Let it be as you say," he replied in sudden decision. "You have proved yourself reliable, on the whole, in matters of your word. I do not think you will break it here."

"Most holy sir, we have a bargain." Maniakes stuck out his hand.

Agathios took it. His grip was hesitant, his palm cool. He sounded worried as he said, "Those of a rigorist cast of mind will judge me harshly for what I do here today, your Majesty, despite the benefits accruing to the Empire from my actions. The schism we have discussed on other occasions may well come to pass because of our agreement: The rigorists will maintain—will strongly maintain—I am yielding to secular pressure here."

"You will know more of ecclesiastical politics and the results of these schisms than I do, most holy sir," Maniakes replied, "but isn't it so that the side with secular support prevails in them more often than that without?"

"As a matter of fact, your Majesty, it is," Agathios said, brightening.

"You'll have that support, I assure you," Maniakes told him.

"Oh, splendid, splendid." Agathios risked a smile and discovered that it fit his face well. "You shall prepare the oath for me and I the dispensation for you, and all will be amicable, *and* you will remain in Videssos the city."

"So I will." Maniakes pointed at the patriarch as something else occurred to him. "The dispensation will need to have a clause rescinding any penalties you've set for the holy Philetos because he performed the marriage ceremony for Lysia and me."

"Your Majesty is loyal to those who serve him," Agathios observed, the smile fading. When he spoke again, after a moment's silence, it was as if he was reminding himself: "Such loyalty is a virtue. The clause shall appear as you request."

"I'll be as loyal to you, most holy sir," Maniakes promised, and the patriarch cheered up again.

Maniakes and Lysia peered through the grillwork that screened off the imperial niche in the High Temple. Maniakes had stored the parchment with the text of Agathios' dispensation with other vital state documents; he presumed the ecumenical patriarch had done something similar with his written pledge not to abandon Videssos the city save under the most dire of circumstances.

"The temple is packed today," Lysia said. Sure enough, nobles had trouble finding space in the pews because so many common people had come to hear the patriarch's promised proclamation.

"Better to let Agathios make the announcement than for me to do it," Maniakes answered. "If I did, it would seem as if I forced the agreement down his throat. Coming from him, it'll be a triumph of reason for both sides."

He started to say more, but the congregants below suddenly quieted, signaling that the patriarch was making his way to the altar. Sure enough, here came Agathios, with censer-swinging priests of lower rank accompanying him and filling the High Temple with sweet-smelling smoke.

When the patriarch reached the altar, he raised his hands to the great stern image of Phos in the dome of the High Temple. The worshipers sitting on all sides of the altar rose; behind the screening grillwork, so did Maniakes and Lysia. They intoned Phos' creed along with Agathios and the rest of the congregants: "We bless thee, Phos, lord with the great and good mind, by thy grace our protector, watchful beforehand that the great test of life may be decided in our favor."

Maniakes took less pleasure in the liturgy than he usually did. Instead of joining him to his fellow believers throughout the Empire, today it seemed to separate him from what he really waited for: Agathios' sermon. His prayers felt perfunctory, springing more from his mouth than from his heart.

Agathios led the worshipers in the creed again, then slowly lowered his hands to urge them back into their seats. Everyone stared intently at him. He stood silent, milking the moment, letting the tension build. "He should be a mime," Lysia whispered to Maniakes. He nodded but waved her to silence.

"Rejoice!" Agathios cried suddenly, his voice filling the High Temple and echoing back from the dome. "Rejoice!" he repeated in softer tones. "His Majesty the Avtokrator has sworn by the lord with the great and good mind to rule the Empire of Videssos from Videssos the city so long as hope remains with us."

Rumor had said as much, these past few days, but rumor was known to lie. For that matter, patriarchs were also known to lie, but less often. The High Temple rang with cheers. They, too, came rolling back from the dome, filling the huge open space below with sound.

"They love you," Lysia said.

"They approve of me because I'm staying," Maniakes answered, shaking his head. "They'd be howling for my blood if Agathios had just told them I'd be sailing day after tomorrow."

Before Lysia could respond to that, Agathios was continuing: "Surely Phos will bless the Avtokrator, his viceregent on earth, for this brave and wise choice, and will also pour his blessings down on the queen of cities here so that it remains our imperial capital forevermore. So may it be!"

"So may it be!" everyone echoed, Maniakes' voice loud among the rest. He tensed as he waited for Agathios to go on. The patriarch had set forth what he had got from Maniakes. How would he present what he had given up?

Agathios' hesitation this time wasn't to build tension. He was like most men: he had trouble admitting he had needed to concede anything. At last, he said, "His Majesty the Avtokrator bears a heavy burden and must struggle valiantly to restore Videssos' fortunes. Any aid he can find in that struggle is a boon to him. We all know of the tragic loss of his wife—his first wife—who died giving birth to Likarios, his son and heir."

Maniakes frowned. It wasn't really the patriarch's business to fix the succession, even though what he said agreed with what the Avtokrator had established. He glanced over at Lysia. She showed no signs of annoyance. Maniakes decided to let it go. In any case, Agathios was continuing: "All this being said, on reflection I have determined that a dispensation recognizing and declaring licit in all ways the marriage between his Majesty the Avtokrator and the Empress Lysia will serve the Empire of Videssos without compromising the long-established holy dogmas of the temples, and have accordingly granted them the aforesaid dispensation."

At his words, a priest near the altar set down his thurible and strode out of the High Temple, presumably in protest. Out went Kourikos and Phevronia, too. The logothete of the treasury was willing to go on working with Maniakes, but not to be seen approving of his marriage. Another priest left the High Temple, and a few more layfolk, too.

But the large majority of worshipers and clerics stayed where they were. Agathios had not presented his bargain with Maniakes as the this-for-that exchange it was at bottom. That probably helped reconcile some of the congregants to the arrangement. And others would be relieved enough to hear that Maniakes was staying in Videssos the city that they wouldn't care how Agathios had got him to do so.

The patriarch stood straighter when he saw his announcement was not going to set off riots under the temple's dome. "The liturgy is ended," he said, and Maniakes could almost hear him adding, *and I got away with it, too.* A buzz of talk rose from the congregants as they made their way out to the mundane world once more. Maniakes tried to make out what they were saying but had little luck.

He turned to Lysia. "How does it feel to be my proper wife

in the eyes of all—" *Well, most*, he thought. "—the clerics in the Empire?"

"Except for morning sickness, it feels fine," she answered. "But then, it felt fine before, too."

"Good," Maniakes said.

If Maniakes stood on the seawall and looked west over the Cattle Crossing, he could see smoke rising from the Makuraner army's encampments in Across. And now, if he stood at the northern edge of the capital's land wall, he could look north and see smoke rising from the suburbs the Kubratoi were burning. Refugees streamed into Videssos the city from the north, some in wagons with most of their goods, others without even shoes on their feet. Monasteries and convents did what they could to feed and shelter the fugitives.

Maniakes sent the religious foundations a little gold and a little grain to help them bear the burden. That was all he could do. With the Makuraners holding the westlands and the Kubratoi swooping down toward the capital, the lands recognizing his authority were straitened indeed.

He visited a monastery common room. For one thing, he wanted to show the refugees he knew they were suffering. The fervent greetings he got made him uneasily aware of how much power his office held over the hearts and minds and spirits of the Videssian people. Had he sailed off to Kalavria, they might indeed have lost hope—though he had no intention of ever admitting that to Agathios.

He also wanted to get a feel for what the Kubratoi had in mind with their invasion. "I just saw maybe ten or twenty," one man said in a rustic accent. "Didn't wait for no more—not me, your Majesty. I hightailed it fast as I could go."

"Saw 'em out on some flat ground," another fellow said. "They weren't bunched up or nothin'—ridin' along all kind of higgledy-piggledy, like."

"They would have got me sure," a third man offered, his face breaking out in sweat as he recalled his escape, "only they stopped to kill my pigs and loot my house and so I was able to get away."

The stories confirmed what Maniakes had come to believe from other reports: unlike the Makuraners, the Kubratoi did not plan to make any permanent conquests. They had swarmed into Videssos for loot and rape and destruction, and spread themselves thin across the landscape.

He summoned his father and Rhegorios to a council of war. "If we can catch them before they're able to concentrate, we'll maul them," he said.

"I ask the question you would want me to ask," Rhegorios said: "Are you looking for us to do more than we can?"

"And here's another question along with that one," the elder Maniakes added. "So what if we do beat them? They'll just scoot back to Kubrat, faster than we can chase them. When they ride north, they'll torch whatever they missed burning on the way south. Even a win seems hardly worth it."

"No, that's not so, or at least I think I have a way to make it not so." The Avtokrator pointed to the map of the region north of Videssos the city that lay on the table in front of him. He talked for some time.

When he was through, the elder Maniakes and Rhegorios looked at each other. "If I'd been so sneaky when I was so young," the elder Maniakes rumbled, "I'd have had the red boots instead of Likinios, and you, lad—" He pointed at Maniakes. "—would be standing around waiting for me to die."

Before Maniakes could say anything to that, Rhegorios declared, "It all still depends on that first victory."

"What doesn't?" Maniakes said. "If we do go wrong, though, we'll be able to retreat inside the walls of Videssos the city. We won't be caught in a place where we can be hunted down and slaughtered." He slammed his fist onto the tabletop. "I don't want to think about retreat, not now." He hit the table again. "No, that's not right—I know I need to think about it. But I don't want the men to know it's ever crossed my mind, or else it'll be in the back of theirs."

"Ah, there you come down to the rub," the elder Maniakes said. "But you're going to try this scheme of yours?"

Maniakes remembered the ambush Etzilios had set, remembered his failure in the campaign up the valley of the Arandos. As Rhegorios had said, he had tried to do too much in both of them. Was he making the same mistake now? He decided it didn't matter. "I will try it," he said. "We aren't strong enough to wrest the westlands away from Makuran. If we also aren't strong enough to keep the Kubratoi away from Videssos the city, I might as well have sailed to Kalavria, because it would be about the only place our foes couldn't come after me. That was one of the reasons I wanted to go there."

"Always Haloga pirates," Rhegorios said helpfully.

"Thank you so much, cousin and brother-in-law of mine," Maniakes said. "Does either of you think the risk isn't worth taking?" If anyone would tell him the truth, his father and cousin would. They both sat silent. Maniakes slammed his fist down on the table for a third time. "We'll try it."

Sunburst banners flapping in the breeze, Maniakes' army rode forth from the Silver Gate. The Avtokrator glanced south toward the practice field where his soldiers had spent so much time at drill. This was no drill. This was war. Now he would find out how much the men had learned.

Scouts galloped out ahead of the main body. Finding the foe would not be hard, not at the start of this campaign. All Maniakes had to do was lead his army toward the thickest smoke. He absently wondered why all warriors, regardless of their nation, so loved to set fires. But finding the foe was not the only reason to send out scouts. You also wanted to make sure the foe did not find you before you were ready.

"Haven't been on campaign in a goodish while," Symvatios said, riding up alongside Maniakes. "If you don't do this every year, you forget how heavy chainmail gets—and I'm not as young as I used to be, not quite." He chuckled. "I expect I'll still remember what needs doing, though."

"Uncle, I'm sorry to have to ask you to come along, but I'm short a couple of senior officers," Maniakes answered. "If Tzikas has a command these days, it's on the wrong side, and Parsmanios—" He didn't go on. That grief wouldn't leave him soon, if ever.

"I am a senior officer, by the good god," Symvatios agreed, laughing again. He had always been more easygoing than the elder Maniakes. "Not quite ready for the boneyard, though I hope to show you."

What Maniakes hoped was that his uncle would have the sense not to get mixed up in hand-to-hand fighting with barbarous warriors a third his age. He didn't say that, for fear of piquing Symvatios and making him rush into danger to prove he could still meet it bravely.

Towns and nobles' villas and estates clustered close to the imperial capital: rich pickings for raiders who managed to get so far south. The Kubratoi had managed. Maniakes' troopers ran into them on the afternoon of the day they had left Videssos the city.

When the scouts came pounding back with the news, the

first question Maniakes asked was, "Are we riding into an ambush?"

"No, your Majesty," one of the horsemen assured him. "The barbarians—a couple of hundred of 'em, I'd guess—never spied us. They were busy plundering the little village they were at, and there's open country beyond it, so nobody's lurking there waiting to jump us."

"All right, we'll hit them." Maniakes slammed a fist down on the mailcoat that covered his thighs. He turned to Symvatios. "Hammer and anvil."

"Right you are," his uncle answered. "That's the way we'll be running this whole campaign, isn't it?" He called orders to the regiments he commanded: no horn signals now, for fear of alerting the foe. His detachment peeled off from the main force and rode away to the northeast on a long swing around the hamlet the nomads were looting.

Maniakes made the main force wait half an hour, then waved them forward. Following the scouts, he headed almost straight for the Kubrati-infested village: he swung his troopers slightly westward, to come on the Kubratoi from the southwest.

That worked out even better than he had expected, for an almond grove screened his approach from the Kubratoi. Only when the first ranks of Videssian horsemen rode out from the cover of the trees did the barbarians take alarm. Their frightened shouts were music to his ears. He shouted for music of his own. Now the trumpeters blared forth the charge.

A lot of the Kubratoi had dismounted. Several of them stood around waiting their turn with a luckless, screaming woman who hadn't been able to flee. The fellow who lay atop her at the moment sprang to his feet and tried to run for his steppe pony, but tripped over the leather breeches he hadn't fully raised. When the first arrow penetrated him, he screamed louder than the woman had. A couple of more hits and he sagged to the ground once more and lay still.

Arrows came back toward the Videssians, too, but not many. Most of the nomads who were on horseback or could get to their ponies rode away from the oncoming imperial force as fast as they could. "Push them!" Maniakes called to his men. "Don't let them think of anything but running."

Run the Kubratoi did. A lot of them outdistanced their pursuers, too, for the boiled leather they wore was lighter than the Videssians' ironmongery. And then, from straight ahead of them, more Videssian horn calls rang out. The nomads cried out in dismay: in running from Maniakes' horsemen, they had run right into the soldiers Symvatios commanded.

Trapped between the two Videssian forces, the Kubratoi fought as best they could, but were quickly overwhelmed. Maniakes hoped they had perished to the last man, but knew how unlikely that was. He had to assume a couple of them had escaped to warn their fellows he was in the field.

As fights went, it wasn't much, and Maniakes knew it. The Videssian army, though, had been without victories for so long that even a tiny one made the soldiers feel as if they had just sacked Mashiz. They sat around the campfires that evening, drinking rough wine from the supply wagons and talking in quick, excited voices about what they had done—even if a lot of them, in truth, had done very little.

"Hammer and anvil," Symvatios said, lifting a clay mug to Maniakes in salute.

Maniakes drank with his uncle. Kameas had wanted to pack some fine vintages for him. This time, he hadn't let the vestiarios get away with it. Wine that snarled when it hit the palate was what you were supposed to drink when you took the field. If nothing else, it made you mean.

"We have to do this three more times, I think," the Avtokrator said. "If we manage that . . ." He let the sentence hang there. Fate had delivered too many blows to Videssos for him to risk tempting it now. He drained his mug and said, "You made a fine anvil, Uncle."

"Aye, well, my hard head suits me to the role," Symvatios replied, laughing. He quickly grew more serious. "We won't be able to work it the same way in every fight, you know. The ground will be different, the Kubratoi will be a little more alert than they were today. . . ."

"It'll get harder; I know that," Maniakes said. "I'm glad we had an easy first one, that's all. What we have to do is make sure that we don't do anything stupid and give the Kubratoi an edge they shouldn't have."

"You've got enough scouts and sentries out, and you've posted them far enough away from our camp," Symvatios said. "The only way Etzilios could surprise us would be to fall out of the sky."

"Good." Maniakes cast a wary eye heavenward. Symvatios laughed again. The Avtokrator didn't.

* * *

About noon the next day, the scouts came upon a good-sized band of Kubratoi. This time they were seen—and pursued. Some fought a rearguard action while others brought the news to Maniakes. He listened to them, then turned to Symvatios. "Move up with your detachment," he said. "Make as if you're at the head of the whole army. While they're engaging you, I'll swing wide and try to take them in flank."

His uncle saluted. "We'll see how it goes, your Majesty: a sideways hammer blow, but I think a good one. My guess is, the nomads don't yet know how many men we've put in the field."

"I think you're right," Maniakes said. "With luck, you'll fool them into believing you're at the head of the whole force. Once they're well engaged with you . . ."

Banners flapping and horns blaring, Symvatios led his detachment forward to support the Videssian scouts. Maniakes hung back and swung off to the east, using low, scrubbily wooded hills to screen his men from the notice of the nomads. Less than an hour passed before a rider galloped over to let him know the Kubratoi were locked in combat with Symvatios' troopers. "There's enough to give them a hard time, too, your Majesty," the fellow said.

Plenty of east-west tracks ran through the hills; this close to Videssos the city, roads crisscrossed the land like spiderwebs. Maniakes divided his force into three columns, to get all his men through as fast as he could. Again, he sent scouting parties ahead to make sure the Kubratoi weren't lying in wait in the woods. Even after the scouts went through safe, his head swiveled back and forth, watching the oaks and elms and ashes for concealed nomads.

All three columns came through the hill country unmolested. There on the flat farm country ahead, the Kubratoi were trading arrows and swordstrokes with Symvatios' detachment. The nomads were trying to wheel around to Symvatios' right; he was having trouble shifting enough men fast enough to defend against them. As the messenger had said, the Kubratoi were there in considerable force.

Their outflanking maneuver, though, left them between Symvatios' troopers and Maniakes' emerging army. The Avtokrator heard the shouts of dismay that went up from them when they realized as much. His own men shouted, too. Hearing his name burst as a war cry from thousands of throats made excitement surge through him, as if he had had too much of the rough camp wine.

The Kubratoi tried to break off their fight with Symvatios' men and flee, but the soldiers from the detachment pressed them hard. And then Maniakes' men were on them, shooting arrows, flinging javelins, and slashing with swords. The Videssians fought more ferociously than they had since the days of Likinios, now almost ten years gone. The Kubratoi scattered before them, madly galloping in all different directions trying to escape.

Maniakes called a halt to the pursuit only when darkness began to render it dangerous. "Like lions they fought," Symvatios exclaimed as they made camp. "Like lions. I remembered they could, but I hadn't seen it in so long, I'd started to have doubts."

"And I," Maniakes agreed. "Nothing like the sight of the enemy's back to make you think you're a hero, is there?"

"Aye, that's a sovereign remedy," Symvatios said. Not far away, a wounded man groaned and bit back a scream as a surgeon dug out an arrowhead. Symvatios' jubilation ebbed. "Heroing doesn't come free, worse luck."

"What does?" Maniakes said, to which his uncle spread his hands. The Avtokrator went on, "Etzilios will know we're out and after him: no way now he can help but know it. He's used to beating us, too. We may not have two fights ahead of us before we put our plan to the full test. We may have only one."

"Behooves us to win that one, too, so it does," Symvatios said.

"Now that you mention it, yes," Maniakes answered dryly. "If we lose, there's not much point to the rest, is there?"

The Videssian army pressed north unchallenged for the next day and a half. They overran a few small bands of Kubratoi, but most of the nomads seemed to have already fled before them. The relative tranquility did not ease Maniakes' mind. Somewhere ahead or off to one flank, Etzilios waited.

When the army moved, a cloud of scouts surrounded it to the front and rear and either side. If Etzilios wanted to strike, he could. He would not take Maniakes by surprise doing it. Whenever the army approached woods, the Avtokrator sent whole companies of troopers probing into them. He was beginning to believe his men would keep on fighting well, but he wanted them to do it on his terms, not those of the khagan of Kubrat.

A scout came riding back toward him. Alongside the cavalryman was a fellow in peasant homespun riding a donkey that had seen better days. The scout nudged the farmer, who said, "Your Majesty, uh—" and then couldn't go on, made modest or awestruck or perhaps just frightened at the prospect of addressing his sovereign.

The scout spoke for him: "Your Majesty, he's fleeing from the northwest. He told me all the Kubratoi in the world—that's what he said—were gathering close by his plot of land, and he didn't care to stay around to find out what they would do." The trooper chuckled. "Can't say as I blame him, either."

"Nor I." Maniakes turned to the peasant. "Where is your plot? How far had you come before the soldier found you?"

When the farmer still proved incapable of speech, the trooper once more answered for him: "He's well south of Varna, your Majesty. We can't be more than half a day's ride from the nomads."

"We'll halt here, then," Maniakes declared. Hearing his words, the trumpeters who rode close by him blared out the order to stop. Maniakes told the peasant, "A pound of gold for your news."

"Thank you, your Majesty," the fellow cried, money loosening his tongue where everything else had failed.

Maniakes and Symvatios huddled together. "Do you think your men can feign a retreat from the Kubratoi and then turn around and fight when the time comes?" the Avtokrator asked.

"I . . . think so," his uncle answered. "You want to make the fight here, do you? The ground is good—open enough so they can't try much in the way of trickery. And if things go wrong, we'll have a real line of retreat open."

"Aye, though I don't want to think about things going wrong," Maniakes said. "My notion was that, if I pick the ground here, I'll be able to set up the toys the engineers have along in their wagons. No chance for that if Etzilios is the one paying the flute player."

"There you're right," Symvatios said. "So what will you want me to do tomorrow? Ride ahead, find the Kubratoi, and then flee back to you as if I'd fouled my breeches like a mimeshow actor?"

"That's the idea," Maniakes agreed. "My hope is, Etzilios

will figure us for cowards at heart. My other hope is that he's wrong."

"Would be nice, wouldn't it?" Symvatios said. "If your boys see mine running and take off with them, the Kubratoi will chase us all back to Videssos the city, laughing their heads off and shooting arrows into us every mile of the way. It's happened before."

"Don't remind me," Maniakes said, remembering his own flight from Etzilios. "Tomorrow, though, the good god willing, they'll be the ones who run."

As he had every night since setting out from the capital, he strung sentries out all around the camp. He wouldn't have put a night attack past the Kubrati khagan. Come to that, he wouldn't have put anything past him.

Dew was still on the grass and the air was crisp and cool when Symvatios and his detachment rode north, as proudly and ostentatiously as if they were the whole of the Videssian army. Maniakes arranged the rest of the force in line of battle, with a gap in the center for Symvatios' men to fill. He had plenty of time to brief the troopers and explain what he thought would happen when Symvatios' men came back. While he spoke, engineers unloaded their wagons and assembled their machines with tackle they had brought up from the city. When they asked it of him, Maniakes detailed a cavalry company to help them.

Then there was nothing to do but wait, eat whatever iron rations they had stowed in their saddlebags, and drink bad wine from canteen or skin. The day turned hot and muggy, as Maniakes had known it would. Sweat ran into his eyes, burning like blood. Under his surcoat, under his gilded mailshirt, under the quilted padding he wore beneath it, he felt as if he had just gone into the hot room of the baths.

Scouts rode out of the forest ahead, spurring their horses toward him. Their shouts rang thin over the open ground: "They're coming!" Maniakes waved to the trumpeters, who blew *alert*. Up and down the line, men reached for their weapons. Maniakes drew his sword. Sunlight sparkled off the blade.

Here came Symvatios and his men. Maniakes' heart leapt into his throat when he spied his uncle, who had a bloodstained rag tied round his head. But Symvatios waved at him to show the wound was not serious. He shouldn't have been fighting at all, but Maniakes breathed easier.

Symvatios' rearguard turned in the saddle to shoot arrows at the Kubratoi behind them. The nomads seemed taken aback to discover more Videssians athwart their path, but kept on galloping after Symvatios' men. Their harsh, guttural shouts put Maniakes in mind of so many wild beasts, but they were more clever and deadly than any mere animals.

Maniakes waited till he spied Etzilios' standard and assured himself the khagan was not hanging back. Then he shouted "Videssos!" and waved his troopers into the fight. At the same instant, Symvatios and his hornplayers ordered a rally from his fleeing detachments.

For a dreadful moment, Maniakes feared they would not find it. Videssian armies had done so much real retreating, all through his reign and Genesios' before it—could the detachment, once heading away from the foe, remember its duty, or would it be doomed to repeat the disasters of the past?

He shouted with joy as, behind the screen of the rearguard, Symvatios' troopers reined in, turned their horses, and faced the Kubratoi once more. Fresh flights of arrows arced toward the nomads. Off on either wing, the catapults the engineers had assembled hurled great stones at the onrushing barbarians. One of them squashed a horse like a man kicking a rat with his boot. Another took the head from a Kubrati as neatly as an executioner's sword might have done. Still clutching his bow, he rode on for several strides of his horse before falling from the saddle.

Of themselves, the blows the stone-throwers struck were pinpricks, and only a few pinpricks at that. But the Kubratoi were used to facing death from javelins or swords: not so from flying boulders. Maniakes saw them waver, and also saw their discomfiture at Symvatios' rally.

"Videssos!" he shouted again, and then, "Charge!" The horns screamed out that command. His men shouted, too, as they spurred their horses toward the Kubratoi. Some, like Maniakes, shouted the name of their Empire. More, though, shouted his name. When he heard that, the sword in his hand quivered like a live thing.

The nomads' special skill was shifting from attack to retreat—or the other way round—at a moment's notice. But the Kubratoi at the rear were still pressing forward while the ones at the fore tried to wheel and go back. The Videssians, mounted on bigger, heavier horses and wearing stronger armor, got in among them and thrashed them as they had not been thrashed in years.

"See how it feels, Etzilios?" Maniakes shouted, slashing his way toward the khagan's horsetail standard. "See how it feels to be fooled and trapped and beaten?" He all but howled the last word.

A nomad cut at him. He turned the blow on his shield and gave one back. The Kubrati carried only a tiny leather target. He blocked that first stroke with it, but a second laid his shoulder open. Maniakes heard his cry of pain, but rode past and never knew how he fared after that.

All at once, the entire nomad host realized the snare into which they had rushed. Etzilios felt no shame at fleeing. The Kubratoi were remorselessly practical at war, and waged it for what they could get. If all they were getting was a drubbing, time enough to pull back and try again when chances looked better.

The usual Videssian practice was to let them go once the main engagement was won, the better to avoid sudden and unpleasant reversals. "Pursue!" Maniakes yelled now. "Dog them like hounds! Don't let them regroup, don't let them get away. Today we'll give them what they earned for invading us!"

The nomads' pursuit from Imbros down to Videssos the city had chewed his force to bits and swallowed most of the bits. That was what he wanted to emulate now. He soon saw it was too much to ask of his men. Because they were more heavily accoutered than the Kubratoi, they were also slower. And, unlike Etzilios' warriors, they were used to keeping to their formations rather than breaking up to fight as individuals: thus, the slower troopers held back those who might have been faster.

So they did not destroy the Kubrati host. They did hurt the invaders, running down wounded men, men on wounded horses, and those luckless enough to be riding nags that simply could not run fast. And, every so often, Etzilios' rearguard tried to gain some space between the rest of the Kubratoi and the Videssians. The imperial army rode over them like the tide rolling up the beach near Kastavala.

Maniakes hated to see the sun sink low in the west. "Shall we camp, your Majesty?" soldiers called, still seeking routine though they had broken it by beating the Kubratoi instead of shattering at the nomads' onslaught.

"We'll ride on a while after dark," the Avtokrator answered. "You can bet the Kubratoi won't be resting, not tonight, they won't. They'll want to get as far away from us as they can.

And do you know what? We're not going to let them. We won't let them ambush us in the blackness, either. We'll have plenty of scouts and we'll go slower, but we'll keep going."

And keep going they did, sometimes dozing in the saddle, sometimes waking to fight short, savage clashes with foes they could scarcely see. Maniakes was glad when his horse splashed into a stream; the cold water on his legs helped revive him.

When dawn touched the eastern sky with gray, Symvatios looked around and said, "We've outrun the supply wagons."

"We won't starve in the next day or two," Maniakes answered. "Anyone who doesn't have some bread or cheese or sausage or olives with him is a fool, anyhow." He glanced over at his uncle. The bandage made Symvatios look something like a veteran, something like a derelict. "How did you pick that up?"

"By the time we get back to Videssos the city, I'll have a fine, heroic scar," Symvatios answered. "Right now, I just feel like a twit. One of my troopers was hacking away at a Kubrati in front of him, and when he drew back his sword for another stroke—well, my fool head got in the way. Laid me open as neat as if a cursed nomad had done it."

"I won't tell if you don't," Maniakes promised. "You ought to be able to bribe the trooper into keeping his mouth shut, too." They both laughed. Laughing, Maniakes discovered, came easy when you were moving forward.

The pursuit went more slowly than it had the day before. Troopers had to go easy on their horses, for fear of foundering them. The Kubratoi gained ground on the imperials, for some of them, in nomad fashion, had remounts available. Etzilios kept on fleeing, though. Now he led the men who had been surprised and beaten and who wanted no more of their foes.

Then, toward late afternoon, a scout galloped back to Maniakes. The fellow urged on his mount as if it had left the stable not a quarter of an hour before. "Your Majesty!" he cried, and then again: "Your Majesty!" He delivered his news with a great shout: "The Kubratoi up ahead, they're fighting!"

"By the good god," Maniakes said softly. He glanced over to Symvatios. The bandage had slipped down so it almost covered one of his uncle's eyes, giving him a distinctly piratical air. Symvatios clenched his right hand into a fist and laid it over his heart in salute. Maniakes turned and spoke to the trumpeters: "Blow *pursuit* once more. Now we give all the effort we have in us. If we can get to the battlefield fast enough, the Kubratoi will take a blow they'll be a long time getting over."

Martial music rang out. Tired men spurred tired horses from walks up to trots. They checked their quivers. Few had many arrows left. The nomads would be in the same straits. Maniakes wished the supply wagons could have kept up with his host. If they had, he would have poured arrows into Etzilios' men till night made him stop.

To his initial startlement, a band of nomads charged straight back toward his forces. Symvatios figured out what that meant, shouting, "Etzilios knows he's in the smithy's shop. Are we going to let him keep the hammer from coming down on the anvil one last time?"

"No!" the Videssian soldiers roared. They were no more enthusiastic about exposing their bodies to wounds than any men of sense would have been, but, since they had chosen that trade, they did not want their risks to be to no purpose. They surged forward against the Kubratoi, who, badly outnumbered, were soon overwhelmed.

Up ahead, Maniakes saw the rest of the nomads battling a force under sunburst banners deployed directly across their line of retreat. "Hammer and anvil!" he cried, echoing his uncle. "Now we come down."

The wail of despair that rose when the Kubratoi spied his force was music to his ears. He spurred his horse into a shambling gallop. The first Kubrati he met cut at him once, missed, then set spur to his own pony and did his best to escape. A Videssian who still had arrows brought him down as if he were a fleeing fox.

"Maniakes!" shouted the Videssians who kept the Kubratoi from escaping to the north.

"Rhegorios!" Maniakes shouted back, and his troopers took up the call. Now that Maniakes' men had reached the field, his cousin, instead of merely holding the nomads at bay, pressed hard against them. Rhegorios' soldiers were fresh and rested and mounted on horses that hadn't been going hard for a day and a night and most of another day. Their quivers were full. They struck with a force out of proportion to their numbers.

All at once, the Kubratoi opposing them made the fatal transition from army to frightened mob, each man looking no farther than toward what might keep his uniquely precious self alive another few minutes. In that moment of dissolution,

Maniakes looked round the field for the horsetail that marked Etzilios' position. He wanted to serve the khagan as he had nearly been served south of Imbros. If he could kill or capture the leader of the Kubratoi, the nomads might fight among themselves for years over the succession.

He saw nothing to show Etzilios' place. As he himself had while fleeing from the Kubrati ambush, the khagan had abandoned the symbol of his station to give himself a better chance of keeping it. "Five pounds of gold to the man who brings me Etzilios, alive or dead!" the Avtokrator cried.

Though the battle was won, and won crushingly, a good many Kubratoi managed to squeeze out from between Maniakes' force and Rhegorios'. Then the light began to fail, which allowed more escapes. No one led Etzilios in bonds before Maniakes or rode up carrying the khagan's dripping head. Maniakes wondered whether he lay anonymously dead on the field or had succeeded in getting away. Time would tell. At the moment, in the midst of triumph, his fate seemed a small thing.

Here came Rhegorios, his handsome face wearing a smile as bright as the sun now setting. "We did it!" he cried, and embraced Maniakes. "By Phos, we did it. Hammer and anvil, and crushed them between us."

"I have two anvils—father and son." Maniakes waved to Symvatios, who sat his horse close by. "So much hope going into this campaign. I had to hope we'd win down south of here, win hard enough and often enough to make the nomads decide pulling back would be a good idea. And then I had to hope you'd put your men in the right spot after Thrax and the fleet carried you up the coast to Varna."

"I almost didn't," Rhegorios said. "The scouts I had out farthest ran up against the Kubratoi fleeing first and fastest. I had to hustle the lads along to get 'em where they'd do the most good in time for them to do it. But we managed." He waved to show the victory Videssian arms had won.

Like most triumphs, this one was better contemplated in song and chronicle than in person. Twilight started to veil the aftermath of battle, but did not completely cover it, not yet. Men and horses lay still and silent in death or twisting in the agony of wounds and screaming their pain to the unhearing sky. The stink of blood and sweat and shit filled Maniakes' nostrils. Hopeful crows hopped not far away, waiting to feast on the banquet of carrion spread before them.

Healer-priests and ordinary physicians and horseleeches strode across the battlefield, doing what they could for injured Videssians and animals. Other men, these still in armor, traveled the field, too, making sure all the Kubratoi on it would never rise from it again. Maniakes wondered if the scavengers could tell the difference between the men who gave them less to eat and those who gave them more.

"May I share your tent tonight?" he asked Rhegorios. "Mine is—back there somewhere." He waved vaguely southward, toward the outrun baggage train.

Rhegorios grinned at him again. "Any man would share with his brother-in-law. Any man would share with his cousin. Any man would share with his sovereign. And since I can do all three at once and put only one extra man in my tent, how can I say no?"

"Can you spare some space in that crowd of people for your poor feeble father, as well?" Symvatios said. Despite the bandage, he didn't look feeble. He wasn't quite the cool calculator the elder Maniakes was, but he had led his troops bravely and done everything the Avtokrator asked of him. A lot of officers half his age couldn't approach his standard.

Rhegorios' cooks got fires going and stewpots bubbling above them. Hot stew went down wonderfully well after the two hard days just ended. Maniakes sat on the ground inside Rhegorios' tent—after some argument, he and Rhegorios had persuaded Symvatios to take the cot in there—and sipped at a mug of wine. He hoped it wouldn't put him to sleep, or at least not yet. Having won his victory, he wanted to hash it over, too.

"Most important is that the men stood and fought," Rhegorios said. "We couldn't know whether they would till we took 'em out and tried 'em. They didn't waste all that time on the practice field."

"That's so," Maniakes said, nodding. From the cot, Symvatios let out a snore. He hadn't wanted to fall asleep, any more than he had wanted to accept the cot, but however willing his spirit, his flesh was far from young. Maniakes glanced over at him affectionately, then went on, "The other important thing we did was land your men behind the Kubratoi. That turned what would have been a victory into a rout. I wonder if we got Etzilios."

"It was a fine idea," Rhegorios answered. "The nomads are

nothing to speak of on the sea. I wish we had run up against some of those little pirate boats of theirs, those *monoxyla*. Thrax' dromons would have smashed 'em to kindling, and we wouldn't have landed an hour late."

Maniakes plucked at his beard. "The Makuraners haven't much in the way of ships, either," he remarked, and then paused to listen to what he had just said. Thoughtfully he went on, "We've taken advantage of that in small ways already, landing raiders in the westlands and so forth. But we could move along the coasts by sea faster than Abivard could shift his forces by land trying to keep up with us. We could . . ."

"Provided we have troops who won't piss their drawers the first time the boiler boys come thundering down on them," Rhegorios said. Then he too looked thoughtful. "We're on our way to getting troops like that, aren't we?"

"Either we're on our way or else we have them now," Maniakes said. "Going over the Cattle Crossing and ramming headlong into the Makuraners always struck me as the wrong way to go about clearing them from the westlands, and a good recipe for getting beat, to boot. Now maybe we have another choice."

"No guarantees," Rhegorios said.

Maniakes' laugh held a bitter edge. "What in life has any guarantees?" He remembered Niphone's face, pale and still, as she lay in her sarcophagus. "You do as well as you can for as long as you can. If we're not going to let the Makuraners keep the westlands, we'll have to drive them out. Making them move to respond to us would be a pleasant change, don't you think?"

"You get no arguments from me there," Rhegorios answered. "I'd love to see them scurrying about instead of us. Can we do it this summer, do you think?"

"I don't know," Maniakes said. "We'll have to go back to Videssos the city and see how long we'll need to refit, how many men we can pull together, how many ships we have. We'd have a surer chance of doing it if Etzilios hadn't jumped on us, curse him."

"You many end up thanking him one of these days," Rhegorios said. "You might never have come up with this idea if he hadn't invaded."

"There is that," the Avtokrator admitted. "Sooner or later,

though, I think I would have. It's the best choice we've got. It may be the only choice we've got. Whether it's good enough—we'll find out."

DEL REY® ONLINE!

The Del Rey Internet Newsletter...

A monthly electronic publication, posted on the Internet, GEnie, CompuServe, BIX, various BBSs, and the Panix gopher (gopher.panix.com). It features hype-free descriptions of books that are new in the stores, a list of our upcoming books, special announcements, a signing/reading/convention-attendance schedule for Del Rey authors, "In Depth" essays in which professionals in the field (authors, artists, designers, sales people, etc.) talk about their jobs in science fiction, a question-and-answer section, behind-the-scenes looks at sf publishing, and more!

Internet information source!

A lot of Del Rey material is available to the Internet on our Web site and on a gopher server: all back issues and the current issue of the Del Rey Internet Newsletter, sample chapters of upcoming or current books (readable or downloadable for free), submission requirements, mail-order information, and much more. We will be adding more items of all sorts (mostly new DRINs and sample chapters) regularly. The Web site is http://www.randomhouse.com/delrey/ and the address of the gopher is gopher.panix.com

Why? We at Del Rey realize that the networks are the medium of the future. That's where you'll find us promoting our books, socializing with others in the sf field, and—most importantly—making contact and sharing information with sf readers.

Online editorial presence: Many of the Del Rey editors are online, on the Internet, GEnie, CompuServe, America Online, and Delphi. There is a Del Rey topic on GEnie and a Del Rey folder on America Online.

The official e-mail address for Del Rey Books is delrey@randomhouse.com (though it sometimes takes us a while to answer).